CHAPTER 1

ENGLAND

Lenny Plant snorted cold Marc.. ..
Proud of reputation the month blew its chill no... s.
Gates rattled, unnerved at the pained howl of naked branches as they clawed the stars. Unruly gusts bullied the fences, ignorant to the plight of spring's new daffodils, for they could yield to the blast no further. Through cheap denim Lenny scratched at himself.

It was late.

Shivering in his shirt Lenny Plant contemplated the gradient before him. He placed one foot deliberately in front of the other – the way he did whenever he was drunk.

People take walking for granted; those able to walk that is, but not Lenny. He appreciated that walking was an incredible skill; desirous of balance, navigational acuity, and current awareness of the terrain under foot. Without discrimination his drunkenness laid siege to each faculty.

The final leg of the return journey from the pub was always awkward. In order to gain the back door Lenny would need to equal the challenge of a treacherous, south facing incline; one whose steepness varied in proportion to the volume of alcohol consumed.

This night Lenny's driveway reared up at him – high as he'd ever seen it.

He readied himself with the clumsy thought of removing the trailing foot from the ground to set it in front of the aforementioned foot, but paused when he heard the shout.

Someone shouted Lenny's name – more like cried his name. The wind chased the dying echo back down Willow Gardens. A shadowed figure, betrayed by half a moon's light, shuffled up the pavement towards him. Lenny Plant smelt tragedy in the village of Locburn.

He braced himself. Closing one eye to check for focusing, Lenny assessed his overall condition. He was drunk alright – but drunk in a different kind of way. Lenny had altered his drinking habits of late – his "drinking style" as he preferred to call it. The word "habit," he felt, associated too willingly with undesirables such as "bad," "dirty," and "disgusting".

For years Lenny had achieved a condition of drunkenness through the combined absorption of red wine and beer. He harboured an unquenchable fondness for both the froth of the hop and the fruit of the vine. The affection, equally divided, ensured that whenever occasion demanded, each commodity was consumed without prejudice to the other.

Now, wading through his fifties, Lenny was beginning to outstrip his capacity to grapple with hangovers. He'd arrived at a situation where his drinking was affecting his drinking style. Lenny was showing up for his fill at The Haydale Arms on a Saturday night, still in a state of recuperation. His drinking companions were beginning to notice how, more and more often, he struggled to keep up with the pack.

Lenny was determined to react in a responsible way and took one of his closest friends into his confidence. Ronnie Dent was an expert drinker. With over forty-five years of successful hard drinking behind him, he was the man you went to see if your habit was affecting your drinking.

Ronnie advised Lenny that the red wine/beer combo was a brute of a mix when it came to hangover severity. He offered that getting drunk on a single brand could solve or at least alleviate his problem.

Ronnie had been getting effectively drunk of late on a premium organic German cider called Pystwiser. At eight per cent by volume the fortified extract of apple packed a punch and, with nothing but the finest ingredients used in its manufacture, was as pure as alcoholic spring water. Lenny would no longer have to rely on concoction to achieve the desired level of intoxication. Ronnie

POOR RONNIE

POOR RONNIE
A tale from the Dales

ANDREW PRICE

YouCaxton Publications
Oxford & Shrewsbury

ISBN 978-1-913425-15-9
Published by YouCaxton Publications 2020
YCBN: 01

YouCaxton Publications
enquiries@youcaxton.co.uk

"Whether skies be blue or they be grey
the shells still burst the same old way
the flag the faith the last bugle call
in whose vain shadow shall perish all."

Lenny Plant 2015

"It's sacred ground we walk upon, with every step we take."

Pagan chant

"The present dies as it's born; an indestructible paradox
ever moving.
It drags the past behind it."

Maxim Yankov 2057

"Fuck off."

Lenny Plant 1978

"Forgive me Father for I have sinned."

Andrew Price 2020

For
Babs n' Aims

ALSO BY ANDREW PRICE

"POOR ENID"

Contents

gave assurance that a straight five to eight pints of the cider would transport Lenny, most pleasantly, to where he needed to be on his own personal scale of inebriation. The purity of the draught would, no doubt, have restorative properties in respect of hangover recovery. Lenny took Ronnie's advice and tonight was his debut session.

Ronnie Dent had been in many different drunken scenarios: 'drunk and disrespectful,' 'drunk in possession of a Blue Winged Macaw,' and 'drunk inside a privet hedge whilst still on his bike.' Most memorable of all, Ronnie became a folklore drink- driver after an incident back in 1978, when Ronnie, his Cortina and three passengers, failed sensationally to make the automotive trip back from The Legion Club to The Haydale Arms:

'I know it's a stupid question, but are ye havin' another one Ronnie boy?'

Dermot Doran let loose a smile tireless of charm. The Haydale's affable Irish Landlord tilted Ronnie's empty beer glass on the sodden bar towel. Its frothy rim grinned Ronnie's way.

'No Dermot,' says Ronnie, straightening out of his familiar bar-side slouch. He screwed his cigarette into the ashtray and reached for the pile of money heaped on the bar. 'I'll nip up the bookies now and get the bets on – a sly one in the Legion and back down for the racing.'

'Ah good on yer Ronnie boy,' says Dermot. 'And don't forget: I want a fiver each-way on "Blue Light" – plus a tenner to win on "Bag of Breath." Make sure ye' put the bets on before ye' get any more of the drink in ye'.

'Are you sure about this 'Bag of Breath' thing Dermot?'

'Sure I saw her run at Catterick last month; she got boxed in an' all so she did. But she was rarin' to go Ronnie boy; I'm telling ye', some focker's been sticking the ginger where they shouldn't be.'

'Ginger eh?' quipped Ronnie, 'we'll see.'

'Don't be long Ronnie boy – first race two o'clock. I'll have the telly on and yer beer on the bar ready an' all for ye'.'

'I'll scoot up in the car.' Ronnie pulled the keys from his pocket and jingled them at the side of his beardy grin.

'Have you not had too much for the driving Ronnie boy? I saw the cops were waitin' up at the roundabout this morning – parked up in the car an' all. I'll have Lynne run you up.'

'I've only had a couple, I'll be right enough,' reckoned Ronnie, his sanguinity borne of four pints of bitter. He turned to a trio drinking at the table behind him. 'Any of you lads fancy a swift one up at the Legion?'

Young Lenny Plant volunteered his interest in the excursion by thrusting his hand at the ceiling. He lowered it smart-like once he realised what he'd done. At seventeen he was still tuned-in to the classroom etiquette of raising an arm before offering an answer. Along with Lenny; Gordon Taylor and Ned Parker also fancied a change of scenery.

The three drinkers supped-off and filed out of the bar after Ronnie. Dermot called to Gordon Taylor, who at twenty-eight was a year younger than Ronnie but slightly more wise in drink.

'Make sure ye get him back down in a taxi Gordon – and with the bets on. I know what he's like once he gets on the cheap piss up there – an' the focker's easy distracted an all.'

Dermot went over to the open window and called out across the car park, 'Missing you already, fellas.'

§

Lenny folded his lankiness into the rear seat of the Mark Three Cortina. The youngest of the four men he'd already maxed-out at six-foot-four. Ned Parker, a chirpy cockney, slid in from the other side to join Lenny.

Ned worked the local building sites laying bricks. A hard-living product of the city, Ned was forty but would look young for a sixty-year-old. His eyes, Blue and Lively, blazed out of a face worn with weather, drink, and fag smoke. Blue eye was blue, and made of glass, Lively eye was also blue – and seemed to mock Blue eye as it swivelled, energetic and enquiring in its socket.

Ned was a comfortable sort to spend time with: laid-back, unassuming – but interested. He'd meandered up-country years ago, happened upon Locburn Village in North Yorkshire, and decided he'd come far enough. He bought a small cottage in the village during the lost forever golden age of affordable housing. Ned was kind, and small and lean – and rough as a pile of broken bricks.

Lenny had been labouring for Ned, cash-in-hand, while he was searching for a full time job. The pair of them had worked and joked together the whole summer. Each was easy with the other's company, Lenny liked Ned, and Ned liked Lenny. Ned had invited Lenny along this Saturday – so they could have a drink – with Ronnie Dent.

Lenny would marvel with undiminishing wonderment at the way Ned laid the bricks: every brick lifted, mortared, and placed with the same easy, seamless movement. Ned got it right first time, every time. Never a fumble did Lenny witness – never a single brick re-laid.

It wasn't just the skill of the brick-laying that so mesmerised Lenny. Ned's whole range of physical interaction with his environment made perfect, graceful sense. From the way he rolled a cigarette, to the way he walked, to the way he fetched a pint glass to his mouth before returning it dead centre of the beer mat without looking. There was a magical, subliminal choreography to Ned's every movement.

His entry into the rear of the car was typically elegant. He didn't clamber awkward into the confinement as Lenny did. He swung the door, curved his torso, and glided his arse onto the vinyl seat. His head cleared the roof without the need to duck – ducking's a startled reaction. Ned's head swooped in-under, stooping no more than needed.

Once settled Ned gave Lenny a knowing wink and nodded at the back of Ronnie's head. He set about organising his smoke. With a dirty fingernail he prised open the lid of a battered tobacco tin. Ned flicked his tongue into it and extracted a pre-rolled fag in the manner of a feeding chameleon. The stickiness of his beery saliva was barely sufficient – but sufficient enough to fetch the cigarette to his lips. In the same instant his free hand produced a box of matches from his breast pocket. Sliding the box open,

Ned removed a match, struck it, and lit-up. The employment of one hand served for the activity – including disposal of the spent match, flicked past Gordon Taylor's ear, and out through the narrow opening of the front passenger window.

In Lenny's young world, only Ned Parker could render the mundane lighting of a cigarette an act of hypnotic elegance.

Ronnie Dent piled himself into the driver's seat, his own fag already installed in a mouth barely visible beyond the shag of a beard out of control. Lenny wondered if beards were flammable, and if they were, was Ronnie's fag capable of starting a bush fire. He smirked as he imagined Ronnie being blasted with a fire extinguisher.

Ronnie handed Gordon Taylor the cash for the bets. 'Look after that lot Gordon while I see if this crate's interested in going anywhere.'

The motor had been abandoned in the pub car park the previous Saturday – it hadn't moved since. The previous owner of the left-hooker was a soldier convicted for dangerous-driving, who in turn had bought it from a lead-footed German salesman who'd thrashed it the length and breadth of the autobahn network. The vehicle had been badly used all its life. Now in Ronnie's charge, there would be no respite from the neglect. These days the Cortina looked weary from every angle. It rested itself on four tyres; three of them bald, the fourth one, there or thereabouts.

Ronnie shuffled himself comfy, dipped the clutch, and slotted the worn key into the ignition. His seat, tired with age, creaked arthritic like.

Ned leaned forward and puffed a chest-full of smoke into Ronnie's hair. The engine churned on twisting the key, greeting the neighbourhood with the mechanical equivalent of a death rattle. Ned's smoke steamed from Ronnie's mop hair as his passengers, resigned to a journey on foot, exchanged hopeless glances.

'Looks like we're on Shanks's pony,' said Gordon, watching the smoke continuing to rise out of the pilot's hair. 'When did you last get her serviced Ronnie?'

'What, the car or Edith?'

'Edith,' countered Gordon.

'I'm there every night Gordon – she wants for nothing.'

'Does she use much oil?'

'Only if she gets it,' said Ronnie, cranking down his window. 'Christ it's smoky in here – can't see out the bastard window.'

The car coughed and backfired, scattering the crows in the nearby field. Ronnie turned the key again. Bemused silence, the nursling of cynical anticipation, befell his crew.

'I'll give it full throttle with a touch of choke – clean out the cylinders,' said Ronnie, implying technical knowhow.

'Hey fellas – it's Flight of the fackin' Phoenix innit. Jimmy Stewart here's gonna clean out the bleedin' cylinders,' joked Ned, referring to the film in which a stranded crew's chances of survival hung on the great actor's pretend skills to restart the engine of a crashed plane.

Of course you're never in doubt as to the outcome – but only because it's Jimmy Stewart stuffing the Koffman starter cartridges into the aircraft's ignition. If it was John Mills they'd have perished in the desert, along with six spent cartridges. John Mills the actor was English, unreliable, and capable of imparting unnecessary tragedy to his fellow actors. Typical among many misadventures: his South Pole fuck-up – along with perforated submarines, bloated with seawater and dead bodies, lying on the ocean floor. Mills possessed a wholesome talent to play the pig-headed English hero – fucking every consequence as he went.

'Shut up Ned, I'm concentrating here,' said Ronnie. Smoke pluming from his nose, his mouth, his beard and his hair.

The engine fired up. Sucking hard on his fag Ronnie examined each of the passengers' faces; his imploring stare hungry for approval.

So – off they went, enveloped in tobacco fog, the four of them; up to the bookies, then onto the Legion Club – for a swift one of course. If you screwed your eyes up real tight, you'd be forgiven for thinking that Ronnie Dent looked a bit like John Mills.

Six miles to the west, suspended above Hudswell Moor, a cumulonimbus cloud the size of Peterborough hung heavy in the atmosphere. As greedily as Ronnie sucked the beer from his glass, so the cloud sponged every drop of moisture from the air around it.

Ronnie knew not of such a cloud, and would likely care not if he did know. What he didn't know, and what he would be concerned to know, was that he had no way of knowing what this type of cloud was good at doing. If he did know, he still wouldn't know that the cloud he didn't know about previously would have a significant bearing on the fate of his driving licence.

§

'Where're you going Gordon?' asked Ronnie as the Legion's swinging doors coughed the boozy quartet out onto the pavement. Gordon had turned right, heading off in the opposite direction to the others.

'We,' emphasised Gordon, 'are going to get a taxi.'

'Gordon,' said Ronnie, feigning an impatient huff. 'I've only had a couple.'

'You've had seven, pisshead.'

'I'm a nervous driver – I drive better when I'm relaxed, you know, with a drink inside me.'

'Tell the doctor about your nerves Ronnie,' said Ned sniggering. 'He'll sign you one of those Drunk Exemption Certificates, so you can drink and drive and tell the cops to fack off?'

'I didn't know you could get something like that,' said Ronnie, his brain half-soaked.

'Can I have a go at driving?' asked Lenny, raising his hand for the second time that day – 'I've had driving lessons.'

Ronnie looked at Ned, who shrugged his shoulders, then looked at Gordon for guidance.

'Don't lose your licence before you've even passed your test Lenny lad; best to let Ronnie lose his,' said Gordon.

'I'm fine driving the car,' protested Ronnie. 'Anyway, look at the queue for the taxis – we'll never get back for the first race.'

'He's right,' said Ned. 'And Dermot's waiting on the betting slips. It's ready to slash it down as well.'

§

The backfire from the passing car caused PC Casey Peasey to look up from his Country Sport magazine. He'd been intrigued by an article on crossbows that featured useful hints on how to avoid nasty accidents with such weapons. Peasey had been troubling himself to think of a non-nasty accident with a crossbow – but was stumped.

One safety tip advised against the practice of polishing a loaded crossbow (whether alone or in company) and cited the misfortune of a Middlesboro housewife, fastened to her own kitchen door by a crossbow bolt:

Her twelve year old son, seated by the kitchen table, had been polishing the trigger-guard assembly when the inevitable occurred. The weapon was a birthday present from an uncle who'd stolen it from another idiot.

The youngster suffered from undiagnosed Attention Deficit Hyperactivity Disorder.

After passing between the mother's clavicle and upper rib cage, the bolt pinned her to the door against which she leaned. On hearing the screaming and cursing, a neighbour came to the rescue. She gave the mother a fag and shared a tin of beer while they waited for the Police Armed Response Unit to show.

The son and neighbour were shot dead; the mother was stretchered to hospital, still connected to a disconnected kitchen door.

'That fackin' cop's seen us Ron,' said Ned, casting the gaze of his seeing eye through the back window. Ronnie had made a meal out of negotiating the roundabout, navigating it in the style of a drunk-driver.

The four occupants had been engaged in a lively debate over the source of the objectionable fumes. Layered in the smoke-filled interior, hung the stench of putrefied food nearing the end of its journey through the alimentary canal. Suspicion soon settled on Gordon – who hadn't helped his defence by declaring earlier that he'd sat down the previous evening to a feast of bangers and mash, accompanied by a mountain of sautéed onions and cabbage.

9

He was also the only one laughing at the smell – the other three retched, and groped for the window winders, like boy soldiers, fumbling with tragic lateness, for their gas masks. Some people laugh at their own jokes – Gordon Taylor laughed at his own farts.

PC Peasey was good at spotting a drunk driver – it was part of his job. He didn't need to be good to spot Ronnie's drunken driving though. Ronnie drunk and drove so convincingly he could make the car behave like it was under the influence.

'What's he doing?' Ronnie squinted in his rear-view mirror. He steered the vehicle with one hand at the top of the wheel, a cigarette mounted between his fingers like a gun-sight. Resigned to the inevitable, Gordon shook his head.

'He's coming this way Ronnie,' said Lenny.

'Just pull over and park-up a while Ron,' said Gordon, 'he's probably not interested in us.'

'Fuck him,' said Ronnie, drawing-in a casual lung-full before exhaling the remainder of his smoky comment, 'we've already missed the two-o'clock at Haydock – we need to be down there for the two-thirty.'

Lenny wondered at Ronnie's lack of concern, and how he prioritised attendance at the Haydale Arms over a rear-view mirror full of police car. Ronnie's ability to perceive his fate, or have any caring for the consequences of his mischief, had been anaesthetised by seven pints of bitter. Alcohol had soothed any pinching anxiety he may have had for his driving licence – or the safety of others.

The beer slushed around Ronnie's stomach; suspended in the warm fizz: three pork scratchings, a lump of chewing gum, and some catarrh he'd snorted back to decongest his sinuses. With little or nothing to absorb the alcohol, a breathalyser test was certain to be an odds-on failure.

PC Peasey rattled his knuckles against Ronnie's window. Ronnie screwed it down.

'You made a right mess of that roundabout back there sir.'

'I think there must be something wrong with the steering officer,' said Ronnie, implausible as drunkenness is to sobriety.

'More like something wrong with the person doing the steering. Have you been drinking sir?'

'Just the one – a pint of shandy as a matter-of-fact,' said Ronnie, in a matter-of- fact kind of way.

Gordon farted, narrowly avoiding a follow-through – up on one cheek he let out a hot, lengthy hiss.

'I have reason to believe you have been driving whilst under the influence of alcohol. I'm going to have to ask you to provide a specimen of breath sir.'

Ronnie wheezed and coughed his response. 'But I'm asthmatic – I haven't the wind in me to blow that hard.'

'In that case, I'm arresting you under suspicion of driving whilst under the influence of alcohol.' The policeman cautioned Ronnie. 'We'll take a urine sample to check for alcohol down at the station.'

Lenny listened from the rear seat; he'd heard of breathalysers, but not of urine tests. He wondered how they would go about taking the piss out of Ronnie. Lenny felt sorry for his bearded friend.

The cop leaned in through the window and reached for the ignition keys. He sniffed long and deep at Ronnie's face for alcohol. Peasey was a teetotal, non-smoking vegetarian; cursed with a weak stomach and recurring conjunctivitis. He was unprepared for the miasmic assault on the vulnerability of his disposition.

First, Ronnie's beer breath: warm and stale, carrying subtle notes of a weeping abscess. Then the smoke: savage, biting away at his eyes. By the time he'd deep-breathed Gordon's gut-turning arse vapour PC Peasey was wishing he hadn't bothered.

Clutching his throat with one hand and rubbing his eyes with the other, Peasey withdrew back through the window. Still stooping he reversed across the pavement with a backward stagger.

The policeman roared vegetarian vomit into the gutter.

'Dirty bastards,' he gargled.

'Language officer,' Ronnie twisted the keys, floored the throttle, and dropped the clutch.

Peasey ran back to his car, radio in hand, coughing and spluttering for assistance.

§

The cloud above Hudswell Moor pissed its piss. It pissed its piss on the dry hard ground. Ground made hard and dry by the long hot summer; ground too hard and too dry to soak up any amount of pissing rain in any amount of a hurry. The cloud pissed its piss.

§

Ronnie Dent, fag clamped in the side of a psycho grin, hammered the car down Back Lane. Worn-out suspension struggled with the rigours imposed on it by the drunken wheelman. The narrowness of the road, its undulations, bends and potholes did their best to throw the wreck from its precarious trajectory. The body shell shuddered, door panels rattled – at the trough of every bounce sparks sprayed from a sagging exhaust. As for the passengers; they'd have been less traumatised strapped into a NASA space shuttle, cowering at the white-hot death roar of Earth's re-entry atmosphere.

Gordon Taylor clung to his seat, knuckles white as his face. No more jolly farting – just for now. 'You're mad Dent, you're fucking mad you are,' he repeated at intervals.

Lenny observed from the rear seat. He reassured himself about Ronnie's state of mind: Surely he can't be mad? He's a sensible grown-up? At twenty-nine years of age he's a proper adult – he's got a beard for fuck's sake?

Up on Hudswell Moor the rainwater poured into Leadmill Beck. In no time the stream had burst its banks. An ugly, ever swelling brown torrent rolled down off the moor.

Ronnie had his course plotted. He'd take the car to the bottom of Back Lane where there was a choice of either turning right into Willow Gardens to access the pub car park via the village green, or carrying straight on to the shallow ford before rounding the corner to pull the car up in front of the pub. The latter option favoured a speedy disembarkation from car to pub where, in a bid to side-step the breath test, Ronnie would claim to have recently downed three large whiskies. He decided to ford the ford – in his Ford.

A high-powered patrol car turned into Back Lane – all blaring horns and blue lights. Peasey followed in his panda car, revenge on his mind.

The raging spate closed in on Locburn Village.

Ronnie had made good progress down Back Lane – he'd worked hard to build-up the momentum, taking full advantage of the gradient and the weight of the four adults. Although it was raining to the West, a drop was yet to fall in Locburn. Ronnie was smart enough to know that the baldness of his tyres maximised the amount of rubber in contact with the dry road, and that this would optimise adhesion. Having lived in Locburn all his life the boozer knew Back Lane better than anyone. A sober driver in a superior car would have been hard pushed to keep pace.

Approaching the ford Ronnie eased off: 'Please keep your seatbelts fastened until the plane has come to a rest. We hope you've enjoyed flying with Dent Airlines and wish you a safe onward journey. Home and dry fellas,' he chirped.

Home perhaps – but not dry.

Leadmill Beck flows through Locburn Village before emptying itself into the River Swale, one mile to the East. During dry spells a child could leap the stream; sudden downpours can see it rise by up to six feet.

Lenny saw it first: foaming dirty water, lots of it, coming at them like it was late for something important. Water doesn't happen like that, he thought, thinking like someone who's seventeen and drunk – so it wasn't actually happening. No need to announce its approach.

It wouldn't have mattered anyway. Having entered the ford the car was at the point of no return.

Ronnie sensed an uncharacteristic sideward motion come into play as the water engulfed the car. Wasted seconds passed before he had half a notion of what was occurring. With a cognitive efficiency impaired by alcohol, Ronnie was immune to the inevitable unfolding of attendant danger. Cocooned in the warmth of inebriation he responded to the situation in the fashion of a clueless drunk. As the car became buoyant and drifted downstream, he switched on the wipers and steered the steering wheel. As a further precaution he switched off the radio, turned on the vehicle's hazard warning lights, and firmly pressed his brake pedal.

Ronnie fastened his seat-belt.

Lenny naively interpreted Ronnie's actions as a formal emergency procedure; one to be followed on driving one's car into a swollen river. He felt confident that the adult at the wheel was somehow in control of things, and would soon be pulling up at The Haydale Arms. Ronnie knew what he was doing, thought Lenny, he's an adult – he's got a beard for fuck's sake.

Gordon had a different slant on the situation:

'You've gone and killed us Dent – I'll never forgive you for this. You're mad, you're fucking mad! Windows down lads,' he bawled. 'Get your windows down!'

Ned Parker, unflustered, wound his window down. 'Good job you ain't got electric windows Ron – you're facked with them once you go in the drink.'

Lenny's feet felt suddenly cold.

'Can we all swim?' asked Gordon.

'Eh,' said Lenny, water rising to his waist.

'The car's sinking – leave the doors shut, get out the windows and swim.' Lenny and Ned complied.

'She's taking on water!' shouted Ronnie, still working the steering wheel, 'I'm going down with her.'

'What about him Gordon?' shouted Lenny, giving a worried nod in Ronnie's direction. Lenny was half out the window but concerned at the plight of the doomed mariner.

'Sod him and his car Lenny. Get out!'

Ned was first out; snaking through the window he pulled himself up onto the roof. The cockney – a quick thinker, wasted no time. Standing up on the roof he leapt from the car and managed a safe landing on the grass bank.

Lenny and Gordon bailed-out into the water. Inspired by a line from Gulliver's Travels, Lenny struck-out with the front crawl and swam "as fortune directed." Gordon just swam for it.

The swirling brew took them where it pleased.

Lenny focused on a clump of vegetation approaching to his left; in a desperate bid to anchor himself to the bank he reached out and grasped a handful of nettles. The current took him further downstream – clutching a bouquet of stingers. The next time someone urged Lenny to "grasp the nettle," he'd have something to say to them.

Ned ran along the bank, pulling off his jacket as he went. He overtook Lenny at the bend and swung a sleeve into the water. Lenny caught hold and Ned hauled him in.

Gordon Taylor swam with the flow. He'd lost his glasses; nevertheless he could see a belt of slower moving water up ahead where the stream had spilled over onto the lower slope of the village green. With what strength he had left he kicked for the shallows. Lenny and Ned saw what Gordon was attempting. They waded back into the water and dragged their friend ashore.

Ronnie and his car were travelling backwards. Were it not for the intervention of the old village bridge the pair of them would have drifted, no doubt fatally, into the River Swale. Britain's second fastest flowing river had claimed the lives of many over the years. The bridge, constructed almost two centuries ago, had a low arch. Today it struggled to swallow the flood water.

The boot of the Cortina wedged itself into the top of the arch. Although full to the dashboard with floodwater, the force of the current held the front of the car buoyant. It bounced on the flow like a speed-boat on full throttle.

Ronnie watched the blurred tree-line rise and fall at the end of the bonnet. He felt doubly sick: a land-locked drunken sea-sickness, together with a nauseous blue light dawning that perhaps this particular game was almost up. One consolation: the betting slips were safe, wedged warm and dry in the captain's shirt pocket.

Up on the bridge, Gordon, Ned, and Lenny tried to coax Ronnie from the car. Oblivious to the arrival of the police, Ronnie stayed put, convinced he was about to awaken from a nightmare.

Gordon took stock. His clothes hung on him, cold and heavy with saturation. Dampness clung to his skin – the only sensory comfort: the warmth of freshly laid shit, steaming from the seat of his pants. He turned to Lenny.

'Lenny, quick – clear off over to the pub, tell Dermot what's going on – we'll deal with the cops.'

Lenny didn't need telling twice; he had an intrinsic aversion to flashing blue lights. Off he galloped.

§

Both horses having romped home, the atmosphere over at The Haydale Arms hummed with jubilation. Dermot Doran had ridden each of them down the final furlong. He'd mounted a bar stool in front of the telly and thrashed at the air behind his arse with an imaginary whip. Amused locals guffawed over their beer as the landlord hollered the thoroughbreds over the finishing line. Overjoyed with his new solvency, Dermot treated his regulars to a celebratory drink.

Lenny Plant, gulping air and wet as the bottom of a pond, stumbled in through the door. The thrum of happy banter stalled as faces turned to observe the sodden teenager swaying by the end of the bar. A puzzled Dermot was first to speak.

'Lenny lad, what's going on?'

Silence followed as Lenny tried to make some reasonable computation of recent events. In order to translate to Dermot, he set his mind on organising a rational explanation. A confusion of thoughts boiled in his head: the alcohol, threats of breathalysers and urine tests, the terror ride, the dawning that they'd almost drowned – then there was Ronnie, still in the car and certain to perish.

Lenny opened his mouth. He tried to explain everything, but offered only an incomprehensible utterance – one crippled with shock and drunken brevity.

'It – it's Ronnie, you know – Ronnie Dent.'

'Yes Lenny – go on,' encouraged Dermot. 'What's happened?'

'He's got – he's got.' Lenny blurted out his useless answer: 'He's got urine in his piss.'

'What the Jesus?' Dermot scratched his head. 'Where is Ronnie?'

'In the river; it was just a stream at first, but it's a river now.'

'What's he doing in the river Lenny?'

'Driving his car – he's got the wipers on as well.'

Drinkers nudged one another, swapping bemused glances.

'What're you talking about Lad? You're not making sense.' Dermot rammed a glass at the optic twice and handed Lenny a large whisky. 'Get this inside of you and tell me what's going on.'

Lenny gulped the whisky, wiped a damp hand across his mouth, and got himself half settled.

'The car's gone in the river Dermot. Ronnie drove it in there and he's still in it. He's drunk and the river's flooded and the cops are there. He's jammed – jammed under the old bridge. Ned and Gordon are trying to get him out but he won't budge; the fucking idiot won't budge Dermot. We've got to get him out.'

Dermot thought a while before startling himself into a bog-eyed panic. 'The slips – who's got the fockin' betting slips? Please tell me Ronnie hasn't got them Lenny lad.'

'Ronnie's got the betting slips Dermot.'

Dermot grabbed the beer pumps, stood on his toes, and cried-out across the bar: 'Six pints to the person who brings me those betting slips!'

The place erupted. In response to the offer of a reward drinkers launched themselves from their seats. Truck drivers Ken Wiggins and Dave Bartle abandoned their darts match while a dart was still airborne. Delia Stark slid off her bar stool. Concerned her boyfriend might make the bridge before her she threw a left and knocked him to the floor. War veteran Victor "The Brad" Bradley thrust his walking stick between the striding legs of his drinking companion Freddie Adler to gain advantage on the rush for the door. Sherry slurper Agnes Rycroft drained her glass and joined the stampede, confident Dermot would convert the reward to a bottle of Harvey's Cream.

Dermot threw Lenny a coat. 'Wrap yourself up Lenny; c'mon to we see what's happening.'

'What about the pub Dermot?'

'Sure there's no one in it.'

Dermot and Lenny made off to the bridge.

§

'I'm not moving till you two fuck off,' ordered Ronnie from the driver's seat. He peered up at the policemen through a half opened window. Ditch-water slushed around the interior – suspended in it: a flotilla of fag ends, an empty beer can, and a used durex.

Sergeant Fox and PC Peasey stood on the bridge, truncheons drawn. Fox was getting frustrated at his lack of success at extricating a harmless drunk from a half-submerged car. The cop cautioned Ronnie – only it wasn't the formal policeman's pre-arrest caution. He leaned over the bridge wall and threatened with a wave of his truncheon, 'We're staying here till you get out of that car you drunken bastard; and the quicker you climb out the less of this you're gonna get.'

The brutal coaxing was having little effect on Ronnie. Gordon Taylor intervened: 'You heard him mate – he's stubborn, okay? If you don't back-off he's going to drown.'

Fox rounded on Gordon and pointed his truncheon directly into his face.

'Listen-up shitty pants, you're obstructing a police officer in the execution of his duty – one more word out of you and you're nicked.'

The crowd from the pub, led by Delia Stark, had just made the scene. Stark, a wayward but smart girl, whose father was a prominent barrister, drew-up in front of the sergeant.

'You know fine well he won't get out of the car while you're standing over him,' Delia nodded at PC Peasey, 'why don't you and him go and wait by your cars and let us get him out?'

'Are you telling me how to do my job madam?'

The fearless Stark put her face within kissing distance of Fox's; she snarled up his nostrils: 'If he drowns because you decline to move thirty yards then I see that as a gross dereliction of duty occasioning unnecessary death. This man is half frozen, disorientated, and temporarily bereft of his capacity for rational thought by virtue of drunkenness. You are the controlling mind in this scenario and therefore abusing your office through seeking compliance by threatening him with violence.'

Stark shot a decent line in high-end bull-shit; she turned and swept her arm at the crowd standing behind her.

'Look at all these police-hating witnesses officer – they're itching to make their statements. By the way, I'll be asking my father Christian Stark to represent the family of the late Mr. Dent when it all goes to court. It's going to look so bad for you in the dock. It'll be in the papers as well; you'll be out on your ear – think about that: bang goes your pension, your lump sum, and your early retirement. Oh – and you won't be able to boss people about any more – not even your fucking wife. You're looking at porridge. A plod in jail – it's not the kind of breakfast oatmeal you want to be munching on Percy.'

The policeman was possessed of a dullness of wit familiar to many of his calling. It proved debilitating whenever it came to summoning spontaneity beyond the prosaic. Delia had him comfortably outmanoeuvred. He'd heard of Christian Leopold Stark – and the reputation that preceded him.

Fox and his colleague backed off. As they did, Victor "The Brad" Bradley leaned over the wall and offered the hooked end of his walking stick to Ronnie. Ronnie took hold and eased himself out of the window; as he did Lenny reached out a lanky arm and grabbed Ronnie's collar. Hauling him over the wall Victor spied the betting slips. Evading the attentions of the police the old war dog removed them to his own pocket – a victorious six-pint grin dimpling his cheeks. 'I'll look after these for you Ronnie.' He smiled a world of sympathy and patted Ronnie's back. 'Just go quietly old boy, there's a good chap; in a week's time we'll all be laughing at this.'

Fox and Peasey marched over from their cars to make the arrest. Delia Stark warned Fox with a prodding finger: 'One mark on him – one mark!'

Lenny watched the policemen load Ronnie into the back of the car: a soaking bundle of despondency Lenny felt for the drenched sot – but only for an instant. Dermot's whiskey marinated in his skull; it went some length to comfort all morbid reflections on the day, convincing the young man that everything would be fine. After all, Ronnie Dent was an adult, he knew what he was doing – of course he did. He had a beard for fuck's sake.

The locals retreated to the pub. Dermot and Lenny followed.

'After all that carry-on you'll be needin' a drink in ye Lenny lad?'

'You don't know where I could get one do you Dermot?'

'I know just the place.' Dermot gave a playful ruffle of Lenny's hair before running-on ahead. 'Last one back's a Protestant.'

Lenny chased after him – drunk, and laughing, and young.

A pair of Russian eyes looked on from the wooded bank opposite. They were the eyes of Vagin Semyon – a time traveller. He'd been sent from the future. He'd been sent to observe Lenny Plant.

All was not well.

CHAPTER 2

BACK TO THE PRESENT

The night, windblown and dark as the inside of a chimney, smothered the neighbourhood. Lenny Plant peered into it. The watery half-moon sulked behind a bundle of clouds.

Lenny was curious. Through eyes blurred with drink and tiredness he watched the lone figure make its way along Willow Gardens. Closer it came; scurrying, staggering – managing an awkward half jog now and then. Lenny heard his name once more, choked-out between tar-lined bronchial gasps. Closer still and Lenny recognised a familiar tangle of human scruff.

Ronnie Dent was sixty-six these days. Lenny couldn't remember when he'd last seen his friend run with a belly-full of drink in him – in fact, all Lenny's life he'd scarcely seen Ronnie run at all. Ronnie walked most places.

Ronnie Dent could be seen to run on special occasions: like to the toilet, with an arse-full of loose shit, or on to the next pub in time for last orders, or to catch a bus to take him to the pub, or else to a waiting taxi, its meter ticking, heading for the same destination. Ronnie ran fastest from the police – and almost as fast from a job interview.

Ronnie walked most places.

'She's gone Lenny – gone for good. You got to help me.' Ronnie clung to Lenny's shirt and sobbed into his chest.

'Ronnie – what's happened?'

'She's gone – gone for good,' repeated Ronnie. 'Come with me; help me Lenny lad, please help me – I've got a plan.'

Lenny cottoned-on; the way a midnight drunk cottons-on to what he thinks is the obvious. 'She'll come back Ronnie; give her a day or two to cool off and she'll be walking back up the garden path pushing that old bike of hers.'

Lenny comforted his friend, knowing fine well Ronnie and his wife Edith rowed more often than Ronnie thought about his next drink.

Lenny had left Ronnie fifteen minutes earlier, in good spirits, full of spirits, clinging to the bar of the Haydale Arms. His old friend had given up on the Pystwiser cider halfway through the evening, defaulting effortlessly to his favourite Scottish tipple. His breath reeked of single-malt apples, sautéed in halitosis.

Lenny had seen Edith too, on his way home from the pub. She'd swept passed him on her bicycle, travelling abnormally fast for a burly sixty-four year-old. Lenny guessed she must have left the house in a hurry as she hadn't bothered to fasten her coat. It flapped behind her like a torn sail.

It was out of context, seeing Edith pedalling her bike at that time of night. As she passed Lenny she called out to him. Lenny was certain he heard what she said: above the roar of the wind Edith had shouted a comment on the weather: "It's a freezer Lenny." That's what she said – for sure.

Now, with Ronnie sobbing in front of him, it was obvious what had happened. Lenny's late-night encounter with Edith was perfectly explainable: she and Ronnie had had one of their humdingers after Ronnie had staggered in through the back door. After saying her piece Edith had stormed off on her bike, likely threatening never to return.

'What am I going to do without her Lenny? I'll not cope – I can't believe it's happened – thought I'd be the first to leave.'

Ronnie was a good bit shorter than Lenny; more so nowadays, courtesy of a stoop brought on by the years. Until recently the majority of his face had long since seen daylight – his eyes, nose and ears being the only features evident beyond a bristle of beard and eyebrows. A low thatch of tangled hairline did its best to converge. In addition, the follicular sprout from his ears and nostrils was nothing less than startling – Ronnie was hirsute in the extreme. Gordon Taylor had once remarked, in the crowded bar of The Haydale Arms, that he dreaded to think what Ronnie's arse looked like – given the state of his face. Ronnie obliged his curiosity by bending over and dropping his trousers. Dermot Doran, presiding, concurred there wasn't a whole pile of difference at either end.

Ronnie had been clean shaven for almost a month. Those who knew him found his new appearance took a bit of getting used to. In a bizarre effort to raise money for good causes Ronnie had allowed his nasal and ear hair to grow unchecked. Eventually such length was attained as to allow Delia Stark to elegantly join the two growths in plaits that looped across either cheek from ear to nostril. To heighten the visual effect Delia threaded a pink ribbon into the join of each braid. Those beholding Ronnie for the first time were overly fascinated by his appearance, and almost always drew-out their money for a donation.

The chagrined Edith had attempted to amputate the unsightliness on several occasions – coming at Ronnie with a pair of blunt scissors. Lenny didn't doubt that the new look, combined with such profligate drunkenness had heightened the intensity of this evening's row.

To date Ronnie had raised total of two-hundred pounds towards The National Church Disembowelment Program: one of many Societal Enhancement Initiatives operated by a world charity called "Flowers for Faith" – more often referred to as "Three F."

Places of worship up and down the country were being bought-up by Three F, courtesy of a statute loophole, created accidentally on purpose, by a nervy Conservative government doing its desperate best to arse-lick public favour. There would be nothing unusual about tonguing the electorate in such a fashion, side for the fact that the country was being run by an invisible proxy.

A Bill titled "Society Right to Own" made it onto the statute books: an indirect reaction to accommodate a burgeoning public awakening on religion, politics, and soap operas.

On transfer of ownership the churches were stripped of their religious furnishings: altars, candlesticks, crucifixes, and all things "pictorial" (stained glass, murals, paintings and the like). Once gutted, the hollowed-out structure would have no religious affiliation.

Flowers for Faith would re-register the building as a Public Institute for Social Science (P.I.S.S.) – in essence: a proactive, problem solving academy executive, its members elected and mandated by Three F to implement the sustainable deconstruction of any aspect of the "community collective" deemed obstructive to the linear development of a cohesive, morally introspective society. Flowers for Faith's Chief Executive, President, and Director Art Schitthelm, tirelessly expounded the maxim that: "A society that serves for the good of all; must be nurtured by the good of all."

Religion would have no place in its cultivation.

Schitthelm, a veteran of two world wars, had reached the ripe-to-rotten old age of one-hundred and fifteen. In a bid to free-up the flow of creative "academy think juice," he'd come up with the idea of having all disembowelled churches licensed to sell alcohol.P.I.S.S. Academies were now opening up the length and breadth of the country; with welcoming news of uptake interest being expressed throughout large swathes of Europe.

Art Schitthelm played squash five times a week.

Ronnie had actually raised four hundred pounds for the cause – however he was a fair sort: Out of the total money he'd collected, he donated two hundred to Flowers for Faith's Disembowelment Program – and two hundred towards financing his drinking and gambling activities. "Charity begins with charity – and some of it ends up at home," he would declare to himself.

Lenny was cold to his bones; he tried to make light of things. 'C'mon Ronnie, it's not the end of the world; we've both been here before – same old routine: down to the pub, get plastered, back home for the mandatory row, wife grabs handbag and does a Captain Oates number – perfectly normal adult behaviour.' Lenny smiled at his friend. 'The rate she was pedalling it must have been one hell of a ding-dong Ronnie.'

'She's dead Lenny.'

'Eh?'

'Edith's at home – dead.'

Lenny promised himself he would have a sober word with Ronnie about mixing whiskey and cider. Edith was alive and well, he'd just seen her, far removed from death, tearing up the street on a pushbike.

'She'd have a hard job Ronnie.'

'What're you on about Lenny; who's Captain Oates?' whimpered Ronnie.

'Fuck's sake,' muttered Lenny to himself. He was eager to conclude the evening, and not in a mood for enlightening Ronnie on the tragedies of early polar exploration.

'Listen Ronnie, she can't be dead; I saw her ten minutes ago, on her bike, pedalling like her arse was on fire.'

Ronnie's pink ribbons fluttered against his cheeks; Lenny wondered how anyone could take the man seriously given the ridiculous celebration of unwanted hair. Appearance alone would alert most rational thinkers to the possibility that any ensuing conversation would have to be seasoned with more than just a pinch of salt. Now here he was, mourning the demise of his wife – when she was still very much alive.

Lenny made to reason further with Ronnie, but stalled himself with a fresh thought: What if it was he who was the worse for drink? What if he only imagined he'd seen Edith on her bike? After all, it's a known fact that drink can mess with your perceptions, your recollections, and your consciousness. Being a newcomer to the Pystwiser, Lenny had been drinking in potent, unchartered waters all evening. He was likely to be unaccustomed to the nature of the cider's intoxicating properties – and how they interacted with synaptic transmissions within the skull.

His expression wrinkled with anxiety; Lenny began to doubt himself. Ronnie clocked the face language, looked up and down the street, and fixed Lenny with a stare that focused three miles beyond the Milky Way.

'I need help with something Lenny,' Ronnie had a cupped hand raised to the side of his mouth – like he was worried someone other than Lenny might be listening in. Someone was.

'Can't it wait until tomorrow Ronnie?' said Lenny, further worried by Ronnie's abrupt shift from his principle distraction, i.e. the claimed discovery of his dead wife. Now there was an added concern: Lenny's long held knowledge that, whenever Ronnie Dent needed "help with something," it was usually something illicit and self-serving.

Ronnie tugged at Lenny's arm. "C'mon Lenny, we can't hang about, she's going cold on us."

With his curiosity and self-doubt sufficiently aroused, Lenny gave up on the idea of telling Ronnie to sod off home. The two drunks made off to Ronnie's house.

§

Using the cover of a hawthorn hedge that skirted the road, time traveller Vagin Semyon watched the pair of them. He had one eye on the front of his chin – the other situated at the top right-hand corner of his forehead. Vagin's arms were attached to his hips and his mouth spoke-out from the left side of his neck. He wasn't born with such disfiguration – Vagin's horrifying deformities were down to the side effects of a "time shunt" accident.

The Russian was a hideous sight.

Those for whom he worked were eager to find out what had caused the accident. With a view to establishing accountability, the Russian President Vladimir Sputum ordered the Head of the KGB's Military Operations Directorate to carry out an investigation and produce a report with a "positive spin" – one that would hold up to internal scrutiny. On the President's insistence the report would carry the title: "Time Shunt Event."

The investigation was completed within a month and a draft of the report sent to the President. It identified various contributing factors, detailing them in technical jargon well beyond the comprehension of most who read it.

To lend the investigation some palatable symmetry the report concluded with an upbeat summary: It declared that much knowledge had been gained to the furtherance of time travel research, and described the "event" as "fortuitous." Vagin's deformities were classified as an "Operational Asset." The upside of Vagin's "new appearance" was extolled as "beneficial to his role," "an inbuilt incentive for any Grade A Surveillance Officer to keep themselves out of public sight and thus optimise their covert status."

The report recommended that Vagin be deducted three months' time travel bonus for his part in the "Event."

Meanwhile, back in 1912, Captain Oates was being kicked to death. The ice wind that hungered to claim him would lose out on its place in history.

It was Saint Patricks' day – Oates' birthday.

CHAPTER 3

RONNIE'S HOUSE

Ronnie and Edith Dent lived in a detached dormer bungalow, left them by Edith's late uncle Bertram in 1976. Immaculate when they took possession, the intervening years would see the house, and its grounds, devolve into a state of unkemptness, floundering somewhere between tired and clapped-out.

Set back from the road, the majority of the property was now shrouded in a giant bird's nest of horticultural negligence, with access to its front door gained along a barely penetrable footpath. If you peered into the front garden's wilderness with determined eyes you could pick out Ronnie's old Cortina; it had become 'as one' with the overgrowth. Ronnie had it recovered from the stream the Monday after he drove it in there – the drink-driver was uninsured, skint and in anticipation of a hefty fine – at least. He left Edith to square the recovery bill, but she was only prepared to pay the breakdown company to tow the vehicle as far as the house. Ronnie and Gordon Taylor pushed the car onto the front garden – which would turn out to be the car's final resting place. With the exception of one person, no one had been in the Cortina since September 1981.

Uncle Bertram would no doubt turn in his grave if he could see the state of disrepair his former house and gardens had fallen into. That would be so if corpses were able to turn in their graves. However, if corpses were able to turn in their graves, then Uncle Bertram's corpse would be incapable of expressing disapproval from his coffin in such a fashion. Uncle Bertram was presented unto the Lord in a state most un-corpse like.

Uncle Bertram, affectionately known as Uncle Bertie; was a short-sighted bachelor who suffered from Chronic Essential Tremor Syndrome. He would best be remembered as an interfering fuss-pot of a steam engine enthusiast who drank Double Diamond from a shivering half-pint glass. His demise at the age of fifty-eight occurred for all to see at the Locburn Village Summer Fete: Uncle Bertie's trembling fingers had a tragically miscalculated interaction with the drive belt on one of his favourite puffers. He was carrying out a delicate and entirely unnecessary adjustment to the belt tensioner when the wobbling Whitworth spanner slipped from the adjuster. He was dragged, involuntarily, and with savage authority, into the flywheel assembly. Uncle Bertie, or to be fair, bits and pieces of him, were scattered about the Village Green – here, there, and everywhere.

Aside from the initial pinching sensation as his fingers fed-in twixt belt and flywheel, Bertie didn't feel a thing.

The Wurlitzer played on.

Some are remembered for their famous last words: Nelson for instance, with "Kiss me Hardy," or Ned Kelly's final utterance, "Such is life." Uncle Bertie could only manage a polite "Whoops."

He went straight to heaven.

In the early days Edith did her best to garden, and clean, and tidy, and cook. However a full time job, together with Ronnie's natural laziness and costly hobbies proved too much of a burden. Her husband had been sacked from numerous jobs over time and had long since attained the status of "unemployable." They'd tried for children shortly after they were married but nothing happened.

The most devoted of partners would have given up years ago; but Edith was stout of spirit, and trundled on through life's undulations with what she had. Ashamed of how her husband presented himself to the world, both in attitude and appearance, and also embarrassed by the state of the house, Edith was reluctant to receive visitors. She did all the visiting, and counteracted the misery of circumstance under which she laboured, by promulgating harmless gossip within the pedalling range of her pushbike.

In spite of everything she remained faithful to Ronnie: a man possessed of an inexhaustible talent for converting money into drunkenness – and alcohol into urine. Ronnie's pension and nefarious fundraising paid, more or less, for his indulgences – Edith's civil service pension covered everything else.

CHAPTER 4

OUT OF SIGHT

Ronnie Dent led Lenny Plant up the garden path. The wily drunk would be leading his friend up several more garden paths before he was through with his intentions. Lenny stooped and weaved his way through the tangle of bush and briar and branch till the front door came into view.

Ronnie coaxed the door open with his shoulder. He spoke in a whisper. 'Are you ready for this Lenny?'

'Come on Ronnie, let's get on with it – I still think you're either pissing me about, or just plain pissed, or both.'

Lenny was muddled with the situation, but took a care to hold steady with his line of disbelief. There was a tangible doubt eating at him though.

'She's in the living room, watching telly she is Len – err, or she was before she, you know, before I found her, well I didn't really find her because I knew she would already be there, because that's where she always was when it was that time of night, but I didn't know she wouldn't be alive any more, like she was before – before, you know – she was dead, like she is now. Does that lot make sense Lenny?'

'Yeah, perfect sense for somebody who's totally shitfaced – fuck that bastard apple juice Ron, fuck it,' Lenny followed Ronnie in through the door, drawing to a halt when he spotted a pushbike parked under the staircase void.

'I didn't know you had a bike as well Ronnie?' he asked, consciously fooling himself, and at the same time not wanting to take another step further into the house.

'I don't.'

'Eh?'

'My bike's long gone Lenny – you know that? I wrecked it when I stuffed it into Archie Cole's privet hedge and got myself stuck in there.' Ronnie waited for Lenny to affirm. 'It was that time I was drunk – remember?'

'Ah, come to think of it I can remember now Ron; once you mentioned you were arseholed it kind of jogged my memory.' Lenny had a go at sarcasm to ease the looming gravity.

'So Edith's got two pushbikes then?' asked Lenny, assigning any remnants of hope to desperation.

'Just the one Lenny,' assured Ronnie, 'just the one pushbike for poor old Edith; to think she'll never ride it again.' He sniffed back his grief and opened the door that led from the hallway into the living room.

As the door opened Lenny's nose fed incoming data to his brain. He had a remarkable sense of smell – half as good as your average dog. Sometimes it was a curse, sometimes a blessing; other times a mixture of both.

Through the open door came many scents. Lenny smelt the underlying base odours any outsider would pick-up when first entering another's home: the welcome smell of the coal fire, the ubiquitous infusion of Ronnie's chain-smoked fags, an old carpet, riddled with the reek of time, the lazy rank of a fart, sphincter-blown into a sofa the day before, still rising, miracle like from its spongy lair. There was the homely waft of a thousand cooked dinners, nestling between the hum of rising damp and foot-sweat.

Above every aroma, Lenny's nostrils drew-in the leaden stench of fresh death. He'd experienced the same smell once before, long ago, back in the hot summer of 1976. A 15 year-old Lenny was standing not ten yards from the old steam engine when Uncle Bertie became entangled.

Warm, fresh death – here it was again, sweet, sickly, streaming up his nostrils, turning his guts. Lenny could hear the telly as he followed Ronnie into the living room: a church minister on a late night current affairs program was warning the public that the Devil was alive and well, and going by the name of Art Schitthelm. The fire, in want of a shovel of coal, flickered low in its grate.

At the far end of a large sofa sat Edith. She looked okay, thought Lenny, on his first acquaintance. Her posture was normal for anyone watching television from the comfort of their settee. She seemed composed, not dishevelled, or in pain, or annoyed, or even dead. Her eyes were open and looking in the direction of the TV. On the arm of the settee Edith had balanced a patterned china plate; on it, two chocolate digestives – a bite taken from one of them. Lenny relaxed a little, feeling that the scene was as naturally domestic for this time of night as one could imagine.

'Hello Edith; I've fetched him back for you,' he announced with plenty of chirp – 'found him roaming the neighbourhood; must've forgotten where he lived.'

Edith didn't respond. Her eyes were unblinking and her mouth hung open. Lenny stepped forwards for a closer look; leaning over the back of the sofa he noticed her left hand opened and turned palm upward. She'd relaxed her grip on the handle of the china cup, spilling its contents onto the cushion next to her.

'Looks like she's nodded off Ronnie,' said Lenny, down to his last ounce of denial.

'How many people do you know sleep with their eyes open Len?'

Lenny shrugged at the question.

'Even ducks have to close at least one eye. She's dead.' Ronnie uttered life's final diagnosis in a tone flat as a fucked tyre.

'Are you sure?'

'Yeah I've checked.'

'Checked – how?'

'I tested her reflexes.'

Lenny was a tad impressed; there was more to his friend than just drink, fags and horses – Ronnie could tell when dead people were dead by testing their reflexes.

'Tested her reflexes?'

'Yeah – watch, I'll show you.'

Ronnie went over to the sideboard and slid a knitting needle from a ball of wool. He returned to Edith's side and jabbed it into her cheek with force enough to leave a Kirk Douglas dimple.

'See what I mean – dead.'

Lenny tried to believe what he'd just seen.

'Christ Ronnie, you can't – that's not how you – she's dead Ron, Edith's dead.'

Numbing realisation took hold; Lenny was left with nothing but his drunkenness to soften the brunt of the shock.

Like a fanfare from hell the wind wailed down the chimney. Lenny shuddered to his guts as he strained to find the composure to prompt Ronnie.

'You need to ring the cops?'

'Cops?'

'Yeah – you know: shiny buttons on black suits, flat feet, handcuffs.'

'I know, I know – what do I want to ring them for? Are they going to bring her back to life or something?'

'It's a sudden death,' said Lenny, 'you've got to report it.'

'What's the difference between a sudden death and a non-sudden death Lenny lad?'

'Like it was with Bertie and the steam engine – that was sudden; the cops have to be informed Ron, believe me.' Lenny looked about the room. 'Where's your phone?'

'Eh?'

The old BT phone sat on a small table in the corner of the room. Lenny spied it, strode over, and reached for the receiver.

'No cops Lenny.' Ronnie got to the phone first. With a tug vicious enough to remove the head from a rattle-snake, he ripped the cable from its receiver. Lenny looked at his friend; unsure of his own mind, and whether startled had the upper hand over confusion.

'What're you doing Ron – what's going on?' Lenny tried to fathom Ronnie's behaviour. Even factoring-in alcohol and bereavement something wasn't right. Lenny had known Ronnie for decades. In all that time, interpreting his friend's climate of mood and manner, both in and out of drink, was reliably easy. For all his faults, Ronnie, his social dogma, and his lifestyle rhythm, were steady as they went.

It was different tonight though: Ronnie Dent was out of tune with himself – and it bothered Lenny.

Lenny had another concern surfacing from the pickled mists of his recent memory: He'd seen Edith on her bike and she had spoken to him – no doubt about it. He was seeing ghosts again. Lenny pushed the worry to one side; knowing fine well it would be back to haunt him later.

'I know we're not keen on the cops Ron, but we're in the shit if we don't inform them.' Lenny got out his mobile phone and squinted at its screen – no signal. Ronnie relaxed when he realised the three of them were incommunicado.

'No signal eh – it's always crap down here,' said Ronnie, a twist of a smile breaking on his face. 'Nobody's in on this one Lenny – just you and me,' Ronnie turned and nodded at his late wife, 'and Edith of course.'

'You're spooking me Ron. How about telling me what you're up to?'

'Sit down a minute Lenny.'

Lenny took a seat at the opposite end of the sofa to Edith. Ronnie sat down between the drunk and the dead, and stared at the fire.

'I can't get by without her Len,' he said with moderate sadness.

Lenny eased a little and offered up his condolences in a series of prosaic one-liners: 'I'm so sorry Ronnie, I wish I knew what to say, I can't begin to imagine what you're going through, at least she died peacefully. If there's anything I can do for you.'

Ronnie chimed in.

'Thanks for that Lenny – actually there is something you can do. I'll come to that shortly.'

Ronnie crisped his tone mid-sentence; shifting from appropriate melancholy to business-like in a breath. He leaned forward and half-turned to Lenny, settling his eyes on him with a sideways look. Ronnie rested his elbows on his knees to facilitate palm rotation for purpose of gesticulation. Financial Advisors adopt a similar posture and mannerism when selling endowment mortgages to the desperate and the unknowing.

'What I'm trying to say Lenny, is that: yes, I am going to miss Edith, and her death has come as a great shock to me – but there's no way I can manage without her.'

'Time will heal your pain Ronnie – believe me. Following death there has to be hope; there has to be faith in the future. Edith would want you to carry on with life and cherish your memories.' Lenny was embarrassed; but only because he was aware he sounded like a priest going through the same old routine sympathy shit.

'Yeah, yeah, I know that Lenny – let's save the routine sympathy shit for when the priest comes – or for when he doesn't come as it happens.'

'Sorry Ron, I was only trying to –.'

'No worries. Now, quiet awhile and hear me out.'

Ronnie set to with his cajolery.

'You've known me donkey's years – we've got up to all sorts of mischief – me, you and the others, but you know what I'm like. Let's be honest Len, I'm a fucking waster.'

'Don't say that Ronnie; I think you're a –.'

'A fucking waster Lenny – I know what I am and I'm comfortable with it, so don't bother blowing smoke up me arse, it's already full of shit.'

Lenny agreed in silence. Ronnie was indeed a waster, a waster full of shit at that. But Lenny loved his old friend – he loved him and he felt for him.

'I can't let Edith go just now Lenny; there're some things I need to say to her – things I should've said long ago. I would have said them sooner, only when I came to saying them I couldn't get a word in lengthways.'

'You mean sideways Ronnie.'

'Yeah, that way as well – Edith never shut up, bless her. Now that she's quiet it's an excellent opportunity for me to get it all off my chest.'

'Do you want me to leave you and Edith alone for a while Ron?'

Ronnie shook his head. 'That would be good Lenny, but the things I have to say, well, they're going to take more than just a while to say.'

'Right – so what do we do?'

'As far as favours go Lenny, I'm about to ask you for a whopper.'

Ronnie paused so Lenny could ask exactly what the big favour was.

'So what exactly is the big favour?' asked Lenny.

'You got to promise – don't be mad.'

'Not fair Ronnie.'

'Edith's staying here with me.'

Lenny stalled as he tried to process the unfolding nonsense. Ronnie waited for a response.

'So you'll be scattering her ashes in the garden then, or maybe sitting them on the mantel-piece in one of those fancy earns?'

'I'm not cremating her.'

'You can't bury her in the garden Ronnie; it's not the done thing.'

'I'm not burying her.'

'Smithereens Smith then; bloody expensive Ron?'

'No way – I'm not having her blown up. How can she stay here with me when she's been blown to pieces in a disused quarry by some new-fangled fad of a funeral service? Anyway, you're right – it'd cost me a bomb.'

Smithereens Smith Afterlife Services had been operating their revolutionary 'non-burn, non-burial' funeral business for almost three years now. The key to their unexpected success hinged on the novel appeal of having ones remains blown up. The avant-garde undertaking, now a national franchise, had grown to take a forty per-cent share of the UK market.

The business was established in 2011 by an Arthur Smith of Gravesend. Arthur was a child when he discovered, at a tender age, that he'd more than just a passing interest in explosives. He'd gained proud possession of his very first box of matches after swapping the jawbone of a dead German pilot he'd unearthed in his uncle's allotment. Arthur had made his grisly find whilst engaged in the business of burying a neighbourhood cat he'd dispatched with his cousin's air rifle. Arthur held the cat responsible for the brutal murder of his pet goldfish.

Little time had passed before Arthur, his matches, and an ordnance factory came into contact with one another. The nine year-old had set fire to a dustbin at the rear of the factory following a busy day lighting fires in a local forest. Arthur had interrupted his homeward sprint from a blazing horizon to stop for a comfort break by the bin compound. Not wanting the last match in the box to go begging, Arthur struck up and tossed it into a bin to see what would happen. When the flames took to the building he resumed his onward gallop.

A balmy September evening back in 1967 saw the people of Salisbury treated to an earth trembling firework display sufficient to kick-start an extinct volcano.

Smithereens Smith's advertising puns thrived on morbid humour: "No smell, no rot – no need to book a plot," "Don't cremate, detonate!" "Go out with a bang." "They'll be thrilled to bits when you're blown to bits," "Ask the Vicar, it's so much quicker," "Don't whiff – send for Smith."

D.U.N.C.E. (The Society of Diggers Undertakers Necrophiliacs Crematorialists and Embalmers), along with the Church and certain environmental pressure groups, were outraged at the practice. They lobbied Parliament to intervene and ban the 'body blasting' immediately.

The Conservative Prime Minister was instructed to order an investigation into the affair; and at the same time encouraged to ensure that the resultant public report would not harm the interests of Smithereens Smith.

The Prime Minister knew what was good for him, and Art Schitthelm knew what was good for the Prime Minister. The Prime Minister knew that what was good for Art Schitthelm was also good for the Prime Minister. Each knew what was good for the other. Of all the goodness that was good for the pair of them, both knew that no badness should come from the good of it.

The report was published and made public. It gave the 'facts,' and concluded that the moral argument had been blown out of all proportion. The church's voice was dismissed as hysterical, and more or less obsolete in a dawning of neo-enlightenment. An environmental study, commissioned on behalf of the Government by Flowers for Faith, produced an independent report providing irrefutable evidence that the process was kinder to the environment than more conventional methods of dealing with death's compost. D.U.N.C.E came out of it badly, being discredited for jealousy, assumption of monopoly, and lack of innovation.

As an acknowledgement to the low carbon footprint generated by the business, gelignite purchased solely for funeral use was zero-rated for VAT. Coincidentally, explosives manufacturing plants throughout all of Western Europe were owned by Three F. The charity maintained healthy market prices by controlling production; they also, covertly, and very precisely, policed who was using it – and to what use they were putting it to. Art Schitthelm saw to it that anyone who utilised anything that went 'bang', to the detriment of decent society, would suffer dearly.

In time to come Smithereens Smith would be floated on the stock market – the majority of its shares being bought up by Flowers for Faith.

'Do you need any frozen food Len?' asked Ronnie.

He stood up from the sofa, groaning at his aches as he arched his back. 'I'm clearing out the freezer. I don't want anything for the grub – you can have it for nowt.'

'No thanks Ron,' said Lenny, still confused and drunk, and picturing himself rolling in through the back door at two in the morning laden with out of date frozen food. 'Sarah's got our freezer full to its throat with oven chips, pizzas and boil in the bag shite we'll never eat – all welded together in a nasty domestic iceberg. You'd need a fucking power-chisel to get at what you wanted.'

Ronnie grinned at his friend. Lenny was intrigued at how different Ronnie looked when he grinned these days. The absence of a beard revealed a new landscape to his various expressions. Ronnie had a slant to his mouth that Lenny had long forgotten about. Having been left with a buckled mandible following a bungled operation to reset a bad fracture, Ronnie lacked some degree of facial symmetry.

Back in 1976 Ronnie had been standing by the coconut shy when he was struck in the face by uncle Bertie's large intestine. The sizeable chunk of Bertie's digestive system, engorged with the previous evening's cottage pie, had travelled across the fairground at forty-eight miles per-hour, before laying Ronnie out for the count.

Lenny studied the sloping grin, the conjoined ear and nose hair, and the pink ribbons. His friend put him in mind of a silly fucker.

'What're you throwing good food out for Ronnie? You'll need it for yourself.'

Ronnie thought before answering. He went to stroke his beard then realised he didn't have one.

'I badly want the space – anyway, there's plenty of tinned stuff in the cupboard. Then there's the peanuts Mervin sticks on the bar at the Haydale – and bits and pieces I can nick from the supermarket. So – big deal, little deal; if you're not interested in the food, I'm chucking it tonight.'

Lenny wanted to go home. 'Right Ronnie; you want to spend some time alone with Edith – fair enough. I'll head off home and leave you to it – but I'm ringing the cops first thing.'

'Hang on Len, wait there – I'll be back in two seconds.'

Ronnie left the room. He went through to the kitchen, grabbed a bin liner, and scurried into the garage. Negotiating his way around years of accumulated junk he got to the chest freezer at the back of the garage. In a hurry Ronnie emptied its contents into the bin liner, nipped round the back of the garage, and dumped the bag into the wheelie bin.

'I'll need a lift before you go Len.'

Ronnie had returned to the living room.

'What with?'

'Edith.'

'Where are you lifting her?' asked Lenny, longing for his duvet, and on the cusp abandoning the situation.

'Not far – just out to the freezer.'

'The freezer?'

As Lenny spoke a penny dropped inside his head – a large penny: When she had ridden past him earlier, Edith didn't say "It's a freezer Lenny," – she said "In the freezer Lenny."

The body fitted neatly into the old chest-freezer: a National Electric Bulk Frost 100 Deluxe, featuring revolutionary rheo-static trickle-volt technology with a three phase econo-freeze matrix lining. It was bought back in the seventies for Ronnie and Edith as a wedding present by Edith's parents. Awful to think their dead daughter would end up in it.

Lenny had taken Edith under the arm pits; Ronnie took her ankles. Lenny had the heavier end by a good margin. Edith Dent had the appetite of two truck drivers. One thing she never did though was eat between meals – Edith had meals between eating. Lenny looked down at her and estimated the majority of the bulk to be made up of breasts; breasts large enough to wet-nurse half the suckling of Somalia.

Lenny had never seen Edith's bosoms alfresco; although he had been informed many times, by her drunken husband, that when unslung the mass/buoyancy ratio was sufficient to confound the dictates of gravity. When Ronnie first met Edith back in 1973, it was her frontage he fell in love with – over the years his preoccupation had endured without falter. Edith Dent had always been on the portly side, but carried herself well. Her enormous breasts and fulsome buttocks lent her a contour that was not entirely unpleasing; either to the wanton letch of the heterosexual male – or the hungry roving of a lesbian eye.

'I can't believe we're doing this,' said Lenny, as Ronnie closed the lid of the freezer.

'It's the right thing to do Lenny and you know it; Edith spoke to you, her ghost told you what you had to do: "In the freezer Lenny." And isn't it more than just a coincidence that I wanted to put her in there as well?'

Ronnie had conveniently developed a strong belief in ghosts the minute Lenny coughed about his encounter with Edith. Once Lenny mentioned what he thought she'd said Ronnie didn't take any convincing. Neither did he need to further coerce Lenny into assisting him.

Four years previously, in the village of Locburn, Lenny had encountered three ghosts inside a week. They had spoken to him – warning him, enlightening him, advising him. Since that extraordinary week, Lenny, formerly a cynic when it came to all things supernatural, believed in ghosts. For very good reasons he took what they said seriously. In this case it was clear Edith wanted to be close to the man she loved; a man she wanted to continue loving beyond the grave – that made perfect sense inside a head swimming with pystwiser.

Ronnie had a less romantic perspective: he wanted her out of sight, but still alive in existence of mind. That is: alive in everyone's existence of mind; including the nosey living minds of the neighbourhood – along with the benevolent living mind of the Civil Service Pensions Agency.

Vagin Semyon hung by his feet from the guttering. Upside-down like a roosting bat he watched through the window as the two men loaded a large woman into the freezer. Vagin clutched a box of frozen fish fingers; their sell-by-date two months gone. He crunched on one of them – and salivated at the size of the breasts.

CHAPTER 5

WHAT WENT BEFORE

Lenny Plant could tell you the exact time and place it all started: 2011 it was, liquid lunchtime, twelve-noon – around midday, last Saturday in the summer of June that same year. Sitting alone at his garden table, that's where he was. Drinking wine as it happened.

That's when he heard the howling of a human being. It was the kind of howling a human being makes when they've amputated three of their toes with a lawn mower.

Two gardens down Enid Byers, a sixty-three year-old widower and Cliff Richard fan, had pulled the mower over her foot. Rotten luck the toes got in the way – poor Enid.

The small village neighbourhood of Locburn was quiet that day, Lenny's wife and daughter were out shopping; others in Willow Gardens were either doing the same, or else visiting relatives, or on their holidays. Fate saw to it that only Lenny would be around to lend assistance to the stricken Enid.

Lenny called for an ambulance. Enid was rushed to hospital – she'd nearly bled to death.

Following the accident Lenny and Enid formed a strong platonic bond. Enid rightly had Lenny down as a likeable pisshead who genuinely cared for her. Lenny wrongly had Enid down as a gentle, sixty three year-old widow, cursed with undeserved misfortune.

There were many things Lenny didn't know about Enid Byers back in June 2011; things better left unknown. Unfortunately, inside a week, get to know them he did.

Blessed with an I.Q. of a hundred and sixty one; the white-haired rose pruner could fly a military helicopter, bench press three hundred pounds, and kill a grown man with a carpet slipper.

Enid worked for Flowers for Faith (Three F). More precisely, she worked for Art Schitthelm's Covert Kill Squad: a team of highly trained assassins.

Schitthelm founded Flowers for Faith in 1965 during a visit to the toilet. The inspiration to form the charity set upon him as he strained to egest the remnants of a Black Forest Gateaux. On pondering the charity's intended utilisation Schitthelm looked to the flush system for inspiration. Whilst pulling the chain it occurred to him that, with the right technology and resources, unwanted shit could be removed effectively and permanently – leaving behind a most desirable and essential cleanliness.

Art had long been troubled at the condition of the World's society. Having witnessed two of the bloodiest wars in history, both fought inside of four decades, he had just entitlement to his concerns.

In spite of the slaughter the human race had remained untaught, and as resolute in its foolishness as it ever was. Profitable change came to weigh insignificant against obscene bloodshed. Any welcome flourishing of sociability or morality was too readily intoxicated with the same old mischiefs: greed was genuine, munificence false, and hatred hungered after hatred. They served to nourish the self-interested designs and actions of a truly sick World community. Spouting their vain promises, demagogic political and religious arseholes still came, and charmed, and plundered, and went.

Art grieved at the indifference, the endemic moral impoverishment, the vicious rot that gorged its bottomless guts on modesty, vulnerability, and decency. Something had to be done – and something would be done.

The subjugation of such misbehaviour would become a central feature to Schitthelm's enterprise. A remedy had to be sought through means other than war, religion, or politics. He set about forming his charity – ostensibly just a charity – however a smokescreen behind which would evolve the antidote.

Art would construct a mechanism to effect sustainable change – and he made a pledge to get things right from the start. As a clock is desirous of its various inner workings that it may show good time – so the underground function of Three F would require hidden components such as technology, stealth and brutality, that it may show society right from wrong.

Fast-forward back to June 2011and Lenny Plant is paying Enid Byers a visit in hospital. He finds her recently out of surgery with a brain muddled by anaesthetic. In her dazed state Enid imagines Lenny to be Cliff Richard and, overwhelmed by the superstar's "gravitas," she confides in him the gory back-catalogue of her own greatest hits with the Covert Kill Squad.

Lenny is at first shocked by what he hears, but as she rambles on he soon settles himself with the reassurance that Enid's story is nothing more than a drug infused fantasy.

As Enid recounts she lets loose to Lenny, in some detail, the clandestine functions of the charity. She also lets him in on the fact that her allegiance to Schitthelm has been compromised after she'd recently discovered her husband Leslie Byers had been assassinated by Three F ten years previous. Leslie had threatened to expose Schitthelm by revealing all to the press. He paid the price with a fatal heart attack – one induced by a dart containing a synthetic aortic coagulant.

Following his death Leslie was sentenced to serve time in purgatory for murdering a dragonfly back in 1961. The dragonfly was one of God's favourite creatures. She took it badly when some idle brat soothed their boredom by splatting one with an elastic band. For his punishment Leslie would haunt the marital home till it crumbled.

Schitthelm had grown suspicious about Enid's loyalty as she'd been spending a lot of her spare time in the company of a corrupt Catholic priest. The wily Father Thomas had long been an outspoken critic of Schitthelm and his voice was fast gaining a sympathetic ear beyond the parish.

To keep adjacent with the situation Schitthelm places Enid under surveillance. When he discovers a new interloper (Plant) showing an abnormal amount of interest in Byers, he becomes concerned enough to have Plant's phone tapped.

Plant duly receives a call from a long-time friend going by the nickname of Dickhead Douglas. Dickhead has just landed a job as a part-time vibrator salesman. He waxes to Plant over the phone about the latest mains powered model: an SD 12 240, complete with a 'Seismic Wobbler' attachment. Douglas brags at how the product is guaranteed to make the Earth move for the other half. Schitthelm listens in and misinterprets what his one-hundred and eleven year-old ears tell him. He convinces himself that Plant and Douglas are international arms dealers.

Schitthelm sends out his top hit-man, Silvestro Savellini, to take care of Plant. Plant is oblivious to the unfolding jeopardy. Whilst engaged in his casual day to day domestics the phlegmatic boozer kills his would be assassin by accident – and without ever meeting him. A murder hunt ensues, with Plant naively assisting the police in their fruitless efforts to trace the killer.

Further attempts to eliminate Plant are unsuccessful, due entirely to an uncanny abundance of good luck, supernatural intervention, and ignorance. Father Thomas is less fortunate: Schitthelm has him killed by a policeman working for Three F.

Lenny encounters the ghosts of Leslie Byers and Father Thomas. They warn him of the danger that stalks him and also inform him that Schitthelm is convinced the Seismic Wobbler is a weapon of mass destruction.

With Schitthelm unable to do away with Plant he accepts that his quarry is invincible – he makes an unprecedented decision to negotiate a deal with an adversary. Schitthelm shows up unannounced in Locburn Village and comes face to face with Plant.

As they chat Schitthelm finds himself warming to Plant, so much so, that he reveals his inspiration behind his fervour to cleanse the World's societies of wrongdoers. The hundred-and-eleven year-old unloads a hitherto untold story about an incident at Ypres during The First World War, and a promise made to a dying comrade.

Plant is touched by Schitthelm's tale and can't believe his luck when the veteran offers an open cheque-book to get him out of his hair. Plant capitalises on the situation, however asks only for charitable favours and donations – and nothing for himself. Schitthelm is impressed with Plant's philanthropism and tells him he is virtuous – an accolade rarely dispensed with by a man so stubbornly principled.

The pair part company, with Schitthelm thrilled at having met Plant. Plant decides to tell no one about the encounter.

Events appear to conclude on Christmas Eve when Plant has a vivid dream in which he bumps into Leslie Byers in his garage. Leslie has recently become an angel after getting out of purgatory early. He informs Lenny that God is female, and goes on to reveal some astonishing details of Schitthelm's family tree. Leslie leaves him a bottle of wine atop the boiler at the back of the garage. He asks that Lenny shares the wine with his family and friends on Christmas day, assuring him that it will taste heavenly.

CHAPTER 6

THE MORNING AFTER

Lenny Plant opened a bloodshot eye – it stared at Italy. Italy stared back. That's what the stain on the ceiling looked like: Italy from two-thousand miles up. A burst water pipe New Year's Day – big panic at the time, but all fixed in a blink thanks to the prompt and professional service of a local plumber: "just the stain to paint over once it dries – a ten minute job Mr Plant," comforted the plumber, his pocket three-hundred pounds the better. The mark survived yet, courtesy of steadfast procrastination.

Lenny had asked his wife, by way of affable curiosity, what the stain reminded her of. At first Sarah played along; remarking that it bore an uncanny resemblance to an unsightly mark left by a burst water pipe. As the stain went unpainted her interpretation changed: she told her husband, on any rare occasion he was on top of her, that the stain reminded her of a shrivelled penis. Off his stroke, Lenny would pledge to paint it the next day, or if not – then definitely the day after.

The hangover was so severe Lenny could feel the pounding before he'd freed himself from the grip of a bizarre nightmare. He'd dreamt a rabble of Greeks had broken into his skull during the night using hammers and crowbars. They'd forced an entry with the intention of stealing the finest china. Once inside his cranium they were instantly overcome by pystwiser fumes. Lenny was most unhappy at what happened next: the intoxicated Greeks defaulted to their cultural predisposition for frenzied crockery smashing.

Now he was awake his mouth felt like one of the Greeks had sneaked in there for a shit halfway through the partying. If that wasn't bad enough the bastard had gone and used Lenny's tongue to wipe his arse.

Lenny moved what inner parts of his mouth he could to work up some saliva, but it was no good – he would have to rise and slurp from the tap. Before easing the duvet aside Lenny turned his head. He was inspired to recall a lyric from an old Squeeze song: "It's funny how the missus always looks the bleedin' same."

Sarah Plant slept, so was unable to observe her husband in some similar critical way. With his puffy red eyes, encrusted with puss-yellow sleep dew – and hair tufted upward either side of his crown; Sarah would have her husband compared to a giant alcoholic rabbit, one moribund with myxomatosis.

Lenny dropped his legs over the side of the bed and let his feet hit the carpet. Draping his arms slack either side he threw his upper torso forwards. At the peak of momentum he straightened his legs, the whole movement generating sufficient energy to hoist him clear of the mattress. That's how you get out of bed when you're six-foot-four and in your fifties. He took an awkward stride to the window and slid his head through the curtains. Twisting his face against the glare of a bright March morning Lenny groaned at the latest job to join the queue: a garden fence laid flat by the wind.

With his reflection shaming him from the bathroom mirror, Lenny drained his bladder and headed downstairs. The phone had rung mid-stream but went unheard beneath the racket of splattering urine. Sarah could have taken the call from the bedroom phone but slept on. It was just as well; a bewildered Ronnie Dent was on the other end, ringing from a call-box in the village. He'd lost his wife for the second time in twelve hours.

Lenny snapped open the blinds, filling the kitchen with a blaze of sunlight. He settled himself at the kitchen table with a cup of tea and a hangover. Roscoe, the wise black Labrador, surveyed him from the comfort of his dog basket.

The principal event of the previous evening wasn't so much forgotten about – more temporarily unremembered. The recollection was there though, due to break the surface at any time. For now Lenny would understand that he'd got himself badly drunk on a rampant German cider whilst in the irresponsible company of Ronnie Dent.

Full strength hangovers subdue most peoples' capacity for clear reasoning, deftness of articulation, and useful industry. Lenny was no exception. Following a thorough brain basting he would endeavour to avoid strenuous thought, intricate conversation, and any mildly challenging DIY activities.

Leaving his mind to the entertainment of useless thought, Lenny tried to work out how much his house weighed. Whilst doing so he carried his gaze over the rim of his cup and across the kitchen as far as the pedal bin. With its lid propped open with compacted rubbish, it gaped back – as if it were mocking him. Lenny tried to recall an image of the pedal bin in a state of emptiness – but no such memory existed. Aside from the day he carried it from the hardware store he was yet to observe the lid in its closed position. It seemed to Lenny that he was the only one that ever coaxed the bin liner out for disposal; a tricky operation if one's to avoid bursting the liner during extraction. A lettuce leaf hung flaccid from the rim; Lenny screwed his eyes up until the bin reminded him of a breathless fat dog with a gangrenous tongue.

Sarah had always struggled with the concept of bin emptying. She coped with the dishwasher, the washing machine, and the bank account – but the pedal bin – even just once in a while?

Lenny heard movement upstairs; his wife was stirring. He knew the routine just by listening and imagining: feet into slippers – parked by the bedside, stretch her arms and yawn, ruffle her hair and on with the glasses, scrutinise her finger nails then up on her feet to scrape her buttocks for a second or two. Into the bathroom, a swish of torrential piss while she unreels a yard of toilet roll – dab the dribble dry. Out to the dressing table, pluck her night gown from the back of the chair and throw it on. Lenny heard the drawing of curtains, to the accompaniment of his wife cursing the flattened fence.

Sarah called from the landing, 'Lenny, I'm doing a wash; do you want your jeans throwing in?'

'Where's my other pair?'

'Washed – virtually found their own way into the wardrobe – hanging on a hanger apparently, hung there by the person who literally picked them off the floor and washed and ironed them.'

'Wow,' whispered Lenny to the dog as he made his wife a cup of tea, 'fancy that Roscoe – hanging in the wardrobe –"apparently" as it turns out.'

Lenny disliked the word "apparently," a useless utterance according to him – "a waste of letters, breath, and noise – it either 'is' or it 'isn't.'" The words "literally," "basically," and "virtually," fell into the same category – apparently.

'I heard that!' shouted Sarah from the top of the stairs. Lenny should have known better – little escaped his wife's ears. Her auditory prowess was peculiar to her gender; a primeval throwback he'd concluded. Lenny theorised that whenever pre-historic man was out hunting and gathering with his buddies, he was settled with the knowledge that pre-historic wife would be tending to the brood, nestled safe in the cossetting camouflage of the pleistocenic overgrowth. Little did his pre-historic brain appreciate, that the survival of the species was precariously reliant on highly evolved female hearing acuity – an essential for the early detection of stalking predators.

Lenny had a similar theory with the 'doggy style' position: It was the only way of having safe sex back in the day. With prowling Sabre Toothed Tigers and swooping Giant Eagles threatening, neither pre-historic man, nor his family, could afford to have him staring lovingly into his wife's eyes during procreation. Having pre-historic woman present to him on all fours meant he could maintain optimum vigilance whilst setting to with the snorting, the foaming, the frothing and the pounding.

Surviving sex, and sex and survival; it was everything.

Lenny struggled to expound to his wife the benefits of ancient style shagging; his reasoning/pleading un-helped by the sterile fact that the only predator in the Plant household was a loving, well fed Labrador. With modern wife refusing to change her position on the position, it looked like 'doggy style' was off limits for the foreseeable – which meant that Sarah would continue to lie on her back and contemplate the stain on the ceiling.

'The fence has blown down,' said Sarah as she loaded the washing machine.

'Yeah I know – that was some wind.'

'It needs fixing.'

'I'll sort it.'

'When?'

'Tomorrow.'

'I'll ring Larry Porter this morning – get him down here sharpish.'

'Let me do it Sarah; he'll charge us a fortune – worse than the plumber.'

Sarah sat down, took a sip, and stuck with the fence issue.

'If it's not fixed today I'm getting him round to fix it. I'll ask him to paint that stain on the bedroom ceiling as well.'

'Sarah, give me a break – I said I'd do it.'

'And the stain?'

'That as well, promise; now settle down and drink your tea.'

'I'll believe it when I don't see it.'

'That's sarcastic darling,' said Lenny sarcastically. He considered some jovial eye contact but allowed his focus to cower off in the direction of the cooker.

'Why don't you try doing stuff, instead of just talking about doing it?'

'I'm always doing stuff without talking about doing it.'

'Like what?'

'The pedal bin for starters; who's the only person in this house that empties it? And I've made you a cup of tea.'

Sarah glanced over her shoulder at the bin then returned her stare to Lenny.

'It doesn't look very empty to me.'

'I was going to empty it.'

'When – no, let me guess: you were going to do it tomorrow.'

'I was thinking maybe this afternoon – or perhaps early evening.'

'See you got pissed again.' Sarah raised her china cup to her mouth, observing her husband in a way he didn't like. Lenny had a go at sounding perky.

'Have you heard of pystwiser Sarah? It's this really strong cider they've just got in at the Haydale.'

'What a stupid name for a drink.'

'Yeah I know; but it's funny right, because they call it pystwiser and it gets you totally pissed – but not any the wiser.'

'Hilarious, have you looked in the mirror at yourself?'

'Earlier on – had to tear myself away for a piddle; took some doing.'

'Too much bullshit; I'm off up for a shower. You need to be shaping to fix that fence Len.'

The phone rang.

'And you can get that as well – if it's Linda, tell her I'll ring her back.'

Lenny heaved himself from the chair. He broke into a reluctant dawdle through to the hallway, purposely stunting his progress in the hope the phone would ring-off – that would suit him. When alone in the house a ringing landline would register in Lenny not the slightest twitch of acknowledgment. He had his mobile, so anyone who mattered could call him on that – though even then he could be fickle.

'Lenny – is that you?' Ronnie Dent's tone was that of a blind man, scared and lost in a thick forest, who thinks he's recognised his friend by the sound of a muffled fart.

'No I'm Dustin Hoffman.'

'Dusting off? I thought Sarah did all that?'

'How come you're calling the landline?' asked Lenny, 'you never ring the landline.'

The majority of Ronnie's calls to Lenny were made from his mobile; usually whilst installed at the pub or the bookies, or if not, at some in-transit location from either to other.

'Some fucker's fucked off with me wife Len.'

'Don't you mean your wife's fucked off with some fucker? You can't blame her Ronnie, not after all these years.'

'Not like that – someone's nicked her – stolen her, burgled her.'

'Wife theft, that's serious Ronnie. When did you first realise she'd been stolen?'

'First thing this morning,' Ronnie paused for a sigh – 'I don't know what the World's coming to Len; I mean, what kind of sicko low-life steals another man's dead wife – from his own freezer as well?'

Like an old central heating boiler, waking to the first nip of September, Lenny's memory recall system fired-up. His mind's eye watched in horror as the latter episode of the previous night played-out in his skull. Brutally roused from its torpor, Lenny's nervous system doused his vascular network with enough cold adrenalin to retrieve a buffalo from death-grip coronary. His intestines reacted in typical fashion, with abdominal spasms pumping hot shit, liquefied by the adrenalin, from colon to large intestine, and back again. Lenny clenched his arse cheeks in a bid to wrestle a twittering sphincter from gaping dilation. Once it had dawned on him that he (and Ronnie) was metaphorically "in the shit," he didn't want the business end of his digestive system rendering a physical manifestation. Lenny was aware it would arouse in Sarah, some stingingly awkward questions, should she descend the stairs to catch sight, and stench of him, standing in a pool of his own steaming slurry, the phone clenched in a fist-full of white knuckles, and a jaw hanging from his face like a back-loader shovel.

Lenny Plant could tell you, over a glass of red, or a pint of the Landlord's best; that involuntary evacuation of one's bowels through fear or panic was not an undesirable symptom of modern life. Humans, men in particular, have been shitting themselves since prehistoric times. In those days projectile defecation was an intrinsic feature of human survival. Having a hungry predator break cover and pursue prehistoric man through the bush would cause his body to release into its system, significant quantities of both Alpha and Beta adrenalin. Alpha adrenalin would act as a sphincter relaxant, whilst Beta adrenalin would stimulate violet muscle contractions in the lower abdominal wall. With most or all predators reliant, to some degree, on a sense of smell to help

locate their prey; a trail of jettisoned excrement sprayed from a
fleeing arse would often send the beast off on a false scent. Also,
with prehistoric man being lighter on foot, an enhanced turn of
speed would further assist in his escape.

Not so much 'fight or flight' – more 'flight and shite.'

'You're telling me Edith's not in the freezer?'

'The freezer's empty Len.' Ronnie shoved another fifty into the
slot.

'I can't believe we're having this conversation.' Lenny scratched
his head. 'When do you reckon she went missing?'

'I went back into the garage – about an hour after you left – you
know, just to say goodnight to her.'

'And she was still there?' asked Lenny.

'Yes – she was absolutely fine.'

'Absolutely fine – have you heard yourself?' Lenny hissed
down the phone at Ronnie; making a point of breaking into
an incredulous half snarl. 'She's dead Ronnie; how can she be
absolutely fine when she's dead? Your wife's died, now she's gone
missing, or stolen, or whatever – and just in case you're out of
touch with current affairs: we're in it up to our ears.'

Ronnie was silent. Lenny took advantage of the verbal downtime
to grope for an explanation – there had to be one. Looking at the
situation from a rational view-point it occurred to Lenny that,
on the balance of all probabilities, no one steals a dead domestic
housewife from a domestic freezer; especially when no one, aside
from the domestic idiots who put her there, knows there's a dead
body in the freezer to start with. Every situation, no matter how
straight-forward or bizarre, has a reason for its rhyme.

'What if she hasn't been stolen Ronnie – maybe she's not dead?
She might have been unconscious, drifted into a diabetic coma or
something. That narcolepsy's a funny thing too. Edith's probably
come-to and climbed out the freezer in the night.' Lenny's fears
eased; he relaxed a little and used his thumb nail to prise a limpet
of snot from the rim of his right nostril.

'Did she suffer from diabetes?'

'Christ knows.'

'Go back and search the bedrooms – search the whole house.'

'Already done it Lenny – Edith's nowhere. And another thing; the front door and garage side door were locked from the inside, with the keys still in the locks – that's the way I left them.'

Till now Ronnie never bothered with household security; he'd leave Edith to lock-up the house on turning-in for the night.

'We'll have to face up to it Lenny, Edith's dead; dead presumed missing.'

'Someone must've had her out through a window?' offered Lenny.

'Impossible.'

'Why?'

'Virgin dust on all the sills.'

Lenny tried his hand at analysis: 'Okay, now we're narrowing things down a bit: We've established Edith's not in the house, and she hasn't been taken away through a door or window – and there's no way the chimney could have been used.'

'The chimney – how do you mean?'

'Santa's not due back till December, and he hasn't been here since last December, so we can't place him at the scene of the crime. In any case, it would be well out of character for him.'

'In what way?'

'Because he brings stuff down the chimney – it's well documented Ron: Santa comes down the chimney, leaves the presents, then fucks off back up the chimney – on his own.'

Lenny couldn't help but let sarcasm take the lead; whatever focus he'd mustered was drowning fast in a confusion of riddle.

'Listen Lenny, I've got a story together.' Ronnie spoke to Lenny like he knew what he was doing – like he'd thought of a great idea of how to solve the mess of a dead, stolen wife, simply by getting a story together. Lenny didn't reply; his brain was struggling to process reality and make sense of it.

'Are you still there Lenny?'

'A story – you mean like Snow White and the Dwarfs, or Treasure Island? I love Treasure Island – fuck's sake.'

'Seven Lenny.'

'Eh?'

'It was Snow White and the Seven Dwarfs.'

'Let's go with that one Ronnie – brilliant! Snow White and the Seven Dwarfs; only in this one there're no seven dwarfs – just Snow White and the Two Fuckwits, co-starring The Evil Queen. Now, let me see; who can be Snow White? – has to be Edith. Christ-sakes Ronnie, Edith's dead, I can't believe it – aren't you upset or anything?'

'Carry on Lenny.'

'What?'

'Carry on with the story – just in case your story's better than mine.'

'Oh it's dead simple: you see the Evil Queen; she's the Chief Inspector heading-up the bewildering case of missing Snow White and the empty freezer. She gets her wicked way and solves the mystery and the two fuckwits get seven years apiece and everyone doesn't live happily ever after.'

'No offence Lenny, but I think my story's a bit more convincing.'

'Are you still pissed or what?'

'Lenny I only wanted to keep her in the freezer for a few months – just so her pension carries on paying into our account; money's tight right now.'

'That's not what you told me last night Ron,' Lenny listened up the stairway. Sarah was in the shower so there was still time to straighten his head out.

It occurred to him that Ronnie had opted to place his wife in cryogenic suspension shortly after he'd staggered in and found her on the sofa. That he decided to do such a thing was undoubtedly bizarre; that he was so spontaneous in conjuring-up a solution for his money worries was coldly exploitative.

But then Ronnie often allowed reckless action take priority over consideration of consequence – especially when drunk. And seeing as he was frequently drunk, he was frequently exposing himself to the consequences of his own reckless action. As with the drink-drive excursion, he wasn't averse to taking someone along for the ride.

Lenny cursed his own drunken stupidity. The paramedics should have been called straight away, along with the police. That's what anyone else would have done, drunk or not. At least Edith would have been pronounced dead with no suspicious circumstances.

That opportunity had long passed.

'I'm going to tell everyone she's left me – and that she isn't coming back. Because that's not a lie Lenny, she has left me, and she isn't coming back.'

'What about her friends and family? They'll want to get in touch.'

'I'll tell her cronies she's gone to her sister's in Canada to start a new life. Her sister's a nasty bitch – cut all her ties over here when she emigrated. No one's going to bother following it up. As for me; I'll have to endure a bit of village gossip for a week or two – but hey-ho.'

'Poor Ronnie,' jibed Lenny, 'all that horrible gossip. What about other members of the family?'

'Apart from her sister there's none, her brother down in Cornwall died last year.'

'How convenient.'

'Isn't it just Lenny? The job's sorted.'

'And if Edith turns up in the meantime?'

'We'll deal with it – if and when it doesn't happen.'

'You mean you'll deal with it Ron; there's no point in two people going to jail when one will do. I'll not spill the beans, but you keep me out of this. As far as I'm concerned Edith's walked out on you for good – all that freezer shit never happened.'

'Changing the subject Len, what're you up-to today?'

Lenny gave up on the correspondence, remembering his friend was impenetrable when it came to sound reasoning, especially in critical situations. Ronnie couldn't help it, that's the way he drifted, somewhere between blind insensitivity and stark oblivion. Along the years Lenny had treated the perceived condition as an ailment, a semi-disability, something Ronnie was born with – so, with semi-disability goes semi-accountability. Once more Lenny would cut his friend a mile of slack.

'I've got a garden fence to fix and a ceiling to paint – and I'm bloody glad to be doing it. Something's got to take my mind of all this bollocks.' Lenny heard movement upstairs. 'I'd better go Ronnie, Sarah's about; if anything turns up ring me straight away.'

'She's not going to turn up Lenny, I just know it. Edith's disappeared into thin air.'

'People don't disappear into thin air Ronnie. She'll turn up – wait and see.'

Ronnie had used his last fifty; the line stuttered half-a-dozen beeps and went silent.

Ronnie was half right, and Lenny was half wrong. Which meant that Lenny had to be half right and Ronnie had to be half wrong: Ronnie was right in saying Edith had disappeared into thin air, however he was wrong in saying she wasn't going to turn up. Lenny was wrong in saying people don't disappear into thin air, however he was right in saying she'd turn up.

CHAPTER 7

TIME

Art Schitthelm looked out over Lake Geneva. Black-suited, and straight and old as a Victorian drainpipe, he stood before a tall, arched window. His eyes swam enchanted through the soft dimming of an eastern vista. Art watched the shades of evening creep on; fan-fared by the distant calling of a lesser spotted speckle-legged hook-billed grape warbler. The crimson hues of a falling sun had set the southern bay a turquoise shimmer; its centre punctuated by a lone yacht. Beyond the headland, Jet D'eau's spouting finger reached skyward, a rainbow trapped in its sparkled arc. To the horizon, alpine snow blushed-up on the mountains, their lower reaches cut through with verdant forest.

Art farted, he knew afternoons grew old and died, they had to; so they could live on in your memory: "Without memories from the past, we have very little to reminisce about." Art said that often; especially when in nostalgic mood.

The view was as fine as any the planet had to offer. The kind of view a holiday-maker takes pictures of so they can bore the folks back home. And the kind of view a retired civil servant you unwittingly stumble across in the pub, describes in relentless detail, not realising you stopped listening the second they opened their tedious gob – just so you could fantasise on stuffing your beer glass into it – a fine view indeed.

Schitthelm's ancient eyes were ancient enough to have seen everything the World could show them; for the World had shown them everything it could: ignorance and understanding, avarice and kindness, compassion and cruelty. Gazing through the window this evening, Art's thoughts dwelt on the passage of time. He lamented the past, worried for the present, and concerned himself for the future of the future. As he struggled to prioritise which of the three tenses he should most care about, he became tense himself – so tense he summoned-up a mental reference to Leo Tolstoy's "The Emperor's Three Questions," for guidance.

It had been many years since Art had read Tolstoy, but his memory held a vague account of how the tale went: The Emperor sought wise answers to his three questions, that he might govern his people with equity. After consulting with several of his senior civil servants, he became almost as clueless as they were – and certainly more clueless and less clued-up than he was before he approached them in his state of cluelessness.

With his solicitations unaddressed the Emperor set off to wander on his own. He walked himself wide and far – then far and wide. Whilst walking on the wide side he came across an old hermit. The Emperor passed the time of day with him at length. Finding the old man to be modest and wise, he ventured to ask him the three questions on which he craved enlightenment.

The first question; the one over which Art pondered: "what was the most important time: past, present, or future?" was asked by the Emperor.

The Hermit answered without hesitation.

He told the Emperor that the present was the most important time; for the past cannot be changed, and what is done now will have bearing on the future.

Up until recently Art would have agreed with the hermit; it made perfect sense that "now" had to be the most important time – but not anymore. The past was now the most important time, way more important than the present or the future. Art churned it over in his mind: If one can gain access to the past and influence it, then they have control over the present and the future. However if one has control over the present and the future, they can't influence the past. That's the way Art saw it. He wanted to see it some other way – but he couldn't. Looking back on what he'd just thought about, Art reflected that, as things presently stood, for the time being, the future lay in the past more now, than at any other time in the past – or indeed, at any time in the unforeseeable future.

Art was a big believer in seizing the moment; he'd spent his life seizing moments. That's how he built his success; that's how he'd welded Three F into what it is today. But seizing the moment was now yesterday's thing. No longer could anyone gain advantage by seizing the present moment. If you reached to seize the moment nowadays, you would find yourself clutching the bankrupt air of the here and now. The highly prized advantageous moment you sought to seize, hung presently in the past, beyond the grasp of almost everyone.

Art was perhaps the oldest person on the planet, and definitely the only surviving soldier to have fought in both world wars. He'd seen and smelt the blood of slaughter, and cried his futile tears onto the worthless mud of a thousand battlefields. He'd heard the teenagers, and bits of them, tattered with shrapnel and lead, howling for their mothers through the fog of gas and gun-smoke.

Art didn't blame the enemy, he respected the enemy. For the enemy wasn't the real enemy; the real enemy was the one that sent them to perish. Society itself was the real enemy; for was it not society that indulged itself in the blind pandering to the vain, greedy, vicious cowards who hungered for glory: Kings, Princes, and Queens, Priests and Bishops, Generals and politicians. Art hated their guts – he hated Jesus Christ too: "The biggest glory seeking shit-stirrer of them all."

Art's wisdom had been cultivated the hard way, nurtured by his raw experience of human brutality. If anybody had justifiable entitlement to custodianship of the past, it would have to be him. He regarded the past as an essential reference point for moral navigation. Without the wake of time, in its unadulterated state, Art would have no guiding star. Tomorrow may not yet belong to him; but the past, up until the present, used to be all his.

Things were changing and it worried Art. Three F's ubiquitous intelligence sources had uncovered irrefutable evidence that the past was now physically accessible, and that time travellers were presently being sent to the past – sometimes successfully.

That such a vicious race had the means to meddle with its own history caused Art great concern. He had no doubt the Russians were teetering on the cusp of creating a global disaster; one that would make nuclear warfare look like a scratchy octogenarian bitch fight at a W.I. cake stall.

Among the archived corridors of history skulked Armageddon; an inverted time bomb, awaiting deliverance.

Things were desperate.

A knock at the door interrupted Art's thoughts.

'Come in.'

Art's son, Horace, half opened the door and peered round it to check if his father was on his own. Art turned from the window. When he saw it was Horace he became annoyed.

'I thought I told you not to knock on se door Horace. You know how it irritates me when someone I know knocks on se door.'

Art Schitthelm's accent alternated twixt cockney and kraut, often haunting the chasm in-between. He was born in Germany in 1900, but abandoned by his mother during a visit to London when he was twelve. Having no surviving relatives back home he was adopted and given British nationality.

Art walked over to his mahogany bureau; he slid a cigar from a silk lined silver case and jabbed it in Horace's direction as he spoke.

'It was only last week I sent out a blanket e-mail to everyone that I know, including you, telling them not to knock on my office door if they already know me. That way I will know that when I hear a knock at se door it will be someone I don't know, and I will think to myself, "that's someone I don't know – I wonder who it could be?"'

Horace stepped into the room and pulled the door shut. 'But father, what if someone you don't know opens the door without knocking, either because they have no manners – or perhaps they intend to kill you?'

Art strode over to his son and punched him in his ninety-four year-old guts.

'You always have to complicate things Horace; even something as straight forward as knocking on se door. Life's complicated enough, so don't try and make it more complicated than it already is.'

Art had recently taken to punching his son in the guts whenever he was frustrated. Horace didn't mind though, he appreciated that being the head of Flowers for Faith was a stressful job, and it was important that his father had some way of releasing his tension. By allowing himself to be punched in the guts Horace felt he was doing his bit for the organisation.

Art used to punch Horace in the face to relieve exasperation; but as years went by he found the hardness of his son's face was causing painful bruising to his ageing knuckles. Art visited his doctor who examined his knuckles. He warned Art that the hardness of his son's face threatened to cause long term damage to Art's knuckles. The doctor was a clever man though; he could see that Art gained huge benefit by relieving stress in such a way. He advised him to try alternating his fists from left to right – then back again, in a bid to reduce wear and tear.

Art took the doctor's advice and at first the results were promising, if a little awkward. Art, being right-handed, found it tricky throwing a left-handed punch with the necessary degree of accuracy. He would often miss his target, which only resulted in exacerbating his frustrations. Revisiting the problem, the doctor recommended that Art and Horace meet for an hour every other day so Art could practise left-handed punches. Art soon got the hang of it, and for a while the problem looked to be solved. However over time both Art's hands began to suffer from the pounding inflicted by the hardness of his son's face. Another visit to the doctor yielded more sound advice. To avoid Horace's face causing permanent damage to Art's knuckles, Art was ordered to desist from punching Horace in the face. Art took it badly but perked up when the doctor suggested that punching Horace in his nice soft guts would eradicate the problem.

Six months on and Art's knuckles were in great shape.

Horace was tired; he slumped onto the chaise longue and watched his father light up the hundred dollar Arturo Fuente cigar. At ten inches long it stuck out from his face like the smoking barrel of a panzer tank.

'Father I think you should consider giving up smoking – I don't want to state the obvious, but it's bad for your health.'

'Couldn't give a fuck Horace,' Art took a long drag and hoovered-in the fumes.

Horace could see his father was in awkward mood; he gave a disinterested shrug of his shoulders and occupied his mind with putting together a recipe for the evening meal.

'Horace, have you ever read se tale of Se Emperor's Three Questions?'

'Not sure,' replied Horace, his mind's eye fixed on chopped parsley and onion salt.

'Can you remember reading anything at all by Tolstoy?'

'Erm – don't know really,' replied Horace, dwelling on the garlic asparagus.

'How about Goldsmith – you must have marvelled at se ingenuity and eloquence of his sophistry?'

'Probably have at some time or other.' Horace had moved on to the crème fraiche fondue potatoes.

Art picked up on his son's lack of interest in a one-sided conversation. He decided to put Horace's attention to the test.

'Did you know Horace, that se lesser spotted speckle-legged hook-billed grape warbler is se only bird that breast feeds its young?'

Horace yawned; he was busy steaming the red snapper. 'Yes father, I already knew that.'

Art marched across the damask rug, over to the chaise longue, and punched Horace in the guts.

'Ha! Caught you out there didn't I?'

'Caught me out – how do you mean father?'

'You're not paying attention to my questions.'

Horace sat up and pretended to look interested. 'Yes I am father; I always pay attention to your questions.'

'Then how come you just agreed that se grape warbler breast feeds its young?'

'Did I really?'

'Yes you burke – you know fine well it doesn't breast feed. How can it breast feed without any proper breasts? I told you all about se grape warbler when you were a young boy: how it spends se day fluttering about se vineyards, gorging on se pinot blanco grapes before perching itself anywhere it can to allow se grapes to ferment in its belly. You and I have sat at sunset numerous times and listened to its drunken warbling. We've laughed at them first thing on a morning, still perched where they were se night before, their heads buried under their wing.'

The lesser spotted speckle legged hook-billed grape warbler is a migratory bird that spends the winter months eating wild figs in North Africa. Come spring-time it heads for the vineyards of the European continent to feed exclusively on pinot blanco grapes. With this variety of grape now being successfully cultivated in some parts of England, there have been reported sightings of the bird raiding vineyards as far north as Huddersfield.

Although despised by grape farmers, the warbler is a protected species owing to its unique behaviour: After feeding throughout the day the bird seeks out a perch where it will remain until the following day. As it sits on its perch, the grapes in its yeast-lined stomach ferment into alcohol. Once the bird is fully intoxicated it breaks into a characteristic drunken warble that sounds uncannily similar to someone with a frost-bitten hair lip trying to whistle Mozart's Clarinet Concerto in A Major whilst sucking on a golf ball. The following morning the bird can be seen hunched-up on its perch, head buried in its wing, dealing with the symptoms of a hangover.

In general the hen bird eats fewer grapes than the cock and lays a clutch of between eighty and a hundred eggs. Most warblers die young; invariably from liver failure.

Art let out a snigger before resuming a serious look. Seconds later he sniggered again; this time the snigger concluded with a stunted yelp. Art turned from Horace, his shoulders quivering with suppressed laughter. Horace saw that something had tickled his father.

'What are you laughing at father?'

'Nothing Horace,' said Art unconvincingly.

'Come on father; you know I hate it when you don't tell me what you're laughing at.'

Art turned to Horace, his lungs full of cigar smoke, and let out a wheezing belly-laugh. Smoke belched from his mouth, cloaking his son's head. Horace coughed and swiped at the smog like he was fighting off a squadron of malaria-ridden mosquitos.

Art was further amused, this time at his son cowering from the fumes. The old man sucked on the cigar hard as he could, 'Here Horace, have some more,' he billowed another plume of smoke at his son. Art resumed his mirth and spoke through his chuckling.

'Thank your lucky stars it's not mustard gas Horace, yes? You didn't have any of that stuff blowing around se army stores back in forty-two, no?'

'It wasn't as easy as you think father – we got bombed you know?'

'That's right Horace; se REME stores did get a direct hit. Luckily you were on sick parade that day; down at se medical centre two miles away.' Art gave a slapstick scratch of his head, 'now what was it you were ailing with? Ah yes – it was your eczema playing up again if I recall.'

Horace side stepped the sarcasm.

'You still haven't told me what is amusing you so father?'

'I don't know if I should tell you Horace – it's a bit disgusting if I'm honest.'

'Father, I'm ninety-four years old, I've heard it all.'

'Horace, you're ninety-four years old and heard fuck-all.' Art leaned over and stared in close at his son's face; he jabbed a thumb at his own chest. 'If you want to know something from someone who hasn't heard fuck-all before, ask me.'

'Okay, I agree, I have heard fuck-all, and you haven't heard fuck-all, so I'm asking you now; what is it that's making you laugh?'

'It's fuck-all really Horace.'

'It can't be fuck-all; if it was fuck-all you wouldn't be laughing at it.'

'You're right Horace, it isn't fuck-all at all; it's just that I keep getting this picture in my head,' Art chortled his way over to the bureau.

'Go on.'

'It's an image of se female grape warbler sitting in her nest.'

'Okay – so what's funny about that?'

'She's feeding her young Horace,' Art feigned sobriety for a moment.

'That's what birds do father, they feed their young; perfectly normal avian behaviour.'

'Not with their tits out son.'

Art collapsed into his captain's chair and bellowed spasms of helpless laughter about the office. 'Just think: all those thirsty chicks slurping away at se pinot blanco breast milk. Can you imagine that Horace? But then I don't suppose you can – you have no imagination – what a tragedy.'

No smile creased Horace's face. He looked beyond the laughter and sensed something was chewing at his father. He waited for the merriment to ease.

'So – you have something important on your mind father?'

'How can you tell that?' said Art, rubbing the tears from his eyes and twisting his face into a curious expression.

'Because you've summoned me all the way here from China – and I'm guessing it isn't to talk about tit warblers.'

Art unwrinkled his face and rolled his eyes at the ceiling. He shook his head – best save the ornithological pedantry for another day.

He'd sent Horace to Beijing two months previous to set up safe-houses for Kill Squad Operatives. Three F were targeting individuals known to be consuming animal parts such as rhino horns and tiger penises for their own gratification: sexual, medicinal or otherwise. After infiltrating the supply chain, from poacher to end-user, Three F's Operations Directorate decided that this particular problem would be best attacked from the 'user' end.

Art insisted that all targets be mutilated 'pre-termination,' in order to maximise the deterrent effect. Already, bodies were showing up in various districts of the Chinese capital, with either their noses or genitals sliced off. Sometimes both were amputated if the 'deceased-to-be' happened to be a dual user. Tiger and Rhino numbers were anticipated to rise steadily – once consumers became too scared to consume. "Nobody buying, nobody killing," declared Art.

'A hypothetical question for you Horace – one that isn't as hypothetical as it first seems.'

'You mean a question based on or serving as a hypothesis.'

'Well remembered Horace.'

'Thank you father,' said Horace, pleased with himself.

'A prosaic quotation from se Oxford dictionary – but never mind,' Art leaned back in his chair and parked his Italian brogues atop the bureau. 'Now listen up. If someone were to travel back in time and kill you, what do you think would happen to your present existence?'

'My present existence?'

'Yes.'

'Well I would say my present existence would cease to exist.'

Art nodded.

'And if someone travelled far enough back in time to kill you before you sired your children – what would happen to their present existence?'

The question chilled Horace. He didn't want to answer it.

'I'll answer se question for you Horace: A Russian travels back in time and they kill you before you've had a chance to father your children – as a consequence you and your children, who now exist in se present, just disappear.'

'You mean disappear into thin air?'

'In an instant Horace; se second your past self is killed, your present being and your offspring melt into se cosmos. There's a name for it: it's known as "Spontaneous Molecular Disintegration." Then there are se people you've influenced since your expiry; that influence, good or bad, evaporates instantly. If you've killed somebody between your expiry and se present, they are reincarnated: "Spontaneous Molecular Reinstatement." Any changes you've brought about since your expiration are undone. Can you imagine Horace, however slightly, se catastrophic outcome of interfering with se past – even in se most subtle of ways?'

'So what is it with the gobbledegook sci-fi time-travel father? You're a pragmatist; someone who's always taken the empirical stance?'

Art paused purposely before answering. Although the ensuing silence was far from deafening, it was almost audible.

'Unfortunately Horace, what I'm talking about is fact – not "sci-fi," as you are so pleased to call it.'

Horace studied his father's face in the desperate hope for a grin and a reprise of the tomfoolery. The expression remained set.

'Are you telling me that the Russians are capable of time travel father?'

'Regrettably, yes,' said Art, exhaling his cigar fumes with a sigh.

Horace stood up from the chaise longue. He took a smart stride to the bureau and glowered at his father over the top of his brogues.

'We warned you father – as far back as the millennium. The Head of the Technical Directorate spelt it out to you: "Neglect to invest in time travel research at your own peril," that's what he said. You should have listened to him – we'd have been upsides with the Russians.'

'Listen to yourself Horace – just because you've watched Dr Who and read some H.G. Wells, you think you're an expert on time travel – anyway, if your memory serves you correctly you'll recall I had him fired.'

'Fired – is that another way of saying you had him shot?'

Art thought about punching Horace in his guts.

'Wrong Horace; first I fired him, then I had him shot – saved us a packet in redundancy payments and final salary pension.'

'How can you say something like that father?'

'I fired him for his temerity; he dared to challenge Three F's long standing, long agreed policy regarding time travel. I had him shot because we discovered shortly afterwards he had an undeclared personal property rental portfolio.'

'So he was a landlord,' said Horace.

'A nasty one Horace: big rent, bad accommodation, not to mention intimidating his tenants. He created a situation – one that was harming society. Do I have to remind you of Three F's commitment to se development and maintenance of good society?'

'Yes please – if you don't mind father.'

Art rose from his chair; he climbed over the top of the bureau to save him walking around it, and punched Horace in the guts.

'Consider yourself reminded son. Now make yourself useful and get hold of Mandy Seymour for me. You'll need to contact her through se internal communication network.'

'Mandy Seymour – I haven't heard that name in a while. Isn't she one of our top surveillance operatives?'

'Correct Horace; I've assigned her to a job in North Yorkshire, England. She's been keeping an eye on our old friend Lenny Plant.'

'Not him again father,' said Horace with disapproving tone. 'I thought you and Plant had settled your differences and called it quits?'

'We did indeed,' said Art, perching his bony arse on the corner of the bureau.

'And I was happy to leave it at that. However something has come up and it's most worrying.'

'Tell me.'

'You remember se Magnetoscope Satellite we launched into space last year to monitor se Earth's magnetic fields?'

'You mean the rocket we fuelled with distilled essence of goat shit to lower its harmful emissions?'

'Se very one Horace; Three F rockets are now over fifty per cent kinder to se atmosphere than any Chinese, American, or Russian rocket, even though se exhaust fumes stink somewhat.'

'Can we get to the point father?'

'Okay; se satellite has been in orbit for over twelve months. For most of that time it's been transmitting balanced readings of se Earth's magnetic fields. Gravitational variations influenced by se moon have shown normal displacements within uniform variation cycles. Then, three months ago, we start receiving inexplicable data: wildly erratic fluctuations in se intensity and duration of magnetic field oscillations.'

'Are we sure the readings are accurate father? At what frequency/distance ratio are the sample readings being taken?'

'Every two seconds at eight-thousand miles radius to se Earth's core you clever dick – and before you ask, there have been no electro-cosmetic storms reported that could have contaminated se data.'

'Don't you mean electro-cosmic storms Father?'

'Fuck off and come over here and listen you pedant!' Art's cigar was half burnt; he stuffed the remaining fifty dollars' worth into the ash tray. 'Now tell me; what's your take on all this?'

'I must admit, the readings do give grounds for concern father – is there any way we can account for them?'

'I tell you what we can account for Horace – and that's se epicentre of se magnetic vortex, whenever we're picking up se erroneous transmissions. We've got geographical co-ordinates that give us a global position within one square meter of its highest concentration.'

'So where are we talking about?'

'A domestic property in North Yorkshire: number two Church Lane in se village of Locburn to be precise – to be even more precise, se garage at se rear of se house.'

'Who owns the property father?'

'A Mr Ronnie Dent – no prizes for guessing who his best friend is?'

'Lenny Plant?'

'Brilliantly guessed Horace; se venerable Mr Plant. Seymour has confirmed both he and Dent were at se address last night, shortly before se peak of se magnetic vortex – it's light years beyond coincidence.' Art took out a fresh cigar.

'Needless to say Horace, this latest intelligence is unnerving. Plant's up to something with this Dent fellow and we need to find out what.'

Horace went quiet – his mind retreating into deep thought. Art left his son to reason. He went back over to the window and listened to the grape warbler singing.

It sounded different this evening – like it had sobered up.

CHAPTER 8

PUB

Lenny Plant was in his wife's good books by a considerable margin. In a single day he'd put up a new fence and painted the stain on the bedroom ceiling. That was some achievement for a DIY hating procrastinator such as Lenny.

As they walked down the garden path, en-route to the pub, Sarah slotted her arm into Lenny's and admired the new fence.

'Oh Lenny the fence looks great – you've even stained it and taken the old one to the rubbish tip. And the bedroom ceiling's painted as well. We've got the newest, bestest fence in the village. I wonder if Edith Dent's noticed it yet, she notices everything?'

Lenny's stomach knotted-up at the mention of the name. Sarah continued with her rambling as they walked down Willow Gardens.

'I've got me a real DIY husband and I didn't even know it; the fence looks like it's been done by someone who knows what they're doing and not you Lenny. I was thinking, we could get the loft boarded out, you know – for a bit of extra storage space; then there's the spare bedroom, I've seen some lovely wallpaper down at Badcock's Interiors.'

'It's Babcock's Sarah,' muttered Lenny, allowing his wife's twittering to fade into background noise. He would let her dream on about further domestic projects for now; that would keep her mind safely occupied, bless her. The loft would remain un-boarded for a time well beyond the foreseeable future. As for the wallpaper, Lenny had last hung a strip of the stuff back in 1989 – and he wasn't too fussed about hanging any more.

He'd gone at the fence with uncharacteristic energy and focus. Normally even minor jobs about the house would drag on for days or weeks, their progression punctuated with distraction, boredom and indifference. If he had several jobs on the go he would flit from one to the other, and then onto something else – like going to the pub.

There were certain home improvement jobs that were well beyond Lenny and he was happy for them to be that way; principal among them: tiling bathrooms, fixing leaking taps, and laying patios. He despised those "good husbands" who held down a full-time job then spent the weekends annoying neighbours by working a jig saw, a hammer, or a drill. Come Monday morning you daren't ask them about their weekend. You dread how they're going to make you feel both inadequate and irritated as they talk you through the whole bastard job.

Today was different for Lenny though. His troubled mind was in dire need of distraction and the DIY work did the trick – for a while at least. Now, walking to the pub, Lenny was back churning the situation over in his head. He presumed Ronnie to be already at the pub, and Christ knows what he'd be blurting out of his drunken mouth. Whatever it was, it was bound to culminate in a confession. Ronnie was never good at keeping secrets.

Lenny tried to anticipate what kind of sentence he'd be handed by the judge once they got to court. Ronnie's brief would advise him to keep the nose-to-ear plaits and wear ridiculously large pink ribbons. That way he could get away with a reduced sentence on grounds of diminished responsibility. One look at Lenny would convince the judge that he had the protagonist in the dock – and that's where the stiffer sentence would be heading. Lenny could see nothing but misery looming on an endless grey horizon.

For the present though, faking normal behaviour in front of Sarah was taking some doing.

They came out of the snicket that led from Locburn Lane and walked across the pub car park towards the pub's rear entrance. The Haydale Arms, over three-hundred years old, looked every bit the quintessential English watering hole. This evening a lazy column of smoke rose from a russet chimney-pot; its sides white-streaked with jackdaw skitter. Though darkness had devoured the last of the evening light, oak-framed windows beckoned visitors with an amber glow.

These days the place was run by Mervin and Diane Daley. They'd bought the pub from Dermot Doran back in the nineties after Dermot and his wife Lynne retired to Ireland. Locals needn't have worried; the transition from landlord to landlord had been seamless. Mervin and Diane took to the helm with confident ease and gelled instantly with their patrons. Today the Haydale Arms was as popular as it ever was.

'Hey-up Lenny lad – evening Sarah,' Mervin Daley offered a chirpy greeting as he walked down from the top end of the bar to greet them. He'd been talking to Gordon Taylor and Dickhead Douglas at the other end of the bar as Lenny and Sarah entered the pub. Straightaway Lenny did a visual sweep at the locals scattered around the bar. He noticed no one going by the name of Ronnie Dent. The seat customarily occupied by Ronnie was conspicuous by its emptiness.

'What're you having Sarah pet?'

'I'll have a large glass of Gavi Conchetta thank you Merv,' said Sarah.

Mervin turned from them with intentions of pulling a cork.

'Lenny, do me a favour and chuck another log on that fire will you? I asked Dickhead to do it half an hour ago and his arse's not shifted,' said Mervin, now crouching behind the bar and rummaging among the clutter on the lower shelf for the cork-screw. He hollered for his wife Diane.

'Diane! What've you done with the cork-screw? I just saw the bloody thing not five minutes ago.'

Diane came in from the kitchen, bothered, dusted in flour, and shaking her head. She picked up the cork-screw from the bar top and slapped it into Mervin's hand.

'Who left it there?' said Mervin in accusatory tone.

'You did,' said Diane in confirmatory tone.

'Good job your balls are in a bag Merv,' called Dickhead from his end of the bar. 'We'd never be done looking for them.'

'The old ones are the best ones,' said Gordon Taylor, raising his glass for a luxuriant quaff of brown ale.

'What balls?' said Diane, returning to the kitchen and leaving her husband to endure the ensuing mockery.

'He's sixty-two,' remarked Dickhead, 'they must be well dangled by now.'

Sarah caressed her glass and giggled like a schoolgirl. With her new fence and painted ceiling she was in a great frame of mind. Mervin, thick-skinned as any landlord, was impervious to the raillery.

'How about you Lenny,' he said with a grin, 'are you still persevering with the pystwiser?'

'You're joking aren't you; that stuff did for me last night,' moaned Lenny.

'So it'll be a large Cotes du Rhone then?' said Mervin; pre-empting Lenny's second choice. He slid a bottle from the rack.

'Yeah Merv,' said Dickhead, walking over with Gordon to join Lenny and Sarah, 'best sort him one now – you know, while you've still got the corkscrew in your hand.'

Lenny fetched out a couple of crumpled notes. 'Get one for yourself Merv – and whatever these two idiots are drinking while you're on with it.'

'He's not all bad is our Lenny,' quipped a grateful Gordon, supping off and handing his glass to Mervin.

'Anyone clapped eyes on Ronnie today?' asked Dickhead. 'He's usually here by now.'

'He's probably got stuck up at the Legion Club Dickhead – a win on the horses no doubt,' said Gordon.

Lenny raised the wine glass to take his first sip of the evening. Before he got it as far as his lips he froze. Outside he could hear the harsh crunching of feet against gravel. Louder and closer it came. Someone was running across the car park towards the pub. Lenny wondered at the inspiration propelling the inbound stranger. He assigned it to the ungoverned thirst of a beer-starved fool, broken into an ale-house canter. Lenny was deluding himself. This was more an urgent, stomping gallop, a rabid haste – likely a harbinger of unpleasantness.

Lenny was beset by a fathomless foreboding; he dearly wanted to be somewhere else – anywhere would do: a North Korean labour camp, a Karachi sewer, Barnsley – anywhere. But Lenny was where he was, like it or not – and like it he didn't.

The door to the bar crashed open startling everyone in the room. Faces turned to see the doorway filled by a man wearing a woman's purple maxi trench coat.

He was bent near double with breathlessness; puffing and panting like he'd just outrun a troop of psychotic baboons, hungry for a spot of deviant intimacy with a close relative. The man raised his head and stared over to the bar.

Ronnie Dent had his eyes open as far as he could get them; they bulged unblinking in their sockets. He'd been running alright; running because he was terrified. So keen was he to evade whatever it was that scared him, he'd cleared the car park in six-point-three seconds – a personal best for him. Back in 1978 Delia Stark had covered the same distance in five-point-nine seconds – ironically on her way to rescue Dermot Doran's betting slips from a beleaguered Ronnie Dent.

During his sprint one of Ronnie's pink ribbons had detached from its ear plait; it swung below his chin from the left nasal plait.

As Ronnie continued to catch his breath, the ever phlegmatic Mervin Daley spoke up.

'Evening Ronnie – let me guess: you've ran all the way here from the bookies, via Dorothy Perkins, to tell us you've backed a hundred-to-one shot?'

If anyone else had barged into the pub in such a state there would be measurably more concern shown by the locals. But it was Ronnie Dent; a man capable, and renowned, for showing up in various states of confusion and drunkenness.

Ronnie continued with his gasping; an expression of genuine horror scrawled across his face.

'Spiderman!' he choked.

'Eh?' said Dickhead.

'Funny name for a horse,' said Gordon, his tone a mixture of sarcasm and curiosity. 'When's it running?'

Lenny stared at Ronnie, clueless.

'Fucking Spiderman, I – I've seen him.'

Sarah spoke, 'Ronnie, how come you're wearing Edith's coat? What's going on?'

'Suits him,' said Mervin, unsure of whether to pull Ronnie a pint, or pour him a glass of sherry.

'Nah,' said Dickhead, 'it clashes with the pink ribbons.'

Sarah turned to Lenny. 'Lenny what's going on – do you know something I don't? I saw Enid at the corner shop this afternoon and she said Edith hadn't shown for coffee. That's not like her – she never misses Saturday mornings at Enid's.'

'True enough,' said Gordon. 'Our Enid called her mobile just after eleven – no reply. ' (Enid Taylor, nee Byers, had married Gordon back in 2012).

Sarah continued. 'And what were you and him up to last night Lenny? Gone two o'clock when you got in,' she spun and fixed Ronnie a brow warped with curiosity. 'Where's Edith Ron?'

Lenny cut-in, nervous of where his wife's instinctive questioning was heading.

'Look, let's calm down a bit and get Ronnie settled. He's not in a fit state to be interrogated. You heard what he said – he's just seen Spiderman; Edith's probably out on a blind-date with Captain America.'

'Yeah Ronnie,' said Mervin, 'shut the bloody door and sit down – you're letting all the heat out.'

Lenny went over to Ronnie and ushered him to a seat. While they were out of earshot he muttered in Ronnie's ear.

'What's the score Ronnie; what the fuck are you going on about?'

'Seen Spiderman Lenny – need a drink.'

Ronnie's fingers trembled against his lips as he sat down. He reached out and took Lenny's wine glass from him, drained it in one gulp, then handed it back. Lenny looked at Ronnie, looked at his empty glass then looked back at Ronnie. If there was anyone who badly needed a drink this evening it was Lenny; yet he was the only one in the pub who'd had not so much as a sniff.

Sarah sat down on the bench next to Ronnie; Lenny took a seat on the other side of him.

'In the wheelie-bin, that's where he was – hiding there.' Ronnie's stare remained locked in the straight-ahead position.

'Okay Ronnie,' said Sarah, draping a sympathetic arm over his shoulder. 'You've obviously over-imbibed on strong waters and it's taken your mind back to your Marvel Comic days. You've experienced a subliminal re-visitation to a dystopian cartoon world featuring criminal freaks and over-blown superhero characterisations, presented in comic-strip fashion to articulate a surreal narrative in a predominantly violent context.'

'Bloody hell Sarah,' commented Gordon. 'I'm impressed – what a fancy way of telling someone they're pissed.'

'Nice one Sarah,' said Lenny, relieved that his wife's half-baked philosophy had her diverted from the initial scent – but at the same time puzzled as to its origins.

'Sprang-out like a jack-in-the-box so he did; scampered off through the back garden and over towards the graveyard – never seen anything like it.'

Edith Dent sat down on a chair opposite Lenny – she looked beautiful.

Gordon handed Ronnie a large whiskey; Ronnie sank it and beckoned another. The expedient application of alcohol worked as an emollient. Ronnie eased-up as his friends worked to nurse him into a semi-communicable state. After some gentle coaxing Ronnie set to with his account of the day – taking a care not to mention Edith.

He told of how he'd been in the house all day, rummaging through cupboards and drawers in the spirit of tidying up. Ronnie had an insurmountable aversion to domestic labour and all present were aware of this. For now though the anomaly would go unquestioned in favour of continuity.

In fact Ronnie wasn't tidying-up at all. He was searching for some premium bonds he remembered Edith buying way back.

His ferreting procured nothing but a worthless pile of letters, bills, junk mail, and old newspapers.

Before heading out for the evening, Ronnie gathered the heap of paperwork into a bin-liner and made off to the wheelie-bin at the back of the garage. He didn't disclose that he'd put on one of Edith's coats earlier in the day because it smelt of her and made him feel close to her. When Sarah asked once again why he was wearing the coat, Ronnie short-circuited his response by defaulting to a half-confused, half-drunk mumble. It seemed to do the trick.

Vagin Semyon had hidden himself in Ronnie's wheelie bin for two reasons: Firstly, it provided an excellent surveillance post. He only needed to use his head to raise its lid a fraction so he could peer out using the eye situated at the top right-hand side of his forehead.

Secondly, with his time-travel bonus deducted for three months, Vagin was both short of money and hungry. So hungry was Vagin he opened a packet of Ronnie's thawed-out economy beef-burgers. They were made from six per-cent mechanically stripped Latvian pit pony, and ninety-four per-cent synthetic bonding triphosphate.

For someone who hadn't eaten properly in days, the burgers were a delicacy. Overly distracted with his feasting, Vagin failed to hear Ronnie approaching. When Ronnie opened the bin lid, Vagin looked up at Ronnie, and Ronnie gaped down at Vagin.

Vagin was startled – Ronnie was petrified.

When you open a wheelie-bin lid you expect to find rubbish – unless the bin men have just been – then there's just a smelly emptiness. What you don't expect to see is someone picnicking on out-of-date burgers, looking back at you through eyes that blink at opposite ends of his skull. Then you see that he's been gorging on the raw meat with a mouth situated on the side of his neck. When he leaps from the bin and scurries off at speed on four limbs that sprout from his hips, you've gone beyond the realms of doubting your sanity.

Ronnie was certain he'd seen what he'd seen. Rendered morose by bereavement and with no drink past his lips since the previous evening, he was sufficiently lucid to trust his senses. The way Vagin had scampered off on all fours reminded Ronnie of a giant spider in a big hurry to be somewhere else.

Vagin Semyon scurried as far as the graveyard and hid in a sycamore tree (unaware that the words "Vagin Semyon scurried" contained more than enough appropriate letters to spell the name of the tree he was hiding in). He was dying. He'd recently acquired the cardio-vascular system of a sixty-four year-old woman – one clotted up over decades with thirty-two thousand litres of full-cream milk, three-thousand kilogrammes of sweet pastries, and six-thousand four-hundred and twenty-two fried breakfasts.

Vagin's prostate gland had gone missing, along with a twenty foot tapeworm he'd acquired through eating raw meat. He noticed his breasts had grown.

Lenny wrestled himself from a shocked daze. He spoke to Edith. 'Edith, I'm sorry – I never meant to –.'

'Quiet Lenny, they'll see you talking to yourself.'

Apart from Mervin, no one in the pub noticed Lenny when he spoke to the fresh air in front of him; neither did they register his wide-eyed surprise. They were too preoccupied with Ronnie's Spiderman story.

'Let me do the talking Lenny; you're the only one who can see or hear me, and time is short.'

Edith was dressed in a skirted white business suit. With angelic discretion it hugged the length and breadth of every elegant curve of breast, waist, thigh and buttock. Lenny could smell honeysuckle, orange peel, and liquorice – three of his favourite scents. Her hair, undyed and lustrous, flowed over her shoulders, as if an angel had lovingly poured a tin of premium grade interior finish Barley Crush polyurethane vinyl paint over her head. Edith's skin was so smooth it made porcelain look like a badly tiled bathroom. The hem of her skirt hung enticingly above the knees, showcasing calves boasting the contours of a brace of North Atlantic salmon.

Edith uncrossed her legs then crossed them the other way – Sharron Stone-like. Lenny could have peered up her skirt but he didn't need to; he already knew what it was like up there. His mind's eye and nose led him up there, up between the thighs of an angel – right up there, as far as he could go: no knickers of course; angels don't need to wear knickers, or thongs, or anything so suffocating. Neither did any component of her genitalia require trussing or containment. With the absence of pubic entanglement the view was unobstructed: a deforested wonder-scape; perfectly proportioned with no tattered hymenal remnants, hanging like hacked liver, after a lifetime of friction, penetration, tear and stretch. There was neither fear nor threat of pungency; the scent of honeysuckle, orange peel, and liquorice endured in every fold, wrinkle and recess.

Lenny imagined her mons pubis, its bald mound a fleshy roundness, sloping away to the symphysis. Then the generously puffed labia majora, like fillets of rainbow trout, perfect in symmetry, and revealing, in the intervening slit, elegant slivers of the pinkest, most succulent looking labia minora. Lenny knew fine well that the prepus, glans, and frenulum of clitoris were arranged meticulously; with the head of the clitoris identical in dimension and appearance – but not colour, to a healthy marrowfat pea. Finally: the posterior labial commissure, concluding its taper to within a perfect inch of the anal sphincter.

If heaven is perceived by the imagination of the imaginer, then Lenny had arrived at its zenith – the vagina of an angel.

Edith cracked Lenny a smile as warm and incandescent as the log fire behind her. She knew what he was thinking about; angels can do that: watch your mind and hear your thoughts. She wasn't surprised though. Lenny's mental pre-occupation with her fanny was a perfectly normal phenomenon that often occurs when a male mortal encounters a female angel. Such contemplation is known in heaven as trans-vangelical cogitation.

Lenny complied with Edith's instructions and remained quiet as she spoke.

'I got to heaven Lenny,' she said; a nuance of proud achievement in her tone.

'Had to spend two hours in purgatory though; years of gossiping you see.'

Lenny wondered what kind of punishment she received. Edith heard him thinking.

'I had to sit and listen to what had been said about me over the years behind my back – some quite upsetting stuff if I'm honest: "Nosey fat cow," "Belle Tent," "News of the World." Then the remarks: "Didn't know hippos could ride bikes?" "I bet she sweats a lot for a fat lass." Served me right Lenny; God doesn't like gossips – bear that one in mind.'

Lenny was puzzled as to why Edith had showed up at the pub; he wanted to ask her where she'd disappeared to. He also felt he owed her an apology for dumping her in the freezer.

Edith chuckled, 'Stop worrying about sticking me in the freezer Len; it's what I wanted for him.' She nodded at Ronnie. 'When I passed you on the bike last night that's what I called out to you, "in the freezer Lenny," remember?' Lenny offered a silent acknowledgement.

'I knew that's what Ronnie would do and why he wanted to do it – I also knew that you would try and stop him. Had to give you a shout from the grave Lenny; I was hoping you would comply with the instructions of another drunk. There's no way Ronnie could manage without my pension – he could have left my body in that freezer for years and taken the money.'

Lenny wondered what God had to say about such rich dishonesty.

'She wasn't too concerned Lenny. I was a dead civil servant, and the way God sees it there's not much difference between a dead one and one that's supposed to be alive. There was a sublime irony in letting Ronnie benefit from the pension.'

Edith continued.

'Think about how you feel about civil servants Lenny – especially retired ones; they're worse than non-retired ones, and different from other retired people. They're instantly recognisable, usually on discount cruises, with their cheap cardigans draped around their shoulders and fake brand sunglasses perched on their heads. When they tell you who they are you want to push them over-board. No one's interested in conversing with a retired civil servant because there's nothing interesting to converse about; they're unremarkable – almost tragic. You bump into a retired deep-sea-diver, a scaffolder, or a burglar, and it's different – you're all ears.'

Lenny oozed quiet acquiescence. It pleased him that he never draped his cardigan over his shoulders, and the only time he wore sunglasses was once a year when visiting the crowded Provencal market of Bedoin. The wrap-around shades allowed Lenny to admire the curvy arses of the pretty French girls without betraying to Sarah the lechery of his focus.

'I'm coming back from Heaven, back to the land of the living Lenny – a lot fitter than I was too. On the downside, I'll have a prostate gland and a twenty foot tapeworm inside me.'

'What?'

'Shush, remember, just listen. Suffice to say you'll need to brace yourself for my reappearance.'

Lenny checked about him to see if anyone had heard – all clear.

'Something unusual has happened; something over which God has limited control. I can only tell you so much; that isn't how God wants it, but her hands are tied to a greater degree. She's trying to contain a situation, a most unfortunate one. There's already been a meeting with Satan; even he's not happy with what's going on. The problem is: both Heaven and Hell are restricted by the laws of the Cosmos, so earthly intervention is extremely difficult. Any measures to deal with the problem have to be taken through an intermediary.'

Lenny wondered what the problem was, and what Edith meant by an intermediary.

'A mortal Lenny, a living being; something has to be done to remove a significant threat to the well-being of humanity. Before you ask me who that living mortal is, I'm telling you that it's you – Lenny Plant.'

Lenny frowned; he found himself teetering on the precipice of total bewilderment.

'The freezer you put me in Len; it has to be destroyed – completely.'

'A freezer – what the bollocks is going on?' thought Lenny.

'It's a rare model: a National Electric Bulko-Frost 100 Deluxe – only two working models left in existence. Believe me, they're deadly and they've both got to go. You see the unusual technology incorporated into the design of that particular freezer means it can be utilised for purposes other than freezing food – and right now there are some dangerous people keen to get their hands on it.'

If that's the case a good workout with a sledgehammer should keep Heaven and Hell happy, thought Lenny; wondering where in the world the other freezer was – and also what it was that made them so deadly.

'Not that easy Len – smashing it to pieces I mean. As I said, I'm coming back from heaven any time now – a freak occurrence. My dead body is back in the freezer and my heart is already beating. When I climb out of the freezer and walk through to the living room I'll fall asleep on the sofa. I'll wake up and have no recollection of what's happened. My last memory will be one of me sitting on the sofa last night doing some knitting and waiting for Ronnie to come home. At first I'll be a little confused, you know, wondering how I'd slept away twenty-four hours. But in no time I'll be back into my normal routine.'

As Edith continued Lenny noticed she was fading from view.

'As far as the freezer is concerned, we've had it for years Len: a wedding present from my parents. Me and Ronnie, we're very fond of it. Sentimentality, that's what you're up against – a strong emotion. We won't take kindly to you showing up with a sledgehammer, spouting a half-arsed story about Armageddon and some angel you've met in the pub. Oh, and by the way, the other freezer; it's somewhere in Norfolk and it's in brand new condition – that's as close as I can get you.'

Lenny exhaled concerned breath from puffed-out cheeks. He scratched his head in the manner of a confused schoolboy gaping at his first erection. He was aware that shit was beginning to occur – the main problem being that the shit starting to happen wasn't your average everyday occurring shit; Lenny had plenty of experience dealing with that form of shit. This shit was a special kind of shit: this was reality shit, blended with supernatural shit, along with some other form of happening conundrum shit – the type of which Lenny was unfamiliar with. Trouble was this shit was due to rear its ugly shitty head any time, in the shittiest of circumstances. Lenny feared the whole situation was going to turn to shit – once the shit hit the fan.

'Lenny, I'm talking to you,' said Sarah, nudging her distracted husband.

'Eh – oh sorry, what did you say?'

'I said: "we need to get Ronnie home" – he's had too much to drink and he's talking nonsense.' Sarah studied her husband. 'You've been staring at that empty chair for an age; where's your mind at Lenny?'

Lenny looked at the chair and saw Edith had disappeared.

Sarah got up from her chair. 'C'mon Ronnie, I'm not resting till your back home and I've seen Edith. Lenny and I are coming with you.'

Ronnie gave Lenny a desperate look, one that only a best friend can interpret. The translated expression read: "I think we're fucked Lenny."

Although Lenny's mind was troubled with the freezer demolition challenge (set him by an angel), he was confident that what Edith told him was right. How could anyone question the words of an angel – even a temporary one? He was convinced that she would be back home, alive and well, when they showed-up with Ronnie. Lenny grinned to himself; he looked forward to witnessing Ronnie's reaction when he sets eyes on a wife returned from the dead.

§

'Something's not right.' Ronnie staggered up the garden path, his swaying deportment steadied by Sarah and Lenny.

'When I left the living room with the rubbish I turned the light out.'

'Are you sure Ronnie?' asked Sarah, 'maybe you're a little mixed-up, what with all the excitement. After-all, it's not every day you get to meet Spiderman then get sozzled for free at your favourite pub – perhaps you just left the light on.'

Lenny was amused; his wife did a great line in sarcasm, usually with him on the receiving end.

'Sarah's right Ronnie; maybe you thought you'd switched it off but in reality you'd unintentionally left it switched on without realising. Or else you'd forgotten to switch it off in spite of originally intending to do so; therefore, for some reason, you've actually failed to remember switching it on in the first place. Then there's always the possibility you haven't a clue either way. Switching lights on and off Ron – it's a funny thing. When you get right down to the nitty gritty, it's fifty-fifty one way or the other.'

'I'm telling you – something's not right,' repeated Ronnie. He was now acting- up at the front door like a nervy thoroughbred reluctant to enter the stall.

'You can leave me now; I'll sort myself out from here.' Ronnie wasn't keen on going into the house – and less keen letting Sarah in. He knew that though his instincts were blunted with booze, hers were pin-sharp. Once inside she'd soon sense something wasn't right.

'Oh shit,' said Ronnie, rummaging in his pockets with exaggerated theatre, 'I must've lost me keys.'

'Don't worry Ronnie; there's more than one way of opening a locked door – watch this.'

Sarah reached for the door knocker.

'I think I'll go for a walk; clear my head.'

Ronnie turned to walk away; Lenny stopped him by looping a long arm around his waist. He would make sure Ronnie was going nowhere but through the front door. Lenny was determined not to miss out on this one: Ronnie had behaved with unrestrained selfishness; oblivious to who or what he compromised. Now it was payback time.

Sarah rattled the door knocker – loud as it would go, Ronnie winced at the echo it sounded in the hall beyond. As a few silent seconds whiled away themselves Lenny bathed in blissful anticipation. He'd already decided what stance he would adopt once Edith materialised: He was going register zero surprise, act normal, and pretend the whole thing didn't happen. It was high time his friend had a decent psychological trauma to deal with on his own. On top of Spiderman he was hopefully going to get a shock that would scare the selfishness out of him for good.

Lenny was annoyed at the discrepancy between Ronnie's remorse and his subterfuge. He tried to fathom where the Spiderman business fitted in. Maybe Ronnie made it up, or else he was hallucinating – perhaps it was the Devil. Whatever or whomever it was, Ronnie seemed to be suitably shaken. Lenny smirked; encountering Spiderman and the living dead in one night – just as well his friend had a good drink inside him.

Footsteps could be heard in the hallway.

'Here she comes now,' said Sarah, a smile of relief dawning on her face. Lenny braced himself.

'It's Spiderman – he's come back for me,' cowered Ronnie.

'Shut it Ronnie,' ordered Sarah, looking him up and down and realising she should have made him remove the coat.

The person on the other side of the door slid back the shut-bolt. The door knob turned tantalisingly slow – the way it does in horror movies.

Lenny could hear a giraffe clearing its throat and thought it out of context – the neighbourhood being noted for its scarcity of African wildlife. Then he realised the racket was coming from inside Ronnie's underpants. His friend was guffing enough gas to bring a large pan of stew to the boil.

As the door creaked open Ronnie's arse fell silent. The light from the hallway reached out into the night, silhouetting the figure standing before them.

At first Ronnie was relieved, but only because he could see it wasn't Spiderman. As his eyes adjusted to the glare the shadow revealed its features. Hair, nose, lips and cheeks – then the body shape: all familiar, but not an exact match.

Edith radiated an aura of youthfulness; she looked twenty years younger; midway, estimated Lenny, between the angel in the pub and her old self. She couldn't have looked more alive if she tried.

Ronnie refused to accept what his eyes were telling him; it was the drink you see – one shouldn't mix their drinks because this is what happens: your senses fool around with you.

Denial lays-on a meagre snack for the desperate; affording but fleeting relief from the hunger of reality.

Ronnie began to tremble, every part of him, his mouth, his feet, and all places in-between. He turned to Lenny and gaped at him with golf-ball eyes. Ronnie expected to see an expression dazzled with total disbelief coming back at him – not so: Lenny looked his usual casual self; he smiled at Edith, a normal easy-going laid-back smile. Lenny could tell Ronnie was checking-out his reaction, and that his friend's bewilderment would now be complete. It was a satisfying and just moment. He loved Ronnie – but lessons are lessons, and they have to be learned; the hard way always being the best way.

Lenny would see to it that the events of the last twenty-four hours be forever banished to Ronnie's booze-soaked imaginings – easier to have it that way; save a fortune on the 'whys' the 'wherefores' and the 'what the fucks.' In time the sot would come to accept the whole sketch as a bad dream.

'Hi Sarah – evening Lenny – how's you two?' Edith greeted them in lightsome tone.

She stepped off the threshold and swatted Ronnie's left ear with an open hand. The stinging slap went some considerable length to providing Ronnie with irrefutable affirmation of his wife's physical authenticity.

'Get in here now!' Edith barked at her husband. Ronnie obeyed. Still half stunned he shuffled past her into the hallway. He was used to being slapped by Edith, but not with this amount of energy; her swing was faster and more powerful by half.

'Sarah – I'll call round and see you for a chin-wag tomorrow,' Edith looked at Lenny, slightly puzzled. 'Are you alright Lenny?'

'Err yeah, I – I'm fine Edith.' Lenny was marvelling at the force of the swipe.

'It's just you look different.'

'In what way?' asked Sarah.

'I'm not sure – sort of sober.'

Sarah laughed, 'You're right Edith – Lenny hasn't had a drink tonight. He's been in the pub and he hasn't had a drink; that's got to be a first.'

Edith bid them both good night, closed the door, and turned her attention to Ronnie. Lenny and Sarah dwelt by the doorstep awhile – purely for entertainment purposes.

A barrage sparked-up as the door closed – a steam-roller rant, withering and progressive, delivered with a steady build-up of volume and derision:

'You couldn't even wake me – all day I've been asleep on that couch and you couldn't even wake me – why didn't you wake me you useless pile of drunken shit?'

'I didn't realise you were alive,' whinged Ronnie. 'I mean – no, I didn't mean – err – Lenny helped....'

Another meaty slap cut Ronnie short.

'Never mind Lenny, don't be bringing him into this – he's sober and you're not.'

Ronnie was half stooped with his arms raised in front of his face; as if shielding his eyes from intense light. That was the cowering, defensive position he adopted on these occasions.

'And what are you doing wearing my coat – into cross-dressing now are we? I can't believe it; all these years married,' Edith turned and spoke to their wedding picture on the mantle-piece, 'turns out he's a bloody fairy – should've known the minute he came home with those pink ribbons hanging from his snot hairs.' Edith returned her glare to Ronnie. 'Look at you – I mean – just look at you.'

Another slap.

Outside Lenny looked at Sarah; he puckered his lips, and wrinkled his nose. Sarah held back her laughter with the palm of her hand.

Edith moved on to their sex life: 'I wouldn't mind if you had a half-decent fuck in you – but there again, how could you? Your dick's marinated in booze twenty-four-seven.' Edith was naturally frugal with expletives, rarely using the 'F' word, and using the 'C' word but twice in her entire life.

'What a fucking cunt!'

Sarah was shocked at the utterance; Lenny was pleased with how things were progressing. Edith really was getting it off her chest.

'Dickhead's getting me some of those blue pills for me willy – he buys them of the intern –.'

Slap.

Edith scratched between her bum-cheeks. Her tapeworm was playing up – all twenty foot of it.

'And let's not forget about my Christmas present you bastard.'

'Edith pet; it – it's the thought that counts.'

'Panty liners, a multi-pack of panty liners,' Edith pondered a second to mitigate. 'At least you wrapped them up.'

'I chose the paper especially for you love.'

Slap.

'No you didn't. Reusable panty liners, what an insult – a box of chocolates would have done!'

Edith had started leaking a year earlier. Being overweight and in her sixties, she was also genetically pre-disposed (via a second Aunt) concerning the suppleness of her pelvic floor muscles.

On the lead-up to Christmas Ronnie had been in the bookies waiting for a Newcastle two-o'clock off that was running late. Scraping around in his pocket with idle fingers he came across a crumpled supermarket receipt. In his boredom he studied the cost of various items. Running his eyes down the receipt his scrutiny settled on a multi-pack of Luxury Lavender Super-Soak easy-form triple-lined panty-liners at £4.99p.

Though Ronnie was no expert on products that deal with such containment, he was a master at extrapolating statistics. Effective study of all aspects of horseracing – from runners and riders, to courses, conditions and trainers, require high levels of statistical/mathematical adroitness. Ronnie applied his skills to fathom an expedient solution to the product/cost/consumption issue of panty liners in his household.

His wife's non-stop chatter caused her vocal chords to dry-out, sometimes mid-sentence – and always several times per anecdote.

Edith counteracted by ensuring a cup of strong coffee was forever within reach during gossip sessions. Ronnie made the computation that such prolific intake of a potent diuretic, combined with the inevitable onset of old age, imposed a strain on her bladder that would become increasingly difficult to manage; a bit like an old dripping tap and no one to fix it.

Absorbing the cost of panty-liners was set to cause an ever increasing drain on the finances, and this worried Ronnie. The solution came unexpectedly; shaped-up in the form of a TV advertisement.

On returning from the pub, late Sunday afternoons, Ronnie would find himself at the loose end of his week. Whilst Edith was doing her rounds, he would settle in front of the TV and watch Channel Seven repeats of Columbo, Miss Marple, Poirot, and the like. Each episode would be interspersed with adverts of a specific genre, that is, ones surreptitiously designed to scare the potential consumer into a product buying mood.

The toothpaste one's a classic: It kicks off with a young, average looking female in a gloomy bathroom, scrubbing away at her teeth with a bog brush coated in low-rent toothpaste. She's gobbing blood into the sink at a rate that begs transfusion – only it isn't blood; it's the pretend stuff used in Dracula movies. The studio's done several takes to elevate the balance of horror/reality to a critical level of credibility; one sufficient to rouse the viewer from their apathy.

The narration is deadly serious, delivered in the gravest of medical terms by a part-time actor. It infers that if you don't switch brands immediately you'll get gum disease and lose all your teeth. You'll be left with smelly breath, and, because the advert doesn't conclude the fate of the young female, the viewer will make a subliminal conclusion that she's bled to death by the bathroom sink.

However hope is at hand. The narrator raises his timbre two octaves as the next scene takes us to a laboratory where everything is sparkly white. There's a most attractive young actress of a woman whose teeth are more sparkly white than the most sparkly, sparkly thing in the sparkly white lab. She expounds the product so enthusiastically through her smiling gnashing teeth you're worried she's going to chew her way out of the TV set.

She's beside herself with pride and excitement, because the actor dentist's just told her how absolutely brilliant and immaculate her teeth are. He's standing in the background wearing a bogus white coat, along with a bright and dirty grin. You just know he's been doing stuff to her – under the gas.

The advert winds-up with her savaging an apple.

Then there's the panty-liner commercial – the one that galvanised Ronnie. It carries similar graphic impact to the toothpaste one; however, due to the anatomical topography it's executed in a half cunning, half subtle style. It begins with your almost happy housewife. She's standing in the living-room of her spick and span house, and one look at her informs the viewer that everything in her life is more or less spick and span: it's obvious the mortgage is paid off, there's a brace of Audis on the drive, the roses have been pruned to perfection, and the new double-glazing will see her and her wonderful spick and span retired civil servant husband to their boxes.

So, we have a perfect but plausible mature housewife; she's around sixty years of age, well decorated, and in good physical nick – that's if you ignore one un-ignorable, minor but major defect with the plumbing.

There's no product dialogue yet; just some cosy verbal pre-amble to loosen you up – and it does the trick. We're only ten seconds in and she's already iconic; the very epitome of where every woman wants to find herself on reaching that age – however without the involuntary fluid loss.

Then, after casting an exaggerated glance over her shoulder to make sure Cecil's still outside waxing the Audis, she steps close-up to the camera and lets us in on her little secret. She does it in a genuine, intimate manner that makes us feel privileged and involved – although with a gravitas that implies word must never get out at the golf club. It centres on her problem, and a decision to switch from one panty liner brand to another, and how it's transformed that which was not well in her otherwise perfect existence.

Next we're straight over to the laboratory for a demonstration by a half-arsed actor masquerading as a lab technician. He's got a Bunsen burner flickering in the background, having just warmed a pint of pretend piss to body temperature. This is where the discretion comes in. The fluid is just dyed water – dyed blue, not yellow. Yellow wouldn't do you see; too much like the real thing. He pours the whole pint onto a wafer thin panty liner and it's totally absorbed – just like a Paul Daniels trick: "You'll like it; not a lot, but you'll like it."

Now the technician pours a pint of the same onto a "conventional" panty liner and it's overwhelmed in a blink. Dribblers the length and breadth of the country are shocked to learn that a product with an absorbency factor of a soggy tea-bag, is all that protects them from unrecoverable embarrassment.

The technician remembers his lines as he tells you the liner is made from a revolutionary micro-poly-fibre that's been treated with duro-plasmic synthetic resin that enables a process known as osmotic fluid retention. Just when you think things couldn't get better the technician delivers the killer blow. He holds the liner over a sink and wrings every drop from it – meantime breaking into an almost mid-Atlantic sales rant:

"Check-out the latest Ultra-Sorb panty liner from Ring Dry Incontinence Products! They're guaranteed re-useable for up to fifty soakings with no lingering after-smell. Once you've filled it, just rinse it out, wring it dry and refit."

Back over to a beaming housewife. "Since I switched to Ultra-Sorb panty liners from Ring Dry Incontinence Products I've never looked back; even my friends have noticed the difference," (The commercial doesn't enlighten you as to how her friends have noticed the difference; you're left to sort that one out with what imagination you have). "They're kinder on my purse too!"

Cut to the next scene where we find the protagonist laughing with her friends at the Salsa class. They're all mature happy housewife clones, clad, anachronistically, in tight jeans, and revving-up to the Cuban Bladder Stomp. You can't tell the Ultra Sorbs are fitted though – no matter how hard you ogle their crotches for bollock bulges and damp spots.

Ring Dry Incontinence Products were currently the market leaders in I.M.S. (Incontinence Management Solutions), and due any day for Stock Market floatation. Art Schitthelm had notified the Prime Minister in advance that Flowers for Faith (Three F) had no interest in buying any of the prospective shares.

The PM was puzzled and Art left him to be that way. Three F's International Business Development Intelligence Unit already had their eyes on another rising star – one whose invention would kick a continent of incontinence products clean into touch. Art's charity had unearthed a gem; an accidental genius of a garden shed tinkerer going by the name of Shaun Swill.

While gluttonous prospectors were buying up shares in Ring Dry; Three F's smart money would invest a modest sum in buying the patent for probably the most important invention since the wheel. Shaun Swill's contrivance was set to eliminate incontinence for good.

In essence, shit wasn't going to happen anymore.

§

Lenny and Sarah strolled home from Ronnie and Edith's. The evening's entertainment, provided chiefly by Ronnie Dent, had left Sarah in jovial mood. Her mind, pleasantly engaged, lounged in a contentment of stained fences, painted ceilings, and wine.

'Lenny,' she said, in the honey-sweet tone she often used as a forerunner to inducement.

'Yes darling,' he replied, sober and half guarded.

'You know the dining room carpet?'

'I know it very well my lovely – walked across it earlier on this evening if I remember rightly. What about it?'

'Well, I was thinking; it's looking a bit tired and tatty.'

'Shabby chic, that's the adjectival phrase you're looking for my rose petal.'

Sarah melted into Lenny's side as they walked. Lenny pondered the likelihood of domestic sex.

'You've done such a good job on the fence and the ceiling; I was thinking, well, while you're on a roll as they say?' She beamed up at Lenny. 'I can just see an oatmeal loop-pile in there – it'll go with the furniture.'

'Perhaps next week; or maybe even the month after honey-pie,' said Lenny, wondering if his wife had ever heard of carpet fitters. As far as a new carpet was concerned he estimated shabby chic to have a good three years left in it – at least.

Lenny had a more pressing issue simmering in his head. The novelty of Ronnie's lambasting had worn off in a few strides. He was now beset with the problem of trying to work out how and when he was going to destroy the Dents' freezer. More awkward still; he was trying to work out how to locate a similar freezer somewhere in Norfolk – and do the same to that.

§

Vagin Semyon sensed he was dying. He crawled into the River Swale and allowed himself to drown. The river was in flood. His body washed downstream into the River Ouse, then into the Humber. A passing dredger minced his corpse in its propellers.

The fish they did feast.

CHAPTER 9

TIME TRAVEL

It would be fair to say that the Russians either invented or discovered time travel. To be more precise, they invented or discovered a bio-physical interaction with magnetic energy known as Cellular Ultrasonic Neutron Transmogrification (C.U.N.T).

Strictly speaking their invention or discovery of time travel was incomplete; as they'd not yet succeeded in sending anyone or anything into the future. The present was a transient reference point, and, in spite of numerous attempts at penetration, it remained unpassable.

"The present dies as it's born, an indestructible paradox ever moving; it drags the past behind it." Maxim Yankov would come to say those words in 2057 – on his death bed.

And so it would go for the Russians. In spite of their efforts history would come to prove that the past had happened, was always happening, and would happen again in the future. As such, any future prospects for time travel into the future – had no future.

If it turned out a time traveller was successfully sent, and subsequently retrieved from the past; they would be returned to the "Rolling Present" and no further. For example: a traveller could be sent from the present at 12:30pm, back to Dealey Plaza, Texas, 12:30pm 22nd November 1963, for one hour, to observe the assassination of a President. If that traveller is brought back to the present after precisely one hour, the time will be 13:30 pm, and the time traveller will have grown older by one hour.

Lee Harvey Oswald was not responsible for shooting J.F.K. It was Igor Andropov; a Russian time traveller who did indeed observe the assassination of the President – albeit through a set of gun-sights. Igor had been chosen for this trip because he was remarkably identical in appearance to Oswald, and also a crack shot. He'd been sent back to 1963. As planned he killed Oswald, assumed his identity, and shot Kennedy.

Igor failed to return from the past – courtesy of Jack Ruby.

So, Maxim Yankov could take the credit for sending the first humans back in time – although in precarious fashion. It was an unbelievable, almost incomprehensible achievement.

For many of those involved, the discovery and development of time travel was a troublesome and hideously barbaric journey from the very start:

Yankov had studied Quantum Molecular Physics at Kiev University back in the late eighties. In time he would come to be known as "Young Father Time" and enjoy a prominence in the history of scientific discovery similar to the likes of Faraday and Newton, the woman who invented the wheel – and perhaps Shaun Swill.

Maxim was born in a remote village on the shores of Lake Baikal in 1967. The youngest of five brothers he was also the brightest. Maxim's mother, although a former circus juggler, professed herself a clumsy individual and claimed to have accidentally dropped all four of Maxim's brothers on their heads shortly after they were born. The alleged cranial percussion had had a noticeable effect on their intellectual and behavioural development; and also served to accentuate Maxim as a personable youngster with perhaps a promising future.

In those remote parts inbreeding was rife. With a population of forty-six Maxim's village was no exception.

Though Maxim's mother and uncle were poor, they were neither un-resourceful nor lacking in industry. By selling homemade pickled pike liver and bear brain chutney – containing no artificial additives, sweeteners or preservatives, and made exclusively using locally murdered ingredients, they scraped together enough money to give Maxim the maximum start in life. When he turned eleven they packed him off to a school in Kiev, hoping that, with a decent education, he might achieve his potential. He attended school in the city and soon became a star pupil.

Maxim excelled in all his subjects; in particular science and biology. He went on to gain a place at the University of Kiev, and it was here that he nurtured his fascination for bio-physical molecular structures and their interaction with magnetic fields.

Maxim's talents didn't go unnoticed. The Russian Institute for Scientific Excellence (R.I.S.E.) employed scouts to visit schools and universities, on the look-out for potential scientists. Maxim was noticed immediately, short-listed, and sent to an assessment centre.

After evaluating Maxim's potential, R.I.S.E. assigned him to The Moscow Scientific Laboratories, to work in their Molecular Research Unit. Within a year Maxim was heading up a Time Travel Feasibility Study, funded directly, and copiously, by the Kremlin. The whole project was given a national security rating of Triple C, and the K.G.B. was issued with strict instructions to monitor every move of those directly involved. Project members were required to wear personal microphones, active 24/7, so that all verbal transactions: professional, domestic, or otherwise, could be recorded.

By 2003 Maxim and his team had assembled what would become a prototype of the World's first time machine. On first acquaintance the shoe-box sized contrivance looked far removed from what anyone might imagine to be a time machine. Mounted on a work bench in the centre of the Institute's principal proofing laboratory, it looked somewhat flimsy, and similar in appearance to a small bird cage. Unlike most of the famous fictitious time machines, Maxim's "Cage" did not itself travel through time – only whatever was placed inside of it.

The cage was made from tetra high-carbon steel, infused with a micro-tungsten alloy, and laminated in an extract of tricyclic plasma filament. A multi-pin socket attached to the side of the cage connected a loom of wires to a complex series of valves, electrodes and gauges.

The whole set-up was powered-up by a standard 240 volt direct current feed with a primary regulation at five milliamps, and a secondary regulation topping out at twenty milliamps. The principal function of the "Maxim Cage" was to contain and mimic a magnetic field that existed at a chosen time in the past.

To have half a chance of fathoming the phenomena of time travel, it is necessary to have an understanding of the behaviour of the Earth's magnetic fields. Maxim discovered that by duplicating a magnetic field that had existed in the past, he could open a corridor capable of facilitating Time Orientated Molecular Transmission.

Like the ocean tides, and changes of season, the Earth's magnetic fields have a measurable rhythm to them whose consistency has remained unbroken for millions of years. The retro-mapping of these fields is of intrinsic importance if one is to even contemplate travel into the past. Maxim Yankov knew this, and, like the ancient explorers who sketched their maps of newly discovered worlds, Maxim chartered the ebbs and flows of the planet's magnetic fields back through the ages.

Along with a team of bio-physio-mathematical scientists, Maxim extrapolated the known values of the Earth's historic magnetic fluctuations. These were entered onto a unique piece of computer software known as a Binary Matrix Evaluation Grid. By inputting a precise location, time, and date in history; anywhere from the present, going back up to 500 million years, Maxim could get a fairly accurate fix on the strength and frequency of the magnetic field that existed at the selected time and place. The reading could be programmed into a Line Output Transformer which would transfer a modulated electrical signal to a Cyclonic Filter and then onto a Chronographic Mixer Valve. Once the cage structure was energised with a magnetic field, it only required the technician to trim the energy/frequency values to attain ultimate assimilation.

Once the magnetic fields were perfectly matched, the molecular structure of anything contained within the cage could be influenced by inducing what is known in time travel as a Molecular Shimmer. This was achieved by switching the electrical feed from direct current to alternating current immediately the synchronisation was attained. When the molecular shimmer reached a critical frequency (precisely 153 megahertz), anything contained within the structure of the cage would displace from present to past, and the process of Cellular Ultrasonic Neutron Transmogrification would be complete.

To retrieve the subject back to the present it was only necessary to reverse the procedure by re-assimilating the magnetic fields and switching back to direct current feed.

As with most ground-breaking science and technology, trial and error is very much the name of the game. Even today, space rockets still explode when they definitely should not, in the face of an age of medical research and experiment, organ transplants still may or may not be successful, and, in spite of Global Positioning Systems and over a hundred years of seafaring since the Titanic sank, captains are still sailing their ships into icebergs.

That's the way it went with time travel: trial and horrific error. At the start things weren't too bad on the error side of things – but that was only because Maxim experimented with inanimate objects.

On the 26th April 2005, an empty cigarette packet became the most famous empty cigarette packet of all time, by becoming the first empty cigarette packet to unofficially travel back in time.

Maxim and his team had reached a point where they felt the cage had been developed to its full potential, and, after spending most of that morning powering up the cage to test the quality and consistency of field strength, they all agreed it was time to see if the time machine would work.

Whilst the team debated what kind of item to trial the cage with, Maxim went out into the corridor to smoke the last fag in the packet. He went to toss the packet into a waste paper basket when he noticed the basket was already overflowing with discarded blue-prints for the time machine.

Maxim looked at the empty packet in his hand, took a couple of drags on the fag, and mashed it out against the doorframe with an excitement close to feverish. He returned to the lab waving the packet above a head, buzzing with boyish anticipation. In the back of his mind though, lurked an Eastern Block fear of failure and its consequences.

The team of technicians huddled around Maxim as his trembling hand placed the packet dead centre of the cage. Once the cage door was secured Maxim ordered the Head Technician to initiate the "power up".

As the energy/frequency values were matched, Maxim held his hand over the electrical converter button ready to switch to alternating current. He eyed each of the team in turn then wished them good luck as he switched the current. The team looked on, half terrified, half mesmerised, as the needle on the dial climbed to the critical 153 megahertz.

A baleful drone could be heard, distant sounding at first, but increasing in intensity until the room moaned with an eerie beehive hum. This was unexpected – as were the small blue sparks that crackled around the fag packet the instant the gauge touched 153.

As the molecular shimmer took hold a couple of the team rubbed their eyes, thinking perhaps their vision was blurring – but that wasn't the case. The fag packet was beginning to fade, its density being eaten away by the shimmer. The hum from the cage was silenced in an instant by a whiplash crack that startled the team.

What seemed like an age of silence smothered the room.

The cage was empty. At first everyone just stared at it – after that, they stared some more. Each wondered to dare – then dared to wonder, at the enormity of the achievement.

"It's gone! It's fucking well gone!" bellowed Maxim, his expression brighter than yesterday's sunrise. His team responded with a roar of jubilation; they jumped up and down, got tearful, and hugged the breath out of one another. Two witnesses from the KGB were speechless with stupefaction. One of them peered under the bench to see if some trickery were at work.

Maxim himself had calibrated the line output transformer with a time, date and grid reference for the molecular transfer. All things being equal, the empty fag packet had been sent back to Wembley Stadium, 3:15 pm on April 11th 1970. Leeds United was playing Chelsea in the FA Cup Final. It was one of the dirtiest finals ever played at the stadium. Leeds defender Norman "Bites Yer Legs" Hunter was more interested in kicking chunks out of the Chelsea players than kicking the ball. At 3:15 pm on that day he'd just homed in on striker Peter Osgood to clean him out with one his classic bone crunching tackles. This was the moment and place Maxim chose to send the packet.

Maxim was a big Leeds United fan and adored the team of 1970. He treasured an old Betamax video recording of the game he'd bought in a charity shop long ago. Maxim had watched the video numerous times and was familiar with all minutiae of the game. He'd chosen the moment of the tackle as the footage gave a good view of the surrounding pitch.

Maxim needed to prove the fag packet had travelled back in time, and he set out to do this in a most clever way: He would play the Betamax video of the game on a large screen, and at the same time, play a TV archive satellite transmission download on an adjacent screen.

The difference between a video recording of an event, and a TV archive satellite transmission, is that whereas a video tape retains the integrity of the original recording, an archived satellite transmission is exposed to the Earth's magnetic fields, and, as far as time travel science is concerned, the transmission is deemed "contemporaneous," which means in this case, it can be adulterated by the present. So, in layperson's terms, understandable to members of different sexes (including transgender etc.): the transmission has the capacity to "update".

Maxim turned on the two large flat screens mounted side by side on the laboratory wall. As planned, one screen would display the satellite transmission of the game – the other would show the video recording.

Maxim set the satellite transmission to 3:14 (one minute before the tackle). He then fast-forwarded the Betamax recording to the same time. Before switching the screens to "play," he briefed the room, including the KGB observers, to scrutinise the scene of the tackle. To make it easier to pick out the detail Maxim played the action in slow-motion.

With graveyard silence the team gazed at the screens.

The weather for the match was fair, with the sun in and out of the clouds. A breeze, five to seven knots blew from the south-west. The pitch was in poor condition, courtesy of The Horse of The Year Show that took place there two weeks previously. It would be the last FA Cup final to be played in the month of April.

The action unfolded tantalisingly slowly: As Peter Osgood gains possession of the ball Norman Hunter can be seen sprinting in from the left of the screen. While Hunter makes his lunge, Osgood can be clearly seen to take his eyes off the ball and cast a distracted glance to his right at something that's just appeared on the pitch. That "something" looks very much like an empty cigarette packet. Osgood's diverted attention is only momentary however, courtesy of the subsequent agony inflicted by Hunter.

Maxim froze both screens at the instant of the tackle. He picked an old umbrella from its rack and used it to point at the screens. It was the same umbrella used to fatally inject a ricin pellet into Georgi Markov's leg in London back in 1978. (The brolly had been left at the lab for reconditioning. It was to be deployed again in the future. This time the owner of the intended leg would be Lenny Plant).

Maxim had talked the audience through the moments leading up to the tackle; a gleeful commentary at first – that was until the fag packet appeared on the left hand screen.

The genius went quiet – then stammered – then stuttered.

'It – it's, uh, it's th – there,' he said, pointing the brolly at the left hand screen. 'A – and it's not there,' he said, pointing at the right hand screen.

"It's there, and it isn't there.' Maxim giggled his words out as he pointed the tip of the brolly alternately from screen to screen.'We've done it folks! We've proved it's there because it isn't there where it wasn't before, but it is there where it is now, and it bloody well shouldn't be there.' The team were momentarily puzzled by Maxim's rambling.

'Don't you see? Osgood did. He saw the packet, our packet, the one we sent back in time. We've sent a fag packet back in time and we can prove it!'

Maxim proceeded to celebrate with a Faginesque jig. Flailing the umbrella around his head, he hopped and skipped around the lab, spinning like a weather vane and spouting gibberish.

Immune to the euphoria of the moment, one of the KGB men took hold of Maxim and wrestled the umbrella from him. He spoke to Maxim in the stern, humourless tone used by all KGB men.

'Careful with the umbrella you fool – it's loaded.'

Celebrations ensued. Champagne was removed from the lab fridge and poured into test tubes, petri dishes, beakers, Erlenmeyer flasks, and any other laboratory glassware that came to hand. One team member, who was trying to cut down on alcohol, used a pipette to administer champagne onto her tongue – five millilitres a squirt. Two of the team paraded Maxim around the cage on their shoulders. He poured champagne down his throat straight from the bottle.

The KGB man rang President Vladimir Sputum at a top secret location to give him the news. The President was in bed. Before answering the phone Sputum uncoupled himself from his latest rent boy and sent him from the hotel room for euthanizing.

Disappointment was afoot.

In order to formally claim the credit for the discovery/invention of time travel – and hence the glory; Maxim would have to prove the authenticity of the achievement to a committee of top scientists.

A week after the fag packet experiment, Maxim made a presentation to the Committee in the Institute's boardroom. Proud as a peacock with an over-developed penis, Maxim stood before the committee. He replayed the recordings – just as he did on the day of the experiment.

The scientists went through each frame several times, and although they were hugely impressed, they ultimately decided that the evidence was not convincing enough for a formal accreditation.

They produced a report giving the reasons for their decision. In brief the report accepted that Maxim had succeeded in rendering a material object "de-materialised," and recommended he be suitably lauded for that achievement.

However it concluded that English football pitches in the Seventies were noted for being litter-strewn, and discarded cigarette packets were not uncommon to be seen wafting about the turf. It went on to state that Osgood's distraction lacked significance, and in any case, was too short-lived due to the intervention of Norman Hunter. In addition, Leeds United's goalkeeper Gary Sprake was cited as an incorrigible litter lout. In a single match Sprake could chew his way through a dozen packets of gum. The goalmouth and beyond were scattered with a confetti of his chewing gum wrappers that could easily be mistaken for a crumpled fag packet.

The report went further to criticise the quality of both the video and the satellite recordings. In spite of enlarged frames and the use of magnifying apparatus, a positive identification of the fag packet could not be confirmed. Had the match taken place in the Nineties, advanced technology would lend clarity and definition, sufficient perhaps, to have swayed the Committee's decision.

The main body of the report waxed with a rousing appraisal of the match itself. The Committee was impressed by the skill, determination, and aggression displayed by the Leeds team. They were bowled-over by the intimidating presence of the likes of Hunter, Bremner, Charlton, and Giles. The report feted Leeds as: "A tribe of warriors made of steel, unafraid, unassailable. Men like these win wars," it declared.

Leeds United drew with Chelsea 2 – 2. They went on to lose in the replay.

Maxim and his team were devastated at the findings of the report. However if there was any consolation to be found, it was the recommendations at the foot of the report. The Committee acknowledged that The Maxim Cage had huge potential, and that Maxim himself was on the cusp of great achievement. It was recommended that the project should not be shelved.

After shrugging off the initial disappointment Maxim and his team went back to the laboratory – blessed with an unlimited budget.

How to prove, beyond all doubt, that the cage could send a material object back in time. This was the challenge that had Maxim biting his nails and scratching away at his head like a troubled child with an infestation of head lice.

He became frustrated – not so much at the problem of proving time travel – more at the fact that he'd bitten his fingernails down to their stumps and was now finding it impossible to impart any scratching sensation to his scalp with a set of blunt digits. Things got so desperate Maxim had to employ a junior lab technician to scratch his head during times of applied concentration – or whenever he was beset with puzzlement. When at home Maxim's wife took on the duty; she was a good woman with long, sharp fingernails. Often Maxim would lie awake in the wee small hours and have her scratch till her cuticles ached.

One morning, at around four o'clock, Maxim's wife was chewing away at his big toenail when Maxim was hit by inspiration. 'Arseny Arshavin!' he shouted, with such excitement he managed to un-wrinkle a month's worth of worry lines from his face. 'That's the answer my darling.'

Maxim's wife was puzzled, 'Are you sure?' she asked, spitting out a crescent-shaped off-cut of yellow toenail.

'Of course I am – I never been so sure of anything since the last time I was as sure as this.'

Maxim's wife rose from their bed, 'You'll have to use one of my Lady-Shaves; those multi-blade things you use for your stubble will rip your arse to shreds.' She went into the bathroom still talking, 'and I've got some scented women's shaving cream somewhere.'

'No, no, no,' he called after her, 'not that. Why the hell would I want to shave my backside? I'm talking about Arseny Arshavin.'

Maxim's wife returned to the bedroom twice as puzzled. 'You'll have to explain Maxim; I haven't a clue what you're on about.'

'It's a proper Russian name – check it out if you don't believe me.'

'What kind of idiot parent gives their child a name like that?'

'I agree darling, no wonder he turned out the way he did,' said Maxim.

Arseny Arshavin was born in Norilsk in 1971. Although his parents gave him a stupid Christian name to go with an unfortunate surname, they loved him to bits. Every rouble they earned was spent on giving him anything he demanded. He soon became a spoilt child, and by the time he reached adulthood Arseny was an obnoxious, self-centred spendthrift, who assumed entitlement to anything he desired: cars, expensive clothes, Black Sea holidays, jewellery and women – all financed by his doting parents.

Arseny had the libido of a heterosexual stallion with three grapefruit-sized testicles. This was a hindrance as he had little success with the opposite sex due to his grotesque personality. His parents were aware of this (his grotesque personality) and it worried them. To keep him happy they bought the services of local prostitutes. In no time sex became a drug to Arseny – he was hooked on hookers. Sometimes he would have up to thirty encounters a week with various "sex workers" in seedy red-light hotel rooms.

On the eve of Arseny's twentieth birthday both his parents died simultaneously whilst lying together in bed. The money they had set aside for overhauling their ageing gas boiler had been spent on a BDSM session for Arseny – the action featured two prostitutes, a sink plunger, and a cricket ball.

Apart from being ironic, the death of his parents would lead to the undoing of Arseny. Without their funding he was left to his own inadequate devices for financing his lifestyle. It didn't take long for him to get through the money he got from the sale of his parent's estate – and although the money had gone, his hunger for prostitutes hadn't.

Arseny took to rape – then to rape and murder. He'd moved to Moscow; the large, crowded city, offered plenty of cover for anyone who was up to no good. He stalked the east-side of the city, south of the river – a backstreet district infested with every kind of human vermin you cared to mention.

Almost two years had passed and Arseny had murdered over fifty prostitutes before he ran out of road. A random DNA test did for him after he was mistakenly arrested for an unrelated crime committed by someone else.

He was tried for the murder of fifty-three prostitutes, found guilty, and sentenced to death by firing squad. The sentence would run consecutively for each murder, which meant that Arseny would end up with fifty-three bullet holes in him (one hundred and six if you counted the exit wounds). He was executed at noon on New Year's Day 1994.

Though Arseny Arshavin had now been dead for over twenty years; Maxim Yankov would use him to prove, "beyond all doubt", that he could send an object back in time.

At the time, Arseny's trial and execution attracted a lot of media interest. Maxim had followed all the news stories right up to the day of the execution. What most intrigued Maxim was Arseny's last request from his condemned cell: a porno mag and a bar of Hershey's Chocolate. The popular American chocolate was difficult to get hold off in that part of the world – even in the Nineties; however Arseny's parents went to great pains to make sure there was always a bar available whenever he fancied one.

Maxim and his team, along with the members of the Committee, and the two KGB observers, gathered around the Maxim Cage. Maxim would send a bar of Hershey's Chocolate back to Arseny's condemned cell. It would appear on his bedside table at 07.00 hours the morning of New Year's Day 1994.

Maxim placed the bar in the cage, set the time and co-ordinates, and sent it on its way. It was crucial that the chocolate bar was returned to the present almost immediately for Maxim's plan to work. This would be tricky as he needed to allow just enough time to let Arseny take one or two bites out of the bar and no more.

The chocolate was sent and returned inside of a minute – still in its wrapper. The team sighed disappointment. It turned out the chocolate did materialise in Arseny's cell; however he'd had his head buried in the porno mag and failed to notice its appearance on the bedside table.

Not to be perturbed Maxim told his team to remain calm and wait half an hour before resending the chocolate. This time they got the result they were looking for. The team gasped with excitement as the bar re-appeared with its wrapper torn open and three segments missing, presumed eaten. Arseny had taken the bait. As Maxim examined the chocolate through the cage wire, he sensed the door to eternal fame was finally creaking open.

In business like tone he addressed his two lead technicians:

'Andrei, get onto your computer – download Arshavin's DNA profile from the main database for cross-referencing. Boris, switch on the film illuminator; pin up the negatives of the rapist's bite indent.' Maxim turned to the KGB observers. He strafed them with a stare that was both superior and derisory. 'You two, keep your mouths shut and pay attention – get ready to run along and blurt it to the President.'

The half-eaten chocolate was removed from the cage and a DNA swab taken immediately from the bite area. The bite mark was scanned by three-dimensional infra-red x-ray and the negatives pinned next to the ones already on the film illuminator. It took less than three minutes to run the DNA sample through the electron scrutineer. Long before those three minutes had passed, Maxim's face was stretching with the kind of grin that must have arced across the faces of Archimedes in his bath, Gagarin in his space capsule, and O.J. in his skin.

The bite marks on the chocolate were a perfect match, and the DNA sample showed a ten million to one chance of the profile belonging to someone else. Maxim had done it. He'd proved conclusively that he could send material objects back in time.

Before the ensuing celebrations had finished, the President ordered that a larger cage be built. Being a lover of guinea pigs Vladimir Sputum was concerned that Maxim might head down the usual research route and try out a few of the creatures, to see how good or bad things were going. The new cage would have to be large enough to accommodate a human – a human guinea pig that is. The KGB was instructed to find a suitable candidate.

§

Timofei Fukim was born in a city. If he were born in a village he would comfortably meet the criteria necessitous to fulfil the role of village idiot.

Village idiots, town idiots, and city idiots have one thing in common – they are all idiots. Young idiots often enjoy a unique status among their peers on account of their idiotic willingness to comply, idiosyncratically and idiotically, with requests from said peers to engage in activities deemed to carry a certain amount of danger.

Timofei wasn't averse to taking risks due to his limited perception of hazard and consequence. Thus he was always the first in the gang to try out the latest kamikaze swing, the depth of the water, and suspicious looking mushrooms. If ever there was a go-cart assembled from old pram wheels and bits of garden fence, it would be Timofei piloting the maiden voyage from the top of the steepest hill in the neighbourhood. An electric cattle fence that needed pissing on – would be pissed upon by Timofei.

Word gets around, and word got around. The ubiquitous KGB soon got to hear about Timofei Fukim and his naïve willingness to participate in all things daring and dangerous. The man from the KGB informed Timofei's parents, on their doorstep, that their son was required to assist the Moscow Scientific Laboratories with some important research work on Cellular Ultra-sonic Neutron Transmogrification. The KGB man ordered that Timofei accompany him immediately, as his presence (or temporary lack of it), was required as a matter of urgency. Timofei's parents were thrilled for their son. The man from the KGB handed the parents a consent document whose terms and conditions section was crammed with print so miniscule, as to be unreadable without the aid of a magnifying glass.

On arrival at the laboratory Timofei was ushered into the main proofing lab where the cage awaited. Maxim told him he was going on an incredible adventure; one he would remember for the rest of his life. Timofei was excited. He stood before the team of technicians wearing his old duffle coat; something he always felt at ease in when engaged in any of his daring-do antics – a sort of comfort blanket and lucky charm all in one.

Timofei fastened the top toggle, pulled the hood over his head, and licked the back of both his hands (three times each hand). As he entered the cage he mimicked a strutting rooster and crowed 'cock-a-doodle-fuck!' Timofei's pre-stunt ritual was complete.

He stood inside the cage, willing and oblivious.

Maxim would send Timofei back into the middle of the previous week. The Institute's corridor would suffice as a location – plenty of closed-circuit cameras with high quality resolution to pick-up his presence.

The cage was powered-up, making its characteristic hum as the frequency increased. As the dial approached 153 megahertz the overhead lights in the lab flickered and the cage shut down. Timofei was still where he was – he'd gone nowhere.

Maxim examined various valves and gauges. He discovered a blown 5 amp fuse on the line output transformer. This wasn't a problem as the lab had a supply of spare fuses. Once the fuse was replaced the cage was powered-up, only for the same thing to happen: another blown fuse. Six more attempts and Maxim had run out of 5 amp fuses. High and low he searched – cursing as he went. In the cage Timofei fidgeted with boredom. Lab technicians were sent off around the Institute in search but returned empty-handed. Not an unblown 5 amp fuse left in the whole place.

When Maxim was informed that the earliest they could expect the next delivery of fuses was the following afternoon, he became overly frustrated. In desperation he headed over to the store-cupboard at the back of the laboratory. Brooms, mops, buckets, and foul language issued as he ploughed through the bowels of the cupboard. Then there was silence; the team watched as Maxim emerged from the cupboard, smiling, and clutching an old kettle. Taking a screwdriver from one of workbenches, Maxim removed the plug from the kettle and salvaged the fuse from it. A 25amp fuse – far too high a rating, however desperation and impatience dictated it would have to suffice.

Once again the cage was powered up – this time it hummed with a greater intensity. The instant the gauge touched 153 Timofei disappeared with a bang loud enough to set the ears ringing. Abrupt silence followed. Maxim sensed something awful had happened. He was concerned at the twisted expression Timofei had on his face the instant before he disappeared.

The closed circuit monitor for the corridor played footage from the previous Wednesday. The team huddled around to watch. After only ten seconds of viewing a puff of smoke appeared at the far end of the corridor; it billowed from nowhere. The team watched intently as the smoke cleared.

On the floor lay a duffle coat; underneath it something squirmed. The team all agreed that things didn't look right and the decision was made to retrieve Timofei immediately.

Within a minute of his disappearance Timofei was back in the cage; his re-appearance announced by another bang.

Even the KGB observers were horrified at what they saw lying on the floor of the cage. The smell was beyond description, simply because it was a smell no person had ever smelt before. It would be the first time in history that human electrons had been subjected to "super-heat searing" due to excessive amplified magnetic wave oscillation. The fuse from the kettle, being rated at 25 amps, had allowed the secondary regulation to exceed its operating ceiling of 20 milliamps, and top-out at 73 milliamps – far too much for a living organism to withstand. On top of this, the extra current travelling through the fuse caused the cyclonic filter to "invert". This meant that Timofei's living molecules would blend with the inanimate molecular structure of his duffle coat during transfer.

Timofei had become his duffle coat, and his duffle-coat had become Timofei.

A putrid sludge of pink and brown steaming flesh, similar in appearance to caramelised cow's afterbirth, covered the floor of the cage. Here and there could be seen flecks of duffle-coat fabric. Bubbles popped on the surface, like a simmering pan of thick broth. Half a dozen charred wooden toggles projected from the mess. One of Timofei's big toes nestled in the middle of it all –

welded to his left eye. The eye blinked several times before seizing into a death stare. A junior technician fainted, while one of the KGB men made off to the toilets in a hurry.

Maxim stared-on. Of all the words at his vocabularic disposal, he could muster only one fit for the occasion: "fuck!"

The two lab technicians with the strongest stomachs shovelled Timofei's remains into a couple of heavy duty bin-bags. While Maxim worked out how to play the event down in his report, Timofei and his duffle-coat were taken to the pathologist's lab for extensive examination and sampling. When all was done, the leftovers were dumped in the laboratory incinerator and turned into ashes and smoke.

Timofei's parents were sent a letter, signed by the President himself. It praised their son for his bravery with a lengthy eulogy. Eloquent prose, garnished with patriotic sentiment lamented how, if it weren't for the sake of national security, the people of Russia could celebrate one of the country's greatest heroes. As a consolation the President enclosed some supermarket vouchers with the letter. Timofei's father noticed that although the vouchers had value enough to provide the family with a month's worth of groceries, the expiry date for their validity was two days gone.

More research and development followed. The new fuses arrived, however there was still an underlying problem. Eventually the cage was retro-fitted with a variable rate thermistor vortex regulator that acted as a separator of animate and inanimate molecular structures. This solved the problem of molecular blending and meant that humans could travel clothed and with equipment if necessary.

More human guinea pigs were sent back in time, highlighting additional teething problems. A student who was studying the Russian Revolution was given the opportunity to travel to 1917 and see it first-hand. He was sent during an intense electrical storm and this was unfortunate. The co-ordinates for his destination were influenced by the abnormal surge in electrical atmospheric activity in the skies above the lab.

Nestor Bogrov ended up twenty-five million miles off target – on the surface of Venus, as it was in 1917. The surface temperature of Venus was much the same in 1917 as it is now. His constitution found the Venusian sizzle of 864 degrees Fahrenheit disagreeable. It took Bogrov just nine seconds to die from thermal stress. Within five minutes his flesh was cooked, tender as any table-bound Christmas turkey. After an hour, Bogrov, or what was left of him, resembled an extinct coal fire.

Then there was Vitaly Shmakov. He was into dinosaurs. Maxim sent him back one-hundred and fifty-million years to the late Jurassic period. Shmakov took with him a packed lunch and a Pentax camera.

The Russian arrived safely and was instantly intoxicated with Jurassic wonderment. Over a period of nearly two hours he snapped pictures of trees and plants. He got a superb shot of a Pterodactyl in flight, and also a Brontosaurus that happened to be trundling by. At midday he took a break and sat on a pre-historic rock to eat his sandwiches.

An Allosaurus was crouching behind a bush three-hundred yards distant. It caught the scent of honey-roast ham as Shmakov prised open his sandwich box. The T Rex look-alike had already been toying with the idea of getting something to eat when Shmakov showed up. As the smell of twenty-first century ham reached its nostrils, the giant lizard switched into hunting mode.

The Allosaurus was an expert stalker of its prey. The fact that the species survived for over twenty-million years bears testimony to this skill. The main feature of every hunt was a stealthy approach that culminated in either a short burst of speed, or a lighting pounce.

Shmakov didn't hear the Allosaurus approaching from behind. It gave him quite a jump when the large toothy head reached over his shoulder. The first bite took the sandwich along with the hand holding it. As Shmakov turned to see exactly where the sandwich (and his hand) had disappeared to, the Allosaurus took a second bite. This disconnected his head and part of his upper torso. The precision of the amputating laceration, courtesy of twenty-five million years of dental evolution, left a neatly cropped forty-eight per-cent of Shmakov, sitting cross legged, on the lunchtime rock. Two more bites and Shmakov's arse and legs joined the rest of him.

The Allosaurus ate the other half of the sandwich, the sandwich box, and also the Pentax. The camera flashed off a picture as the lizard held it in its mouth – the subject: Shmakov's legs disappearing down the dinosaur's throat.

President Sputum decided it would be a good idea for a Russian to be the first person to reach the South Pole.

Maxim meant to send Ivan Gromrinskykobacachovaskiov ("Gromy" to his friends) back to Antarctica, November 14th 1911 – a full month ahead of Amundsen, and two months ahead of Scott. The destination was supposed to be 90 degrees south – The South Pole.

Maxim did a brief research of polar exploration the evening before sending Ivan. He'd had a bottle of vodka for company as he studied the facts surrounding the famous race for the Pole. The alcohol had affected the clarity of his memory recall, causing Maxim to get his time, dates and co-ordinates in a bit of a muddle.

Ivan entered the cage with a pole and a mallet. The Russian flag was attached to the top of the pole. Lower down the shaft Maxim had fastened two letters – one for King Haakon, and one for the King of England.

Ivan and Maxim had already agreed that five minutes would be more than enough time for Ivan to securely drive the flag pole into the ground. This estimation factored-in the usual time travel disorientation experienced on first arrival – normally around thirty seconds.

The visit to the South Pole, being so brief, meant that Ivan wouldn't need to wrap-up in cumbersome thermals. An extra cardigan and a pair of gardening gloves would provide sufficient protection from the Antarctician snap.

A hungover Maxim entered the date and co-ordinates into the machine. Off went Ivan; down to the South Pole – a tad off-target, and far too late.

Amundsen had made it to the South Pole on the 14th December 1911. Scott's ill-fated mission arrived on the 17th January 1912. On discovering he'd been beaten to the most isolated and inhospitable place on Earth, and also realising that he and his four colleagues were destined to perish on the way back, Robert Falcon Scott became the most pissed-off person in the world. More pissed-off than any person has ever been pissed-off in the entire history of persons being pissed-off.

Maxim had unintentionally set Ivan down on the Ross Ice Shelf at 18:30 hrs on 17th March 1912. His position: 81 degrees 32 minutes south, was nearly four-hundred miles distant from the South Pole. Captain Lawrence Oates had just walked out of the tent, informing his friends that he was off for an evening stroll. On exiting the tent Oates emphasised how unsure he was of the duration of said stroll.

Maxim had promised sunshine and a temperature of minus 18C, along with a wind speed of approximately 4 knots – meteorologically speaking quite balmy for those parts.

Ivan felt like he'd been hit by a locomotive made from the bowels of Beardmore Glacier. He was greeted by a granite-splitting fifty knot wind-chill of minus 41C. The mallet and pole froze instantly to each gardening glove.

Before Ivan could take stock of his new surroundings, Captain Oates had staggered into him. Oates was clad in the typical livery of an early twentieth century polar explorer. His thick, heavy thermals, made him look twice his size. Encrusted in snow, and shuffling through the blizzard with frostbitten toes, his deportment was reminiscent of a classic Frankenstein creation – one cross-stitched with an Egyptian mummy that's shit in its bandages.

The Russian was still assimilating. In his confusion he convinced himself he was being attacked by an abominable snowman. He struck-out with the mallet and clobbered Oates on the side of his head. Oates was close to death anyway. He crumpled to the ground in the obedient manner of someone who's just had their temple smashed-in with a two pound mallet.

Ivan set-to with the kicking; he kicked Oates till he was lifeless.

Back at the laboratory Maxim was trying to retrieve Ivan; this time he'd entered the correct co-ordinates for the South Pole. A pile of genuine Antarctic snow was all that came back.

Once Ivan was sure he'd killed the abominable snowman, he hammered the pole into the ground and waited to be retrieved. He froze to death ten feet from the body of Oates.

The Ross Ice Shelf, 17th March 1912: one Englishman, perished virtue of the incompetent, arrogant fool who took him there; and one Russian, perished virtue of the flawed genius who sent him there.

CHAPTER 10

THE FREEZER

As well as sending people back in time the Maxim Cage was capable of teleporting humans to various destinations in "present time". This meant that, in an instant, a human could travel from Vladivostok to New York without the need to bother with trains, planes, boats or automobiles; nor worry about being obsequiously polite with ill-bred American immigration officials. Maxim only had to enter the geographical co-ordinates, stabilise the magnetic field, and leave the time as 'present', to send Russian spies anywhere in the world. This method of travel was known as "Level Transfer".

There were still problems though. Both with time travel and level transfers. Over-exposure to the molecular shimmer associated with dematerialisation/materialisation, meant that travellers ran a high risk of gaining a deformity. All well and good though – as far as the KGB were concerned. The odd deformity was a small price to pay, given the benefits to be reaped for the Mother State.

The delivery zone accuracy was another problem. Spies sometimes materialised in the wrong street, or even the wrong room, and, on one unfortunate occasion, in two rooms at the one time.

Maxim noticed that Vagin Semyon's most recent transfers to Locburn Village were achieving a hundred per cent success rate for pin-point delivery.

When Maxim first sent Vagin to spy on Lenny Plant, he'd set the co-ordinates for an old abandoned farmhouse on the outskirts of Locburn Village. Maxim would end up being delivered to the septic tank buried in the grounds of the farmhouse. The tank was made from steel and had a favourable interaction with the magnetic field generated by time travel. Vagin would materialise in the tank and emerge through the access cover, his presence safeguarded by the isolation of the farm.

There was a drawback with the delivery zone though. The heavy stench of age matured human shite clung to him for several hours after he climbed from the tank. To avoid olfactory detection, Vagin had to waste precious time hanging around the farm until the reek dissipated sufficiently. On top of this, the delivery zone was only good from 1965 to 1976, after which the farmhouse was renovated by new owners. The old septic steel tank was replaced by a plastic one. Plastic would turn out to be a useless medium for forming any intimacy with magnetic fields generated by time travel.

Ronnie's old Cortina would provide the delivery zone for time travel from August 1978 (when it was abandoned in Ronnie's garden), up until September 1981. Its body, constructed from poor quality steel, provided a half-decent interaction with the magnetic field. Side effects were a problem with this zone however – Vagin's skin would break out in rusty scabs shortly after materialisation.

Going into the autumn of 1981 the car's doors began to seize and this made them noisy to open – also exit and entry were becoming tricky due to the unchecked proliferation of nettles and briars. Any spying on Lenny post September 1981 would involve the churchyard being used as a delivery zone. The churchyard wasn't the ideal location in terms of accuracy. Vagin could show up anywhere in its two acre grounds. To reduce the chances of being seen, delivery and retrieval were usually done under cover of darkness.

Recently Maxim had taken a risk, and, without consulting the KGB, he fed-in the co-ordinates of Ronnie's barely frequented garage for the delivery zone. Maxim felt sorry for Vagin and decided delivery to the garage would protect the spy from the vagaries of the weather. On his return Vagin informed Maxim that he'd been transferred to an old freezer at the back of the garage. He also commented on how it was the smoothest transfer he'd ever done, with little or no disorientation, and no apparent worsening of his already hideous disfigurement.

As more transfers were made to the garage it dawned on Maxim that the freezer was an ideal receptor vessel for time travel and level transfers; both in terms of accurate delivery, and reducing side effects. Since the freezer had been in Ronnie's garage since 1977, it provided a broad time span to get spies, undetected, into and out of Locburn Village. Plenty of time for the KGB to find out what exactly was going on between Lenny Plant, Art Schitthelm, a pisshead, and a freezer.

Although Maxim's scientific instincts informed him that domestic freezers were excellent receptor vessels, they neglected to tell him that not any old freezer would do. If Maxim's instincts were pin-sharp, they would let him know that only one particular type of freezer was up to the job – and that there were only two such freezers left in the whole of human ken.

Ronnie and Edith's National Electric Bulko-Frost 100 Deluxe, with its three phase econofreeze matrix lining and rheo-static trickle-volt technology, was indeed a rare specimen. To understand the reasons for its existence, and also the rationale behind its technological specification, one needs to look back at what inspired the man responsible for its creation.

§

Mick Frost came into this world with a soft landing. On exiting his mother the new-born dropped as far as the softly sprung passenger seat of a GMC 360 one ton pick-up. Mick was born to Afro-Caribbean parents in Death Valley, Nevada, the day Adolf died.

Mick's father, Jack, had refused to pull the truck over to assist his wife with the delivery. He was keen to make good progress to Stovepipe Wells where his mother had made one of her excellent pumpkin pies. Every Monday afternoon Jack's mother would lay a pie to cool on the window ledge – there it stayed till a ravenous Jack showed.

They'd set off from their home in Cactus Springs half an hour earlier to make the two hour trip across Death Valley to Stovepipe. Mick's mother, Bertha, had begun with contractions earlier that day and ideally (essentially) should have remained at home for the birth. Jack assessed his wife's status. He estimated her contractions to be no more frequent than the intermittent mating call of a hump-backed bush weevil; and her dilation to be somewhat less significant than a corn snake's gape. Extrapolating his observations, Jack calculated there was ample time for the journey.

Jack loaded Bertha into the pick-up and off they went. Thirty minutes into the journey and Bertha had her backside perched on the passenger window sill. She was half-in and half-out the cab. At the same time Mick was half-in and half-out of his mother. Bertha splayed her legs inside the cab, adopting, as best she could, a position appropriate for the occasion. She'd hooked one foot under the dashboard, and anchored the other in Jack's armpit. Her upper body leaned out the side of the truck. Bertha gripped the lip of the roof panel and howled across Death Valley. The truck trundled along in 107 degrees heat at 52 mph. To distract him from his wife's hollering, Jack kept his eyes glued to the road and sang Lucille Brogan's 'Shave 'Em Dry'.

At twenty-one minutes past midday young Mike Frost came into the world. Jack surveyed Mick as he bungeed at the end of his umbilical cord. A bouncing baby boy no less – perfectly formed, with ten fingers, ten toes, and a healthy pair of lungs.

Jack's singing tailed-off halfway through his third rendition; for what he saw dried his throat and twisted his guts: a head smothered in hair as red as a Nevadan sunset – one viewed with bloodshot eyes through a glass of Shiraz.

Mick's skin was freckly and milky-white – as freckly, and milky-white, as the freckly milky-white skin of Albert 'The Beef-Pole' Cockfoster – Cactus Spring's ginger-haired milkman.

Along with his friendly disposition, Albert packed a penis of equine dimensions. Home alone wives could often assess his proportions as he walked up the garden path – depending, that is, on which way the wind blew his trousers. He'd fucked his way around Cactus Springs and its environs, his life milk spawning a small army of gingers. Albert was North America's first ever milkman to deliver chilled milk, in glass bottles, straight to the neighbourhood doorstep.

§

Bertha could do nothing but pretend to be lost for an explanation. She knew fine well that anyone – including Jack, who put black and black together, could never get ginger. Jack didn't need an explanation. He knew, equally fine well, that black plus black, always gets black. With his appetite sufficiently suppressed he turned the truck around and headed back to Cactus Springs.

Jack dropped Mick off at the home of his biological father; clarifying his understanding of the situation by kicking Albert in his ginger balls. Climbing back into the truck, Jack found his appetite restored. He took the road back to Stovepipe Wells with Bertha.

Along the way Jack and Bertha discussed the situation. They decided to give their marriage another go, agreeing that there would have to be certain changes in the relationship. Jack made Bertha promise that from now on the only kind of milk allowed over the doorstep of the Frost household would be of the powdered variety. To appease Jack further she pledged to make pumpkin pies every bit as good as her Mother-in-Law.

For his part, Jack agreed to buy a penis enlarger and dye his hair ginger.

§

Albert was a good biological father to all fifty-nine of his gingerlings. Each was well clothed, well fed, and well educated. Albert was a fair man; he allowed them all equal liberty to pour as much milk on their breakfast cornflakes as they fancied.

As soon as he was old enough to understand, Albert sat down with Mick and explained, in detail, the provenance of his existence. The explanation included a brief appraisal of his non-biological father. Better to be straight right from the start – that was Albert's philosophy. Mick reacted to the news of his lineage without too much fuss and carried on with life as before. He had only one request, and that was the right to retain his surname of Frost. This would lend him some distinction from his brothers and sisters.

Being fair skinned meant Mick had to be careful when out and about in the sun. The briefest of exposure was enough to turn him from white to pink quicker than you could stir strawberry jam into a rice pudding.

To help protect him from the sun's scorching rays, Mick would rub Albert's double-cream into his skin immediately after breakfast. The cream was astoundingly efficient at preventing sunburn. Mick always looked forward to the evenings when he would lick the cream off those areas he could reach with his tongue. The cream tasted unique: baked sour by the heat of the sun, and also salty with body sweat, it was a flavour that imparted immense pleasure to the taste buds.

It wasn't long before all Albert's offspring were using his double cream in such a fashion. It put a sizeable smile on the milkman's face when, every evening before tea, he observed fifty-nine ginger heads at the dinner table, nodding in unison as they licked their hors d'oeuvres.

Mick was the brightest of all the siblings. He suggested to his biological father that he should have a go at making the cream and selling it to his customers. Albert gave his biological son a genuine biological hug and set-to the following morning.

A large vat of double cream was left for a day in the sun to mature. Towards evening Albert instructed his sweaty children to bathe in the vat. Once they'd finished, a level cupful of Utah rock-salt was stirred into the cream in order to nuance its saltiness. The cream was then scooped into cartons by the ginger workforce, sealed and chilled.

Cockfoster's Sun-Matured Salt 'n' Sour Cream went down the throats of the neighbourhood a storm. Locals couldn't get enough of the stuff. Word spread throughout the County, throughout the State, and eventually, throughout the land. When it became public knowledge that the cream could also be used as an edible sun-block, Albert was approached by a global cosmetics company keen on marketing a range of his sun-creams. They planned to enhance their appeal with varying scents, flavours, and protection factors. On the table for Albert – a multi-million dollar deal.

Albert found himself in a win-win situation. He rose to become the second wealthiest milkman in the world – the wealthiest being an Argentinian milkman, turned cheesemonger, named Roberto Garcia. Roberto made his fortune as a producer of artisanal full-flavoured soft cheese made from non-pasteurised greyhound milk. His fortune exceeded Albert's by ninety-eight dollars and forty-two cents (currency adjusted).

Mick was sent to university to study thermo-dynamics. After passing-out with honours he returned to Cactus Springs, both to help with the family business – and also to try and solve a problem.

Things had got to the stage where Albert was becoming a victim of his own success, and it was all down to temperature, demand, and logistics. Getting the Salt n' Sour supplied to the entire USA was proving challenging – especially during the summer months. Delivery trucks would drive through the night to get to different states; however, keeping the cream sufficiently chilled during transportation was becoming a headache for Albert.

Mick read the situation well and told his father he had an idea to solve the problem. He persuaded Albert to provide funding for a project he had in mind. Albert had amassed a fortune, and harboured no qualms about investing in anything that might enhance the performance of the business – he also had every faith in Mick.

A fabrication works was set-up to convert wagon trailers into mobile refrigeration units. Mick was Chief Engineer; he applied his knowledge of thermo-dynamics to fit out the trailers with ground-breaking refrigeration technology.

The storage compartments were lined with a three phase econo-freeze matrix lining of zinc-based aluminium blended steel. The material would give good insulation, but more importantly, it was capable of accommodating voltage amplification due to its three phase matrix set-up. This meant that, when fed through a rheo-static trickle-volt module, the truck's diminutive twelve-volt electrical system could be magnified ten-fold, and provide sufficient current to power-up the refrigeration unit.

A revolution was born. Chilled food transportation had arrived, and it was here to stay. Mick Frost set up his own company: National Electric Bulko-Frost. Their refrigerated trailers could transport chilled foods to anywhere in the country. Once other food manufacturers caught wind, they didn't want to miss out. A stampede ensued as orders for the trailers flooded in – not only from the States, but from all over the world. Soon Mick's company was fitting out aircraft and ships with the refrigeration units. From humble beginnings in the small town of Cactus Springs, chilled food distribution had spread throughout the World. Mick Frost, like his biological father, had become a millionaire.

When things get as good as they can get, they often turn out to be too good to be true. Unfortunately this was the case with the fates of both the double cream, and the refrigeration businesses. A bizarre combination of factors would conspire to destroy the two enterprises within a decade – the culprits: a substance called Freon, stubbornness, artificial additives, cholesterol, and Russian time travellers.

Although the refrigerated trailers were revolutionary, they were expensive to build, both in terms of time and materials. They were also heavy, and this reduced the payload capacity. An aerosol refrigerant known as Freon was now available on the market. This allowed cheaper, lighter materials to be used to manufacture refrigeration units. The advent of Freon rendered three-phase econ-freeze trickle-volt technology redundant overnight.

Mick Frost could have easily re-tooled the manufacturing plant and jumped on the Freon bandwagon – however he was impossibly stubborn. He convinced both the shareholders, and his workforce, that Freon technology was nothing but a passing fad, and no match for his home-grown econo-freeze technology. In reality Mick was overly proud of his ownership of the patent. He harboured a paranoiac self-assurance that other companies were most covetous of it.

The order book emptied, never to refill.

At the same time, Albert's Sweet n' Sour Double Cream was busy running its course. Food manufacturers were now using a vast range of artificial additives such as sweeteners, colourants, and flavourings, to enhance and mimic all manner of foodstuffs. The Sweet n' Sour Cream, being so popular, was an obvious target for imitation. It was sixties America; availability and choice had rendered the consumer's taste buds more fickle than an impressionable hormone-ridden schoolgirl in a classroom full of Paul Newman lookalikes. The leading food companies had in their laboratories, a legion of chemical engineers. They could make anything taste like anything.

As time rolled by Sweet n' Sour cream took up less and less space on the supermarket shelves. Come the end of the sixties, it was barely a memory.

All of Albert's children were employed by either of the businesses; and all of them had devoured gallons of the cholesterol loaded cream over the years. Like many Americans of that era, they didn't know when to stop putting stuff into their mouths. Morbid obesity reigned in the workforce, and every one of them, Albert included, became candidates for cardiac arrest.

If things weren't bad enough, Russian time travellers began showing up. They were desperate to get hold of the highly guarded technology behind three-phase econo-freeze refrigeration.

They kidnapped key members of the workforce and used horrific interrogation techniques to try and extract information. The time travellers, like Vagin Semyon, were disfigured one way or another, and sometimes in severe cases, both one way and another. Either way, they were equally menacing to behold.

With hearts weakened by the vascular sludge of cholesterol, the kidnapped ginger-haired food dumpsters arrested and died – often before any torturing had commenced. The time travellers simply scared them to death.

With a depleted workforce and an empty order book, Mick Frost made one last attempt to resurrect the marketability of his three-phase econo-freeze technology.

On returning from a trip to England, a close friend of Mick's had commented on how small the English fridges were; in particular the freezer compartments contained within the fridge.

'No wonder those Brits are so goddam skinny Mick,' joked his corpulent friend, 'ain't enough space in those freezers for a single tub of tango-toffee- flavoured ice vanilla substitute.'

'I love that stuff,' replied Mick, 'the aspartame and saccharine really complement the toffee effect; whilst the L-Thirteen vanilla flavouring marries well with the tango-citric T-Four emulsifying agent.'

Mick went into work the following morning, tired through lack of sleep. He'd been up all night thinking about what his friend had said about the diminutive English freezers.

Mick sat down in the boardroom to address his production team – he had an idea:

'We're gonna' make one mother of a freezer – and trial it on the English market.'

'You using econo-freeze technology, or Freon?' asked Gerrard, Mick's half-brother and Lead Technician.

Mick gave Gerrard the kind of look you give your best man after he suggests a threesome to liven-up the honeymoon shag.

'We're using econo-freeze – period!' exclaimed Mick. 'Don't use the Freon word in this boardroom ever again.' Mick was now looking at Gerrard like he'd vomited over the wedding cake.

Mick had spent the wee small hours thinking his idea through. He convinced himself that a jumbo freezer was exactly what the English needed.

It was the early seventies, and Mick knew the Brits were having a rough ride. The Nation was struggling to cope with power cuts, fuel rationing, dockworker strikes, and Alvin Stardust.

Mick also knew that British shopping habits were changing with the times. Supermarkets were sprouting up around the country. Traditional food shopping in the high street was in decline – no need to haul your shopping up and down either side of the street as you visited the butchers, the green-grocers, the bakery, and the chemists. Most families owned a car. You could drive to the supermarket, get all the shopping in one go, and throw it in the boot.

Frozen food was becoming ever popular. If you had a big enough freezer, you could brim it with frozen food and feed your family for a month. With only one monthly shop to worry about, the nation could save time and fuel. The three-phase econo-freeze technology, with the matrix lining and trickle volt supply, meant that the freezer would use very little electricity, and also retain its chill for long periods between power cuts.

So that's where Mick's innovative thinking had headed: a commodious freezer; that's what every British household lacked.

The factory was re-tooled within a month. Within another month it had produced a primary batch of one-thousand chest freezers. These would be exported to England as a 'market tester.' If they sold well the factory would go into full-scale production. The Marketing Director suggested two target areas for outlet networks in the UK – one in Norfolk, the other in North Yorkshire.

What Mick didn't factor-in to his considerations, was the indestructible British Bulldog spirit. Many of his potential clientele had endured the horrors of a vicious war: bombing, black-outs, evacuation, and rationing, to name a few. Power-cuts, striking dockworkers, and fuel rationing were a mere bagatelle in comparison.

Beyond a dozen fish-fingers, and a half-filled tray of ice cubes, frozen food wasn't an issue for the British. As for Alvin Stardust – he was tolerable. The only thing that truly bothered the British was the British weather; about which they would moan frequently. Mick Frost and his company could do nothing to remedy that.

The freezers were shipped to the Norfolk and North Yorkshire retail outlets on a sale-or-return provision. Of the thousand units exported, nine hundred and sixty five came back to Cactus Springs unsold. The freezers were too expensive and far too bulky for the average British household. A total of thirty-five had been purchased – fifteen in Norfolk, twenty in North Yorkshire. Over the years the freezers found their way to the rubbish tip – with the exception of two.

The ones returned to America, having no marketable potential, were scrapped. In the spring of 1976 the National Electric Bulko-

Frost Company went bust. Albert had used what was left of his fortune trying bail-out his son's business, but to no avail. The following year the creamery went under. Albert had a massively fatal heart attack in sympathy.

Mick Frost suffered the same fate as his father, dying in 1979 at the age of thirty-four. By 1982 all of Albert's children were dead – their combined vascular systems blocked with enough cholesterol to kill three Bull Elephants. Both the dairy and the freezer factory were demolished in 1984.

These days the forty-acre site accommodates a retail park. It boasts franchises such as FC Mega-Burger, FB Super-Size Fashions, and a FF Gastric Band Express, featuring a 24/7 drive-through fitting service.

Once he'd realised the business was doomed Mick destroyed all electrical and engineering diagrams for the freezers. He de-registered his patent and burned any paperwork and certification that related to it. Mick Frost was determined that no one should benefit from his brainchild.

So thorough was Mick in burying all traces of econo-freeze trickle-volt technology; the only way to unearth it would be to lay your hands on one of the two freezers left in existence. That way you could strip it down and work out how it was constructed, from what it was made of, and how it functioned.

Both Art Schitthelm and the Russians were now aware of the freezer in Ronnie's garage, and both were equally keen to gain possession of it. Schitthelm wanted to put it 'beyond use.' The Russians wanted to mass produce the freezer and flood the Western market. That way they could transfer and level transfer their spies, undetected, cheaply, and with devastating effect. The initiative would be code-named "Operation Deep Freeze".

Neither Art nor the Russians knew that there was another freezer somewhere in Norfolk. Neither did they know that Lenny Plant intended smashing the pair of them to pieces.

Lenny owned a ten-pound sledge-hammer.

CHAPTER 11

SLEEP

Lenny Plant couldn't remember being as tired as this. Even the thought of potential sex with Sarah failed to give him any lift. The last twenty-four hours had caught up with him, overtaken him, and left him for played-out. He wasn't used to lifting bodies into freezers, erecting fences, and painting ceilings. Not in such a short space of time anyway.

Lenny was physically spent – but he could deal with that kind of tiredness. A decent night's sleep and he'd be up and running next day. It was the orgy of bizarre nonsense romping around inside his head that had him mentally exhausted. It mocked his grasp of reality, crippled his capacity for rational thought, and troubled him senseless.

It would help if he could talk things through with someone – but he'd already agreed with himself that the business with Edith should be consigned to secrecy. In any case, if he did spill the beans, who would listen? And who would believe? How would Lenny go about articulating the unfolded events to a sympathetic ear? Perhaps the best tactic would be to start with the most believable bits, get his listener on board, then work his way through the fantasy stuff – before moving on to the totally insane.

He'd kick-off with the bit where they find Edith dead on the sofa; because although that's shocking, it is totally believable. Then he'd ease-in the part about hiding the body in the freezer – just so her husband could go on claiming her pension? For sure it'd go down like a concrete dingy at a buoyancy contest, but it wouldn't be the first time someone's stored a body in a freezer for some reason or another.

Edith disappears without trace or reason? Well, unless there's magic involved, it has to be body theft or, after a two millennia hiatus, rising from the dead is back in vogue.

Now the tricky bit: Edith shows up in the pub as an angel – with no knickers – only it isn't fancy dress night. She mentions she's about to become host to a prostate gland and a twenty-foot tapeworm.

Before disappearing into the cosmos Edith informs Lenny that the freezer is a threat to humanity and has to be destroyed. Trouble with this part of the story is Lenny is sober as a cold stone – so blame can't be laid at the boozy doorstep.

Finally, the crème de la crème: Edith does in fact rise from the dead. She's unaware of her visit to Heaven, or that she's upstaged JC in the modesty stakes by dying quietly, with no cross, no nails, no glory, and no neurotic fuss.

Dying has done her good; she glows with youth and vitality. Her breasts are now a manageable size, and her weight is down by four stone. Edith's intestines do indeed sport a twenty-foot tapeworm, doing its level best to absorb those pesky additional calories. Her pelvic floor muscles are piss-tight, and when she does go, she has a strong, steady flow – so there's no problem with the prostate.

For a while Lenny re-considered his self-imposed vow of silence. He contemplated blurting all to Sarah under the old 'problem shared, problem halved' comforter. But Lenny knew even his wife would doubt his sanity – and he couldn't blame her. He also thought about visiting the confessional and off-loading to the spiritual side; Lenny was a Catholic by birth so that might carry some weight.

But then Art Schitthelm and Three F had converted most places of worship to P.I.S.S. Academies. The nearest church was now over a hundred miles away. Lenny could show up at the village's Public Institute for Social Science and get it off his chest there; but the locals would just write it off as Comedy Night.

Lenny had to accept there were only a few who had the capacity to listen, believe, and empathise. He needed to track down an acid head, or else a drunk –or maybe a struggling science-fiction writer.

With that thought on his mind Lenny turned down Sarah's offer of a cup of tea. He went to bed. He slept. And he dreamt.

CHAPTER 12

THE MEETING

Maxim Yankov eased open the heavy oak door. He eased it open with the timid reluctance of a person none too fussed about passing beyond it. Behind the door waited three dangerous men – they had awkward questions in need of urgent answers. It had been a long day and time had wound itself close to midnight.

At the far end of a table thirty-foot long sat Traktor Popov, Head of The KGB. To his right sat his Operations Director, Victor Pavlov; to his left, Vasily Vasiliev, Director of Intelligence. Halfway down the table sat the stenographer; a sober looking woman, plainly dressed, wearing heavy-framed specs. She had her hands poised either side of a keypad and puffed on a drooping cigarette without removing it from her lips. In each of the far corners of the room stood a KGB guard, both of them packing a side-arm.

Hugging a folder full of notes to his chest the genius stood quiet and motionless in front of the door he'd just closed. He noticed how his presence had smothered the hushed mumblings at the head of the table. Four sour faces surveyed him through an atmosphere choked with silence.

It was the stenographer that unnerved him the most. Bottomless dark brown eyes, magnified by stout lenses, pierced him through. The body posture was upright and starch rigid. Maxim noticed her face: long, flat, and heavily pockmarked. It put him in mind of a tank-shelled tenement block.

After a gestational pause worthy of a freshly inseminated elephant, Traktor Popov spoke up. He growled at Maxim.

'Mister Yankov, you're two and-a-half minutes late. I detest tardiness; especially from someone who deals in the commodity of time.' The stenographer commenced prodding at her keypad.

'The traffic was awkward a – and I didn't want to drive too fast,' replied Maxim, trying to mask his nerves. 'Anyway, better to be late in this World than early in the next,' he joked uneasily.

Popov grinned at each of his Directors in turn. His face was unaccustomed to revealing any prolonged expression of amusement. It obediently defaulted to its standard KGB misery; a look slightly less genial than a staring corpse. He squared Maxim with cruel eyes thatched-over with bird's-nest brows.

'Early in the next World you say mister Yankov? We can arrange that for you, no problem – and earlier than you think.' The Directors chuckled in unison.

'Sit down Yankov,' ordered Popov. Maxim made to walk up the side of the table to take a seat next to one of the Directors. 'Not up here!' bellowed Popov, 'down there at the bottom of the table – you sit in the bad boy's chair, yes?'

Maxim seated himself as instructed. Popov and the Directors opened their files.

'We have problems mister Yankov. It's the President – he's not happy.'

'I'm sorry to hear that, I –,'

'Shut-up!' barked Popov, 'you've been acting outside of protocol, with the net result that things are turning to shit. Sputum's taken a dim view; he's ordered an investigation. As for me – I'm tired of making excuses for you. The South Pole debacle was bad enough; but this latest incident – the one with the fat lady,'

Maxim cleared his throat. 'We had no way of knowing Plant and his friend were going to dump her in the freezer. Vagin said he tried his best to get her out but she was way too heavy. With only two minutes left for the level transfer deadline he had no choice but to get in with her.'

'And you end up transferring an unclassified into a grade 'A' security State laboratory.'

'But she was deceased Mister Popov,' pleaded Maxim.

'And a good job for you. Are you sure she was dead?'

'Positive,' lied Maxim, 'still warm maybe, but definitely dead.'

'Do we know who she is?' asked Popov.

'We found no ID on her; and Vagin was too incoherent to debrief.'

'So why didn't you alert The Director of Intelligence straight away? That's procedure and you know it.'

'We've never had to deal with such a situation. Anyway, that's exactly what I did. I rang his emergency line. It rang for over fifteen minutes; there was no response, no one picking up.'

Popov looked at his Director of Intelligence pointedly.

'Is this correct Mr Vasiliev? An unanswered emergency call from a grade 'A' State laboratory? We can easily check the line.'

The Director shuffled in his chair, a tad uncomfortable.

'I must have been on the toilet or something. If I'd have heard it ringing of course I'd have answered it.'

'Fifteen minutes on the toilet Mister Vasiliev? What were you doing? Are you constipated or something?'

'Something I'd eaten Mister Popov – a bad bout of food poisoning,' said Vasiliev, giving his belly a sympathetic rub.

'Ah I see,' said Popov, sarcastic. 'Well it's good to see you've made a speedy recovery comrade.'

Vasiliev furrowed an already furrowed brow and gave Popov a puzzled look.

'I'm referring to this evening's exertions at the dining table with the hog fricassee and a bottle of sixty-eight Laffite you imbecile.'

Vasiliev had in fact heard the phone ringing in the early hours of the morning – but he was too engrossed to answer. Having taken delivery of a parcel the previous day he was busy breathing life-size dimensions into an inflatable male doll.

Popov shook his head and returned his attention to Maxim.

'Your notes state you have the cause of death down as cardiac arrest – she died from natural causes yes?'

'That's right,' said Maxim. 'We couldn't perform a full autopsy – we didn't have the resources. And taking her halfway across the city to a State Mortuary was out of the question. We took a few blood samples to confirm cause of death. Interestingly her samples revealed abnormally high levels of the male hormone, testosterone.'

'I'm not interested in testosterone Yankov. I just need you to guarantee that Plant played no part in her death?' said Popov.

'Absolutely, it was death by natural causes.' lied Maxim.

'Because that's what's going on the report. Plant has become a big enough threat as it is; if he's started killing people then we've got a major headache. The last thing we want is Locburn Village crawling with the police.'

Maxim braced himself to deliver some bad news.

'There's been another development. I err – it's just come to light in the last hour or so that – um, it's Vagin Semyon you see – he's – I think, well I know he's – .'

'He's what Yankov? Out with it,' said Popov, annoyed with Maxim's hesitance.

'He's expired.'

'You mean he's dead – why don't you just say "he's dead?"

'He's dead.'

Popov took a deep breath and exhaled slowly. He was about to blow his gasket. The two Directors stiffened-up in their chairs.

'Have we any idea what's happened to him?'

'His transponder implant showed all vital signs extinct at 19:25 hours their time.'

'And when you level transferred him back to Locburn; how did he seem?' asked Popov.

'He seemed healthy enough – that's if you ignore the disfigurement,' said Maxim. 'He did look different though; put on a bit of weight around his upper torso if I remember rightly. Man-boobs – I think that's what they call them.'

'Did we get a fix on the location at 19:25 hours?' asked Vasiliev.

'Yes,' said Maxim. 'The River Swale, one kilometre north-west of Locburn Village.'

'And where is he now?' said Popov.

'We don't know,' replied Maxim.

'The transponder should still be transmitting his geographical co-ordinates – am I right?' asked Vasiliev. 'What's happened with it? Has the battery gone flat or something?'

'Impossible,' said Maxim, 'the nuclear power cell fitted to Vagin's transponder is good for thirty years – he only had it fitted last August.'

'Where was his last known position?' said Popov.

'The River Humber, close to the Humber Bridge. There was no fading of the signal like you would find with a flat battery. The transmission terminated instantly; we had a signal go from full strength to zero in a blink.'

'So why would that happen Yankov? Do you have an explanation?' asked Pavlov.

'When this has happened in the past it's been down to sabotage,' said Maxim. 'My conclusion is that someone's removed the transponder and destroyed it.'

Vasiliev spoke up. 'But these transponders Yankov – they're implanted deep inside the skulls of our spies aren't they?'

'That's correct,' said Maxim. 'It's a surgical procedure – we go in through the base of the cranium.'

Popov clenched his fist in readiness for crashing it down on the table.

'You mean to say someone's butchered their way into Vagin's skull and removed the transponder?'

'I would say that's the most likely scenario Mister Popov.'

Both Vasiliev and Pavlov scratched their heads, like a pair of puzzled school kids.

Popov bashed his fist full force on the table.

'Look at the pair of you!' he bawled at his Directors, 'Scratching away at your heads like you haven't got a clue. It's obvious what's happened. He's been assassinated – Plant's done him in.' Popov swivelled in his chair to study the large map of Yorkshire on the wall behind him. 'He's killed Semyon barely one kilometre from the delivery zone and taken his body to the Humber Estuary for disposal. Before he throws Semyon off the Humber Bridge he rips the transponder out of his skull.'

Vagin's transponder had in fact stopped transmitting the second it was smashed out of his cranium by the spinning propeller of the dredger. For a while it floated in the water, attached to a piece of Vagin's brain. It was swallowed by a seven-pound cod that happened to be swimming by.

Popov nodded wisely. 'This is textbook stuff – brutal and efficient.' He turned back to the table and leafed through the report.

'All of you; turn to page sixty four,' ordered Popov. He allowed a minute or so for the others to remind themselves of the content.

'You will see that our surveillance of Plant back in the summer of two-thousand-and-eleven gives an account of how a top Italian hitman named Silvestro Savellini was taken-out by Plant with an empty wine bottle. Savellini worked for Three F. Over two hundred successful hits behind him and Plant stopped him in his tracks with a bottle of wine.'

§

Late in June 2011 Lenny Plant had been crossing the hospital car park after visiting his neighbour Enid Byers. She'd severed three of her toes in a gardening accident. Enid had worked as a Kill Squad Operative for Art Schitthelm's Flowers for Faith (Three F). She'd recently discovered that Schitthelm had had her husband Leslie assassinated by Three F for threatening to talk to the press.

Savellini had shot Leslie with a poisoned dart that induced a cardiac arrest. Leslie's death certificate revealed he'd died from a heart attack. The Coroner worked for Three F. Schitthelm was now concerned that Lenny Plant's association with a disenchanted Enid was in danger of compromising Three F security.

As Lenny had crossed the hospital car park he noticed an empty wine bottle lying in the gutter. Obsessed with sell-by dates, Lenny lifted the bottle to look for an expiry date. Having noted the sell-by date good for another six months Lenny hurled the bottle over a fence into a disused bus depot next to the hospital. Savellini was waiting in the depot with a loaded dart gun. He'd been sent to eliminate Lenny. The bottle struck Savellini on his top lip, knocking two front incisors into the back of his throat. Lenny was oblivious to the hit-man as he choked to death.

Only two people witnessed the incident: Schitthelm's wheel-man, waiting nearby in a getaway car – and Vagin Semyon, the Russian time traveller. He had been observing Lenny from a hospital wheelie bin.

§

Poplov shook his head, slow and grave.

'They should have listened to me,' he said, regretful.

'Who are they?' asked Maxim.

'The October Committee – I warned them about Plant.' Popov exhaled with a sigh. 'Ever since Vagin surveyed him talking to Schitthelm back in two-thousand and eleven I got a bad feeling about the man. We could have killed him several times – we still can. You Yankov; you only have to send a traveller back in time and remove Plant. Then we will have rid of all this nonsense.'

'It's a good idea,' humoured Maxim. 'But travelling to the past and killing someone like Plant is sure to give us a bigger headache in the present. We need to remember the mess we created when we shot Kennedy.'

'He's right,' said Pavlov. 'Retro-assassination is not suitable for Plant. We still have no idea how well connected he is. The impact risk is way too high.'

Maxim nodded, relieved that Pavlov had remembered the recommendations of the October Committee.

'Okay,' groaned Popov. 'I take your point.'

Popov stared at his report and thought for a while.

'Well, Mister Yankov. Seeing as there's no sign of you sending anyone into the future in the near future, we're presently left with one option.'

Maxim and the others waited to hear what Popov had to say.

'We take care of Plant in present time.'

'Why such a hurry to kill Plant Mister Popov?' said Vasiliev. 'Keeping him under observation may throw up some more clues as to his association with Schitthelm.'

'Plant is onto us, he knows what we're up to – it's obvious.' said Popov. 'He's playing games with us, taking the piss if you will.'

'I'm not with you,' said Pavlov.

Popov let out a sigh of exasperation. 'Let me spell it out to you comrades: Plant has dumped the fat lady in the freezer as a prank – just to let us know that he's one step ahead of us. He knows we have time travel capability, and he knew there was a level transfer due – so he killed her and dumped in the freezer.'

'But she died from natural causes Mister Popov,' interrupted Maxim.

'I'm not one bit convinced Yankov. Yes, we'll put that on the report, but there's no doubt in my mind that Plant killed her as part of his prank. He's making a statement: he knows we're using the freezer as a delivery vessel for level transfers, he knows Semyon's been watching him, and he knows we plan to steal the freezer. I'll also wager he knows about Operation Deep Freeze, and it's highly likely he's reporting everything to Schitthelm. So – how many reasons do I have to give you? Plant knows too much, he has to go, non-negotiable.'

Nobody said anything. Not for a while at least. The stenographer's fingers froze mid-action in response to a silence heavy enough to subdue any attempt at challenging the Head of The KGB.

When he felt the silence had worked its effect, Popov spoke.

'Okay, we enter onto the report that the fat lady died from natural causes, and that Semyon died from death by misadventure: he fell into the river and drowned. I'll sign it off and forward it to the President. One way or another we've got to cool this situation down. Yankov, I want you to ready the cage for a level transfer. We'll be sending one of our finest to deal with Plant.'

'Who did you have in mind?' asked Vasiliev.

'We'll level transfer Leo Smirnov over to Locburn today. He'll take his brolly with him.' said Popov.

'We're not doing a Georgi Markov number on him are we?' said Pavlov, disapproving.

'And what's wrong with that?' asked Popov. 'Smirnov is a master of stealth – he'll sneak up on Plant and jab him in the leg with the tip of the brolly. The ricin pellet gets injected into Plant's leg, and two or three days later he dies from what looks to be a fever.' Popov cracked a grin, one undiscernible from genuine amusement, wind pain, or the strained expression one is overcome with when ridding themselves of an awkward turd.

'I've watched Smirnov practising on convicts. You should see how he does it – it borders on slapstick. He goes to walk past his victim – as if he's in a hurry, like in a busy street, or a shopping mall, or anywhere that's crowded with people. He pretends to half-trip and accidentally on purpose stuffs the tip of the brolly into the intended leg.' Still grinning Popov waited for a reaction.

'And guess what happens then?' he asked, with a glee that rendered him close to human. When no one spoke he chuckled out his response. 'Bobski soon won't be your uncle.'

Pavlov interrupted Popov's psychopathic merriment.

'The brolly thing's so yesterday – we have lots of other alternatives at our disposal: the electric pellet, the expanding headache tablet, the hybrid funnel web spider. I could go on.'

The electric pellet was invented in 2008. It was originally the idea of a cross-eyed Crimean farm labourer called Grigory Pawlinski. Grigory was at breakfast one morning when his attention was drawn to a competition advertised on the back of a packet of cornflakes. Entrants were invited to come up with a novel idea of how to a kill large, warm-blooded creature (roughly the size of a human being) with the minimum of fuss.

Grigory was tired of hammering a bolt through a pig's forehead in order to slaughter it. It was a messy business that had only a seventy per-cent first-blow kill rate. Frequently the pig would sense impending doom and shift at the last second, causing Grigory to miss the bolt and strike the hand steadying the bolt.

If Grigory was full of vodka he sometimes failed to hit the bolt squarely enough to drive it sufficiently into the pig's brain. This resulted in a drunken Grigory having to chase two-hundredweight of pissed-off bacon around the farm yard with a bolt protruding from its forehead.

When people get severely drunk they often see double. Because Grigory was cross-eyed he saw quadruple when overly inebriated.

When he was this intoxicated he had only a one-in-four chance of hitting the correct bolt. If he did hit the correct bolt, but failed to drive it far enough into the pig's head, it would result in a severely drunken Grigory having to chase four pissed-offpigs, totalling eight-hundredweight, each with a bolt protruding from their forehead.

Grigory fathomed that, with today's technology, a gun could be designed to fire a high voltage pellet into the pig and electrocute it instantly. He filled in the entry form and sent it off.

A panel of KGB weapons experts judged the thousands of entries and awarded Grigory's idea first prize. He won a signed picture of the President. Meanwhile the Kremlin's Weapons Research Centre was tasked with converting the idea into reality.

A semi-automatic air pistol was designed, small enough to be easily concealed about the person. It fired a pellet the size of a garden pea at a velocity of two-hundred metres per-second. The head of the pellet contained a muli-latex cross-wrap copper capacitor that could hold a charge of thirty-thousand volts. A magazine of six pellets slid into the butt of the pistol. The pistol was whisper silent in operation and had an effective range of sixty metres. Once the pellet penetrated the skin the whole thirty-thousand volts was discharged and the pig would die instantly from electrocution.

Almost a decade on and the pistol has been in frequent and effective use by the KGB. Back at the farm cottage the President's signed picture hanging on the wall has faded. Grigory drinks as much as he ever did and still kills his pigs with a hammer and bolt.

The expanding headache tablet was an in-house invention. The Kremlin Weapons Research Centre had been experimenting with cellular compression techniques in order to shrink objects which could later return to their original size. The technology would come to provide for many applications.

One of the junior engineers suggested compressing a quantity of chalk-based calcium nitride to the size of a paracetamol tablet. The engineer in question spent many hours as a child pulling wings and legs from various insects.

When the tablet was ingested it maintained its compressed size until it entered the stomach. Once in the stomach the calcium nitride reacted with the point five per-cent of hydrochloric acid we all have in that part of our digestive system. In less than a second the tablet would expand to its original dimensions – roughly the size of a Saint Bernard.

The Bio-Weapons Laboratory came up with the hybrid funnel web spider. They'd spent two years researching deadly spiders and found two species that were equally venomous. One was the Giant Venezuelan Tarantula; the other was the Sydney Funnel Web. Although the Giant Tarantula was deadly, it had a docile temperament. Any idiot foolish enough to handle the creature could get away with being bitten if they were sufficiently gentle with it. Some imbeciles even kept them as pets.

The Sydney Funnel Web, in comparison, was an aggressive spider that would go out of its way to bury its fangs into anyone who went near it. It was capable of pouncing, and would bite repeatedly. The male spider is particularly feisty during the breeding season, when it becomes highly mobile. Australians normally remember to check inside their shoes before donning them as the funnel web's fangs are powerful enough to penetrate a toenail.

The Bio-Weapons Laboratory harvested eggs and sperm from either species and cross-fertilised them. Eventually they bred a spider, comparable in size to the tarantula, however with an attitude ten times shittier than a conventional funnel web. The spider had to be secured in a cage at all times, save for when it was released into the house, or office, or car of the intended victim.

To date the spider has claimed ninety-two victims, the expanding headache tablet, ninety-four, and the electric pellet, fifty-seven. Two spider-bitten victims currently lie in deep comas. The National Office of Statistics are holding back on publishing the latest State Enemy Eradication Figures in the hope that both victims will die and peg the spider level with the headache tablet.

§

At the mention of sending a hit man with an umbrella Maxim spoke up.

'I don't think we will be able to send personnel with any kind of equipment for the time being Mister Popov – or anybody clothed or wearing jewellery for that matter.'

'What are you trying to tell me Mister Yankov?' said Popov. 'Not more bad news I hope.'

'There's a technical hitch with the cage; more precisely the vortex regulator. It's over-heating you see.'

Popov shook his head. 'A vortex regulator,' he asked. 'What does that do?'

'It prevents animate molecules mixing with inanimate ones, and mutual exchange of living, with living molecules. You will recollect the misfortune of the protagonist in the sci-fi film called "The Fly."' replied Maxim.

'Eh?'

'Turn to page sixteen of the lab report for last month – halfway down the page, the incident with Timofei Fukim and his duffle-coat.'

Popov read for a few seconds. He shuddered when he recalled the tragedy.

'And when did you first discover that there was a problem with this – this vortex thing?' asked Popov.

'When we got the blood test results back from the lab.'

'You mean Semyon's and the fat lady's?'

'Yes, we analysed them straight away. We were curious because it was the first time dead and living tissue had travelled together.' said Maxim.

'And what did you find?' said Popov, becoming interested.

'There has been an interaction – a molecular exchange between Semyon and the fat lady.' replied Maxim. 'We believe that's what caused the vortex regulator to over-heat. Before we send anyone else we've got to fit a larger capacity regulator to avoid any kind of molecular blending.'

Maxim and his team would discover in the coming weeks that, when a body dies, its molecules are still 'viable' for up to twelve hours. In terms of Cellular Ultrasonic Neutron Transmogrification 'viable' means that living cells and viable cells will readily combine.

When Edith and Vagin were level transferred together, there was an intimate molecular exchange. As the viable dead cells have twice the absorbency factor of living cells, it meant that Edith's molecular infrastructure sponged at the healthy molecules of a man in his prime. Unfortunately for Vagin most of Edith's unhealthy cells were deposited in his molecular infrastructure. Unfortunately for Edith she absorbed a tapeworm, and prostate gland, belonging to Vagin.

When Maxim saw the blood test results he was reluctant to let Vagin know of the findings. He hastily level transferred him straight back to Ronnie's freezer in Locburn. Because the vortex regulator hadn't cooled sufficiently Vagin had a partial molecular exchange with his crusty underpants – this rendered him suicidal.

After returning Vagin to Locburn, Maxim went to ring the Director of Intelligence for a second time. Before he got to the phone he looked over at Edith lying on one of the examination gurneys. He was startled to see her cheeks colouring up, and one of her toes twitching. Maxim went over to Edith. He got out his pen torch and shone it in one of her pupils; he recoiled in shock as the pupil reacted to the light. Maxim's attention was drawn to Edith's head of grey hair. Before his very eyes he could see each strand turning a deep brown, and at the same time taking on a healthy sheen.

Having sent his technicians home for the evening, Maxim was alone in the lab with Edith. In his confusion the genius rightly wondered if she was coming back to life. In a state of panic he wheeled the gurney over to the cage and bundled her into it. Fortunately for Edith the vortex regulator had cooled sufficiently to prevent a molecular exchange with her clothing.

By the time Edith was transferred back into the freezer, Vagin had already vacated it. Her heart began to beat, strong and steady. Climbing out of the freezer Edith experienced the typical disorientation caused by a level transfer. In the midst of confusion she staggered through to the lounge and fell asleep on the sofa.

While her drunken husband was recounting his Spiderman experience in the pub, Edith woke-up in the same place she'd died less than twenty-four hours earlier.

Maxim thought it better to keep Edith's suspected resurrection out of his report.

'Why don't we send Smirov naked on ahead of his clothes and umbrella? We can send them immediately afterwards.' said Vasiliev. 'That way there won't be any of this molecular blending you talk about.'

Maxim thought about Vasiliev's proposal. Before he could answer Popov spoke up.

'Good idea Mister Vasiliev – problem solved. We'll get Smirnov over here straight away. Vasiliev, you can brief him. Yankov, you get the weapon's people to check the umbrella over for function. Make sure Smirnov takes some spare ricin pellets with him.'

Popov leaned back in his chair and allowed himself a grin. 'At last comrades, a big problem solved before it gets any bigger. Once Smirnov gets over to Locburn it shouldn't take him too long to locate Plant. Then it's just a simple matter of jabbing him in the leg with an umbrella – what could be easier?' Popov rubbed his hands together.

'With Plant out of the way we can get at the freezer. I've got our logistics team in place over there. They'll show up in a delivery van when the house is empty, deliver a replica freezer, and take the old one away. Once we have the freezer in our possession we can get rolling with Operation Deep Freeze.'

CHAPTER 13

THE CARPET MAN

'Lenny,' Sarah called from the bathroom, 'There's someone at the front door.'

'You don't say,' Lenny shouted back from the sitting room. 'I wondered what was causing the door knocker to go rat-a-tat bastard tat – and why the doorbell kept going ding fucking dong.'

'Less of your language Mister Plant,' said Sarah, in a tone stern enough to put him off swearing for the short term. She walked through to the bedroom and reached for her hair dryer. 'I'm busy up here, so go and answer it. It's probably the carpet fitters.'

Lenny didn't mind a reasonably firm rat-a-tat-tat at his door from any kind of visitor, whether a canvassing Liberal Democrat, a Witness belonging to Jehovah, or even a member of the North Yorkshire Police Force. And he didn't mind any kind of visitor who opted for pressing the doorbell to save them rattling the door knocker. But any kind of arsehole who rattled at the door whilst ringing the doorbell, was simply, well, just an arsehole.

Lenny's aversion to someone knocking at the door, and someone ringing the bell of same door at same time, was somewhat at odds with Paul McCartney's joyous musical celebration of the same phenomenon. However when one considers the polarity of the two men's circumstances, it's easier to understand the social contradiction:

Millionaire Mac tickles away at his Steinway in a room the size of a large semi-detached. He's likely bored to the extent where he's gotten himself close to shitless, when he hears someone a knocking and a ringing at the door. How fortuitous; in a millionth of a moment, Millionaire Mac is inspired to knock-out another million seller.

He warbles to his servants that someone's a knocking and a ringing at the door; asking them to do him a favour and let 'em in. Macca seems ignorant to the fact that the servants, being servants, are tuned-in to recognising, and reacting, without being bid by their Lord, to the percussive or melodious resonances a visitor offers with either their knuckles, a prodding finger – or in this instance, both.

Then Millionaire Mac's clever-dickedness kicks-in. Before a servant can get to the door, Macca's trilling out the identities of the people waiting to be let in. He already knows who the visitors are – but how? Perhaps he's seen them through the window, walking up the gravelled drive. Or else he's been expecting them at that time because he's already invited them.

It turns out that most of them are family members: Mac's sister Suzi and his brother-in-law Michael for example. However there're a handful of unlikely luminaries midst the throng. Phil and Don Everly have showed up, probably for a singalong with Macca, so that's plausible enough.

But then there's Uncle Ernie – as in 'Wicked Uncle Ernie,' the Tommy Rock Opera pervert responsible for the lowering of the bedsheets and the raising of the nightshirts. If Macca were a little more prescient he could have invited Jimmy Savile along as well, just to help Ernie out with the nightshirt business.

Maybe Jimmy is there though; it's just that Millionaire Mac can't shoe-horn his name into the cosy lyrics.

The biggest surprise has to be Martin Luther. Not the reformist who nailed his list of theses to the door of a Wittenberg church in 1517; but the poor fucker some fucker shot through the neck in Memphis in 1968. It's unbelievable; Martin Luther King has risen from the dead, or whatever twilight dimension he's been haunting for the past umpteen years, and decided to do a bit of visiting. Bless him, he's made a genuine effort to come and see Millionaire Macca and that's really ever so nice.

Unfortunately the pragmatic side of the listener's brain will not entertain such a frolic with fantasy. The punters will work it out in a trice and smell a pair of morally corrupt rats. It's Jimmy and

Ernie you see. They've unearthed Mr Luther King and fetched his remains along for reasons known only to them; reasons that can do nothing but invite an orgy of depraved conjecture.

On the other side of life's railway track we have Lenny Plant. He's busy sitting in a sitting-room the size of Millionaire Mac's broom cupboard, applying full concentration to a scab on his left elbow. Having monitored the scab periodically over the week in order to assess its level of maturity, Lenny observes there's sufficient crusting to allow it to be coaxed off. Removal of the scab would have to be done with great care and precision, so as to avoid any drawing of blood. If blood is drawn it would cause another scab to form.

Because of the person rattling and ringing at the door, Lenny has to postpone the removal of the scab. This annoys him almost as much as the din of the ringing and the rattling.

Lenny's black Labrador, Roscoe, can't be bothered barking to announce the arrival of the visitor. Like Lenny he's irritated at the racket, and also the idiot creating it. He groans and trots off to the kitchen in search of tranquillity.

Unlike Millionaire Mac, Lenny's never met the person standing on his doorstep, and, unlike Mac, he dislikes them. However Lenny is far more astute than the socially naïve Mac. Before he opens the door he's already profiled the stranger on the other side: Male, short of arse, and a problem with it. He's covered in tattoos he pretends not to regret, and drinks cheap Australian lager. Has to be ex-army, nothing above the rank of Corporal mind, sufficient office for a loud-mouthed asinine apprentice drill-pig, endowed with intellect enough to grasp the bigotry he gleans from the low-rent, fuckwit, wannabe rightist arse-wipe tabloid, the one with Sudoku and tits included, untastefully infused with appropriate nuances of prejudice fashioned to appeal to the rancid shite lodged in the confines of his shallow noddle.

Lenny opened the door.

'Carpet fitters – come to fit your carpet sunshine. We haven't got all day so show me to the dining room at the double.'

Before Lenny could usher him to the dining room the carpet man pushed past him, all five-foot-five of him. He walked up the hallway like he owned the place.

'Can't hang about, running late we are – bloody protesters cluttering up the High Street outside the council offices. If they want to do something about the homeless they should get rid of all these bloody immigrants. And these fuckers on benefits – get the lazy bastards out to work – oh, and don't get me on about these rich bastards and the tax avoidance. It's hard working people like me who get shafted by the tax man – every time. We all need to be paying our taxes, the bleedin lot of us.'

He spun on his heel when he got to the end of the hallway. 'You need any other carpets fitting don't be ringing Rosenstein's for a quote, coz I'll beat any quote they give. I'll under-cut them, even if I have to make a loss – the greedy big-nosed money-grabbing fucks. If you want to do cash I can knock you a few quid off.'

Sarah was still upstairs; she had the hair dryer on at full speed so was oblivious to the diatribe.

'Man United won again,' said the carpet man, standing by the dining room door. 'What team do you support then? You're not a Leeds man are you?'

'I can't stand football – and I hate footballers slightly less than I loathe football fans,' replied Lenny, wishing he were somewhere else.

Being interested exclusively in the sound of his own voice, the carpet man took little notice of Lenny's comment.

'We signed Rubens last week – a hundred million. What a player. He's the top scorer for Israel's national team you know – a real nice bloke too by all accounts; done well for himself, bought a fourteen bedroom town house in Belgravia and registered it to a company in the British Virgin Islands. More money than God – you should see his yacht, twenty million quid. He leases it to himself from another company his accountant told him to set up on the Isle of Man; saved him four million on the VAT. The guy's switched-on alright.

'He's my son's hero. I got him the new team strip for Christmas
– bolloxed me wallet for three-hundred quid though. It's an extra
hundred see, that's if you want the signed poster of him posing in
front of his yacht.'

Lenny showed the carpet man to the dining room, wondering if
he ever paused to draw breath.

'Your Missus gave me the measurements in metres and
centimetres sunshine. No good to me that. Got to be feet and
inches; I'm old school: miles, gallons, feet and inches – fuck metric
– every inch of it.'

'I see,' said Lenny, surprised. 'I'll just nip to the garage; there's an
old tape in there somewhere.'

'No need,' said the carpet man. 'I've got an imperial tape in the
van. It's hardly been used but I bet it's older than yours – follow me
a second.'

The carpet man marched back to the front door and shouted to
a young lad sitting in the passenger seat of his transit van.

'Troy! Off your arse and fetch the tape,' he ordered, 'at the
double you horrible little turd.' The carpet man spoke to Lenny.
'The P.I.S.S. Academy sent him – it's their Youth in Work
Scheme. They're paying me to train him to fit carpets for the next
eight weeks. He's not a bad lad, too easy distracted though. Got
Asperger's – I think that's what they call it.'

Lenny watched from the doorstep as Troy opened his door and
slid off the passenger seat. He walked to the back doors of the van.

'I wanted a laser tape but they don't do them in Imperial.
Everything's metric nowadays, I can't get me head round the
bastard,' moaned the carpet man. 'There was a time when I could
do metric – but I've never been the same since Orderly Sergeant
Trotter kicked me in the head on purpose – out of order he was. I
copped for his size twelve after morning parade. Fucking Officer of
the Day went and noticed a speck of dandruff on me collar.'

A grin, warmed by the memory of revenge fulfilled, crested
on the carpet man's face. 'Got me own back though; walked into
a boozer in Rochdale fifteen years later and who's standing at
the bar but retired Sergeant Trotter. Not so orderly nowadays –

more drunk and disorderly. Pretended I was glad to see him after all those years. On his own he was – zero authority and short of friends he never had. The bastard was only too pleased to see me. I put on a show of false congeniality and talked about the army days like we were best buddies. I drank-off and bid him farewell. He thought I'd left the pub but I went into the bogs and waited for him. Anyway – in he comes for a piss, and I give him a brand new look.' Lenny eyed carpet man, concerned. 'Sorted his face out with a corkscrew I always carry with me.'

Carpet man pulled a corkscrew from his pocket. He held it in a clenched fist so that the screw protruded from between his fingers.

'A very present help in times of need,' he said, articulating well beyond his intellect, 'sorts out all me road-rage issues as well. Never mind Trotter's fizzer, you should've seen the state of the bogs; there was claret everywhere.'

He returned his attention to Troy.

'Show him how it works Troy – and no fucking about,' said carpet man, nudging Lenny and winking.

The youngster took hold of both handles and swung the doors open. Lenny thought he caught a trace of a smile on the young lad's face.

Troy reached an arm into the van, took hold of something, and walked steadily backwards. Lenny watched.

Troy had the end of a white tape pinched between his finger and thumb. The tape looked shiny and new. Clearly marked in feet and inches it continued to extend from the rear of the van. As Troy walked backwards both he and carpet man eyed Lenny for a reaction.

Lenny craned his neck to get a better look inside the van. As he did, he got a better look inside the van.

What came into view caused Lenny to look away. He looked away because acute denial informed him that what he was looking at was not actually happening – and could not actually be happening. Lenny looked at the bird table in the garden, because he could see that, by looking at the bird table, he was looking at something that made perfect sense to look at. Finches and sparrows, blackbirds and robins, any bird that fancied, could alight on the table to eat the seeds scattered on its surface. Seeds scattered there by a person, or persons, who derived pleasure in watching various birdlife fluttering, chirping, pecking, and, from time to time, being ripped to pieces by the local sparrow-hawk.Yes, the bird table made sense and fitted-in with rational consciousness; much the same way as a pillow case, a steering wheel, or a new hair-do.

'Don't let go of it you little twat,' ordered carpet man. Troy looked at Lenny, sniggered, and let go of the tape. Lenny had turned his gaze from the bird table back to the van.

'It's like when I eat spaghetti,' laughed Troy.

'Fucking Asperger's,' groaned carpet man.

The tape slid through the air like a recoiling snake. Back towards the van it went. Before it disappeared, the last three-foot whiplashed against the plump white arse-cheeks flanking the sphincter from which it was pulled.

Although still gripped with shock, Lenny had to agree that the tape did indeed slap at Edith's buttocks in a manner not dissimilar to a lengthy strand of spaghetti being slurped into the sauce stained chops of a mischievous brat.

'Morning Lenny,' called Edith, cheery. She was kneeling on all fours.

'What the f–, Edith,' Lenny stared at the carpet man, unsure of what kind of stare he should use to stare at him with. He'd never had to react to such a situation and so was at a loss whether to stare in disbelief, horror, disgust or bewilderment. Lenny played it safe and stared at him with a mixture of all four.

'Tha – that's n – not right,' stammered Lenny.

'Just some part time work Lenny,' said Edith, 'cash-in-hand as well.'

Edith was wearing a mini-skirt and no knickers, presenting Lenny with a similar genital vista to the pub angel; albeit from a different angle and much less subtle. She was un-bald. Troy had slid the hem up her back to gain access to the end of the tape worm.

'I had to mark it out with indelible ink,' said carpet man.

'You – you marked it out in edible ink?' mumbled Lenny.

'No,' laughed carpet man, 'I said "indelible ink" – you wouldn't want to eat that bastard.'

Carpet man spoke to Troy. 'Can you remember how long the tape is Troy?'

'Twenty-foot long – but we have to add an extra three-feet-two inches,' explained Troy.

'So what's the longest length of carpet we can measure with it?'

'Twenty-three feet and two inches,' said Troy, proud of his knowledge.

'Where do you get the extra three-foot-two inches?' asked Lenny.

'Tell him Troy,' ordered carpet man.

'That's the distance from the tip of Edith's nose, to her bum-hole.'

Carpet man smiled, 'He says bum-hole because he struggles with the word sphincter – got a lisp you see.'

'I still don't understand,' said Lenny, referring to the whole situation. Carpet man misread his confusion and set to explaining the extra three-foot-two inches.

'When we measure-up a room, we have Edith on all fours and get her to touch her nose against the wall. We then extend the tape across the room to the other wall and take a measurement – in feet and inches of course. We add three-foot-two inches to the reading at the sphincter.'

'This can't be right,' said Lenny. 'You can't treat another human being like that – it, it's degrading.'

Troy had pulled the tape back out and was about to let it go again. Lenny shouted at him.

'Pack it in! Stop it – stop it right now. You mustn't do that, stop, don't let go of it, stop!'

Lenny heard his wife's voice. 'Lenny, wake up.' Sarah was shaking his shoulder.

'What – what's going on?'

'Wake up, you've been dreaming – sounded like a nightmare.'

Lenny sat bolt upright in bed. He checked his elbow.

'What's up with your elbow?'

'I haven't got a scab on it.'

'What?'

'They forgot to take the skirting-boards into consideration.'

'What are you talking about?' said Sarah, trying to fathom the link between a scab and a skirting-board.

'They need to subtract the total thickness of the skirting boards after they've added the three-foot-two inches to the bum-hole measurement,' said Lenny, still half-in and half-out of his dream.'

Sarah looked at Lenny and chuckled with a hand over her mouth.

'What's up with you?' said Lenny, yawning and frowning.

'You said bum-hole.'

'So?'

'The proper name is sphincter.'

'Try saying that with a lisp,' said Lenny.

'Sssthpincsther,' replied Sarah, before a laughing fit.

Lenny smiled at his wife, she could be fun. 'That was a weird one Sarah. So bizarre – but it seemed so real.'

'What was it about?' asked Sarah, snuggling into Lenny's side.

'You don't want to know,' replied Lenny, not wanting to get her on to the subject of carpets. He glanced at the bedside clock.

'What day is it?'

'It's Sunday morning and you've got to get your two hours in at the Academy.'

CHAPTER 14

THE P.I.S.S. ACADEMY

The Public Institute for Social Science (affectionately known, and often referred to, as the "Piss Academy") requires that every member of its parish attend the Institute for an average of two hours per-week over each calendar year. There's a six week allowance for holidays and family emergencies. Membership is mandatory and all ages are required to attend. Members who non-attend for any lengthy period shall give good reason for their absence and strive to redress the shortfall.

The housebound are provided for with the National P.I.S.S. Academy TV Network. Those both housebound and completely deaf can activate the subtitle button on their TV remote. Anyone housebound, completely deaf, and illiterate, are catered for with sign language interpreters doing their stuff at the bottom right of the screen. The hard of hearing are entitled to an inner ear amplification service, provided free of charge, courtesy of Three F. A complimentary pre-insertion wax purge is included in the service.

Each member has their own P.I.S.S membership card which they swipe over an electronic timer at the entrance to the Institute on entering and exiting. By swiping the card the total time spent at the Institute is logged. The card also entitles its owner to discounts of up to ten-per-cent on purchases of any commodity that contributes to environmental or social sustainability. Some examples of products that qualify are books (apart from bibles), high-end wines, and line-caught tuna. Examples of products that don't qualify for the discount are golfing accessories, plastic conservatories, and ferrets.

The majority of churches in the country had been bought-up by Three F (Flowers for Faith), and, under the direction of Art Schitthelm, subjected to a National Church Disembowelment

Program. The Institute in Locburn Village was formerly Saint Mary's Catholic Church.

Up until the summer of June 2011the incumbent priest was Father Thomas; a corrupt man who took every opportunity to abuse his position of trust in the community. He financed an extravagant lifestyle through blackmail, people trafficking, sham marriages, and stealing lead from the church roof. Thomas was also strident in his criticism of Art Schitthelm. Sunday sermons would find him in the pulpit, bellowing anti-Schitthelm diatribe to a bemused congregation.

Schitthelm put up with Thomas's rantings until he tired of him. Sergeant Savage, a policeman on the Three F payroll, shot Thomas with a dart containing a blood thickening agent. Thomas died of a heart attack shortly afterwards.

Once Thomas was out of the way Schitthelm installed one of his New Era Ministers at Saint Mary's. Minister Arthur Kelly was employed by Three F as a half-arsed priest cum change manager. He would oversee the transition from a church to a Public Institute for Social Science.

The churchgoers were surprisingly easy to win over, as were other parishioners up and down the country. Indeed the broader public were mostly welcoming of many of the social projects Three F were introducing nationally. Art Schitthelm would often chant, 'Three F are changing things that matter, that change things that matter,' and he was getting results – much to the chagrin of politicians, police chiefs, local councillors, and religious leaders.

Art Schitthelm and Three F had set out to cure the ills of society – ills such as poverty, greed, religion and ignorance. Art despised ignorance, at first labelling it a two-headed snake, before reproaching himself and publicly apologising for demonising snakes.

Seeing no harm in demonising demons, Art renamed ignorance a 'two-headed demon,' a metaphoric insinuation of the entities ignorance, and ignorant. Ignorance being a condition of unawareness – a crippling social laissez faire, and ignorant being a multi-faceted, multi-dimensional trait, that manifested itself in the individual: an ignorant bastard, fucker, or cunt of whatever sex. Somewhere between ignorance and ignorant, were ignorant 'what's-its-names,' who were either unaware of their ignorance or just plain ignorant ignoramuses.

Art was campaigning to have religion officially listed as the eighth deadly sin, citing it as an unnecessary source of social aggravation: "Religion is the sperm of the Devil, the Devil's sperm – the sperm that comes out of the Devil. And when the Devil cometh, ye shall know about it," Art had his New Era Ministers preach these words at Institutes up and down the country.

'Opposites attract,' so the old saying goes. As far as greed and poverty were concerned Art was in complete agreement. However they made terrible bed partners, with Poverty being eternally shafted, from every angle, by Greed. No matter that Greed fucked, sucked, slurped and gorged – still it hungered.

"There will dawn a day when both greed and poverty shall feed from the bowl of equity, and the bowl shall brim with sugar and shit. Thus," says The New Era Minister, "shall it be. For verily I say unto thee, that he who feedeth on the sugar and the shit, shall tasteth both in equal amounts."

§

Lenny Plant walked down Church Lane on his way to the Institute. He was alone. He'd swipe-in just before ten to catch the Sunday Morning Current Affairs Argument.

Every Sunday morning (including Sundays that fell on Christmas day, and Easter Sundays) any issues or disputes that affected the local community could be publicly quarrelled over in the main church hall. The New Era Minister would chair the argument from the pulpit. It was his responsibility to mitigate, resolve, or call the police.

Issues that failed to reach a conclusion after three consecutive Sundays would be forwarded to the nearest disembowelled Cathedral (The former Cathedral of Durham served for Locburn), where a panel of Senior New Era Ministers would sit in judgement. On the rare occasion that Senior Ministers were unable to bring matters to a close, a report of the whole affair would end up on Art Schitthelm's desk.

Each Sunday the argument started no sooner than the tenth chime of ten o'clock, and finished on the twelfth chime of midday. It commenced and concluded precisely at these times, oblivious to pleasantry or insult. At the instant of chime twelve there would be prompt silence, and all present would vacate the hall. This was a strict imposition – a Schitthelm idea. He deemed such a measure imperative in order to impart discipline to the Institute's schedule: 'Se individual gatherings, activities, and events, must contain themselves within themselves. That way everything will not outgrow anything else, and each will belong in its own dimension, so that neither one encroaches upon se other, and vice versa.'

If Lenny swiped-out for midday, or shortly afterwards, he'd have his two hours logged for the week. As for Sarah, she'd get her two hours in at the Ladies' Hod-Carrying Class from six till eight that evening.

This Sunday's debate was over an ongoing local issue; ongoing since the previous Sunday when the clock struck twelve at the height of an intense row. Today the Minister was anxious to bring the matter to a close, fearing it had the potential to run into a third Sunday and perhaps beyond. He'd never had an argument forwarded for scrutiny by Senior Ministers. He knew that if there was no joy with them, it would be bound for the attention of Art Schitthelm – perish the thought.

Minister Arthur Kelly knew he was in a tight spot with this particular local feud. At the previous week's argument he'd had a taster of its divisive effect on the community. It involved the living and the dead, the pedigree of certain parishioners, the eco-system, and a moral compass pointing any which way.

The disagreement was over the gravestones in the churchyard, and it was heading beyond boiling point as more locals allowed themselves to be sucked-in to the debate. As for Lenny, he'd already decided he wouldn't get involved. With no members of his family buried in the yard, and other things crowding his mind, he thought it better to stay out of this one.

§

The western side of the churchyard boasted a formidable rookery. The birds had built their nests high up in a canopy of ash, beech, oak and horse chestnut. As it was the start of the nesting season there was plenty of activity at the site –and more so this year than any other. The previous year a local farmer had cut down three acres of woodland in a neighbouring field, "because he needed logs for his fire." The de-forestation was reported to Three F's Environmental Protection League and the farmer had a nasty accident involving a chain-saw shortly afterwards.

With the rookery at the felled copse destroyed, the homeless rooks migrated to the churchyard rookery. Things were busy.

As with any other living creature in possession of an arsehole, rooks shit. And when you're a rook, you never, as the old saying goes, "shit in your own nest." The graves and gravestones sited directly under the rookery were being shat upon from a great height, and this is possibly the worst way to be shat upon – especially with rook shit, as it splatters on contact. Those visiting the graves, either to pay their respects, or tend to them, were noticing that there was now twice the likelihood of experiencing the phenomenon of shit happening.

Minister Arthur Kelly had made the unnerving discovery that the avian shit that hits the gravestone, spreads ten times further than the conventional shit that hits the proverbial fan.

Those members of the parish with loved ones buried under the rookery were seeking the same kind of shit-free grave-visiting enjoyment experienced by some of their fellow parishioners, i.e. the bereaved that frequented graves outside of the 'shit-zone'.

Their demands were simple enough: 'get rid of the rooks.'

§

Minister Arthur Kelly climbed into the pulpit with the willingness of a condemned man ascending the scaffold. His expression was identical to one he was wearing at the end of the previous Sunday's argument – a look you'd expect to see haunting the face of someone awaiting the outcome of a test for a suspected gonococcal infection.

As the last few seats were taken a dozen or so parishioners were left standing – the place was packed. Lenny had managed to bag a seat at the rear of the hall, close to the entrance. He needed a sharp exit on the twelfth strike so he could beat the Sunday lunchtime rush for the bar at The Haydale Arms. There was the option of having a drink in the Institute's bar, situated in the vestry, but he didn't want to get caught up in any residual crossfire between the shit-free and the shat upon.

'Okay everyone!' shouted Minister Kelly, his volume over-hauling the agitated thrum of several conversations, 'you know the rules: no discussion till the tenth chime – so let's get settled.' The mutterings dutifully faded with the exception of one individual.

Spinster Lilly Gillespie was the village trouble-maker. Every village has one. With numerous chips on either shoulder, she constantly strove to make all existence as miserable as her own. Gillespie didn't like to see people getting along – or even rubbing along. She much preferred to have them at each other's throats, and was only too willing to help things along to that end. For her there was nothing like raising another's hackles for putting a shine on the day. People's business was her business, which meant that she never missed The Sunday Morning Current Affairs Argument.

'Shut it Gillespie!' snapped Minister Kelly, leaning over the pulpit to thrust a seething expression at her. It was three minutes-to-ten and Kelly was determined to brief the hall before kick-off. Gillespie closed her mouth, making do for now by broadsiding him with a vengeful scowl.

'Right, listen-up the lot of you. We're sorting this one out today. Any of last week's nonsense and I'm calling in the police.'

Kelly raised his mobile phone so all could see it. 'Just to show you I mean business, I've already dialled-in the first two sixes. For the duration of the argument my finger will be hovering over the third six. And we all know who comes calling when we dial three sixes?'

'You wouldn't dare,' scoffed Gillespie.

'Gillespie, you acidic old trout; I'll make sure it's your name I give them.'

At Kelly's insult to Gillespie the congregation murmured with an assortment of chortles and giggles. It heartened the Minister enough to half undo his knotted expression. Gillespie turned to Agnes Rutter, a similar aged dim-witted lady with whom she'd formed a dissonant friendship.

'Did you hear what he just called me Agnes?'

'Yes – yes I did. He called you an acidic old trout Lilly.'

Three nines got you the North Yorkshire Police; three sixes got you an alternative: Three F's own Private Police; employed, trained, and paid for by Three F. Visually they were hard to tell apart from the regular police. It was the way they dealt with the problems to which they were summoned that made the distinction. The clock began to chime.

By the ninth chime Gillespie had her mouth open. At the sound of the tenth it went into overdrive.

A person speaks at an average narrative rate of around a hundred-and-twenty words per minute, and a mutual conversational rate of approximately eighty-five. This is a broad estimation that accommodates a rate of delivery infinitely variable for many reasons: mood and situation may influence the speaker's pace, as well as confidence or inhibition. The frequency of interruption to draw breath differs significantly between individuals; so that a clean-living long-distance yodeller will manage more words per inhalation than an asthmatic chain-smoker with pleurisy and a missing lung.

Progress of speech may be impeded by afflictions such as a stammer or Tourette's. Nose pickers will not achieve the word count of those who abstain from the habit. Inebriation is perhaps the most debilitating to coherent and efficacious delivery of speech. A fully intoxicated Ronnie Dent can slur as little as eleven words per minute; most of them rendered incomprehensible by the condition visited upon him by the misuse of strong waters.

An auctioneer in full flow can exceed two-hundred words a minute; whilst an auctioneer with an Ulster-Scots accent can hit three-hundred. Halfway between a drunken Ronnie Dent, and a sober auctioneer from Aghadowey, we find Lilly Gillespie.

Gillespie (de facto shit-zone) started on Kelly. 'You won't get out of this one Kelly – ha! – not today, not next Sunday, not any Sunday – can't see the Senior Ministers doing any better either. Beaten by bird shit, that's you – ha! You'll never live it down – never. Schitthlem won't like it – ha! Think I'll twitter him a line; let him know how things aren't going.'

Kelly cut-in. 'You make any effort to contact Art Schitthelm and you're in breach of protocol. You know the rules Gillespie; rules put in place by Three F. We have three Sundays to try and sort this, after that it goes to the seniors; if they are unable to conclude – then, and only then, does Art Schitthelm get involved.'

Gillespie, seated right under the pulpit, turned to the congregation. 'Looks like Schitthelm's going to get involved – ha!'

Terry Bradley (shit-zone) called out from the back; he was a reasonable sort. 'I know we talked about getting rid of the rooks completely,' he said, sympathetic, 'and that didn't go down too well with those whose graves are not affected by the defecation. So can we consider a cull? You know – reduce their numbers without actually killing them all off. If we could get the population down to roughly last year's level the amount of defecation would be more manageable.'

Ben Crawford (shit-zone) spoke-up. 'Don't sell-out Terry – fuck that lot,' he said, referring to the shit-free collective with a mixture of disdain and a sense of freedom. He felt it liberating to be able to swear in what used to be God's house. 'And it's shit we're talking about, not defecation. Vermin shit Terry. Don't try and sanitise shit by calling it something else – shit is shit.'

Kathy Davidson (shit-free) had a go at Ben Crawford. She spoke with the affectation of a school teacher chastising her pupil. 'There's no such thing as vermin these days Crawford, every living thing is necessary. The rooks have a right to live in the rookery, it's their home. And they have a right to rear their young. We mustn't disrupt any part of the eco-system.'

Here and there a shit-free head nodded in agreement.

Ben Crawford spoke directly to Minister Kelly. 'Listen to her,' he said, jerking his thumb in ridicule at Davidson. 'She wouldn't be spouting that eco-babble if she had a grave covered in bird shit – none of that lot would.'

'Stop referring to us as "that lot," implored Mark Bailey (shit-free). 'We're all one congregation, one parish, one society.'

'Hark the apprentice vicar,' called an obvious shit-zone voice from the throng.

The comment attracted a ripple of shit-zone sniggering.

'Who said that?' asked Bailey, wounded. He swivelled his head this way and that to scrutinise various shit-zone faces.

'Never mind,' said Crawford. 'Let's talk about what you've just said: "one congregation, one parish – one society."'

'And what's wrong with that?' asked Bailey; smarting with indignation.

'You see us all as one do you?' interrogated Crawford. 'Will you stand on that declaration?' Crawford directed his question part at Bailey and part at the shit-free.

'Of course I will,' replied Bailey, regaining composure. He rose from his seat to observe the hall. Inflating his chest he spoke to the congregation with the piety of an archbishop.

'I'd like to think I'm a man of principle – someone who sticks by what they say. And I do say we should unite to solve this issue. It's nobody's fault that some of the graves are situated under the rookery, it's just the way fate has dealt out the circumstances. I empathise entirely with my fellow parishioners who have their loved ones buried in that particular area. This problem has –.'

Gillespie intervened, pointing at Bailey whilst cracking a sarcastic grin at Kelly. 'Watch-out Kelly, this one's after your job – ha! He can't do any worse than you mind – even though he couldn't keep his job on the local council. Had to leave – ha! A little discrepancy with his expenses; I know because Councillor Sherman told Agnes when she was cleaning his office, and Agnes told me didn't you Aggie – ha!'

Agnes shrivelled with embarrassment then secretly wished to evaporate as she noticed Councillor Sherman (shit-zone) machine-gunning a stare from across the aisle.

Minister Kelly gripped the sides of the pulpit; fantasising he was gripping Gillespie's throat. 'Gillespie, will you please let people finish what they have to say.'

'Yes,' agreed Crawford, eyeing Gillespie with disgust. 'Carry-on with what you were saying Bailey,' he beckoned.

Bailey's face was crimson with a blend of rage and embarrassment. Most people would have given up at this point. But he resumed, inspired by the sound of his own voice, and driven with intrinsic narcissism. 'This problem has brought us together, and what brings us together must bind us together. Most of us have loved ones buried in the grounds of the former church; so let's look at this as an issue that we face together and solve together. The graves under the rookery are just as sacred as the ones outside of it. Don't let the soiling cause us to fall out. And anyway; I didn't have to leave – I was invited to resign.'

'Yeah-right,' jibed Gillespie, oblivious to her friend Agnes, who'd started weeping a mix of tears and nasal discharge into a crumpled tissue.

Bailey ignored Gillespie. He swept his eyes over the congregation in search of approving faces.

'So,' said Crawford, 'you say the graves are all equally sacred – does that mean they are equal in all other respects?'

'Yes, why shouldn't they be – aside from a few bird droppings there's no difference?'

'And you say we shouldn't be falling out over a few bird droppings?'

'That's exactly right,' said Bailey earnestly. 'I don't know what all the fuss is about.' He raised his palms to face the ceiling in the manner of a priest about to give his blessing. 'We're above that – all of us.'

'So would you say the graves are situated under the rookery – or would you say the rookery is situated above the graves?' asked Crawford.

'I'm not with you,' said Bailey.

'What came first, the graves or the rookery?'

Bailey scratched his head. 'Well, the graves I suppose; some of them date back to the sixteenth century.'

'So let's cut the trees down, or exterminate the rooks, or both,' suggested Crawford.

Neighbouring farmer Harley Chapman (shit-free) raised his left (recently bereaved) arm.'I don't recommend cutting the trees down,' he said gravely, 'not unless you want a visit from The Environmental Protection League.'

'You started all this Chapman. You and your bloody chain-saw,' said Crawford.

'Yeah, but look at him now,' squawked Gillespie, 'his chain-saw days are over. He's armless – ha!'

Gillespie's jeering earned her an unexpected murmur of laughter. Chapman didn't respond.

Harry Fowler (shit-zone) threw in a comment. 'He's stumped for an answer.'

'Bit of a saw point,' called a voice from the back. Even some members of the shit-free were now laughing.

'Surprised they didn't call in the Special Branch,' enjoined Crawford.

'If you ring them you've got make a trunk call,' returned Fowler. The volume of laughter increased.

'Fuck off Fowler,' said Chapman.

'Fuck off yourself – it's just as far,' back-answered Fowler.

'I'll swing for you Fowler you bastard,' said Chapman, rising from his seat.

'With which arm?' said Fowler, rising from his seat also.

'Order gentlemen please!' hollered Minister Kelly. 'Sit down the pair of you!'

Both men took their time to sit down, staring each other out as they did so.

While the congregation settled themselves Kelly requested that Crawford continue with his questioning of Bailey. The Minister sensed Crawford was heading somewhere with his line of interrogation. Perhaps he was working on backing Bailey into a corner.

Kelly disliked Bailey, almost as much as he hated Gillespie. The ex-councillor was a habitual plunderer of moral high-ground; deploying his chameleon-like sensibilities and synthetic charm to court any public approval that might be up for grabs.

'How's your Uncle Cedric?' asked Crawford, with sarcastic conviviality.

'Pardon?' said Bailey, puzzled.

'A guy named Cedric who happens to be your uncle. He may have forgotten you; but surely you haven't forgotten him?'

Bailey's Uncle Cedric was eighty-seven years old and resided in a third-rate care home in Stockton on Tees. It was the cheapest care home Bailey (in possession of power of attorney) could find for the dear old man. Bailey was Cedric's only nephew and sole remaining blood relative. He stood to inherit a small fortune from Cedric's estate. By getting the cheapest care available, Bailey was doing his utmost to preserve the amount of inheritance due to come his way.

Bailey had a soulless wife. The pair of them spawned a daughter who, like her parents, was born without a conscience. All three conspired to tell anyone who asked, that Cedric was receiving the highest quality of care in an exclusive care home in Harrogate.

The previous year Bailey was overjoyed when he received a phone call from the local police. They'd responded to a call from the concerned manager of a nearby supermarket. Cedric had been staring at a bottle of lime cordial for over an hour.

Bailey had cheerfully observed for some time, the decline in his uncle's mental acuity. The incident with the lime cordial brought his wildest dreams to life. Bailey promptly took Cedric to the doctor, who solemnised that Cedric had a virulent form of dementia and would last, at best, a year. Bailey, his wife, and daughter, reacted by putting on an ostentatious display of false grief before scouring the internet for a cheap and nasty care home. With Cedric safely installed, the Baileys set to with stripping their uncle's house of any article that aspirated the merest whiff of value.

'I know who my uncle Cedric is Crawford – I just don't understand what he's got to do with all this.'

'He's in a bad way is poor old Cedric,' said Crawford.

Bailey shrugged his shoulders and turned a tone on Crawford – one nuanced with belittlement. 'It's no secret my uncle has advanced dementia; sadly there's nothing that can be done to change that. However we're doing our best to keep him as comfortable as possible during what is probably the darkest time of his life.'

'Yeah I've seen,' said Crawford.

'Eh?' said Bailey. He sensed an uneasy twinge in his guts. It dampened any short-term potential for further pontification.

'I went to visit him yesterday,' said Crawford.

Bailey's composure was startled out of him; he unleashed a series of panicky questions at Crawford. 'You went to visit him? Why? How dare you. What's he to do with you Crawford? How did you find out where –,'

'My niece works in the care home – she remembers Cedric from when she was a kid.'

Bailey's left eyelid twitched, the same way it twitched when he was confronted about the sizeable anomaly with his travelling expenses. Minister Kelly noticed how Crawford had got the ex-councillor squirming. Bailey was the antagonising mouthpiece for the shit-free and Kelly was keen to see him subdued. Bailey decided to tell a lie.

'We only put him in there last week as a temporary measure – they're decorating the care home in Harrogate, a – and the paint fumes were affecting his breathing.'

'Bullshit – he's been rotting in Stockton since last August.'

Some members of the shit-free were now exchanging murmured comments whilst looking disapprovingly at Bailey.

'Minister Kelly,' protested Bailey, in his choicest of plaintive tones. 'I really don't think this line of scrutiny is relevant – neither is it fair. It's a personal encroachment on my private affairs and it's detracting from the real and very important issue at hand.'

Kelly didn't want to let Bailey off the hook; however, he needed to demonstrate to the congregation that he was presiding with equity.

'Mr Crawford, I have to ask you, is there any relevance to the point you're trying to make?'

'Very much so Minister,' said Crawford confidently. 'If you'll allow me to continue a little further I can demonstrate the relevance.'

'Very well Crawford, carry on – but please, get to the point.'

'Thank you Minister,' said Crawford politely. He turned to face Bailey.

'Your uncle Cedric, regardless of what care home he's in, has little time left in this world. Am I right?'

'Yes, you could say that,' replied Bailey begrudgingly.

'And you'll be burying him in the graveyard here at Locburn – yes?'

'That's the plan. That's where Cedric wanted to be laid to rest.'

'Chosen a plot yet?' probed Crawford. Bailey disliked the question. The Minister liked it.

'Really Minister, this is preposterous – what right has he to ask –,'

'Answer the question Mister Bailey,' ordered Kelly.

Bailey gave his answer reluctantly. 'Yes, of course we've got a plot for him.'

'Whereabouts in the graveyard?' asked Crawford.

Bailey turned to Kelly. 'This is personal stuff he's asking me Minister. I'm at liberty under my statutory rights to refuse to answer.'

'Actually you're not,' said Kelly.

'I think you'll find I am – I know the law.' retorted Bailey. Kelly pinned him with an officious stare.

'Mr Bailey, I draw your attention to Section Nine of Three F's Floating Policy on Articles Held in Open Debate.' Kelly quoted from memory. 'It states that: "All articles, or subject of articles raised for, or relating to, a designated debate or subsequent argument or quarrel, that takes place within the allotted time for such exchanges at a licensed Public Institute for Social Science, shall not be compromised or bound by any Statute that provides for the protection of disclosure of such information that may affect the resolution of said article or articles." Kelly offered Bailey half a grin and waited for his response.

Bailey had another go at wriggling free. 'That's ridiculous, I'm not aware of any such imposition on my rights.'

Kelly came straight back at him. 'The Manual for Conditions of Institute Function is freely available on the bookshelf in the bar; there's also a copy in Braille, and an amplified audio version online. There's absolutely no reason for anyone not to take a blind bit of notice – or for it falling on deaf ears. So answer the question Mr Bailey. Whereabouts in the graveyard have you reserved the plot in question? And think carefully before you answer. I'll warn you that I have the plan of the graveyard with me in the pulpit – which means I know where all the bodies are buried, as they say. I also know where all the reserved plots are, and who reserved them. So you could say Mr Bailey, that I already know the answer to the question I've just asked you.'

Bailey answered with a subdued mumble, 'the eastern side.'

'A little louder Mr Bailey,' provoked Kelly. 'The people at the back may not be able to hear you.' The Minister was starting to enjoy himself.

Bailey unwillingly raised his voice. 'The eastern side.'

'Correct answer,' said Kelly. 'I've checked with Mrs Scraggs anyway – you came in and booked the plot earlier this month; and while we're on with the subject, I have to remind you that we're still waiting for payment. Back over to you Mr Crawford.'

Crawford stood up from his chair. 'Just in case any of you didn't hear; Mr Bailey has reserved a burial plot on the eastern side of the graveyard.' Crawford spoke to Bailey. 'When you say the eastern side Bailey, you mean as opposed to the western side?'

'Obviously,' grunted Bailey.

Crawford spoke to Minister Kelly. 'Minister – you mentioned you've got the plan of the graveyard with you?'

'Yes – yes, I have it right here.' Kelly eagerly produced the plan from inside the pulpit and scrolled it open.

'Do you mind if I trouble you for a couple of details from the plan?' said Crawford.

'No – not at all Mr Crawford; it's no trouble at all,' said Kelly, only too keen to assist Crawford with the destruction of Bailey.

'Might it be the case,' asked Crawford, 'that there are no plots left on the western side, and that's why Mr Bailey has had no choice but to make do with reserving a plot on the eastern side?'

'Good question,' said Kelly. 'There are plenty of plots available on the western side Mr Crawford.'

Crawford addressed the congregation. 'For those of you who aren't familiar with the geographical set-up of the graveyard: the western side of the graveyard is situated under the rookery, and the eastern side, in contrast, is not situated under the rookery. If anyone is having difficulty telling west from east, then as a rough rule of thumb I suggest you use the gravestones as a guide. The ones on the west-side are covered in shit, whereas the ones on the east are not covered in shit.'

'I think we can do without the sarcasm,' said Kathy Davidson, standing up from her chair to look down her nose at Crawford.

'What a coincidence you should look down your nose at me like that Davidson,' retorted Crawford. 'I was looking down my nose at you in exactly the same way on Friday afternoon. Yep! – looked straight down it as I watched from my bedroom window. There's an excellent view of Robbie Clarkson's back door from up there – I get to see all the comings and goings.'

'Ha!' said Gillespie.

Davidson said nothing. Her face turned from pale vanilla to sunburst red. She was having a secret affair with Clarkson that wasn't as secret as she'd hitherto believed.

Happy that he'd silenced Davidson, Crawford spoke to Minister Kelly.

'Could it be Minister, that the plots on the west-side are more expensive than those on the east-side?'

'Interesting that you should ask that question Mister Crawford,' said Kelly. 'I was going to announce later on that we've discounted the price of the west-side plots by fifty percent as from Monday. The Committee of The Inner Atrium agreed at last month's meeting to the reduction as a compensation for the bird fouling. Prior to Monday however, the plots are all the same price.'

'Hang on a minute,' said Bailey, suddenly annoyed, 'you mean to tell me that The Committee of The Inner Atrium agreed last month to the price reduction, and you've left it till today to tell us?'

'That's right Mr Bailey,' said Kelly. 'Do you have a problem with that?'

'I do actually. I've paid a thousand pounds for a plot, when I could have had one for five hundred. I'm five hundred pounds out of pocket.'

'Let me remind you Bailey, that we're still awaiting payment from you. You've paid nothing, so how can you be out of pocket?'

'Well I'm changing my mind,' said Bailey firmly. 'I want a plot on the west-side.'

'You signed the Contract of Purchase Bailey; you've bought an east-side plot and you're going to pay for it,' said Kelly.

Crawford smiled.

'Scraggs should have told me when I booked the plot,' whinged Bailey. 'She must have known.'

'I've already spoken to Mrs Scraggs Bailey,' said Kelly. 'She tells me you were quite specific about your choice of plot.'

'Nonsense,' said Bailey.

The Minister called to Ernie Rushden at the back of the hall. Ernie was the duty usher. 'Ernie, is Mrs Scraggs in the building anywhere?'

'She's drinking in the vestry Minister. Would you like me to go and fetch her?'

Kelly thought for a second. 'No, no, it's alright Ernie; she'll be half-cut by now. If necessary we can get her in at the start of next week's argument – just to substantiate.'

'Very good Minister,' said Ernie, his manner reminiscent of Wodehouse's Jeeves.

'For the sake of continuity I'll quote Mrs Scraggs' exchange with Bailey verbatim,' said Kelly. 'She said, and I quote: "When I asked Mr Bailey if he had a preference for any particular plot, he got shirty and asked me if I was stupid or something. He then said what kind of person in their right frame of mind would want a headstone covered in rook manure?" unquote.'

Bailey was furious. 'You're out of order Kelly! I – I feel like I'm on trial here. This whole thing's all a load of – of –.'

'Rook-manure,' interrupted Lilly Gillespie.

A medley of laughter and mob raillery struck-up. Gillespie shouted over it.

'That's right, the same rook-manure that covers the grave of my dear father!'

Bailey turned his raw frustration on Gillespie. 'You rancid old cow Gillespie. Tommy's not your dad – you're a bastard! Uncle Cedric told me about your real dad – Danny Danger-Bollocks. There's plenty of shit on his grave alright.'

Gillespie, seated in front of Bailey, climbed onto her chair and leapt at him with astonishing athleticism. She wrapped her legs around his midriff and sank her false teeth, Tyson-style, into his left ear. Her friend Agnes Rutter had finished sobbing. 'Fancy that,' she said to the lady on her left, 'Lilly's a bastard – a nasty one at that.'

One-armed farmer Harley Chapman took advantage of the distraction and punched Harry Fowler on his nose. Kathy Davidson marched up to Ben Crawford and spat in his face. Neighbours Norman Chegwin and Alan Griffiths (both shit-free) decided it was high-time they settled a ten year dispute over a budgerigar. With fists clenched tighter than a robin's arse they set to pummelling each other's faces.

With both his trigger fingers eaten away by childhood meningitis, Danny Dangerfield (shit-free deceased) was unable to go to the war. During the years of The Great Post-War Penis Shortage, Danny sowed his wild oats wherever he found demand. It turned out the demand was as high as Danny's sperm count (his ninety-eight percent rate of first time impregnation earned him the nickname Danny Danger-Bollocks). At the height of a national cock shortage Danny did his level best to fill what gaps he could. As a result of his efforts Lilly was conceived in the June of 1949.

Minister Kelly observed the melange of violence from the pulpit; he dialled-in the third six. To prevent any of the shit-zone getting slapped about, he'd provide the police with the names of the principle shit-free trouble-makers.

The morning had turned out better than expected for Kelly: Bailey, Gillespie, and Davidson, had had their come-uppances, and Ben Crawford had put in a blinding performance (for which he would be generously rewarded in vestry beer vouchers).

Aside from that, Kelly had already put a surreptitious plan in motion, one that would go some way to ameliorating the rook problem: His cousin Adrian O'Kane lived in the next village. Adrian was a member of The Richmond Small-bore Rifle Club and owned a .22 BSA Hornet bullet rifle. The weapon was fitted with telescopic sights and a silencer; on discharge it was close to silent. Adrian rarely missed the bullseye.

Minister Kelly had already given Adrian the spare key to back door of the church tower. As the congregation argued, kicked, spat and punched, Adrian slipped in unnoticed and ascended the spiral stairway that led to the belfry. At the top there was a slotted west facing window that would provide an excellent position for sniping at the rookery. As the rooks settled in their nests, Adrian would pick them off; the bullet from his rifle passing straight through them. The birds would die in situ.

Kelly planned to inform Crawford about the arrangement over a drink in the vestry that evening. Crawford, in turn, would enlighten the activists among the shit-zone – swearing them to secrecy. At the following week's Sunday Morning Current Affairs Argument, the shit-zone would feign acceptance that things were the way they were, and would remain so.

At being let in on the secret however, they could rejoice forevermore at the superiority of their understanding – over the exquisite ignorance of the shit-free.

CHAPTER 15

LUNCHTIME PINT

Lenny Plant walked down Church Lane. Mandy Seymour watched him. And Leo Smirnov climbed out of the freezer.

Lenny was in no hurry. He'd left the Academy as the violence broke out, incurring an hour's shortfall on his attendance as he swiped his card. He wasn't too worried though, he'd sort of pre-empted the scenario and had already set aside an hour on Wednesday evening when The Royal Society for the Prevention of Cruelty to Mosquitos would be making a presentation. Wendy Taylor, President of the local branch, was due to give a talk on how a rare species of mosquito (The Red-Backed Night Sweat) had successfully been re-introduced into North Yorkshire. The species was hunted to extinction in this county almost four centuries ago. Locburn's village pond (recently registered as a Site of Special Scientific Interest) was now the site for a much publicised breeding program. By all accounts Wendy would be revealing bite-marks to her arms and legs from the creatures.

Mandy Seymour was one of Three F's top Surveillance Operatives. She'd parked her car further up Church Lane, opposite the village store. From there she got a good view of the entrance to the P.I.S.S. Academy.

Mandy was the kind of person who never stood out in a crowd, not even a small one. She was of average height, with average build, and average looks. Her hair was of average length, and when she spoke she sounded plain average English.

If you were looking for the ultimate average, then you'd need look no further than Mandy Seymour. However, if you did go looking for Mandy Seymour, and eventually found her, you would never notice how brilliantly average she was, simply because she was so bloody average in the first place. Whenever Mandy came or went, no one noticed her coming or going. Stand yourself alone in the middle of a ploughed field, and you wouldn't see Mandy approaching till she stood on your toes. When it came to covert surveillance, average was the name of the game. Mandy Seymour had it in spades.

To complement her averageness, Art Schitthelm had hired for her an average family saloon.

The moment Three F's Magnetoscope Satellite started picking up wild fluctuations in the Earth's magnetic fields, Art Schitthelm had despatched Seymour to the location of the strongest signal – Locburn Village. When she reported that Lenny Plant was in the vicinity of the latest magnetic vortex transmission, Schithelm instructed her to tag his every movement.

Leo Smirnov had had a smooth level transfer. He waited naked by the side of the Dents' freezer while Maxim Yankov level transferred his clothes and his umbrella. The house was empty. Ronnie was at The Haydale Arms watching Mervin Daley pour him a pint, Edith was at Enid Byers' house, discussing her remarkable invigoration.

Smirnov had studied the intelligence report on Plant devoutly. Vagin Semyon's observations on his subject's comings and goings, his lifestyle and habits, were meticulously recorded. They would greatly assist Smirnov in locating his target. Smirnov would head for the pub. He dressed, picked up his brolly, and climbed out of Ronnie's garage through a loose roof panel formerly used by Vagin.

As Lenny turned into the snicket that led to the pub car park, he saw two police cars and a riot van heading down Back Lane towards the Institute. Some of the villagers were in for a roughing-up. Lenny would have found the rook-shit debacle hilarious if it wasn't for the bleak mood thrown upon him by recent events. One thing for sure – before the day was out, he'd have to do something about Ronnie's freezer.

It was an unusually balmy day for March; a warm front, blown up from North Africa, felt like someone had fixed the outdoor central heating after it had broken-down the previous November. As he crossed the carpark to the pub, Lenny slung his jacket over his shoulder, loosened his tie, and undid the top button of his shirt. He quickened his pace across the car park, pystwiser on his mind.

From March to October Mervin Daley opened at eleven o'clock on Sundays. The better weather tended to bring people out, and, with the pub situated on the Coast to Coast walk, there was the increased likelihood of thirsty walkers happening by.

As Lenny entered the pub he paused for a second to allow his eyes to adjust to its cosy dimness. Although he was early the usual suspects were already present at the bar. Ronnie, Gordon Taylor and Dickhead Douglas were half-way down their respective pints.

'Hey-up Lenny lad,' said Dickhead with a smile. 'What're you having?'

'I'm a bit dry Dickhead – it'll have to be a pint of the Pystwiser.'

Dickhead went to request Lenny's pint; before he could open his mouth Mervin had the glass under the spout. 'Already on it Dickhead,' he said, winking at Lenny.

'That's what you call prompt service Len,' said Gordon. 'Larry Nugent's not that sharp behind the bar of the vestry.'

'That's because he's too busy straining to get a look up Scraggsy's skirt,' said Dickhead. Gordon shook his head and heaved a disapproving sigh. Dickhead continued. 'She does it on purpose you know; perched on the barstool in her mini-skirt, folding her legs and rolling around on her arse cheeks. Old Larry's so distracted he keeps missing the glass.'

'Trust you to notice something like that,' said Gordon, wincing. 'Scraggsy in a mini-skirt – makes you want to have your mind's eye poked out.'

'She's a right one you know – got herself thrown out of Giuseppe's Italian last Christmas.'

'How come?' asked Ronnie.

'Don't tell them Dickhead,' pleaded Mervin, familiar with the tale. Dickhead ignored him.

'She went in there with her new boyfriend, and she's already half-trolleyed. Giuseppe's got his nephew over from Italy and they're training him up to be a waiter. Anyhow, the young lad goes over to Scraggsy's table to take the order, and she plumps for a ribeye steak. When he asks her how she wants it done he has difficulty understanding that she's asking for it to be served rare. Scraggsy runs out of patience and before Giuseppe can intervene she hitches her skirt and opens her legs. "Rare as that," she says to the youngster.'

'What happened then?' asked Ronnie.

'The youngster was startled, dropped his order-pad. Giuseppe blew his onion – started swearing in Italian and threw the pair of them out. The nephew went back to Italy and got a job as a mechanic.'

'Do you have to tell us all this crap Dickhead?' asked Gordon.

'It's not crap,' retorted Dickhead. 'Ask Jordan Dalrymple if you don't believe me; he was sitting at the next table.'

'Bloody disgusting,' said Gordon.

'Come on fussy pants,' chided Dickhead, 'she's not bad for her age – I'd put a mix into her.'

'You'd stick a mix into anything,' said Gordon, 'a rolling doughnut if you could catch it.'

'Never again,' said Dickhead, 'the sugar granules get behind your foreskin.'

'Alright, alright,' said Mervin. 'Tone it down fellas.' As he handed Lenny his pint a young woman pulled up at the bar. She'd broken cover from a group of students drinking at a table in the snug. They'd been staying at a youth hostel at the top end of the village during the week and had frequented the pub most evenings.

'Excuse me bartender,' she condescended in a privileged accent. 'This straw you've given me is useless.'

Mervin was taken aback at the bartender reference. 'What's wrong with it?'

'It's obviously not working,' she said, as if it were obvious. Mervin took a dislike.

'You are using it correctly I take – one end in your drink and the other in your mouth? Perhaps you've got it the wrong way around,' said Mervin, purposely abandoning his bonhomie. He scratched his head and glanced at the shelf under the bar. 'I'm sure there're some operating instructions here somewhere.'

'It's made from paper and it's gone soggy; therefore unable to transfer fluid from the glass to my mouth,' she said, upping the sarcasm.

Mervin gave a passive shrug of his shoulders, a silent concession to the weight of young intellect clutching the flaccid straw. Suspecting he'd lose out if he took the issue further, he handed her another straw.

'A plastic straw please – if it's not too much trouble. You've been giving me paper straws all week and every one of them has gone soggy.'

'We don't have plastic straws,' said Mervin.

'What kind of a place is this?'

Lenny listened-in. He could see Mervin was pissed-off and struggling to be civil to a customer. Lenny was annoyed too: a young woman, supposedly well educated, her life in front of her, and she's moaning about a bloody straw. If only she could have look inside his head and witness what real agonising worry and responsibility was like. He'd had enough of awkward people for one morning so he decided to intervene.

'Listen love,' he said, turning and stooping to get his face intimidatingly close to hers. 'Straws are for toddlers and quadriplegics – and plastic straws are bad for the eco-system.'

The student stood her ground and responded out of a stroppy mouth. 'Rubbish.'

Uppity little cow thought Lenny. He put on his best mock Yorkshire accent.

'Tha's right Luvvie – rubbish. You see a lot of these 'ere plastic straws end-oop as rubbish in t' sea where t' whale lives. T' poor old whale comes swimming along, scooping oop t' plankton wi' his big gob and t' straw gets stuck in his fookin' tonsils and t' poor booger chokes to death tha' knows. Next thing is luvvie, t' whale's lying t' wrong way oop on t' beach at Scarborough, and t' kids are poking at it and there's bloody flies and a reet stink all over t'shop.' Lenny continued, 'So, luvvie, t' best thing is ta' place tha' gob round t' rim of t' glass, form t' hermetic seal and reduce t' atmospheric pressure in tha' silly gob, and sook at t' contents.'

Lenny raised his glass between his face and hers. 'Ere luvvie, watch this.' He drained his pint in one go, burped up her nostrils, and thudded his glass on the bar. 'Not a bloody drop spilt tha' knows.'

The student looked at Lenny bewildered, spun on her heel, and made off, straw-less. Lenny called after her. 'Tak' hod an sup lass.'

Lenny was in a bad frame of mind. Ronnie and Dickhead sniggered into their pints.

'Nice one Lenny lad,' said Mervin.

'The youth of today,' said Gordon wisely. 'What chance have we got?'

Mervin nodded in agreement. 'Don't these students watch the news or read the papers? Plastic's getting a pile of bad publicity lately. I've had to pay extra for wooden chopsticks for Thursday's Chinese night – you and Sarah are coming aren't you Len?'

'Looking forward to it Merv,' said Lenny. Trying to sound like he was looking forward – not only to the Chinese night, but everything else the future had coming to him.

'You alright Lenny?' asked Mervin, detecting an uncharacteristic distance in his friend's voice.

'Yeah,' said Lenny unconvincingly. He feigned the source of his concerns. 'Bit of a scrum-down at the piss club this morning – Kelly had to call the Three F cops in.'

'Not that crow-shit business?' moaned Gordon.

'Actually it's rooks' business?' corrected Ronnie; his most recent mental traumas gone for a stroll in a fog of German cider. 'You know – the business that comes out of a rook's arse.' The old soak giggled like a schoolkid.

'Fuck's sake,' groaned Dickhead.

Mervin reached into a box on the shelf and handed Lenny a pair of the chopsticks along with a bowl of peanuts. 'Here, get some practise in.' He reached for Lenny's glass. 'Fancy another one?'

'Might as well,' said Lenny, taking the chopsticks.

'My round,' said Gordon, 'four pints of Pystwiser Merv – and one for your good self.'

Mervin pulled the pints, lined them up on the bar, and put a straw in Lenny's glass.

Mandy Seymour walked into the pub unnoticed. Avoiding the bar she took a seat in the far corner by a sash window partly opened. From her bag she removed a slim glass and a small bottle of plain tonic water. Mandy unscrewed the bottle top and poured its contents into the glass. Her movement was slow and smooth – she made no sound. Reaching back into her bag she withdrew a straw from its lining. The straw was made from neither plastic nor paper, but from carbon fibre. Mandy handled the straw with care as she inserted it into her drink – she knew how much it cost Three F to manufacture such a straw. At two-hundred millimetres long and with a bore of four-point-five millimetres, the dual-purpose straw could be used for both sucking and blowing through. In the wrist cuff of her jacket Mandy carried five darts, their points coated with a blend of curare and novochoksi 3.

Mandy was a non-smoker, born with an unusual birth defect. With three healthy lungs she could blow such a dart up to sixty feet with pin-point accuracy. Once the dart penetrates the skin, death promptly follows with a minimum of fuss.

The bar was filling steadily. By the time Leo Smirnov walked in it was close to packed. Customers were queuing three-deep to order drinks and food, and the air was thick with the hum of a dozen conversations. Lenny and his cohorts had retreated to the far side of the bar where they drank cider and gossiped. Lenny was having limited success plucking peanuts from the bowl but persevered anyway.

Smirnov had been practising certain phrases in polished English: "Oh I'm awfully sorry sir – are you alright?" "Here, let me buy you a drink." "I must have tripped on the carpet or something." "A pint of bitter please," These would be the words he'd use to placate Lenny after he'd faked a stumble and prodded the tip of his brolly into his victim's leg. The toxin injected into Lenny's leg would take a day or two to kill him.

Smirnov joined the crowd at the bar and started to shuffle his way towards Lenny. His target was ideally situated: standing, distracted in conversation, with his back to his assailant. Leo blended-in well; dressed in a pair of smart corduroys and a white shirt, he wore a tweed jacket and stood in a pair of Savile Row brogues. His tatty old umbrella served to complement his Englishness. Smirnov took a step closer to his victim, raising his umbrella slightly and angling its tip towards Lenny's calf.

Mandy Seymour was expecting Smirnov; she recognised him the instant he came in through the door. She knew exactly what he intended to do and how he was going to do it.

Back in Moscow Maxim Yankov had on his team a Three F sleeper. Dmitri Yeltsin was a Latvian bio-physicist who'd become disenchanted with the Sputum regime many years earlier. Three F's Foreign Intelligence Network had infiltrated The Russian Institute for Scientific Excellence shortly after it was formed back in the eighties. Their mission was to subtly probe for any of its staff that might have leanings towards Three F's controversial, but ever burgeoning doctrine of social engineering. Dmitri Yeltsin risked his life to provide Three F with vital intelligence on key persons and activities within the Institute.

Dmitri had already uncovered a critical development in Russia's time travel program: the recent discovery that an obsolete seventies chest freezer contained the technology essential to flood Western Europe and North America with teams of spies, activists, and assassins. Maxim Yankov and his team were already building a new cage that would send Transfer Pods to strategic locations on the planet. The pods, capable of accommodating several humans along with any necessary equipment (a Victorian mangle for instance), would be manufactured using technology plagiarised from Ronnie's freezer. They would be sent back in time to significant moments in history.

With Operation Deep Freeze Vladimir Sputum planned to create a Russian Empire fit to rule the planet. This would be achieved through changing the past. Already the Kremlin had targeted certain prominent people and events in history: Admiral Nelson, Emmeline Pankhurst, and Shakespeare, would be assassinated in their infancy. A hybrid species of long-toothed woodworm would chew its way through The Golden Hind – and Henry VIII was destined have his tackle wound through a Victorian mangle by a French prostitute on the eve of his first stag night.

The whole of existence had room enough for one ultimate being – and that would be Sputum. To this end all Gods would be un-invented. As for Jesus Christ, he would be denied crucifixion and forced to die of old age.

As Smirnov stepped within striking distance, Seymour withdrew the straw from her drink and loaded a dart into its breech. She held the straw in her mouth and placed its tip just above the surface of the tonic water. Her eyes were locked on Smirnov; one more step towards Plant and she would blow the dart into his neck. Schitthelm needed Lenny Plant alive, and Seymour was there to protect him. In this context the straw was both a life taker and a life saver.

Smirnov tightened his grip on the brolly. He went to make his stumble and died. He died so instantly he was still standing at the moment of his death. He fell to the floor – not forwards, or sideways, or backwards. Offering no resistance to gravity he fell as vertically as Newton's apple.

Seymour's dart was still in the straw; she was puzzled but remained calm. The Three F surveillance operative saw that Smirnov was not breathing and knew he was dead. She noticed that there were no visible injuries, and, as far as she could see, no-one had made physical contact with him. Seymour would have put his cause of death down to natural causes – perhaps a heart attack or stroke, if it weren't for the fact that he looked alert and healthy the moment before he collapsed. One thing she was certain of: with Lenny Plant standing just a few feet away, Smirnov's death had to have something to do with him.

The instant before his death Smirnov was indeed alert and healthy. Even though he was on the cusp of performing an assassination, his blood pressure was normal and his heart rate below sixty. His death was as bizarre as it was instantaneous.

As the bullet entered his left earhole, Smirnov was the epitome of health and vitality. By the time it perforated his left eardrum,

Smirnov became deaf in that ear. In the following nanosecond the projectile had smashed its way through the middle-ear ossicles before continuing its onward journey through Smirnoff's lower brain. Whilst speeding through his brain the bullet destroyed the lower median axial gland. This component of the brain controls heart function, and it was at this point that Smirnov became clinically dead. The bullet exited his head through the right earhole and Smirnov dropped like a stone. The entry and exit wounds were so perfect they were undetectable to the eye – in one ear and out the other. As Smirnov's heart had stopped in an instant, no blood came out of him.

Half a second earlier the bullet had had embarked on a remarkable journey. On leaving the muzzle of Adrian O'Kane's rifle, it headed for its intended target: a hen rook sitting on her eggs. The bullet hit the bird in the upper back, bounced off its sternum, and exited through its anus. The round then skimmed the top of a gravestone which sent it off on a south easterly trajectory towards The Haydale Arms. In through the part-opened sash window it came, hissing through the air towards Smirnov's skull. On leaving his right earhole the bullet flew under Mervin's nose and buried itself in an upright oak timber at the corner of the bar. Mervin heard the faint thud of the bullet hitting the woodwork, but put the source of the sound down to a cupboard door closing in the kitchen.

As Adrian O'Kane squeezed-off the round he had no way of knowing he'd issued a Russian hit-man with a one way ticket to Hell. Oblivious, he carried on shooting at the rooks. The bullet would remain buried in the oak timber until the pub catches fire in 2098. If the projectile were subject to forensic scrutiny, the results would reveal traces of avian excrement, earwax, and the brains of a Russian.

As Smirnov hit the floor there was a moment's silence. Everyone in the bar turned to look at the lifeless stranger. 'Somebody, call an ambulance!' shouted a woman as she crouched down by his side.

'I'm on it,' responded Mandy Seymour, making a show of getting out her mobile and dialling. She called for Three F's own ambulance service, then rang Art Schitthelm immediately afterwards. Her phone was a standard issue side-valve modular analogue, fitted with a transmission scrambler that back-fed through a nibbler filter. Communications made to or from it could not be intercepted on any network scanner.

§

Art Schitthelm had arrived in Manchester an hour earlier. He sat in a swivel chair while a make-up artist fussed over his face. He looked in the mirror – but not at himself. He'd long since tired of his own reflection. Art watched his son pacing up and down behind him. Horace was anxious, and for two good reasons: firstly, his father was due to appear as the main guest on The Dimblewit Debate, a monthly current affairs program hosted by a millionaire called Derek Dimblewit – secondly: there had been no word from Seymour for over an hour.

Art's side-valve mobile rang. He waved the make-up girl out to the corridor before answering.

'Seymour – any news?'

'Yes boss, it's the Russian.'

'Se one Dmitri warned us about?'

'Yes, he came into the pub carrying an Odessa Mark Two Umbrella. Dmitri was right, he was looking for Plant.'

'And did he find Plant?'

'He homed-in on him straight away; the bar was crowded but the Russian identified him immediately.'

'What happened?' asked Art, sitting up in his chair. Horace had stopped his pacing.

'He's killed him boss.'

Art was momentarily stunned. 'Killed him – how?'

'Hard to say boss; one second he's standing at the bar, the next he's dropped to the floor.'

Art was both saddened and annoyed. 'I can't believe it,' he said solemnly.

'We needed him alive – he had vital information.'

Seymour was puzzled. 'But boss, you gave me firm instructions to take him out if he attempted the hit.'

Art became slightly more puzzled than Seymour. 'I didn't mean him, I meant se other one. Please don't tell me you've blown a dart at se wrong person.'

'I haven't blown a dart at anyone boss, I never got the chance. Someone got in before me and killed him.'

Art was getting impatient. 'Who got in before whom Seymour – talk some sense to me?'

'I think it was Plant,' said Seymour.

'What se blinking fuck are you going on about woman? Are you trying to tell me Plant has killed himself before anyone else could get in before him to do it?'

'Plant's alive boss.'

'He's alive!' exclaimed Art with some degree of jubilation. 'Brilliant.'

He stalled for a second to gather his thoughts. 'So who is dead?'

'Se Russian – I mean the Russian. He was going to move on Plant, I had the straw in my mouth ready to dart him but he collapsed and died on the spot.'

'You're sure he's dead Seymour?'

'No doubt about it boss; he's not breathing, he's staring at the ceiling, and the colour has left his face.'

'Hmm – so you think Plant did it?'

'It couldn't be anyone else – Plant was the closest person to him when he collapsed.'

'And what was Plant doing se moment before se Russian fell?'

'He was fiddling with a pair of chopsticks.'

'Chopsticks you say?'

'Yes boss; he was trying to pluck peanuts from a bowl on the bar.'

'Most intriguing,' said Art.

'So what's the score Boss?'

'You're asking me what se score is Seymour – I'd say it's two-nil to Lenny Plant.'

'One-nil don't you mean?'

'Two-nil for sure Seymour – we've just had some fresh intelligence from Dmitri. Se Russians have changed se operational status of Vagin Semyon. They've placed him on their M.P.D. register.'

'Missing presumed dead?'

'That's right – according to Dmitri, Semyon's disappeared and his cranial transponder has ceased transmitting. Plant's done him, no doubt about it.'

'So what's our next move boss?'

Art snapped into focus. 'I take it you've called our ambulance service before you rang me?'

'Yes boss, they're en route.'

'Well done Seymour, you've followed procedure. Are you able to get to se umbrella and secret it away? We don't want se local cops getting their hands on it.'

'I'll sort it boss.'

'Good girl – once we get him into se ambulance se paramedics can remove his transponder and disable it. We'll take him straight to se pathologist's lab. I can't wait to find out what Plant's done to him.'

'I better go boss, the ambulance will be here anytime and I need to secure the umbrella while everyone's still distracted with the commotion.'

'Okay Seymour. E-mail your report to my phone immediately then continue to keep track of Plant's movements. Update me immediately if there are any other developments.'

Art put the phone down and turned to Horace. 'Plant has struck again Horace – he's sorted two Russians in as many days.'

'When you say sorted, you mean he's killed them father?' asked Horace.

'That's right Horace; he's killed them – dead no less.'

'How?'

'We don't know yet; Plant is such an enigmatic killer – he's also spontaneous. There's no sign of se first one, se Russians can't locate him. I'd guess Plant's removed se transponder from his head se instant he killed him.'

'And the second one?'

'Killed in a crowded bar; Plant must have taken him out se instant he made his move. Se Russian had a poison tipped umbrella and Plant had nothing but a pair of chopsticks.'

'Most intriguing,' said Horace.

'That's what I said,' said Art annoyed.

'Pardon,' said Horace.

Art banged his fist on the table. 'I said "that's what I said,"' said Art.

'Eh?'

'When Seymour told me Plant had some chopsticks, I said "most intriguing," and when I told you Plant had some chopsticks you said "most intriguing," I said "most intriguing" first and you went and copied me! Why don't you think of your own things to say instead of copying me all se time?'

'Sorry Father, I didn't realise – it was a bit thoughtless of me.'

Art gave a sympathising sigh. 'It's alright son, I understand – it was a bit thoughtless of you.'

'I said that,' said Horace.

'Said what,' said Art.

'I said "it was a bit thoughtless of me" and you said the same thing. Now it's you who's copying me.'

'No Horace; you said "it was a bit thoughtless of me," and I said "it was a bit thoughtless of you," entirely different.'

'You're always in the right aren't you? You never admit it when you're in the wrong,' said Horace scolding his father.

'That's right Horace – I am always in se right. I never admit it when I'm in se wrong. So why don't you go away and piss-off somewhere else and leave me alone. I need to brief se ambulance crew.'

CHAPTER 16

THE AFTERMATH

Lenny Plant left the pub once the paramedics had taken the man in the Savile Row brogues away in an ambulance. They'd got to the scene in less than ten minutes and took over from Gordon Taylor who was giving resuscitation. Before putting several drips into the Russian they ripped his shirt open and placed the defibrillator pads on his chest. 'Shocking – stand clear!' shouted the lead paramedic as he squeezed-off the pads. The patient convulsed and the assistant paramedic took his pulse.

'We've got him back!' she said triumphantly.

The pub erupted with a roar of jubilation, accompanied by an energetic round of applause. Many of the patrons went to the bar for extra drinks to celebrate the saving of a life. Amid the commotion no one noticed Mandy Seymour stoop and take the brolly.

The paramedics had in fact, put a current of ninety-thousand volts through the Russian's chest; enough rampant electricity to stop the heart of a Blue Whale.

Art Schitthelm had contacted the ambulance crew as they were on their way to the Haydale. Although Seymour was confident the Russian was dead, Art instructed the paramedics to make doubly sure. He couldn't take the risk of the assassin regaining consciousness and having another go at Plant. As best they could, Three F had to do their utmost to keep Lenny Plant alive.

Once they'd loaded Smirnov into the ambulance the paramedics set about removing the transponder from his skull. Once removed, the data on its tracking function was downloaded and the transponder duly destroyed.

Back at the P.I.S.S. Academy the Three F police had confiscated Lily Gillespie's false teeth. A sergeant, sporting a tilted grin, crunched them into the ground using a classic ankle-twist boot-screw motion. Gillespie looked on with caved-in cheeks and a mouse-hole gape. They issued her with a prohibition notice banning her from wearing dentures for six months. She also received an on-the-spot fine of a thousand pounds. Kathy Davidson was fined a thousand pounds for spitting at Crawford, plus an extra thousand pounds for having an affair with a married man. In addition she was given a five-hundred pound fine for being careless enough to have been found out.

Crawford was fined five pounds for snitching on her in a public place, (Minister Kelly secretly gave Crawford the fiver to cover the fine).

All fines issued for misdemeanours committed at P.I.S.S. Academies went towards the upkeep of the vestry bar.

One-armed farmer Harley Chapman was ordered to wear a mitten for a week. He also had five acres of land taken from him by Three F under a Compulsory Confiscation Notice.Budgie brawlers Chegwin and Griffiths were ordered to get into training for a ten-round boxing match, scheduled to take place at the Academy four weeks hence. Tickets for the bout would go on sale at twelve pounds each (twenty for a ring-side seat). The loser would buy the victor a budgie of his choosing.

CHAPTER 17

ROAST PORK

'What exactly happened?' asked Sarah as she sawed her knife through a stout slice of gristle and roast pork.

Lenny took a sip at his Cotes du Rhone. 'Had to be a massive heart attack – one second he's standing behind me, next he's dropped to the floor like a sack of spuds.'

The drama at the pub had distracted Lenny from his worries sufficient to evade his wife's scrutiny of his emotions.

'That poor man – was he by himself?'

'Mervin saw him come in on his own; said he looked fit and well.'

'It just shows you,' said Sarah, now wrestling the pork around with a vigour that forced near a dozen garden peas to the outer extremities of the plate. 'You never know when your number's up.'

She paused to watch Lenny take another sip of wine. 'Surprised you haven't had a thumper yet, the amount you drink.'

'The Syrah and Grenache components have a beneficial effect on arterial health,' said Lenny, with gravity sufficient to subdue any further observations on his drinking. 'It's also a stress reliever. If you want a stressed-out, ill-tempered husband then I'll stop drinking. Anyhow, I reckon if he wasn't in a crowded pub he mightn't have been so lucky.'

'So he collapsed, what happened then?' asked Sarah.

'Denise Crossley took one look at him and shouted for an ambulance. Gordon downed his pint started giving him resuscitation – Dickhead was chanting 'Staying Alive' by the Bee Gees to keep Gordon in rhythm with the chest compressions.'

'That's so brave of him,' remarked Sarah, finally amputating a bite-sized chunk of pork.

'Not really,' said Lenny. 'Mervin had to tell him to shut up – sounded more like a pissed Barry White than a sober Barry Gibb.'

'No, I meant how brave of Gordon to give CPR. How come Denise Crossley didn't do it? She's supposed to be a nurse.' Sarah had her fork poised in front of her mouth. In addition to the pork, she'd mounted half a roast spud and a gravy-coated carrot baton on its prongs.

'She couldn't do it,' said Lenny, 'had her hand in a bandage.'

'What's happened to her hand?'

'She had it in the till of the hospital's charity shop.'

'I'm not with you,' said Sarah, looking confused and lowering the clutched fork, still loaded with food, to the side of the plate.

Sarah was in the habit of doing that whenever she was engaged in conversation whilst eating. It annoyed Lenny because he'd convinced himself that she'd subconsciously picked-up the practice through watching soap operas:

Whenever there was a scene shot in the local café, or a cramped and tastelessly furnished kitchen/dining room, the actors would sit down to a Full English, or else a meal of some significance, as it's been prepared by a silly, talentless, whingeing cockney tart, "wiv awl the twimmings," in the name of a worthless pre-watershed shag they'd had between the Brentford Nylons the night before.

The food is laid at the table, and in comes a bald-headed short-arse, grunting, groaning, and strutting like he's hard as fuck and twice as handsome. Once the stupid cow has had a good snog of his stubbly fat face, they take their seats by the table and set to with the vacuous, recycled dialogue.

The scenario implies hunger is at hand – it has to be. They've been up all night, greasing-up the bedsheets with body fluids; and have likely pledged, after a breakfast of oral sex, that they're going to save themselves for tonight's meal.

As they chat and grunt a big deal is made of carving up various bits of food. Every now and then the fork is offered-up to their faces, only to be returned to the table, denied by a gob already full of empty utterances. The viewer looks-on indifferent, both to the frustration of hunger gone in want, and the better life that lies beyond their inane preoccupation.

'I was talking to Vince. He told me not to say anything about what's happened.'

'So now you're going to blurt it all out to me?'

'You're my wife. I can tell you – it doesn't count.' Lenny put the glass to his head, emptied it, and refilled.

'Tell me then.'

'Are you going to put that fucking food in your mouth or what?'

Sarah raised the fork to within an inch of her lips.

'Thought the wine was supposed to be a stress reliever?'

'Why do you do that Sarah – is it because that's how they do it on Children's TV for Adults?'

'Do what?'

'Mess around with your food. What's wrong with putting it straight into your mouth once you've got it onto the fork?'

'Because I don't want to gulp it down like you do; it's not good to rush your food.' Sarah was keen to usher Lenny on with the main topic. 'Are you going to tell me what happened to Denise Crossley?'

'Put the food in your mouth and I'll consider it.'

She pulled a face and bit the food from the fork. Lenny had an image of Ronnie's freezer barge its way into his head and he didn't like it. Sarah noted the distraction in his face and feared he might deviate. She pushed her foot into his crotch and jiggled it playfully. 'Come on Plantey – tell me about Denise Crossley.'

'Okay, but not a word to anyone.'

'Cross my heart.'

'Whenever she worked the afternoon shift on the ward she would go in early and cover the lunch-break in the charity shop. She'd volunteered off her own back – only for half-an-hour or so, but everyone thought it was really sweet of her.

'Anyhow, after a month or so the shop manager notices the takings are down on certain days. The hospital installs a covert camera above the till and the rest is history. Vince said she'd been going on spending sprees lately – coming back with handbags and shoes she doesn't really need, because, like you, she has a wardrobe brimming.'

'Fancy,' said Sarah, intrigued. 'I never thought Denise would do something like that.'

'She's going through the change,' said Lenny, his ignorance fortified with alcohol. 'Women of a certain age do that sometimes – usually end up shoplifting. They caught Julie Ryder coming out of Boots with ten quid's worth of corn plasters – and that was just two days after she'd turned fifty.'

'What a knob you are Plant.'

Lenny took a sip of red and shrugged his shoulders. He was drunkenly content with his theory on the relationship between behavioural transition in middle-aged women, gender-specific psycho-hormonal degradation, and shoplifting.'

'So what's the connection with her bandaged hand?'

'She went for a disciplinary – gross misconduct. Normally in the NHS that's an automatic dismissal, but things have changed.'

'You're losing me here Lenny,' said Sarah, puzzled.

'Eat some more food and pay attention.'

Sarah speared a whole roast spud and thrust it into her mouth. Chewing with comical exaggeration she leaned across the table and stared, wide-eyed, at Lenny. His wife's mockery amused him.

'All HR functions within the NHS have been contracted-out under a PFI, since January.'

'What's a PFI?'

'A Private Finance Initiative – if any government department feels they can save money, or get a better service by creating a public-private partnership, they tender-out the work, or project, to private companies. That's what they've done with their HR.'

'Who's got the contract?' asked Sarah.

'Three F – they've already got a Front Line Support Service contract with the police, the fire brigade, and the ambulance service. The NHS needed a more robust Human Resources infrastructure, to deal with recruitment, promotions, disciplinary issues and the like – so they got an independent external body to take it on, you know, impartiality and all the rest of it.'`

'You're telling me Three F dealt with Denise?'

'Yep – Vince said they got her in front of a disciplinary board – two women and some bloke they'd fetched up from London. She tried denying it at first. Vince had given her some pre-interview coaching – told her to make out she wasn't very good at mental arithmetic. Anyhow, they let her crap-on for a while, knowing she wasn't aware they'd caught it all on camera. When it was obvious she wasn't going to come clean they showed her what they'd filmed.'

'She should have just owned-up; that's what I'd have done.'

'Yeah, like the time you owned-up to reversing your car into Alan Pearce's Mondeo – once you realised there was no one about, it was a case of first gear and fuck off.'

Sarah was embarrassed. 'That was different.'

'How?'

'Pearce is an arsehole.'

'True enough,' agreed Lenny. 'In their summing-up they told Denise that if she had confessed, they'd be looking at something a lot less punitive.'

'I'm starting not to like the sound of this Len,' Sarah took a hasty slurp of Gavi. 'Tell me what happened next.'

'They gave her a choice: she could either take instant dismissal, with all the shame that went with it; or she could take a punishment fit for the crime, keep her job, and nothing more would be said of the matter.'

'You're going to tell me she took the punishment?'

'Had no choice; she couldn't afford to lose her job. Vince has just re-mortgaged the house to pay for the "brag-factor" holiday in the Maldives. And she's signed-up a PCP on a "brag-factor" two-seater Merc. Then there's Jodie – she's off to Hull "brag-factor" University.'

'Thought she was "non-brag-factor" pregnant?'

'You can still go if you're pregnant – so long as you're female.'

'Don't be stupid,' said Sarah.

'Do you want me to finish the story or what?' said Lenny, becoming impatient with the meandering conversation.

'Take a stress-relieving drink of wine and carry on darling.'

Lenny went on.

'The bloke from London, along with the larger of the two women, led Denise into the charity shop. They locked the door and shut the blinds. Denise told Vince it all happened so quickly.'

'You're going to tell me something awful?' said Sarah, bracing herself.

'The woman got hold of Denise's hand.'

'Her hand?'

'Yeah, the one she'd had in the till.'

'And?'

'She put it back in the till,' said Lenny.

'Then what?'

'The man from Three F slammed it shut.'

'My God,' said Sarah, shocked.

'With his foot.'

'That's terrible – poor Denise.'

'She's broken three of her fingers – well, to be fair, Three F have. But at least she got to keep her job. They told her if she revealed anything to anyone they would have her back in front of the Board. Once she'd calmed down they opened the shop back up and sent Denise on her way to A&E. She had a four hour wait before they could treat her. Immediately they had her fingers reset and her hand bandaged, she was instructed to finish her shift?'

'And what about him?' said Sarah.

'Who?'

'The man in the pub.'

'Ah, we're finally back to him are we?'

'I saw the ambulance go flying past. Good job Edith wasn't coming the other way on her bike,' said Sarah.

'The paramedics showed up and took over from Gordon. They put the defibrillator on him – one click and he's fired up again. You should have been there Sarah. The whole pub roared when the paramedic said they'd got him back – a magical moment, no doubt about it.'

Sarah sighed with relief. 'A life saved – how wonderful. Do you think he's going to be okay?'

'For sure,' said Lenny confidently, 'he's in good hands.'

The Three F Mobile Pathological Laboratory was parked up in a disused lorry park five miles south of Darlington. Leo Smirnov was lying inside it.

Leo was missing the top half of his skull. It lay beside him on a stainless steel tray.Fifteen minutes earlier the ambulance had rendezvoused and transferred his still warm body into the back of the mobile lab. Leo's transponder was salvaged, down-loaded, and destroyed. Inside of another fifteen minutes the lab would move on – that was procedure. Three F knew that once a transponder had been destroyed, the Russians would show-up in an hour or so at the site of the last transmission.

CHAPTER 18

THE DIMBLEWIT DEBATE SUITE

(PART 1 DEREK DIMBLEWIT)

Lenny Plant finished loading the dishwasher and took himself through to the living room. Bloated with Sunday roast, red wine, and pystwiser, he sank into the comfort of his sofa. Sarah was in the hallway, gossiping on the phone to a friend from work.

Lenny slid his hand in through the fold in the sofa where the arm rest met the seat cushion. He rummaged for the TV remote because, most always, if not discarded on any convenient surface, that's where it resided, somewhere in the bowels of the sofa. After inserting his arm to elbow depth Lenny came across it. He switched on the TV and settled himself for The Dimblewit Debate.

The Dimblewit Debate, a topical debate show with a difference (a nasty one), went out the last Sunday of every month. Hosted by Derek Dimblewit the show regularly pulled a national audience of over twenty million and, aside from a couple of soaps, was the most talked about show in the country.

After surreptitiously starting out as a benign chat show-come current affairs program; typically featuring a mixture of vacuous B-list celebs, sacked cabinet ministers, and stunt community leaders – the show purposely devolved into an orgy of humiliating interrogation; it's staple: a controversial main guest, baited in a fashion fit to appeal to the ignorance of the viewing public.

The studio was arranged so that the main guest sat centre stage in a spotlighted chair. In front of them, uncomfortably close, a crescent shaped desk and a panel of guests headed by Dimblewit. The audience sat either side of the desk; their seats arranged in ascending pincer-like rows so that the main guest was flanked left and right. To accommodate the broader audience there was a hashtag facility for the opinionated arm-chair public.

The set was pretentiously unpretentious as to its function; even when empty it bristled with the menace of an execution chamber – the main guest seating accommodation being somewhat less alluring than the high-voltage variant.

Most of the main guests invited to appear on the show would waste no time in declining the offer, knowing they had little chance of surviving the humiliation, and resultant annihilation that awaited them. The audience were pre-selected members of the public, the majority of whom swelled the ranks of bullies, trouble-makers, and 'dull normal' retired civil servants, obsessed with their inconsequential points of view and goaded by a feverish compulsion to mouth them off on prime time TV. Their questions could be directed straight at the main guest, or else by proxy to one of the panel members, who in turn would do their utmost to amplify the ante.

The line-up of panel guests would change with each show, although their calling was much the same: politicians, senior members of the church, high profile business leaders and nasty professors. All had one thing in common: a hunger for the ruination of the main guest.

Tagging the show as a debate was obtusely wide of the mark. Its sole purpose was to intimidate, expose, humiliate and destroy. The sociopathic Dimblewit revelled in it all.

The main guest could be anyone, so long as they were prominent in the public eye and had a stock of penetrable notoriety – perceived, imagined, or otherwise. To even contemplate the invitation they'd need to be foolhardy, blindly narcissistic, or else supremely confident. The ones that proffered optimum entertainment were those endowed with a psychological constitution crippled with some or other neurosis – a functioning mental illness – like an American president. Typical among requisite traits were an inordinate blend of arrogance and ignorance – along with a corrupt sense of personal value.

§

Dimblewit's rise to TV fame was unexpected. After leaving university with a soggy degree in English literature, along with no sense of career direction; he landed a job with a local newspaper that paid him three-hundred pounds a week to provide the dialogue for a daily comedy cartoon strip featuring a horse-racing commentator with a stutter.

Whilst working for the newspaper Dimblewit witnessed an armed robbery. Three masked Hungarians, wielding sawn-off air-rifles, raided a supermarket in West Drayton and made off with a hundred-and-ninety pounds' worth of tinned dog food. One of the robbers had been in the supermarket the previous week buying cheap cider. He noticed any amount of tins marked "Ruffmeat" arranged in a promotional stack next to the deli counter. "Ruffmeat" is a slang word for caviar in certain parts of Hungary. The robbers estimated their haul of around two-hundred tins to have a black market value upwards of twenty-thousand pounds. Dimblewit had been in the supermarket at the time, swapping price tags on aftershave products.

A local TV reporter showed up looking for eyewitnesses to interview. Dimblewit presented himself and fizzed with excitement as he gave an exaggerated but riveting account of the action.

That evening the head of a TV production company happened to be watching the news and caught the report of the robbery. He was instantly impressed with how Dimblewit behaved in front of a camera; the young man had a beguiling confidence about him, an infectious enthusiasm that radiated out of the screen.

The producer and his team were putting together a weekly show that would follow the romantic escapades of people at work. 'Heart-Throbs in the Workplace' would be crafted to provide pre-watershed titillation for grown-up teenagers, frustrated bingo grannies, and amateur wankers of any sex. The show would cast Dimblewit as a cocky tyre fitter, doing his pretend level best at preventing a blond divorcee receptionist from getting into his overalls. The show was a moderate success; however it got Dimblewit the exposure he craved.

In 1998, after spending ten years as the country's most popular celebrity tyre fitter, Dimblewit was given the opportunity to replace Gerry Flaxman, who hosted the Flaxman Show. At the time Flaxman was being investigated for his involvement in paying large sums of money to influential guests in return for them giving scripted answers to politically sensitive questions. The show had healthy viewing figures and Flaxman had long been suspected of conspiring to use it as an instrument for swaying public attitudes on key national and global issues.

Flaxman was having difficulty explaining how he had come to own a multi-million pound property portfolio that turned out to have been purchased using dirty foreign currencies filtered through offshore company accounts. It came to light he was being bankrolled by a consortium of wealthy businessmen with extreme right-wing leanings.

At the time of the scandal Three F was already conducting its own investigation into the persons involved. These days Sir Gerry Flaxman gets about in a wheel chair, its steering controls operated by his tongue. All fourteen of the wealthy businessmen have been on a missing persons register for the better part of twelve years.

The BBC agreed to sign Dimblewit for a trial run of six shows to see how it went with audience numbers – because, at the end of the day, that was the pant-creamer for the Executive. Art Schitthelm hated them for it. He was relentlessly punctual in reminding the corporation as to its shallowness: "Fuck se content, look at se tune-in."

Following the Flaxman controversy the Beeb was left at a loose end with the monthly afternoon prime slot. It was desperate to win back its audience and needed a prompt reaction to maintain continuity with a winning theme. In the end it was decided to soften things up a little. A production team was put together and tasked to create a new show, with a new format, and a new anchorman.

The team worked day and night – within a month the new show was oven-ready.

Dimblewit was briefed to use his fake charm to get the audience on-board; keep things cosy show-biz crap-chat for a while. The BBC had to tread carefully; they were aware The Television Regulatory Commission was now extra vigilant after coming under criticism for the way they handled the Flaxman fall-out.

Dimblewit performed well. Over the first six months he pushed the viewing rates past the ten million mark and the show was earning rave reviews.

In the sixties and seventies the programme could have held its own without any content tweaking. Back then the audiences were more docile and less distracted: just three channels to choose from – and no remote control to flick through a legion of shows, films and documentaries. Once settled in the armchair your average punter would have to haul their arse back out of it to press a button, twist a dial, or bash a fist, to see what was happening on either of the other channels. Mobile phones and I-Pads were unheard of – so no hand held media device to divert the attention, or less occupy an idle finger. In those days a black and white screen drew the gawping stare. A nose-full of crusty snot, for many, entertained a restless digit.

The Twenty-First Century audience was a different creature – its attention span had shrunk. As quickly as it tired, it hungered.

The Beeb were aware of this from the start. Their strategy was to allow the show to morph, episode by episode, into the lust-quenching cringe-fest the viewers craved. Give the public what they want, only don't give it to them – ram it down their insatiable, low-rent throats: controversy, scandal, shame and depravity by the bucket-load. And if something didn't fit – make it fit.

The show had been televised from different venues around the World. This month it would be coming from the Media City Studios in Manchester:

'Good afternoon and welcome to The Dimblewit Debate, with me Derek Dimblewit. This month we're coming to you live from the vibrant city of Manchester – home to the world's most famous football team, and the country's highest average rainfall. As usual we have a studio audience made up members of the public along with a panel of four guests.'

Dimblewit spoke through immaculate white veneered teeth that shone out of a show-biz tan. His smile carried all the compassion and sincerity of a grinning croc. Today the grin was as wide as it had ever been: Art Schitthelm had been lured onto the show – which meant the viewing figures were sure to be the best yet, and that Dimblewit was destined to reach a career high-point.

The only problem with this particular career high-point was the steepness of the slope that led, both to it, and from it. So deliriously self-absorbed was the show host, he failed to consider that things might one day back-fire. As Dimblewit had Schitthelm in his proverbial gunsights – so Schitthelm had Dimblewit in his non-proverbial gunsights.

Over the months Schitthelm had received several invites to appear on the show; all of them sent by Dimblewit himself. Schitthelm turned him down with a purposely annoying politeness every time. The Head of Three F did not reply to the invites personally. He had his private secretary send a telegram offering profuse thanks for the invitation along with a watery excuse for his inability to attend – excuses like taking his seventy-year-old grandson to Santa's Grotto, a hospital appointment to check his sperm count, and celebrity ribbon-cutting at the grand opening of a wasp sanctuary.

Dimblewit disliked Schitthelm – Schitthelm disliked Dimblewit even more.

§

'Our main guest this month is Art Schitthelm, controversial head of Three F, the world's biggest, and allegedly, richest charity. He'll be facing some pertinent questions from both the audience and our panel of guests. For those of you at home, don't forget to use the hash-tag at the bottom right of the screen to ask any question you like about Schitthelm and his charity's nefarious dealings.'

Art Schitthelm sat in the chair; a spotlight shining vertically down at him. He looked at Dimblewit, and yawned.

Dimblewit was about to introduce the panel of guests, but stalled – only for a second or two, but stall he did. Such a hesitation would have gone unnoticed by everyone, including Dimblewit himself, were it not for the fact that he was Derek Dimblewit, the ultra-confident, shoot from the hip, cocky show presenter.

The yawn had taken Dimblewit by surprise. Main guests never yawned in your face when being introduced onto the show – far too uptight with fear. The panel of guests witnessed the yawn; along with the studio audience and twenty-eight million viewers. Camera three caught it perfectly. It was strategically positioned at the start of every show to pull optimum focus on the terror stricken main guest. It never failed to treat the public to their hors d'oeuvres as high-definition wide-screens beamed darting eyes, perspiration sparkled foreheads, and a medley of tics and twitches. Digital stereo sound-around echoed stomachs groaning with nervous indigestion, shallow breathing, and, on two occasions, the squeaking of clenched cheeks on the black leather seat.

Schitthelm finished his yawn but kept his stare locked onto Dimblewit. His seated posture oozed nonchalant relaxation. He wore the kind of expression you'd expect to see on the face of someone contemplating the arrival of cigars and brandy.

Smartly suited as always; Schitthelm had a thick silver mane combed back from the temples and forehead. If you had to guess his age you'd peg him at a young sixty. He looked healthy and at ease, however alert.

(PART 2 MULLINGS & RAMSBOTTOM)

'On our panel of guests this week we have the Senior Police Force Commissioner Trudy Mullings, The Right Reverend Rodger Ramsbottom, Health Minister Max Pilmoor, and the President of the British Golfing Society Sandy Irons.' Dimblewit turned and nodded to the guest on his right. 'I'm going to start with Trudy Mullings.'

Mullings, a dark-haired closet autocrat, with an over-sized bovine-like head, eyed Schitthelm with a look of superiority and disdain. Schitthelm smiled indifference back at her.

'Mister Schitthelm,' she mooed at him, 'can you explain why the Fair and Open Competition rules were overlooked when Three F came to be awarded the PFI contract for Alternative Police Support?'

Art Schitthelm took his time to answer. He looked at his watch then drilled Mullings with a stare that bounced off the back of her eyeballs.

'There was no competition – fair, open, or otherwise.'

Mullings, Dimblewit, and everyone else, waited for Schitthelm to continue – he didn't. The show's producer spoke to Dimblewit through his earpiece. 'Ask him to be more specific Derek, and give us some momentum – get the bastard talking.'

'Mister Schitthelm, expand please,' prompted Dimblewit. 'The Home Office Commission for National Contracts have published the figures for all tendered contracts and – correct me if I'm wrong Police Commissioner – there appears to be a whole bunch of zeros next to Three F's bid.'

'That's right,' said Mullings, nodding a half scowl at Schitthelm, 'Both Safe 'n' Secure, and Public Security Services, lodged competitive, realistic tenders, along with comprehensive method statements and resource allocation pledges. Three F have committed to just two sentences to cover resource allocation and method statement; it's an insult to public intelligence – and the tax-payer. They've been up and running for three months now and we don't know anything about financing, application, or operational policy. Serious questions have to be asked as to how – and why, the government have awarded the contract to Three F.'

'So Mister Schitthelm,' said Dimblewit, 'what were the two sentences you offered-up to support your so-called tender?' He half-smiled, sarcastically, at his guests, the camera then the audience. 'I'm sure the audience can't wait to hear them.'

Schitthelm reached into his breast pocket and removed a gold cigar case. He opened the case and leisurely mouthed-out the number of cigars to himself. Dimblewit was unaccustomed to such phlegmatic disregard for the high-octane tension his show generated. He went to prompt Schitthelm.

'What's wrong Schitthelm?Looking in your cigar case for somewhere to hide – too embarrassed or ashamed to –?'

With perfect timing Schitthelm cut-in."Embarrassed" and "ashamed," you utter se words with such easy familiarity Mister Dimblewit. But that's understandable – you being a dealer in both commodities.' Schitthelm still had his cigar case open. 'I hear business is good – you're making a pile of cash out of ruining people. I've no doubt you lavish every penny on yourself.'

The Right Reverend Rodger Ramsbottom butted-in with formal tone.

'I assume you intend to have a cigar?'

'Do you really?' said Schitthelm, with a righteous dose of ridicule.

'You obviously haven't read the studio's broadcasting terms and conditions you signed-up for. If you had you would know smoking is strictly forbidden in here Mister Schitthelm.'

Art Schitthelm snapped his cigar case shut with the ferocity of a triggered rat-trap. It caused the man of the cloth to flinch. The Head of Three F gave a firm response to the pious rhetoric. 'You "assume" I'm going to smoke, Right Reverend? Is not assumption se weakest form of faith? You could have at least presumed; that's what a man of stronger faith would have done, he'd have presumed I was going to smoke. You played it safe – you cowered behind an assumption.'

The Reverend didn't have a handy response. Schitthelm shook his head and grinned at him. 'You obviously haven't read se terms and conditions in se Bible. If you had you would know neither Jesus nor his dad assumed or presumed anything.'

An embarrassment of silence followed. The show's producer barked down his microphone at Dimblewit. 'Get a grip Derek! You're letting things drift. He needs to be answering questions.'

Dimblewit couldn't hear the producer's instructions; his earpiece was whistling and chirping with interference. Back in Moscow the Intelligence Services were monitoring English TV. Once Dimblewit had introduced the show he'd given away the exact whereabouts of Art Schitthelm. Maxim Yankov was hastily trying to level transfer a Russian hitman into a steel recycling bin situated in the yard at the back of the studios. The strength of the magnetic field was interacting with the studio's audio-electrics. A confused Dimblewit fiddled with his earpiece.

Schitthelm answered Dimblewit's question. 'Two sentences were all that was needed to convince se committee we had se superior tender. Se document is in se public domain, so there's no big secret. However, I quote se two sentences: "Three F guarantee to offer a superior service. We'll bring benefit, not cost, to society."

'Does that mean no cost to the taxpayer?' asked Mullings. 'Or have you just used a cosy two-sentence semantic to charm a government hell-bent on cutting spending to the bone?'

'There will be zero cost to se taxpayer Mullings – if you're clever enough to do se maths you will find zero cost beats se other two quotes by a considerable margin.'

'So where's the money coming from? Are you trying to tell us you're operating a national police support infrastructure on fresh air?'

'I'm not trying to tell you anything Mullings – I'm telling you there will be no cost to se taxpayer. Three F will pay for se service.'

Dimblewit had gathered himself. 'It's some charity that can lay its hands on eight-hundred million Schitthelm.'

'Eight-hundred you say?' said Schitthelm.

Dimblewit gave a quick glance at his notes. 'I'm going on the bids tendered by Safe 'n' Secure, and Public Security Services: eight-hundred million, and eight hundred-and-twenty million respectively for a two year contract.'

'Three F have allocated one-hundred-and-fifty million pounds to se service for se first year. We feel it's an excellent opportunity to invest in our overall Societal Enhancement Initiative.'

'We'll be revealing later in the show how and where Three F are making such vast sums of money,' said Dimblewit. 'But for now I'd like The Police Commissioner to continue.'

Mullings resumed. 'I'm sure you're aware Mister Schitthelm; that you have until the end of next week to publish your first quarterly performance report. There is a stiff financial penalty for a breach of contract – any sign of it yet?'

'Sorry to disappoint you Commissioner, but we have se report ready for submission. I was studying it only last night.'

'No, no, I'm not disappointed,' back- pedalled a disappointed Mullings. 'It's good you have the report ready. Are you prepared to give us a preview?'

'Of course,' said Schitthelm, eager. 'I'll start with our Neighbourhood Open Door Scheme. We've already got fifteen villages and six small towns participating – so far se results have pleased me?'

'They've pleased you?' parodied Mullings. 'Fifteen villages and six small towns – well – that's the Isle of Wight covered.' The audience laughed at the comment. 'What about the rest of the country?'

'We didn't want to jump-in with both balls exposed – se way you did when you green-lighted se New Generation Policing Initiative without trialling it first. Now you've shelved it, blown sixty million, and blamed se Chief Constables.'

Mullings wasn't too bothered about the balls reference; she didn't like the rest of what Schitthelm said.

Dimblewit intervened. 'Mister Schitthelm! No obscenities on my show – you signed the Pledge of Conformity for daytime TV transmission. You owe The Commissioner an apology.'

'Your right Dimblewit – I apologise,' said Schitthelm. 'I was out of order inferring that Se Commissioner had balls, when in truth she has none at all.'

Before Dimblewit could have another go at Schitthelm he had the producer back in his ear. 'Never mind her bollocks Derek! Get Schitthelm to tell us about the open door thing.' The interference from the partially successful level transfer from Moscow had now subsided; which meant that the level transfer was complete.

'Okay Mister Schitthelm,' said Dimblewit. 'Give us the low-down on your Neighbourhood Open Door Scheme.'

'We carried out an in depth survey – se way we do with any new initiative we plan to launch. We asked se public what they felt was lacking in today's methods of policing, and also se society that's being policed – they were extremely forthcoming and I'm grateful to them. We looked for patterns in their responses and found one of many recurring comments that caught our interest: People were lamenting se times when se neighbourhood could leave their back doors open without fear of being burgled, raped, or murdered – or even worse, burgled, raped and murdered – however not necessarily in that order.'

Schitthelm continued. 'We've managed to convince residents in se selected neighbourhoods to leave their doors open day and night – just like you could in se old days. At first they were nervous and that was understandable. Once they found out se methods we were going to use to police their neighbourhood they responded with total cooperation.'

Mullings spoke. 'I fail to see how leaving your back door open proves anything – it's just an invitation for criminals. As for these so called "methods" you've deployed to police these areas, well, one newspaper has summed them up as "absurdly controversial" and, quite frankly, I'm finding it hard to disagree.'

'That's because neither you nor se newspaper have seen se Quarterly Performance Report. Se figures will speak for themselves and ease se concerns of anyone gullible or foolish enough to believe se fairy-tales they read in se papers. You'll see how our Thick Earhole Policy and Discretionary on Se Spot Penalties and Punishments have been instrumental in giving back confidence to se public. Restoring public confidence, improving society – that's where we're heading. That good people in se neighbourhood can leave their doors unlocked – well, I can't think of a better performance indicator.'

Schitthelm casually examined the fingernails on his right hand as he waited for somebody to comment.

'Moving on to your Thick Earhole Policy?' said Mullings. 'We're getting reports that Three F officers are summarily swatting youngsters around their heads. That's assault in my books.'

'That's correct,' said Schitthelm confidently. 'In your outdated books it is assault; in my books it's Reasonable and Justifiable

Corrective Action at Source. By se way, I'd like to make it clear that se policy specifically applies to law-breaking teenagers aged between thirteen and nineteen – and then only for first time offenders, because, as yet, no one has reoffended.'

'You're slapping these kids about at the scene of the alleged offence,' said Mullings. 'What's happened to arresting them, formally charging them, and bringing them before the magistrates?'

'It's outdated, costly, and ineffective.By se time they get to se court any remorse they may have harboured is all but diminished. They've had plenty of time to think of an excuse, blame someone else, or have a brief get them off se hook.'

Art gave Mullings a satisfied grin. 'A hearty slap around se lughole imparts a savagely instant lesson in se relationship between accountability and consequence.'

'Are you slapping young females as well?' asked Mullings.

'Pardon?' said Art.

'Are Three F officers hitting female teenagers?'

'Oh yes,' said Art reassuringly. 'Se policy is not gender specific. At Three F we're very much committed to equal opportunities, and respect that women have se same rights as men.' Art chuckled, 'Can you imagine se public outcry if only se boys were getting thick earholes. Se feminists would have a field day.'

'This is unbelievable,' said Mullings.

'Your disbelief will evaporate as soon as you see se figures in se quarterly report Mullings. For instance: se number of un-stolen bikes in these neighbourhoods is up fifty-four per-cent on last year's figures.'

'What kind of statistic is that?' asked Mullings, her tone hysterically overdone with incredulity.

'Se corresponding quarterly report for last year – that's your Force's report by se way Mullings – which, incidentally, was released six days beyond se deadline, and with no resultant penalty; gave se number of stolen bikes for se same locality as twenty-one percent up on se previous year.'

Art allowed fifty percent of his thoughts to become intoxicated with a rampant design involving his girlfriend. Having his mind thus furnished, the leader of Three F developed a forty-eight percent swelling of a potential semi-on. Easing back in his chair he purposely, and irreverently, parted his knees. For sixty-five percent of a second, and against a three percent minority of her will, Mullings ogled the twenty-five percent overall enhancement to his package – pretending, or estimating maybe, the increase to be sixteen percent short of what she imagined ninety percent of the viewing public thought it might, or perhaps ought to have been.

'We've introduced a more positive way of presenting statistics,' said Art. 'By encouraging se residents to let us know if they haven't had their bikes stolen; or haven't been attacked, or murdered; we get a positive statistic rather than a negative one. Our free-phone line is forever busy.'

(PART 3 SANDY IRONS)

The Producer got back onto Dimblewit. For the first time in any of the series he was concerned that the main guest was getting the upper hand. 'Derek – drop Mullings – she's fucking clueless. Get Sandy Irons fired-up with the golf course fiasco.'

'Thank you Commissioner,' said Dimblewit, becoming slightly fed-up. 'I'd like to bring-in Sandy Irons at this point. The President of The British Golfing Society has an army of his members thoroughly teed-off at Three F's latest Phase Two Societal Enhancement Initiative. Over to you Mister Irons.'

Sandy Irons adored himself: a blond, lantern-jawed Ron Ely lookalike; predictably clad in designer golf livery and doused in aftershave with an up-market stench that rivalled Dimblewit's. Sitting confident and upright in his chair he tried Schitthelm out with an intimidating steely blue-eyed stare. Schitthelm reciprocated with a stare that was notably steelier, and excessively more blue-eyed. Irons opened his mouth; Schitthelm opened his first.

'You're going to moan at me for ploughing-up your golf course – then lose se ensuing argument and make fool of yourself.'

Irons started on Schitthelm. 'What you've done beggars belief Schitthelm – we placed our trust in you and you've openly abused it; you're nothing but a con-man.'

'What have you got to say to that Mister Schitthelm?' asked Dimblewit, hoping that Irons' impending tirade would go some length to provoking Schitthelm.

'It takes a con man to know a con man,' said Schitthelm, casually looking down at his lapel and taking his time to flick-off a speck of fluff. 'You see, I know something about Mister Irons that he doesn't know that I know about – if you get my drift?'

'What's going on Schitthelm?' said Dimblewit, picking up the scent of a scandal and not too bothered about whether Schitthelm or Irons came off the worse. Irons went to cut-in; once again Art beat him to it.

'We ploughed-up Ruislip golf course – all ninety-four acres of it.'

Irons appealed to Dimblewit. 'Three F promised they would take care of the club for us. Now we've got over five-hundred members with no golf course – he's even ploughed-up the driving range.'

'Sounds to me like criminal damage Schitthelm,' said Dimblewit. 'Are you going to get a thick earhole?' Dimblewit stole a ripple of laughter from the audience.

'How can it be criminal damage Dimblewit?' said Schitthelm. 'If your researchers had done their pre-broadcast homework they'd have briefed you on the golf club's recent history. Three F own se golf course. We paid clean, honest money for it.'

Dimblewit nodded weakly.

'Clean, honest money,' repeated Schitthelm with barely concealed disdain. 'When was se last time you came across any of that stuff Dimblewit?'

Dimblewit was both embarrassed and puzzled. 'Mister Irons – how come you guys sold it to Three F?'

Art answered the question ahead of Irons. He knew the golfer to be an accomplished bull-shitter; and the only way to deal with a bull-shitter during a debate is to get in there first.

'Se club's finances had been badly managed in recent times; to se point where it was on se cusp of bankruptcy. Irons approached us asking for money.'

'You mean a loan?' asked Dimblewit.

'That's correct,' said Schitthelm. 'Three F are keen to develop businesses that have what we call "Worthy Potential". Our Finance Division offers zero interest loans where appropriate. Se banks might not like it but I don't care – they've bled se taxpayer for long enough.'

'But you've just stated that Three F have bought Ruislip golf club Mister Schitthelm?' said Dimblewit becoming more confused.

Irons managed to interrupt. 'They said they would sort us a loan – then went back on their word. Next thing we know Three F have bought the club from under our noses.'

'We were willing to give them a loan – but first, as with all business loans of this magnitude, we get our forensic accountants to scrutinise all se businesses' previous transactions. They're extremely thorough – even more so when they spot something that doesn't add-up. Our analytical systems can access all national and international monetary transactions and transfers – we're streets ahead of se Inland Revenue. Se only thing is, in this particular case, we didn't inform se applicant at se time. That's why Mister Irons was, until now, blissfully unaware that we'd gone through se accounts with se finest of toothcombs.'

Irons' face took on a troubled expression. Schitthelm was expecting it – Dimblewit noticed it.

'What's up Irons?' asked the presenter curtly. 'All of a sudden you're looking a little under par.'

Schitthelm turned his face and spoke to the studio audience. 'I've left it until now to inform Mister Irons that, due to what we uncovered, there was no way we could advance a loan. You see Se President of the British Golfing Society was covertly instrumental in facilitating se financial amalgamation of all British golf courses three years ago. Everything went well at first. However two years ago a former girlfriend of his was appointed as National Club

Accounts Manager.' The audience settled a curious gaze on Irons. A corpse-like pallor bleached the golfer's face. Schitthelm resumed.

'That's when large sums of money started to go missing – when I say missing, I mean transferred into a Private Offshore Trading Fund. Mister Irons is fully aware of se requirement to make known, at se first bi-monthly meeting of se Group Committee, of any appointment that may undermine se individual or combined interests of se course network. We accessed se minutes of all se meetings and found no such declaration had been made concerning his ex-girlfriend's appointment. We've handed our findings to se Inland Revenue. If I'm not mistaken Mister Irons, I believe se Fraud Squad are waiting outside to arrest you immediately after se show.'

Sandy Irons thought about the situation. He ripped the microphone from his Pringle jumper and bolted from his chair. The club-swinger galloped out of the studio, whiffs of aftershave swirling in his wake.

The producer had his wits about him. Seeing Irons do a runner down the studio corridor, he set about capitalising on the unexpected drama. After instructing one of the mobile camera crew to chase after Irons, he prompted Dimblewit:

'Roll with it Derek; and don't worry about Irons. If they're waiting to arrest him we'll get it filmed – an extra million viewers plus a newsreel scoop. Ask Schitthelm what's the game with ploughing-up the golf course.'

Dimblewit, obviously ill-at-ease, cleared his throat and shuffled his jacket by its lapels. Schitthelm looked typically unfazed.

'Well viewers,' said Dimblewit, 'looks like Mister Irons has some kind of issue with misappropriated funds. We'll try and get you an up-date on that later. Meanwhile I'd like Art Schitthelm to explain why he's ploughed-up a perfectly good golf course.'

'Three F have been working closely with se Society of Golf Widows for some time now. These are men and women who've lost their husbands, wives, or partners, to se game of golf.

'Like gambling and excessive drinking, golf is a highly addictive and destructive habit. However, unlike gambling and alcoholism, golf is not an illness – it's a pre-meditated act of selfishness.'

'How do you work that one out Mister Schitthelm?' asked Dimblewit, genuinely curious.

'Se sport is most pernicious to se wellbeing of se family unit, and therefore detrimental to se interests of a healthy society. There are too many self-indulged parents and partners habitually absent from se home in pursuit of se activity – so, when attendance on se fairway supersedes family welfare, we see it as our duty to take remedial action.' Schitthelm's tone was one of plausible concern.

Dimblewit sensed his main guest was not being completely open about the whole issue. He challenged Schitthelm. 'I can't help but think that Three F intended buying the golf course all along. It was just fortuitous that Irons happened to show-up with his self-imposed predicament and naively hand it to you on a plate.'

Schitthelm gave Dimblewit a respectful nod for his observation.

'We're all entitled to our lucky breaks Mister Dimblewit – you're right; we drafted our Reassignment of Use Program for se country's golf courses over ten years ago,' Art let out a proud sigh at the memory, 'such vision.

'However we couldn't just barge in with a pile of money and start buying-up these places – not without raising eyebrows in all se wrong places. We were looking for an opening – a credible way in. It was Three F's Intelligence Services that initially flagged-up Irons back in ninety-eight.'

'What was he up to?' asked Dimblewit.

'Selling double-glazing with menaces – we've had tabs on him ever since.'

'So – now you've ploughed-up the golf course, what're you going to do with it?'

'Turn it into a nature reserve,' said Art proudly. 'Three F will restore indigenous flora and fauna to every inch of se ninety four acres. We plan to have educational guided tours for families and nature studies for schools. Se project will be funded entirely by us and will benefit not only society but also se eco-system.'

'Seems pretty radical,' said Dimblewit. 'What about the members of the club?'

'I'm taking this opportunity to give an advance warning to every golfer in se British Isles. By midday tomorrow Three F will take ownership of all golf courses. We start ploughing at one minute past noon.'

'Wait a minute Schitthelm,' said Dimblewit. 'There must be over a million golfers up and down the country. What's your message to them?'

'Three F have already considered their impending plight.'

'You don't say,' said Dimblewit patronisingly.

'Of course we have – we're sensitive to their needs, so they're being offered three options.'

'Go ahead,' invited Dimblewit.

'They can either find another hobby, volunteer to work on their new local nature reserve, or simply get on with their lives. At se end of se day they have only themselves to blame. They elected Irons as their President: a greedy, sociopathic, duplicitous narcissist; he's bankrupted all se country's golf courses. Thanks to se intervention of our Intelligence Services we've been able to stop him in his tracks.'

'Your Intelligence Services appear to be well clued-up Mister Schitthelm,' commented Dimblewit. By now there were several members of the studio with their hands in the air, keen to ask Art Schitthelm questions.

'I'm so proud of our Intelligence Services; I'd put them up against any in se world: Russia's GRU, se CIA, MI6 – we're better than any of them.'

'Surely not,' countered Dimblewit with a sarcastic chortle.

'Want a bet?' said Schitthelm cocky. 'I'll give you a demonstration right now.'

'This should be a laugh,' scoffed Dimblewit.

'Not really,' replied Art, 'here – watch this.'

Art turned to face the studio audience. 'I see some of you are aching to ask your questions. I'm guessing they're nasty, awkward questions and you've been up half se night rehearsing them. You see, nasty, awkward questions are usually asked by nasty, awkward people.'

Art counted those with their hands raised. 'There's fifteen of you with your hands raised. Three of you are involved in extra marital affairs, two are on se take at work, one of you paid to have a neighbour murdered back in November ninety-four, another is blackmailing a gay bricklayer, and one of you is not who you say you are.' Art eyed the relevant person(s) in turn. 'We have someone taking bungs from a property developer for passing off planning applications, a bogus doctor, a director with a phoney degree, and a sheep-shagger.' Art scratched his head and frowned. 'I can't just remember what se remaining three of you have been up to – but no doubt you will jog my memory once you ask me your question.' Art smiled proudly at Dimblewit. 'How's that for intelligence?'

'What's happening Derek?' asked the show's producer. 'The whole show's going to shit. Do something – ask him about his family – or his war-time memories – anything.'

Art continued to address the studio audience. 'A little tip for all you budding current affairs show hosts: Before you ask a searching question, see that your own house is in order – and beware the person from whom you seek se answer.'

Within a few seconds all fifteen hands were lowered. Viewers at home kept their suddenly un-itching fingers well away from the hash-tag button.

'So – would anyone else like to ask me a question? I'm all ears.'

Observing the audience's appetite for enlightenment to be somewhat dulled, Art turned his attention back to the panel of guests.

'It's getting a little quiet for a chat show. Perhaps some of se panel guests would like to say something? What about you Reverend? Maybe you'd like to bring us up to speed on se difference between a Reverend and a Right Reverend; or maybe you'd like to tell us about what you got up to at Se Priory Hostel for Teenage Boys back in se spring of nineteen eighty-two?'

The Reverend was flustered. 'I – I resent your tone Schitthelm, it – it's preposter – I mean, how dare you? This is – it's'

Schitthelm let Ramsbottom splutter to a halt.

'Would you like me to tell them Reverend? And while I'm on with it, I can let se public in on Mullings' secret hobby – and also se tenuous link between Mister Dimblewit, a one-legged Paraguayan prostitute, and a forged UK entry visa.'

(PART 4 MAX PILMOOR)

Dimblewit, Mullings, and The Reverend exchanged uneasy glances. Before the producer could give any instructions to a dumbfounded Dimblewit, Health Minister Max Pilmoor spoke to Art Schitthelm.

'Mister Schitthelm,' he said politely. 'There was something I was keen to clear up with you.'

'Of course Max,' replied Art with a friendly smile. 'If there's anything you need clearing up – anything at all, please don't hesitate to ask.'

Three F's Intelligence Services had investigated Max Pilmoor. It turned out he'd only stepped out of line once in his life. When he was ten years old he stole a Mars Bar from the corner shop in his village. Once rumbled Max became deeply ashamed of what he'd done. He learned from the experience and grew up to be a kind, compassionate, and charitable family man. He was possibly the only virtuous politician in the world. Max Pilmoor was unaware that Art Schitthelm had great respect for him.

The Health Minister, a local chap, was a last minute substitution for Transport Minister Laurie Driver, whose chauffeur had got him stuck in a twenty mile tail-back on the M6 due to a pothole the size of a kids' paddling pool. Driver had originally booked a premium business flight from Glasgow airport, but had to make alternative arrangements following spontaneous strike action by ground crew over pay and conditions. Determined to make the show he used his Civil Service Privilege Card to heavily discount a priority first class ticket on the train, only to get notification that the service had been temporarily cancelled. As a last resort he called his chauffeur.

Max Pilmoor spoke earnestly to Schitthelm 'It's just that you gave a recent interview to World Health Magazine and left us all in suspense when you announced Three F had found a cure for a major post-digestion health issue.'

Art's face lit-up.

'That's right Max!' he exclaimed. 'Thank you for reminding me.' Art glanced at Dimblewit. 'As a matter of fact I can't think of a better place or time to announce some great news – not just for se nation, but for se whole world.'

Art was animated, his excitement barely containable.

'As you can see; my excitement is barely containable – and that is a coincidence. Because what I'm going to talk about is self-containment; or should I say, an embarrassing lack of it.

'We've been looking at a problem that's been causing your department a pain in se backside for quite some time Max. And I'm confident we've got it plugged.'

The producer instructed Dimblewit to let Schitthelm carry on; hoping he would burn up time by immersing himself in a lengthy monologue.

(PART 5 SHAUN SWILL)

'Before I continue, I'd like to give credit to a young man called Shaun Swill, without whom we would not be where we are today in se fight against IBE. Shaun came to us with a dead frog, a car battery, and a brilliant idea. Three F were so impressed we got him to register a patent on it. We then paid Shaun a handsome sum for his idea – along with promised shares in future profits.'

Art told the tale of Shaun Swill to an audience too intimidated to interrupt.

§

Shaun Swill was born in Northallerton in 1990 to Welsh-American parents. His father Theo was a Faith Healer, and his mother Bronwyn a part-time Soothsayer. Shaun had unconventional childhood memories. In his formative years he'd witnessed his father's futile attempts at healing the gullible, the desperate, and the curious – and he'd listened to his mother's hysterical predictions howled up and down the busy High Street.

Shaun's mother longed to go full-time with her soothsaying but was unable to. Ten years previously her live-in mother Gwyneth began suffering from IBE and, as with most cases of incontinence, once it begins – it begins, over and over – again and again.

Money was tight in the Swill household, and for good reasons: Shaun's father charged for his faith healing services, but most of the time he found himself refunding the fee when his professed healing powers imparted zero benefit to the recipient, Bronwyn was forever paying fines for disturbing the peace, and the toothless Gwyneth ate the full value of her pension in baby food.

To help save money Bronwyn used terry nappies for her mother; and hand-washed them daily to avoid using electricity. The Swill's washing line was forever a-flap with nappies – their fragrant, fresh snow-whiteness a paradoxical reminder of Gwyneth's ungoverned discharge.

One evening Theo tried performing his faith healing on Gwyneth. He stood before his seated mother-in-law and placed his hands on her head. Theo instructed Shaun and his mother to stand either side of Gwyneth and chant "hallelujah praise the Lord." At the top of his voice Theo called out at the ceiling, "By the sacred powers vested in me by the Lord God almighty, I banish the demon in our sister – be gone forever to the fires of Hell o evil spirit."

Theo's strident utterance was accompanied by a fanfare of trumpeting shit. The "evil spirit" declared its failure to arrive in Hell as Gwyneth expurgated in the usual fashion.

§

Of all the subjects Shaun took at school biology was his favourite. One day the teacher Mister Nicholson was demonstrating an experiment first carried out by an eighteenth century Italian physicist called Luigi Galvani.

Galvani (the name from which derives the word "Galvanise") discovered that the muscles in a dead frog's legs would contract when he passed an electrical current through them.

Shaun Swill was both fascinated and inspired when Mister Nicholson duplicated the experiment in the classroom. The teacher used a twelve-volt battery to pass an electrical current through the creature. He'd bashed its brains out five minutes before the start of the lesson so as not to traumatise his pupils.

When Shaun witnessed the frog's legs kicking lifelike, an idea leaped into his head.

That weekend Shaun caught a frog, strangled it, and borrowed the battery from his father's Vauxhall. He went along to his local P.I.S.S. Academy where, between three and four o'clock every other Saturday, The Young Inventor's Hour took place.

Shaun arrived unaccompanied to find two other budding young inventors waiting with mum and dad to present their ideas. Fourteen year-old Sebastian Walker had come up with the idea of a safety feature for motorists whose cars were built before air-bags were fitted. He'd fetched along a stout white pillow with two eye-holes cut into it. Sebastian had attached an adjustable head-strap to either side of the pillow.

Fifteen year-old Andrew Palmer had come up with an idea to save time, money, and inconvenience in the examination and diagnosing of certain genital disorders. With his X-ray chair patients could have their nether regions X-rayed at the doctor's surgery without having to remove any items of clothing.

Andrew's chair was just an ordinary adjustable swivel type you'd find at any computer workstation. The clever bit was the seat. Andrew had removed the padding and replaced it with a compound of cathode-ray magneto granules and mercury sulphate crystals, bound in a flexi-stretch lead electro-plasma membrane. The seat was powered by two Triple A batteries and could take up to seventy X-rays before they needed replacing. The X-ray images could be relayed instantly to the doctor's display screen.

Doctors up and down the country could have such a chair in their consulting rooms. While they were consulting with the seated patient they could, surreptitiously, discreetly, or otherwise, view the images of their subject's undercarriage without them having to undress.

Whilst the P.I.S.S. Academy Assessment Committee were not so enamoured with the pillow idea; they were impressed enough with the X-ray seat to have it patent registered and forwarded to the National Clinical Research Agency.

Once Shaun Swill had demonstrated his twitching frog's legs he was asked by the P.I.S.S. Academy Assessment Committee as to what use his idea was to be applied.

Shaun informed the committee that he'd come up with a permanent cure for IBE (Involuntary Bowel Evacuation); stating that, aside from the obvious misery, the condition costs the NHS over three-billion pounds annually, downturns the annual GDP by almost two-point-six percent, and raises harmful greenhouse emissions by point-eight percent globally.

'No shit!' exclaimed the committee's lead assessor.

'Hopefully sir,' replied Swill.

Shaun proposed that two electrodes could be surgically implanted either side of the anal sphincter, in such a way that they were in relevant proximity to the pelvic floor muscles. (The strategic positioning would enhance both faecal and urine retention capability).

Shaun convinced the committee that the implant could be done as a day surgery procedure, carried-out under a local anaesthetic: A sensor wire could be routed under the skin, from the sphincter region, to a small socket stitched into the skin somewhere on the lower torso. A pocket-sized battery pack could be discreetly carried about the person, and a lead from the pack would plug into the socket.

As Shaun continued to explain his idea it became obvious to the committee that he'd spent a lot of time thinking the whole thing through:

A sensor, built-in to each electrode, would monitor the level of muscle tension in the sphincter and pelvic floor. Whenever there was a sudden drop in tension – a typical and pressing forerunner to a BME (Bowel Malfunction Event); the sensor would send a signal to the battery pack, which in turn would energise the electrodes to send a current through the lower pelvic regions. The resultant clamping effect of relevant muscles would ensure the containment of any potential discharge.

The Committee were so impressed with Shaun's idea they contacted Art Schitthelm's office directly. Art didn't have to think twice; he gave immediate instructions for Three F to develop and trial the idea.

§

Most people know that the Beaufort scale measures wind speed – and that the Richter scale measures the intensity of earthquakes. However few people are aware that there exists a clinically recognised scale for measuring the severity of gastric malfunction. A Bulgarian seamstress named Kalinka Krapov (1898- 1979) came up with the idea of using a graduated scale to quantify the magnitude of an unwanted, unexpected gastric event. The Krapov Scale was officially recognised by the World Health Organisation in 1972 as the universally accepted measurement for IBE.

The scale ranges from zero, through to ten; with 'zero' being classified as 'Normal, socially acceptable gastric function,' and 'one' being rated as 'partially mitigated, however unintentional moist flatulence.'

A score of 'two' indicates 'Mild aerosol-borne faecal staining to undergarments,' (sometimes referred to as a 'flavour blur') with 'three' classed as 'Unreliable flatulence.'

'Vivid partial-fluidic staining to undergarments (more commonly known as a 'wet fart' or a 'follow-through') comes in at number 'four'. By the time we get to number 'nine' we're looking at 'Projectile diarrhoea,' (a voluminous and energetic faecal expulsion often accredited to the transitory 'next morning' side effect of gratuitous ingestion; the most common propellant being an aggregate of curry and lager). Ten indicates 'A permanently uncontrollable and recurring state of catastrophic gastro/urinal discharge (most usually encountered in care homes for the elderly).

§

In a matter of five months Three F had developed a prototype of Shaun Swill's invention. Given its portable dimensions Shaun asked that it be named "The Pocket Sphinculator."

Trials commenced immediately and results were most pleasing – for the main part that is. Three F's Medical Research Unit had selected a subjective cross-section of IBE sufferers, ranging on the Krapov Scale from one, right through to ten.

After a month of trialling the results were analysed. The Pocket Sphinculator had performed well – with only a couple of easily rectifiable exceptions concerning side effects and product design.

The main side-effect experienced by many of those involved in the trials was a radical change to their deportment whenever the electrodes were in 'activated' mode. Whilst tolerable in the privacy of their own homes, it drew embarrassing attention from onlookers when out in public. The current from the electrodes caused a degree of spasm in the upper thigh and gluteus maximus muscles, causing a normal stride to change most noticeably to a half swagger, half skip, in a manner that would be hypothetically essential if George Bush Junior were to perform hop-scotch on a catwalk whilst clenching one of Jimmy Carter's peanuts in his arse-cheeks.

The problem with product design was easily solved soon after the launch of the trials. The first batch of sphinculator battery packs didn't have a low battery charge indicator fitted. This wasn't so much of a problem with sufferers rated at category 'four' or less on the Krapov scale; but was an unacceptable flaw for those pegged higher up the scale. One high category patient had his battery run flat on him while he was queuing at a busy check-out in his local supermarket. As a result he suffered a full-on category 'nine' gastric malfunction causing the check-out, along with the ones immediately either side of it, to close as dismayed customers fled the scene in a stampede of disgusted howls and suppressed retching. A category 'eight' patient was involved in a similar incident whilst dining-out at a Michelin starred restaurant in Bromsgrove.

Three F reacted immediately to both problems; training patients in the discipline of Cognitive Reactive Physiotherapy to counteract the change in deportment, and fitting every battery pack with a 'low charge indicator' that gave a full half hour's DDB (deaf, dumb and blind) warning by simultaneously sounding a shrill alarm, a sensory buzzer, and a flashing red warning light.

(PART 6 LENNY PLANT)

Art Schitthelm concluded his story, claiming victory for Shaun Swill and Three F over IBE. Jointly they had restored to sufferers the freedom cruelly taken from them by the condition. Both Shaun and Three F would make a fortune from the invention. Shaun could do with his as he pleased – Three F would reinvest their share in more projects to improve society.

Derek Dimblewit looked concerned. He'd had several gastric incidents since Christmas and worried that he himself might end up having to be fitted with a sphinculator. If he did he knew that once the press got hold of it they'd destroy him with ridicule. Derek could see the headlines already: "TOP SHOW HOST IN GASTRIC MELTDOWN," "DIMBLEWIT CREATES BIG STINK ON SHOW," and "CELEBRITY GETS BUM DEAL WITH THREE F." For sure his career would come to an abrupt and embarrassing conclusion.

As he was about to introduce series of questions about Three F's alleged involvement with the disappearance of a disgraced judge; a metallic clattering could be heard echoing in the corridor that led to the back of the studio. Louder and nearer came the racket – until a well-built gentleman dressed-up as a fake recycling bin staggered onto the set.

Although the audience gasped moderate surprise; Dimblewit was relieved at the distraction and reacted with a jovial grin. He knew that in studio number two "The Reckless Bud Sanderson Show" was in full swing. Bud was an incorrigible practical joker and his show featured a medley of tricks played on fellow celebrities, studio audiences, and any unsuspecting member of the public beyond.

Bud had inflicted his stunts on Dimblewit several times in the past. Dimblewit didn't mind – he lapped-up the attention. In any case, both millionaires were good friends – they regularly played golf together.

The costume department could have been well praised for the job they did on Pietro Poslowski. The fake recycling bin get-out fitted so snugly you'd think it was part of him.

Unfortunately the bin was part of Pietro.

Maxim Yankov had been ordered to level transfer Pietro the instant the Russians discovered Art Schitthelm was at the Manchester studios. Maxim hated being rushed when carrying out a level transfer – the more time spent on attention to detail, the better the chances of a successful transfer.

Pietro Powslowski was ushered into the laboratory and hastily briefed while Maxim set-up the co-ordinates. A syringe containing enough novochoski 3 to put-down a dairy herd was thrust into his hand. His instructions were simple: "Once transferred to the refuse bin, make your way to studio number one, locate Schitthelm, and stick the needle into his neck."

KGB Operations Director Victor Pavlov had showed up at the laboratory along with Director of Intelligence Vasily Vasiliev. Having never viewed an assassination on a prime-time show, they had a TV set tuned in to The Dimblewit Debate. The pair of them ate cheesy puffs as they gazed at the screen with psychotic anticipation.

In a state of confusion Pietro Powslowski shuffled towards Dimblewit. Dimblewit was still smiling at him, wondering how this particular practical joke was going to turn-out. In a haze of disorientation Pietro had half forgotten what Art Schitthelm looked like. Standing over the seated Dimblewit he surveyed the chat show host and estimated him to look near enough identical to his target.

Pietro buried the needle its full length into Dimblewit's neck and squeezed off the plunger. Dimblewit's expression changed accordingly. He rose from his chair with the emptied syringe hanging out of his neck. Staggering towards the audience, purple-faced and eyes bulging like they were ready to burst, he mouthed the words "help me." Dimblewit dropped to his knees, keeled over sideways, and died.

§

Lenny Plant leaned forward in his sofa to study the TV more closely. With a booze-soaked brain he was having difficulty determining whether Dimblewit was dead or just fooling around. Before Lenny could judge one way or the other the transmission shut down. Following a considerable silence an announcer came on screen. "We apologise for being unable to bring you the rest of the Dimblewit Debate. Stay tuned while we show a classic episode of One Man and His Dog from nineteen seventy-nine."

CHAPTER 19

BACK IN THE FORMER U.S.S.R

Traktor Popov arrived at the Moscow Laboratories in a state limousine half an hour after the syringe went into Dimblewit's neck. He emerged from the back of the vehicle and jogged up the chalk-white steps that led to the main reception. Two KGB guards flanked him. Popov was furious.

The Head of KGB had arranged an emergency meeting after viewing the killing of Dimblewit. He barged into the boardroom and marched to the top of the table to take his seat. With an expression set into a contortion of rage Popov glowered at the three men already seated.

Maxim Yankov had arrived in the room shortly before. He'd received the phone call from Popov as he and his team were dragging the smouldering wreckage of human recycling bin from the Maxim Cage. As before, he took a seat further down the boardroom table. To Popov's left and right sat Vasili Vasiliev and Victor Pavlov. No stenographer was present this time – Popov wanted the detail of this particular meeting off the record.

'What a mess,' said Popov, his tone a blend of anger and despondency. 'What a bastard mess.'

Maxim Yankov was quick with a response. He slid a picture of the dead Powslowski up the table to Popov. 'That's what happens when you rush a level transfer,' he said, his tone loaded with accusation. Maxim was getting tired of being put under unreasonable pressure from the KGB whenever carrying out both level and retro transfers. After the previous meeting he promised himself that from now on he was going to be boldly argumentative with Traktor Popov.

Popov studied the picture of Powslowski with noticeable reluctance. He shoved it away, like it was a plate of his least favourite food.

'I told you as much on the phone,' said Maxim firmly. 'We needed time to get a tighter grid reference on the recycling bin. If you'd have given us the extra fourteen minutes we requested, we'd have had the precise satellite co-ordinates.'

Popov's dislike of Maxim had intensified over the last few weeks. Dawning over the arrogance of his ignorance was the realisation that, as much as he was commonplace and replaceable, Maxim Yankov was unique and unreplaceable – "Geniuses don't grow on trees," Sputum had told him at their last meeting.

Popov defended himself. 'Fourteen more minutes and Schitthelm could have left the studios – the opportunity would have passed us by – then where would we be?'

'We wouldn't have a dead celebrity, a dead agent, and the threat of compromise,' back-answered Maxim. 'The BBC may have cut the transmission when they realised something was wrong; but don't doubt they'll have kept the cameras rolling. Powslowski's dematerialisation is probably being studied by MI5 as we speak – plus their forensics team will have the syringe in the lab. Give them an hour or so and they'll confirm Novochoksi 3 was used.'

'So?' challenged Popov.

'So – there's only us and North Korea makes the stuff. They'll discover the syringe was manufactured in Vladivostok – and one glimpse at Powslowski will tell them he doesn't look remotely like any North Korean. I'm telling you now the President will be lucky to fib his way out of this one.'

Popov, unaccustomed to Maxim being so outspoken, was temporarily silenced. As he tried to compose himself, the Head of Intelligence Vasili Vasiliev thought it timely to hit Popov with some more unwelcome news.

'Leo Smirnov is dead,' he said flatly

'What did you say?' said Popov, wishing he hadn't heard the utterance.

'Yankov has informed us his transponder showed all vital signs of life extinct at precisely thirteen-fifteen hours. Less than an hour later its information had been downloaded onto a rogue system then destroyed.'

'This just gets better,' said Popov shaking his head. 'Do we have any idea who downloaded it?'

Popov was hoping Vasiliev would tell him it was MI5, the CIA, or maybe Mossad – anyone but Three F or Lenny Plant.

'We have no doubt it was Three F, Mister Popov,' said Vasiliev. 'They took Smirnov from the pub in one of their ambulances. The signal for the download registered approximately forty-five minutes after the ambulance departed.'

'Damn Three F!' shouted Popov before promptly composing himself. 'Do we know if he died from natural causes, or was he killed?' The Head of The KGB realised immediately the futility of his question.

'What we do know for certain is that Lenny Plant was in immediate proximity at the time of his expiry,' said Vasiliev.

'And what about Plant,' said Popov – 'did Smirnov manage to stick him with the umbrella before he died?'

'We're fairly sure he didn't. As for who killed Smirnov, we have a pretty sound theory to go on,' said Vasiliev.

'And whose theory is this then?' asked Popov. 'It can't be Einstein's because he's dead – he's dead, just like Smirnov.'

'It's a theory we've come up with after studying some security camera recordings,' said Vasiliev. 'We've managed to get a multi-wave satellite signal hacked into the CCTV camera in the pub car park. It shows the comings and goings at the entrance to the pub.'

'Carry on,' said Popov, becoming tired and impatient. He slouched in his chair and rubbed his face into his palms.

Vasiliev rose from his seat, picked up a remote control from the table and switched on a TV screen perched at the end of the table. He talked the footage through:

'We've got Plant, unarmed and on his own, entering the pub just before midday,' he said, before fast forwarding the recording. 'Then, at thirteen- zero-five, we see Smirnov arrive with his brolly.

Between the opening of the pub and the time of Smirnov's death, fifty-two people are seen to enter the pub. They all happen to show-up in groups of two or more. If Smirnov's been assassinated by a lone wolf then there's no sign of an individual suspect entering or leaving – aside from Plant that is.'

Although Mandy Seymour was operating solo, she made sure she entered the pub tagging along with a party of three. A true professional she was aware of the car park camera. Mandy melted her blandness into the scenario by participating in some small talk about the mild weather.'

'You suspect Plant is our lone wolf Mister Vasiliev?' asked Popov.

'Who else could it be?' said Vasiliev. 'We've already established he's killed Semyon – now we find him in the same building as Smirnov at the time of his death.'

'I agree,' said Popov, 'he's a wolf alright – but I'll wager not such a lonely one. I've suspected all along that Plant is a Three F asset; Schitthelm is his master. Anyway, have you considered those already in the pub; the owners, the kitchen and bar staff? Have we run any intel-checks on them?'

'Already done,' replied Vasiliev 'there's nothing doing – just ordinary people in rhythm with their lives. Lenny Plant is the only one with form.'

'And the Dent chap, the one who owns the freezer?' asked Popov.

'He's not capable,' said Vasiliev. 'The man's forever drunk.'

'So what is this theory you're talking about?' said Popov.

'I'll come to that shortly,' said Vasiliev, continuing with his analysis. He wound and rewound the recording as he spoke:

'The picture definition is excellent – you can see for yourself the general mannerisms of the patrons: all of them naturally relaxed; their behaviour totally in context with the occasion of visiting an English pub. There are none of the signatures we look for in suspects readying for a hit; no nervous contemplation etched on their face, no cautious glancing over the shoulder, no agitated movement.'

Vasiliev rewound to the moment of Lenny Plant's arrival. 'But then we have Plant. Just look at the expression on his face – so stern. You can even see the furrows on his brow.' Vasiliev froze the frame. 'This is obviously the look of a man with a lot on his mind. The expression you see here is one of grave premeditation – typical of the one you'd see on the face of many an assassin.'

'Are you sure about this Vasiliev – you're telling me unequivocally that Plant did it?

'Oh I'm sure alright – even more so when I compare the manner of his stride on entering and leaving the pub.'

'I'm not with you,' said Popov.

Vasiliev set the recording running again. 'You can see he's walking to the pub with purpose in his stride – the gait of someone with something important to do. No doubt about it, Plant's on a mission and he means business.'

Lenny Plant did indeed make his way across the car park with furrowed brow and hasty stride. On top of his freezer worries he was thoroughly hacked-off with the P.I.S.S. Academy debacle. The "purpose" Vasiliev observed in his stride was one inspired by a yearning for the soothing effects of pystwiser.

Vasiliev wound the recording on. 'Now look when he leaves the pub shortly after Smirnov's death. He's a different person. The lines of anxiety have left his face – he's totally at ease. And see how he makes his way across the car park – in particular the fashion of his deportment, almost arrogant I'd say.'

'Hmm,' said Popov, brightening slightly. 'Maybe he's walking differently because Smirnov has managed to stick him with the umbrella?'

'Unfortunately not,' said Vasiliev. 'Look at his cheap white chinos. There's no damage or blood in the vicinity of his right calf.'

'Why his right calf?' asked Popov.

'Smirnov always goes for the right calf – he's superstitious like that. Without exception he's secured all his brolly hits with a right calf puncture. It's become his trade mark.'

'Are you sure?'

'Positive,' asserted Vasiliev, 'I can safely say the only holes in Plant are the seven God gave him.'

'Seven holes,' grumbled Popov. 'What the hell are you talking about?'

'You know,' said Vasiliev with a laddish grin, 'his arsehole, his knob-hole, his ear -.'

'That's enough!' snapped Popov.

'Sorry Sir,' said Vasiliev.

'Fuck's sake,' said Popov.

'All I'm saying is that Plant's nonchalant swagger speaks volumes,' said Vasiliev. 'I've seen that kind of swagger before.'

'And where exactly have you seen this kind of "nonchalant swagger" before?' asked a cynical Popov.

'John Wayne,' replied Vasiliev.

'You mean the draft-dodging bag of wind and piss who starred in all those Westerns.'

'Yes.'

'Explain please,' ordered Popov.

Vasiliev explained. 'I'm sure you're aware Sir, that the new Grade 1 State Master's Degree in Espionage now requires a thirty-thousand word thesis on the behavioural conditioning of A list actors by Hollywood to portray an illusion of American compassion and valour?'

'You mean falsifying American history and culture through film – the cinematic propaganda that distracts from the atom bombs, the carpet bombing, and the slaughter of an indigenous noble race?'

'Exactly Mister Popov,' said Vasiliev. 'The countless number of times you see John Wayne empty his Winchester into the bronze belly of an Apache who's packing a blunt bread knife – so brave.'

'What's this got to do with Plant?'

'Well, whenever you see John Wayne kill someone, take note of the way he struts away afterwards – that walk of his. He's been coached to walk that way, an arrogant, proud swagger – it's a statement, somewhat similar to the victorious rutting stag, proudly marching from a bloody encounter for a well-earned bag-emptying session with the nearest doe.

'Plant's killed someone, so he's subliminally influenced by his childhood exposure to cowboy western film culture.' Vasiliev replayed Plant's exit from the pub. 'Look at the boastful stride as he leaves the pub – Plant is walking just like John Wayne.'

In actual fact Lenny Plant did walk a bit like John Wayne when he was half pissed. When he was fully pissed he walked like Buddy Overstreet with two in-growing toenails.

'Bugger me, you're right Vasiliev,' said Popov, astonished. 'Plant's killed Smirnov. He's killed the man we sent to kill him, and now he's doing the John Wayne victory stroll.' Popov scratched at his scalp puzzled. 'But how – how's he done it in a crowded bar – do we have any idea?'

Maxim spoke, 'The transmission showed his heart stopped instantly.'

'So then it's got to be a heart attack,' said Popov.

'Impossible,' said Maxim. 'All his vital signs were perfect right up until the instant of his death: a regular heart-beat, normal blood pressure. Both his heart and brain function were terminated in a microsecond. There's no doubt,' said Maxim gravely, 'whatever Plant's done to him, it was as efficient and effective as anything we've come across.'

'This is not good,' said Popov, after a moment of thought. 'Plant's done two of our top operatives in as many days. He has to be stopped and topped. I suggest we act immediately to take care of him and secure the freezer.'

Popov turned to Victor Pavlov, the KGB's Director of Operations.

'Is your team with the delivery van in place Mister Pavlov?'

'They're stationed two miles away in a disused warehouse just outside Richmond,' affirmed Pavlov.

'And is the replacement freezer inside?'

'All ready to go Mister Popov.'

'Vasiliev,' said Popov, 'we're going in today. Do you have an optimum time for us to swap the freezers?'

Vasiliev opened an intelligence log he'd fetched with him. It contained the entirety of Vagin Semyon's observations in and around Locburn Village.

'I'd say 19:00 hrs is most the opportunistic time Mister Popov.'

'Is there any reason for that particular time Mister Vasiliev?'

'Going by Semyon's log, Mr and Mrs Dent are creatures of habit: she leaves the house on her bicycle every Sunday evening at precisely 18:00 hrs – he sets-off on foot for the pub at approximately the same time. She returns at 21.30 hrs, and he staggers back any time after 22:30. That gives us more than enough time to swap freezers.'

'Are you sure?' asked Popov.

'Semyon's logged all the comings and goings since he started observations – without exception there's no deviance to their routine.'

'Very good, 19:00 hrs it is then.'

'And what about Plant?' asked Victor Pavlov.

Popov spoke to Maxim. 'Mister Yankov, I need you to carry out one more level transfer to the freezer before we seize it.'

'I'm going to need more –,'

'I want him there at 18:00 hrs prompt Yankov!' shouted Popov down the table. 'That's a full one hour before we make the swap.' Popov gave Maxim a nasty smile he'd been saving especially for him. 'Between now and then you have more than enough time – so there'll be no excuses for any fuck-ups.'

'Who do you intend sending?' asked Pavlov.

'That fellow you were telling me about last week Mister Pavlov,' said Popov, scratching his head in a bid to provoke his memory. 'I can't recall his name just now. You had a nickname for him – the animal or something.'

'Ah – you're thinking of Animal Androvski, the unbeaten bald-headed bear boxer from Bulgaria.'

'That's him,' said Popov cheerfully. 'He's our man.'

Animal Androvski had had forty-seven fights with wild bears, all won inside of the scheduled twelve rounds. Thirty of the fights were with Brown bears, sixteen with Grizzly bears, and one with a Polar bear. His fight record ran as follows: 41 by way of knock-out, and 7 by way of technical knock-out. There was 1 non-starter due to the challenging bear running off through the crowd when it caught sight of Androvski standing in the ring growling and flexing his biceps.

'Mister Pavlov,' said Traktor Popov. 'Get Androvski over here immediately; we'll have him thoroughly briefed before Yankov transfers him. He can take care of Plant while we concentrate on switching the freezers. Once we have the freezer in our hands we can abandon Locburn for good.'

'Are we sending any weaponry with Androvski?' asked Yankov.

'No need,' said Popov, 'Androvski can beat a Polar bear – he'll have no problem killing Plant with his bare hands.'

CHAPTER 20

REPLICA

'Locburn Village Petro,' ordered Art Schitthelm from the back-seat of the S Class, 'and no hanging about.'

Petro Pushkar, Three F's top wheel-man, responded immediately. He gunned the Mercedes out of the studio car park and onto the busy streets of Manchester. Pushkar wasn't a second too soon – wailing towards the studios from all directions was every available patrol car in the city.

On Art Schitthelm's insistence the Three F police would have no involvement in this one. The moment the syringe went into Dimblewit's neck, Art calmly drew out his side-valve mobile and rang Three F's Director for UK National Police Support. He ordered the director to assign a 'zero response' status to the incident; stating that this particular show was over in more ways than one.

'We're going to Locburn father?' inquired Horace, sitting next to his father. 'Isn't that a tad dangerous?'

Art laughed at his son. 'When you're as old as me, danger is a tad less dangerous than it used to be Horace – nowadays it's actually a tad safe. You're no spring chicken, so danger should be fairly safe for you as well.' Art smiled to himself. 'Danger obviously doesn't bother Lenny Plant too much – he's in se thick of it all. I can't work out whether he's brave, stupid, or a tad oblivious.'

'Perhaps he's a mixture of all three Father?'

'Whatever he is Horace, we will soon have no use for him – Plant has served his purpose.'

'He's served his purpose?' said Horace, curious.

'Yes Horace. Either wittingly or unwittingly he's been exceptionally efficient at stalling se Russians. His activities have given our Intelligence Directorate a much needed breathing space to uncover exactly what it is they're up to.'

'You're talking like you know something.'

'Oh I know something alright Horace,' said Art with confidence, 'se last forty-eight hours have proved to be most fruitful. I was going to discuss se recent developments earlier with you – but first I wanted to be sure of se facts.'

'What facts?'

'Dimitri Yeltsin, our sleeper in se Moscow Laboratories, has discovered that se Russians are teleporting agents to an old seventies chest freezer in se back of Ronnie Dent's garage.'

'Teleporting – isn't that what they do on Star Trek?'

'That's about se height of it Horace; for once you're more or less on se ball – problem is; se Russians know that, due to se freezer's unique construction, it can also be used as a receptor vessel for sending their agents back in time.'

'Time travel,' said Horace, staring in dazed wonderment at his father. 'You mean like Jules Verne, and doctor what's his name?'

'Doctor who?' asked Art.

'Yes Father – that's him, Doctor Who.'

'Horace, you are se most childish ninety-four year-old person I've ever known. Now be quiet and listen-up. We've confirmed se freezer's location is at se precise epicentre of se magnetic field fluctuations we've been investigating.

Dimitri has informed us that se freezer is an extremely rare model; a Bulko- Frost 100 Deluxe made by a long disbanded company called National Electric. Our Technical and Intelligence Directorates have been researching both se company and se freezer. Information is scant to say se least – however we do know that it's se technology that's gone into se construction of se freezer that so much interests se Russians.'

Horace scratched his head intrigued. 'That's incredible Father – a humble domestic appliance leftover from the seventies. What kind of technology are we talking about?'

'That's where se Russians are snookered Horace. There are no archived engineering diagrams – neither any technological specifications. We've searched se length and breadth of se internet and come up with very little. Se model was an oddity, built as a tester for se British market. Its over-engineered construction meant it was bulky and comparatively expensive. On top of that se product was out of context with se British socio-domestic trending of that era.'

'And what was the socio-domestic trending of that era?'

'Striking dockworkers, Alvin Stardust, and fish fingers,' smiled Art. 'Anyhow, se unique construction of this freezer, along with its rarity and lack of provenance, mean that se only way se Russians can understand its innermost workings is to gain possession of it.'

'I don't understand how Lenny Plant fits into it all Father. What's his interest in the freezer?'

'At first we thought he was up to speed on se freezer's uniqueness – its potential as an accessory for time travel.Turns out he's been using it to store a dead body,' said Art, matter-of-fact.

'A dead body,' said Horace half startled, 'we need to get Three F police involved.'

Art could only offer a languid shake of his head. He despaired at his son's chronic long-term congenital short-sightedness. 'Horace, you're forever not in search of se bigger picture, and eternally in danger of never finding it. Se Russians are on se brink of tampering with history to gain global domination, and you're worried about a body in a freezer. Plant's probably got bodies stored in freezers up and down se whole of se bloody country – big deal. He's in se killing business and that's what happens. From time to time dead bodies manage to find their way into freezers.'

Art frowned with annoyance. 'Of all se freezers in all se country he had to dump a body in this one.'

'Do we know who it is in the freezer?' asked Horace, in the manner of an immature ninety-five year-old, half excited at the prospect of a guessing game. 'My money's on a Russian spy; Plant's been into bagging them lately.'

'Some inconsequential portly lady,' said Art. 'Seymour got a good look at her; about as far removed from a Russian spy as one could imagine.'

'So Seymour's clapped eyes on the freezer?'

'More than just clapped eyes Horace; she's taken detailed photographs of it. Se instant we realised Plant was at se address on Friday night I instructed her to try and gain access to se property. She managed to get to se rear of se house and hide in se overgrown garden for a while. Around zero one-hundred hours she sees se light come on in se garage. From se bottom of se garden she could just make out Plant and Dent struggling with something heavy.'

'I'd have sneaked right up to the window for a proper look,' said Horace with bravado.

'Of course you would Horace,' humoured Art. 'But it would have been too cold and windy for you – and think of all those nasty stingy nettles, and also se prickly briars.' Art formed a mental picture and chuckled. 'Big fat clumsy you, crashing around in someone's back garden in se dead of night – anyway, haven't you forgotten? You're afraid of se dark.'

'Not any more Father – I've gone a whole week with the light off,' bragged Horace.

'Well done son – well done. However Seymour couldn't go to se window because se deformed Russian was already peering directly through it – hanging upside-down from se guttering as it happens. Once se garage light went out Seymour stamped her foot on a fallen branch in order to crack it. She startled se Russian and he cleared-off. As it turns out Plant left se property shortly afterwards, so Seymour wasted no time in climbing into se garage through a loose roof panel. She took a quick look inside se freezer then took several photos of it – such a quick-thinking girl.'

'So we've got pictures of the freezer – are they of any use?'

'Very much so Horace; se minute we got them I sent them off to our fabrications facility, along with orders to construct an exact replica. I demanded they have it ready for delivery within twenty-four hours. They've done well – eighteen hours later and we've got a dead ringer.'

'Does it actually work?' asked Horace.

'Off course,' replied Art. 'Obviously it doesn't have se same technology – but in every other way you can't tell it from se original. Se fabrication team have even replicated a scratch on se front of it. Mister and Missus Dent won't notice any difference.'

'So we're going to swap the freezers?'

'Yes Horace – and se better se sooner. We have to consider se obvious fact that se Russians will be equally keen to seize se freezer at se earliest opportunity. Time is very much of se essence.'

'What about the body?'

'It's gone. Seymour went to se address yesterday evening after she'd seen Ronnie Dent sprinting up Church Lane towards se pub. She got back in through se roof and saw that se freezer was empty. Plant's obviously disposed of se body.'

'So when do we make the swap?'

'This evening – se delivery van is ready and waiting at a nearby location. We go in at 19:00 hrs.'

'What about Ronnie Dent and his wife – err, Miss, Mrs – I've forgotten her name,' said Horace scratching his scalp.

'Mrs Dent?'

'That's right Father, Mrs Dent – how come you know her?'

'Through her husband Horace.'

Horace nodded. 'It's a small world,' he said, wisely. 'What if they're at home when the delivery van shows up?'

'Seymour guarantees se house will be empty at that time. I read her e-mail just before the start of Se Dimblewit Debate. She mentions how she listened-in to Dent's conversation with his cronies in se pub prior to this afternoon's suspected assassination. At one point he was talking about his arrangements for se forthcoming evening. He clearly stated that both he and his wife were creatures of habit, and that they left se house at six o'clock every Sunday to go their respective ways. She's an incorrigible gossip, punctual with her parish – and he's an accomplished piss-artist, unfaltering in his attendance at se beginning second of every opening hour. '

Art's side-valve phone rang. It was Lance Hart, Three F's Head of Pathology. Art had instructed him to call him the minute Leo Smirnov's post mortem had concluded.

'Lance – you have some news for me?'

'Yes Mister Schitthelm – we have the results of Leo Smirnov's post mortem.'

'What have you found?'

'Well, for sure he didn't die from a heart attack – physically speaking he was in peak condition.'

'So he was killed as we suspected?'

'Oh he was killed alright.'

'How?'

'His lower median axial gland has been compromised.'

Art was lost. 'What's one of those?'

'It controls your heartbeat,' said Lance.

'I see,' said Art, suddenly anxious to know whereabouts of his own axial gland. 'And where would one find one's axle gland?'

'It's situated at the base of the brain.'

'You say it's been compromised – how?'

'A comprehensive insult to the integrity of its life supporting function due to an unmitigated and conclusive single excursion through the lower brain tissue by a foreign object,' replied the pathologist, in a tone a doctor would use to inform his patient of a minor skin infection.

'Layman's terms if you please Mister Hart.'

'Well, to me it's typical of a bullet passing through the skull – but I'm not entirely convinced.'

'Why so?' said Art, intrigued.

'There are no exterior witness marks to the skull – neither any obvious signs of entry and exit wounds. Whatever's gone through this man's head has entered his left earhole and exited his right one – clean as a whistle. The conclusive obliteration of his lower median axial gland meant that his heart stopped beating instantly, so no bleeding. I've read the supporting notes in Mandy Seymour's e-mail. She states there was no blood or brain tissue evident in the vicinity. Even the patrons were oblivious to any signs of danger – an off duty nurse at the scene suspected a heart attack and CPR was administered.'

'Are you ruling-out a shooting?' asked Art. 'Because we've got our satellite hooked-in to se car park camera, and it clearly shows our main suspect Lenny Plant entering and leaving – he definitely wasn't packing.'

'Seymour states there was no gunshot, neither anyone wielding a pistol,' said Lance.

'Perhaps a sniper with a silencer?' suggested Art.

'Impossible; according to Seymour the interior of the pub was too dimly lit, and the bar overcrowded with lots of movement. A professional sniper wouldn't touch it. Anyway, where did the bullet end-up after it exited his head?'

'Good point,' said Art, thoughtful. 'This is most strange indeed.'

Horace was listening-in, 'Chopsticks,' he said.

'Pardon?' said Art.

'Seymour mentioned Plant had a pair of chopsticks on him.'

'Did you hear that Lance?' said Art laughing. 'Sherlock here has it all worked out – Colonel Mustard's innocent because Professor Plant did it in se bar with se chopsticks.'

Lance Hart was silent.

'Horace loves a game of Cluedo,' joked Art, before wondering at the lack of response from the pathologist.

'Are you still there Lance?'

'Yes I'm still here,' replied Lance. 'I think Horace might have something.'

'You're kidding?' said Art.

'A chopstick is sharp enough to penetrate the soft tissue of the inner ear, and long enough to traverse the skull from one ear to the other. The bore of the wound is more or less consistent with the shaft diameter of a chopstick.'

'My word,' said Art astounded. 'You're saying Plant's done him with a chopstick?'

'It is possible. However it would require a remarkable combination of speed, timing, and accuracy – along with an intimate knowledge of the anatomy of the brain. You're asking me if this is how Smirnov was eliminated; I'd say, given all the facts, it's the only logical explanation. Plant obviously knew he'd been targeted; so there we have both the motive and the means.'

'Se motive and se means?' queried Art.

'Yes,' said Hart, 'self-preservation plus a chopstick.'

'It's a wonder no one noticed him do it – I mean se bar was crowded,' said Art, still not totally convinced.

'I'm moved to quote Muhammad Ali when he was accused of flooring Sonny Liston with a phantom punch,' said Lance Hart.

'And what did he say?' asked Art.

'"Everyone blinked at the same time,"' quoted Hart.

Art laughed.

'It's a reactive killing by a highly skilled operative. If it's okay with you Mister Schitthelm, that's what's going on the report.'

Art nodded to himself, satisfied at Lance Hart's conclusion. 'That's fine Lance – good work. Be sure to send me a copy of se report.'

Art returned the mobile to his breast pocket and sighed. 'It's a shame we can't recruit Plant for our hit squad Horace; his spontaneous ability to kill anytime and anywhere with se most basic of weaponry is astonishing – I mean, a chopstick for Christ's sake.'

'Why don't we ask him if he's interested in a job Father? If we offer a decent package he might be tempted.'

'A package?' said Art.

'Yes – you know: a six figure salary, bonuses, car user allowance, private health care scheme and an inflation-proof pension, along with forty days annual leave plus public holidays, oh – and a company mobile.'

'That would be an insult to se sensibilities of a man like Plant; such obscene largesse. You describe se kind of package se government awards a senior civil servant. Only if I had it my way I'd have se mobile packed with C4 plastic, just so it blows his fucking useless civil servant brains out se minute I dial him.' Art smiled fondly at the idea.

'I would love to recruit Plant Horace, but he's far too dangerous – he also knows too much. There's every possibility he could become a liability, and right now Three F can't afford a liability – inflation-proof or not.'

'I'm worried he might show-up at the Dent's house when we go in to swap the freezers,' said Horace.

'There's no "might" about it Horace. Plant won't take kindly to us or se Russians snooping around on his home territory. He will make an appearance for sure – that's why we're bringing Ugo along with us.'

Ugo Dragonetti, son of an Italian trawler man, was sitting up front next to Petro Pushkar. Ugo was six-foot-six and weighed twenty-eight stone – most of it muscle. The giant could smash a man's skull with one punch.

In spite of Ugo's startling physical development, the organ in occupancy of the space between his ears took up remarkably little space.

'We're going in with se two delivery men Horace – me, you, and Ugo. I've no doubt Plant knows both Three F and se Russians are going to make a move anytime, so he also will be eager to make his move. Ugo will take care of Plant se second he shows.'

'What exactly do you mean when you say "Ugo will take care of Plant" Father?'

'Plant will be neutralised Horace,' said Art gravely.

'Don't you mean "eliminated" Father? Isn't that the term we use when we brief a Kill Squad Operative?'

'For any of se usual miscreants, that term would suffice, Horace. But Plant is unique – a total one-off. We need a special kind of solution for him. But don't worry yourself son, Ugo knows exactly what to do because I've already told him exactly what to do.'

As Petro Pushkar lined the Mercedes up on the M60 slip road, Art Schitthelm leaned forward and spoke calmly to him. 'It's time to show us what se five-hundred horses under se bonnet can do Petro. If we don't get to Locburn Village by 19:00 hrs, then we must at least die trying.'

Petro tightened his grip on the steering wheel; with his right foot he unleashed-all five hundred horses.

'I'm scared,' whimpered Horace.

'Scared of what?'

'Lenny Plant – he frightens me more than World War Two.' Horace gave his father a pointed stare. 'Aren't you scared?'

'Not scared Horace; nothing scares me anymore. I'm worried though, worried sick for se welfare of all society. At any cost se freezer must be in Three F's possession this evening. For it to fall into se hands of se Russians is unthinkable. Without doubt se next few hours will be se most crucial in se entire history of humankind.'

§

Such a coincidence then, that Three F, like the Russians, should plan to seize the freezer at 19:00 hrs on the same day.

Lenny Plant also, had just decided that 19:00 hrs would be the most opportune time for him to smash the freezer to pieces.

A perfect storm was brewing in the village of Locburn. It would be the ultimate storm – save for one minor, but major oversight.

CHAPTER 21

CHERRY AND CHERUB

Lenny Plant watched One Man and His Dog. He was on the cusp of dozing-off but couldn't quite disengage his brain sufficiently for sleep. He felt like he was in a cinema with several different movies running simultaneously. Whenever he attempted to make sense of one situation, another fathomless set of affairs barged in to take its place. It didn't help that he was coming down off the alcohol; it had rendered him more morose than he could remember.

He'd already made the decision to be at Ronnie's house for seven o'clock – along with a sledgehammer concealed in an old sack. If he set-off at around six and took the back alley that led from Church Lane past the rear of the church to the pub car park, he could hide the sack behind the wall that skirted the east end of the churchyard. This would allow time for the sinking a couple of courage bolstering pints in the pub before making his way over to Ronnie's – remembering of course, to retrieve the sledgehammer as he went.

The least conspicuous way of approaching the house would be through the bottom end of the churchyard that bordered Ronnie's back-garden. Lenny knew both Ronnie and Edith would be out of the house well before seven, and that gaining access wouldn't be a problem – Edith always kept a spare key under an old plant pot by the front door.

Lenny estimated that half-a-dozen hefty blows with the sledge should suffice to reduce the freezer to scrapyard status. By his own reckoning he could be in and out of the house in less than three minutes.

Apart from his deep-freezer worries, there were other hefty concerns endlessly recycling in his mind. Lenny thought about his own future – presuming he had one. If he could destroy Ronnie's domestic appliance and get away with it, surely everything would return to normal. But what existed beyond normal? Having just listened to Art Schitthelm talking about the pocket sphinculator, Lenny pondered the ultimate destiny for his own gastric health. If he did become incontinent would he be faced with the unenviable decision of having to choose between nappies or a pocket sphinculator – or perhaps decline both options in favour of random pant shitting?

Lenny thought about his grandmother's final days, fading away in the Eventide Care Home for the elderly. Was he also cursed to end his days in some old folks' home, staring at a wall and marinating in his own excrement? Then there was the inescapable stench that hung in every part of such resorts: a vile medley of boiled cabbage, old age, piss and shit. With his highly developed sense of smell Lenny feared he would be unable to accustom himself to the odour.

And when he did die, would he go to Heaven, or Hell – or would he languish for half an eternity in purgatory? Thinking back to the previous evening Lenny wished he'd had more time to ask Edith's angel what it was like in Heaven. Like most people he had his own preconception of what it was like up there. He'd been told as a child that heaven was a place of unending paradise, inhabited by harp-strumming humans with wings attached to their backs; decked-out in white robes, and fluttering, carefree, from one fluffy white cloud to another fluffy white cloud.

Now, as an adult, Lenny was struggling to comprehend a state of unrelenting bliss. How could one be happy all the time? If you were eternally happy you would have no consciousness of what it's like to suffer a condition of misery. There has to be a reference point for every state of mind; a counterbalancing mood to validate another's existence. Happiness and misery; surely each must possess the capacity to prevail with equal authority.

Lenny's eyes were beginning to close. Fed-up with One Man and His Dog he picked up the remote and selected a random channel.

The Mary Cherry Sunday Cook-Up had just started. Lenny decided to give it a go. The show this week was due to feature Jon Wallace and Greg Torode as special guests. Unfortunately the pair of them had to cancel at short notice. Jon had bitten his top lip off two days previous in an eating accident; and Greg was in Harley Street having his teeth re-sharpened after they'd under-performed at a televised Steak and Chips Festival.

Mary stood in her capacious country kitchen, surrounded by acres of work surfaces, along with quarter of a million pounds' worth of meal making equipment. There were mixers, mincers, blenders, and whiskers; tenderisers, rollers, skewers, blow torches, and liquid nitrogen; split-level grills, ovens, and fridges; spice racks, hanging ladles and spatulas; pots, pans, bowls, and enough knifes and daggers to furnish half the vermin of Hackney.

Mary was a dab hand with the blade – dexterous, swift, and precise; the ingredients didn't stand a chance. With the knife clenched in her gnarled fingers she could slice, dice, chop, disembowel, fillet, carve, and skin – all the while smiling and talking to the camera.

She was eighty-one these days; blue-eyed, sprightly and alert. The make-up department had done her up a treat. Mary boasted a visage layered with several coats of foundation, dabbed with rouge, and topped-off with a thorough powder-dusting. Complemented in red lipstick, mascara, and eye-liner, her face resembled a half-eaten wedding cake.

Mary smiled at the camera and struck-up. 'Good afternoon to all you lovely people, and welcome to my country kitchen for this week's Sunday Cook Up.'

Mary leaned forward slightly, widened her eyes, and spoke in a half whisper using a tone that would have you think she was letting you in on a cheeky secret.

'Do you know I've lost count of the number of times I'm asked by people of a certain age if there's a special recipe for those of us fretting over surviving the stomach churning odours of the care home? Well I'm pleased to say I've come-up with something that's cheap and easy to cook, and that requires only the most basic of ingredients.'

The camera drew-back to reveal the work surface in front of Mary.

To her right there was a large cabbage and a chopping knife. To her left; six tins of supermarket 'own brand' lager, a packet of rat poison, and a decent sized saucepan.

'Today's offering is a highly aromatic dish called Merde de Choux. It should take you around twenty minutes to prepare – however, with a long simmer to cook. Hopefully the aroma will infuse your house and help you become accustomed to the inescapable God-awful stench that awaits you in the care home.'

Mary introduced the ingredients: 'So, we're going to need one large cabbage, finely chopped, a bladder filled with six tins of discount lager, a stomach bursting with fully digested food, and a family pack of rat poison.'

Mary reached for the cabbage. 'Okay, so take the cabbage and gently peel off the outer leaves. Discard these unless you want to use them as a garnish.'

Setting-to with the knife she had the cabbage reduced to a pile of shreds in seconds.

'You need to empty the entire contents of your stomach into the saucepan – then carefully drizzle a bladder full of urine into the pan so that the excrement is completely covered.'

Mary put the knife down and lifted the saucepan. Smiling proudly, she tilted it towards the camera for the benefit of the viewer. 'Here's one I did earlier.'

Placing the saucepan in front of her she scooped up the cabbage and dumped it into the mix.

'Next, cover the pan and bring to the boil on a medium heat. Once you've got it boiling, reduce heat, and leave to gently simmer.'

Cutting to the next scene, Mary informs us that the ingredients have settled to a simmer. She lifts the lid from the pan and tantalises the viewers by stooping for a lengthy sniff at the steamy vapours that billow into her face.

'Ooh,' she coos through the mist, 'that absolutely stinks to fuck.'

Mary replaces the lid and smiles at the camera. Lenny notices the hot steam has caused the make-up to melt down her face.

'So – there you have it; my Merde de Choux. Left to simmer one pan should be more than enough to scent an average three bed semi-detached for around two days. If, after this time, you feel there's no way you're going to get used to the honk, swallow the entire packet of rat poison.'

Lenny shook his head disgusted. He picked up the remote and selected another channel. The World Above Us with David Attenborough had not long started.

Lenny had great respect for David Attenborough – "The most virtuous man on the planet," he would often declare. Of any human being Lenny knew, only David Attenborough could be trusted to tell you things the way they really were. Lenny believed his every utterance:

The sky behind David was a perfect sky-blue. He stood before the camera on the whitest cloud Lenny had ever seen. Attenborough began in his wonderful, mellifluous, unhurried style:

'This week The World Above Us comes from the outskirts of Heaven, where we arrive to find the unfolding of an ecological disaster. As we know the paradise of heaven is famed for the whiteness and fluffiness of its clouds; but it's these very clouds that are under threat of permanent damage due to acidic erosion. If nothing is done to check the rate of cloud erosion, the number of clouds affected by this problem looks set to double over the next decade.'

As he spoke, an angel with a harp swooped over his head. Attenborough, slightly startled, ducked, gave a jolly chuckle, and continued.

'To even begin to change things here we need to create a responsible attitude towards the environment; because, as things stand, attitudes don't exist in heaven. For an angel to have an attitude would be anathema to the concept of paradise.'

The camera panned to an angel that had just alighted on the next cloud. As it strummed its harp Attenborough took advantage to describe the species and its habitat.

'Although angels may vary in age – from juvenile cherubs to mature adults; all angels enter heaven as a cherub. Once here they age until they reach thirty-two years – the same age as Jesus when, in a bid to substantiate his narcissism, he got himself nailed to a couple of planks of six-by-four.

'There is only one species of angel; to have a superior, or inferior breed, would degrade the high principle of equality in paradise. The temperature in heaven is permanently ambient, so there's no heat or cold to trouble the senses. There is no wind up here, and save for the strumming of harps, everything is quiet and peaceful. The sun shines every day in heaven, and the sky is always intensely blue. The weather in heaven is always the same – always very nice.'

Attenborough pointed to the angel perched on the neighbouring cloud.

'You'll notice that the angel's face bears an expression neither happy nor sad. The expression you do see is one that sits exactly half-way between happy and sad – it's a sort of – well, a nice expression.

'The criterion for entry into heaven is strict. The inhabitants here need to have led a previous life of absolute virtue and moral cleanliness. They're all extremely nice people who've never put a foot wrong; and here in heaven they've got their reward – it's simply a nice place to be.'

Attenborough turned to the camera – he looked genuinely concerned.

'The food here in heaven is nice and uncomplicated: apples, grapes and bananas. The angel feeds on the fruit at a steady pace; so that it neither feels hungry nor full – just nicely contented.

'Sadly, it's the diet of the angel that's at the root cause of the environmental issue here in heaven. You see, the fruit is high in acid content, and the basic digestive tract of the angel has difficulty in processing it. Once an angel has digested its food, it deposits its acidic droppings onto any convenient cloud. Over time the cloud erodes and gradually loses its fluffiness. Once a cloud becomes un-fluffy it makes it difficult to perch on as its surface is now extremely slippery.

'To get a better understanding of the problem we have to look more closely at the anatomy of an angel's bowels. Not only does an angel have the wings of a bird, it also shares the same avian digestive system. When God created the angel he wanted it equipped with intestines that would provide the most graceful way of disposing of faeces and urine. To have angels evacuating their bowels by unceremoniously hoisting their gowns and squatting on a cloud, would be detrimental to the image of paradise. Then, there was the ever present temptation for angels to wipe their backsides with their robes – or even worse, rub the crease of their buttocks along the white, soft fluffiness of a cloud. How un-heavenly for clouds to be streaked with such unsightly marking.

'Disposing of urine was equally concerning for God. Urine splattered on a snow-white cloud, would look much the same as piss-holes in snow-white snow. And through what kind of aperture would the angel relieve itself? God had desired that all angels be of universal gender, and so would have identical equipage for expunging bodily waste.'

Lenny Plant was puzzled at what David Attenborough was saying. He'd seen Edith's vagina and it looked just like a vagina – and her bum looked just like a bum. What Lenny didn't realise was that Edith had not fully morphed into a cherub due to the fact that there was still cellular activity in her mortal body. In any case, Lenny saw what his mind wanted to see. And he imagined what he saw, to be what he thought it would, or should, or ought to be. Attenborough continued:

'After studying the many different digestive tracts of various earthly animals, God opted to fit the angel with the stomach-to-anus digestive system of a Rhode Island Red chicken. He'd observed the animal disposing of its waste and noted how the one orifice served for the expulsion of both urine and faeces in a single, swift squirt. And the discharge itself: a milky white compound that would blend in with the clouds. Another appealing characteristic was that the chicken didn't indulge in any of the usual animal theatrics during excretion – no squatting, no cocking of the leg, no lifting of a tail. The casual manner with which the creature rids itself is so sublime that the bird continues with its day-to-day business, oblivious to the motion – even the chicken's nonchalant strut is unfaltering at the instant of evacuation. Neither is there any change to the expression on its face. How un-heavenly would it be to behold an angel's heaving grimace when straining out an awkward stool: the bulging eyes, the sweat-beaded forehead, flushing deep red, and centre-lined with a throbbing blue vein?'

The camera shifts to a nearby cloud that's been substantially eroded by the acidic droppings. It pulls focus on a cherub trying to scale the side of the cloud.

'Here we witness the distressing site of a cherub attempting to climb the face of a heavily eroded cloud. The young angel desperately flutters its underdeveloped wings as it scrambles up the slippery slope. Just as it reaches the top, the cherub loses its grip and slides back down to the bottom of the cloud. Once again it commences to crawl up the side of the cloud. As it flaps its wings and claws its fingers into the cloud, you can't help but notice the look of hopeless anguish on its innocent little face. To make things worse, the surface of the slope is being further eroded due the cherub depositing its own droppings.'

The camera draws back so that we see Attenborough standing between the two clouds.

'The mature angel perched on the neighbouring cloud surveys the cherub with the usual contented expression. It strums its harp and is completely oblivious to the cherub's relentless struggle. On entering paradise, the capacity to recognise desperation and futility is completely neutered. As the cherub struggles to ascend the cloud it becomes apparent to the mortal onlooker that there will be no conclusion to its plight. Heaven is for eternity; which means this particular cherub is destined forever to never reach the top of the cloud.'

Lenny Plant watched horrified. He prayed quietly that God would send him straight to hell. He wondered what ultimate fate awaited David Attenborough – thoroughly good and decent man that he is. Surely he was destined for a one-way ticket to paradise – God forbid.

The World Above Us portrayed a disturbing image of heaven. Attenborough, a man incapable of misrepresentation, had revealed the place for what it was, is, and always shall be: an eternal, vacuous shithole, abundant with emotional and sensory deprivation.

§

Lenny felt Sarah shaking his shoulder. 'Lenny, wake-up, it's half-five – I'm off to my hod-carrying class.'

Slowly surfacing from his shit-themed nightmares, he sighed with relief once it dawned on him he was still on planet Earth. The credits for One Man and His Dog scrolled up the screen.

Lenny set about clearing his head, to the backdrop of his wife issuing a blizzard of domestic instructions: 'When you clear off to the pub don't leave the telly on stand-by – and you need to put the bin out for the bin men. Make sure you empty the pedal-bin too, oh – and take your key with you in case I pop over to Linda's afterwards. If Enid Taylor rings before you leave make an effort to answer the phone – tell her I'll be round tomorrow with the spring and summer fabric samples. Your breath stinks and I've left the hot-pot recipe for Dianne next to the toaster – make sure you take it with you. Try not to get drunk, you've got work tomorrow.'

Sarah pecked her husband on the cheek and left for the P.I.S.S. Academy. Lenny checked his breath by exhaling into a cupped hand to sniff the trapped fumes. He reckoned the smell to be in the same league as Mary Cherry's Merde de Choux.

Lenny brushed his teeth and took a shower in a bid to liven his senses prior to dulling them once more, courtesy of 2,272 millilitres of pystwiser.

CHAPTER 22

BACK TO THE BOOZER

Lenny Plant was nervous. He checked around for anybody who might be about then dropped the sack, containing the sledgehammer, over the low wall at the rear of the graveyard. The church bell had just sounded six, so he had exactly one hour to sink a few pints, make his excuses, and head over to Ronnie's house. He took a deep breath and headed for the Haydale.

Six o'clock was also the time Animal Androvski, the bald headed bear boxer from Bulgaria, was due to be level transferred into Ronnie Dent's freezer. His instructions, issued personally by Traktor Popov, were uncomplicated: "Find Plant. The moment you see him, kill him."

§

'I still say it was all part of the show – Dimblewit's pulled one of his stunts just to get the viewing figures up,' said Dickhead Douglas.

'Looked pretty convincing to me,' said Mervin Daley, polishing a beer glass and holding it up to the light for scrutiny. 'Delia Stark showed me it this afternoon – she's got one of those I-Pad things. I reckon someone's come back to settle an old score and stuck him with a syringe; probably loaded with some poison or other – serves him right.'

The Haydale Arms was almost empty and that was normal for this time on a Sunday. The lunchtime diners had long left for home and the general knowledge quiz wouldn't be starting till eight-thirty. Mervin welcomed the lull; it gave him a chance to unwind and have some chit-chat with his regulars.

Dickhead took a swig from his freshly poured pint and wiped the froth from his mouth. 'I don't understand why the BBC haven't announced anything if that's the case – why all the silence? I mean, see how quickly they shut the show off. And then sticking One Man and His Dog on – it was like they panicked or something.'

'I don't know Dickhead,' said Mervin wisely. 'One thing for sure, we'll find out if he doesn't turn up for next month's show.'

'Suppose so,' resigned Dickhead. 'He's finished anyway. Schitthelm's destroyed him and the show – a bloody good job done.'

Lenny Plant walked in. On his way over to the pub he'd come up with what he thought was a brilliant plan to conceal the weight of responsibility he was shouldering: best to behave normal – just like he did every Sunday evening at the pub: phlegmatic, affable, and oozing with natural conviviality. It was essential that nothing about his manner betray his intention to save the world by carrying out a vicious act of criminal damage on a best friend's domestic appliance.

As he approached the bar Lenny noticed Mervin surveying him over the top of his specs. Mervin often looked at people in this manner – Lenny included. It was just that this particular evening, with his head wired-up like a Burmese telephone exchange, Lenny picked-up on it and got the wrong message. He also felt he was being studied by Dickhead Douglas, who coincidentally, had his gaze locked on to him whilst taking a casual draw on his pint. With two of his best friends eyeing him; one over the rims of his glasses – the other over the rim of his glass, Lenny felt paranoiacally ill-at ease.

'What's wrong – how come you're both staring at me?'

Mervin and Dickhead continued with their innocent scrutiny. With no immediate response in terms of facial expression or dialogue, Lenny's irrational suspicion deepened.

Ronnie Dent appeared in the doorway. As he looked across the room and saw Lenny he had a flash-back to Friday night/Saturday morning. Ronnie became momentarily confused as he struggled to convince himself that a resurfaced nightmare was nothing more than a resurfaced nightmare. Whilst burying the recollection in the depths of his skull he stared at Lenny.

Lenny's eyes darted from Ronnie, to Dickhead, to Mervin, and back to Ronnie. 'What's wrong?' repeated Lenny – emphatically this time.

Mervin, Dickhead and Ronnie swapped glances.

'Eh?' said Dickhead, his genuine naivety gone undetected by Lenny.

'You're all staring at me.'

Mervin had noticed the previous evening that Lenny was behaving out of character. It concerned him because Lenny Plant consistently behaved in character. At lunchtime too, the landlord had detected that Lenny was somewhat off his beat.

It hadn't escaped Mervin's attention that Ronnie Dent had also been acting strangely of late – although with him it was less easy to distinguish whether the behavioural and emotional discrepancy was influenced by drink or reality –Ronnie being a permanent resident on the sliding scale of inebriation.

Like any seasoned landlord Mervin knew his regulars well; from sobriety to drunkenness, he was familiar with the commensurate changes in mood and manner. He wondered if it was more than just coincidence that both Lenny and Ronnie's change in behaviour had occurred at the same time.

'You alright Lenny?'

Lenny went on the defensive. 'I'm alright – why shouldn't I be?'

'I'm not sure,' said Mervin, upping the suspicion in his tone. He nodded at Ronnie. 'It's just this last day or so you and him been acting strangely.'

'There's nowt wrong with me,' protested Ronnie.

'Nor me,' enjoined Lenny.

'You think so?' challenged Mervin.

'It's you Merv,' said Lenny. 'You're picking-up on stuff that isn't there – delusional – even paranoid. Now can I have a pint of pystwiser please – and one for Ronnie?'

Mervin decided it was time to have his say. As he pulled the pints he addressed Ronnie first: 'You came charging in here last night wearing your wife's coat, with one of your stupid pink ribbons dangling from your snotter. You start crapping-on about how you've met Spiderman – in a wheelie-bin of all places. Everyone makes a fuss over you and you lap-up the attention – along with any drink you can lay your hands on. This lunchtime you're boozing merrily away and not one mention of Spiderman?

'Then there's you Lenny: Friday night you were fine when you came in here – no different to normal. But last night you handed your drink to Spiderman's mate here then spent half-an-hour having a conversation with an empty chair. I could half understand if you were pissed; but you didn't have a single drink past your lips – and that really worries me. You've been coming in here for as long as I can remember; never seen you leave without a drink in you.'

'Yeah, but Merv –,' interrupted Ronnie.

'Quiet while I finish,' said Mervin firmly.

'I saw how the pair of you reacted this lunchtime when that poor fellow collapsed. Neither of you showed any emotion. Everyone else was genuinely concerned – even Dickhead, insensitive as he is, but not you two – it was like you were removed from it all. If I had to guess I'd say you've both been up to something.'

Lenny started to blush.

'You're blushing Lenny,' said Mervin. 'Are you going to tell me what's going on?'

Lenny could feel his face heating up. His palms began to sweat.

'It's too bloody hot in here Merv,' moaned Lenny, 'that's what it is – too bloody hot.'

Mervin placed Lenny's pint on the bar. Lenny took hold and drained it without coming up for breath. Ronnie watched approvingly and did the same.

'Pystwisers all round Merv,' said Ronnie before a hearty burp. 'And get one for yourself.'

'I'll have a drop of red if you don't mind Ronnie – very decent of you,' said Mervin.

Ronnie took a long slurp of his second pint the instant it was handed to him. He stood the glass on the bar and spoke with unhurried sincerity.

'I think I know what it is.'

'What "what" is?' asked Mervin.

'What's causing all this funny business – that's "what".'

Lenny became increasingly agitated as he wondered at Ronnie's next utterance.

Mervin humoured Ronnie. 'So what, exactly, do you think it is?'

Ronnie reached for his glass and took another lazy swig. He levelled his gaze at Mervin.

'Pystwiser's what it is.'

'Pystwiser?' queried Mervin.

'Yep,' said Ronnie affirmatively. 'Everything was fine before you got that stuff in Merv. Now half the village is drinking it and suddenly there's a whole load of weird shit going on.' Ronnie gulped-back another mouth-full. 'Weird shit Merv – no doubt about it.'

Ronnie licked the cider from his lips, savouring the "delicately structured apple-zing aftertaste." 'Oh – and just for the record – I'm still half convinced about Spiderman – and how come I can't work out why Edith's looking thirty years younger.'

Mervin was somewhat taken aback; he was keen to defend his cider. 'For your information that's been one of Germany's premium ciders for over seventy years.' He pointed to the faux coat of arms mounted on the front of the hand pump. 'See – look at the date: nineteen-thirty-eight, that's when the brewery was established.'

Dickhead commented, 'Hang-on a minute Merv. You're telling us that back in nineteen-thirty- eight the Krauts were knocking this pystwiser stuff back?'

'Well obviously Dickhead – why go to all the trouble of brewing it if you're not going to drink it?' Mervin paused and looked quizzically at Dickhead. 'Why – what are you trying to say?'

'Look what happened a year afterwards – they go and start a war on the rest of the World.'

'Don't be daft Dickhead.' said Mervin, curtly. 'You can't blame pystwiser for World War Two.'

A combination of bizarre circumstance and half confusion tempted Lenny to side with Ronnie and Dickhead. He decided, conveniently, to blame everything on the pystwiser.

'I think Dickhead and Ronnie are onto something here Merv.'

'Come-on lads,' said Mervin, eager to change the subject, 'don't you think you're getting a little hysterical?'

'No way,' said Lenny. 'What about all that business at the P.I.S.S. Academy this morning? The village neighbourhood, punching, kicking, and biting each other; I've never seen anything like it: grown-up people squabbling and fighting over rook shit. I know most of them – ordinarily they're peaceable folk, able to sort their differences out in a civilised manner. But lately they've turned vicious,' Lenny paused for effect, '– and there's only one common denominator I can come up with.' There was another brief silence before Lenny concluded his observation. 'Just about all of them have consumed pystwiser at some time or other over the past week or so.'

Mervin went to speak. Ronnie spoke first.

'What about Terry Driscoll?' he announced – eager to promote the speculation.

'What about him?' Mervin asked.

'He was in here last Sunday night drinking the stuff. He goes home and pisses in the kid's tropical fish tank.'

'What the hell did he do that for?' said Mervin.

'You tell me,' challenged Ronnie.

'How come you know he did that?' asked Dickhead.

'Did what?' said Ronnie.

'Piss in the fish tank,' reminded Dickhead.

'Oh – right,' said Ronnie, straining to maintain the dialogue and at the same time commencing a familiar descent into oblivion.

'Young Tom got out of his bed when he heard a commotion downstairs. He came down and caught his dad in the act. Belinda told Edith about it Monday night – then Edith told me.'

Terry Driscoll had staggered home the previous Sunday – he'd downed seven pints of pystwiser. His bladder, more usually accustomed to accommodating half-a-dozen gin and tonics, was new to the pystwiser experience. On reaching his back door Terry found himself in agony. The cider had stretched his bladder to the size of a Pygmy's head.

After wasting a crippling thirty seconds fumbling with his key to unlock the door, Terry had no time to reach the bathroom upstairs. Realising the house had retired, and neglecting, in his drunkenness, to consider the kitchen sink, he staggered across the living room to the aquarium.

Though his way was lit by its soft glow, he collided with various pieces of furniture on his drunken approach. Terry's younger son Tom had heard the commotion from his bed. He ventured downstairs in time to witness his father shaking the remnant amber droplets from the end of his pecker. Terry hastily zipped himself up and offered Tom a fiver to keep his mouth shut. Tom demanded a tenner and the deal was done.

Next morning however, young Tom descended the stairs to be greeted by the sight of his angel fish – and his guppies, floating belly-up on the yellow-tinted waters. The child fled back up the stairs in tears to tell his mother. Tom got a thick ear for taking the bribe – his father received an athletic kick in the whereabouts of the scrotum.

'Hey Dickhead,' said Lenny, brightening slightly. 'Tell Merv what Harry Nesbit did on Tuesday night.'

Dickhead Douglas, halfway through a draw on his pint, swallowed it back in a blink. Boasting an expression straining with excitement, he couldn't wait tell his tale.

'Well you know he was in here till closing time Merv?'

Mervin nodded.

'And he was full-on at the pystwiser?'

Mervin nodded again.

'So he goes home and accidentally buggers Audrey.'

Mervin's mouth opened. Dumbfounded he struggled with a response. Ronnie filled the verbal down-time.

'He buggered Audrey?'

'Yes,' beamed Dickhead, joyous of his knowledge.

Ronnie creased his brow and scratched at his chin. He was trying figure-out what his mind's eye was revealing to him.

'What – annually?'

Dickhead was puzzled for a moment. 'Err – I think it was the first time this year Ronnie – or any other year come to think of it.'

'He means anally,' corrected Lenny.

'Well how do you think he buggered her?' said Mervin, his indignation swelling by the second.

Ronnie was still trying to process the information. 'How do you accidentally bugger someone?'

'I asked Harry the very same question when he confided in me,' blurted Dickhead. 'He reckoned the pystwiser affected his aim – but he's also concerned that there was a latent intention on his behalf to actually do it.'

'Poor Audrey,' said Ronnie, genuinely half concerned. 'How did she take it?'

'Up her arse,' said Dickhead, before an eruption of raucous laughter.

Mervin shook his head disapprovingly. With a sigh of resignation he threw his arms in the air and turned to stare at the till. As Dickhead Douglas hollered his laughter about the bar, a seed of doubt was sown in the landlord's mind.

Perhaps the lads were right? Maybe the pystwiser was to blame for everything?

CHAPTER 23

SLEDGEHAMMER

Lenny Plant left the pub; it was ten-to-seven. He took the back alley down to the path that skirted the graveyard. Halfway along the path a gap in the laurel bush brought the entrance to the P.I.S.S. Academy into view. Lenny quickened his pace when he noticed several Three F police officers entering the academy in a hurry. Further down the path he retrieved his sledgehammer from behind the wall.

Mandy Seymour had spotted Lenny leaving the Haydale Arms. She immediately contacted Art Schitthelm to report that Lenny Plant was on the move and heading in the direction of the Academy.

Schitthelm was closing in on Locburn Village. He estimated his time of arrival to be shortly after seven. He told Seymour to keep the Haydale under surveillance in case Ronnie Dent should decide to leave the pub early and head for home.

Immediately afterwards Art contacted his police who were waiting close by. He instructed them to intercept Plant should he show up at the Academy. If it turned out Plant was actually heading for Ronnie's house, then Art could have Ugo Dragonetti deal with him.

The Three F snatch-team had parked their van in a disused farm track at the head of Back Lane. On receiving Art's prompt it would take them less than three minutes to arrive at Ronnie's house to make the swap.

The Russian snatch-team waited for their signal. Decked-out as white goods delivery men, they'd parked their van in a disused warehouse two miles outside of Richmond. Once they received the go-ahead they could reach Locburn inside of five minutes.

Their latest briefing had been given earlier that afternoon via a coded satellite cell-phone transmission: Bear basher Animal

Androvski would be level transferred to the freezer at 18.00 hrs. He would take care of the main threat to the Russian operation by killing Lenny Plant prior to the swap deadline of 19.00 hrs.

If the Russians did happen to encounter any Three F personnel, they were suitably prepared: each packed a 9mm pistol, half a dozen stun grenades, a cage full of hybrid spiders, and a pocket-sized flame-thrower – rated with an intermittent two-second "spit-range" of twenty metres.

At precisely 18.55hrs they would receive the signal to head for Locburn Village. Immediately on arrival they would gemmy the rear garage door and promptly remove the freezer. In the back of the van was an exact replica of the original freezer. Just like Three F, the Russians planned to exchange freezers and leave the Dents none-the-wiser. Once they'd secured the freezer the team would head for Teesside Airport. There the appliance would be transferred onto a cargo plane bound for Moscow.

§

Like a youngster, newly learned in the pedestrian discipline of road crossing, Lenny made several cautious glances up and down the pathway. Satisfied he'd come thus far unnoticed, he breached the thinnest part of the unkempt hedge at the bottom of Ronnie's garden.

With four pints of pystwiser inside him, Lenny felt he was well up to the job of destroying the freezer. He stalked his way to the front door, casting furtive glances in every direction as he went. Stooping to fumble under the plant pot for the key, he heard the church bell chime. Momentarily unsure of the time-line on a shaky schedule, Lenny paused to count off the seven chimes.

At the toll of the first chime an eternity of embarrassment was born for the Russians – for they could not hear the bell. And if they could not hear the bell, they could not possibly count its chimes.

Turning the key as gently as he could, Lenny eased the door open. Once the hinges had ceased their mutinous creaking, he loitered on the threshold to detect for any presence within.

Over the years Lenny had become intimately familiar with the aura that dwelt in the Dent household – however, of the countless times he'd been in the place, he'd never visited the residence when it was unoccupied. He breathed in deep through his nostrils and listened hard for anything that didn't belong. Everything smelt and sounded as it should be – the faithful drip of a kitchen tap was all that greeted the ears.

Pulling the door shut behind him, Lenny slipped into the hallway. He could see Edith's bike was missing from under the stairs, so she was definitely out and about. Even though he was satisfied the house was empty, Lenny exercised a measure of caution by calling-out with modest volume, 'anyone in?' No one answered.

Petro Pushkar parked the Mercedes at the top of Church Lane outside an unoccupied property that was up for sale. Art, Horace, and Ugo Dragonetti alighted from the car. Art instructed Petro to leave the engine running, in preparation for a speedy departure.

The Three F snatch team pulled-up outside Ronnie's house. They reversed their van into the driveway as far as the overgrowth would allow. Lenny was now in the back kitchen, ready to open the door that led into the garage. He failed to hear the arrival of the two vehicles.

A neighbour who lived further down Church Lane noticed the van pass by the front of their house. Parcel delivery vans, being ubiquitous in all areas of the country, were not an uncommon sight in the village. The neighbour paid it little attention.

Lenny stepped into the garage and pulled the door shut. The freezer stood before him. Although he felt strangely intimidated by its presence, he was at the same time relieved – relieved that he'd finally reached the moment he'd been dreading for the last twenty-four hours. Tightening his grip on the hickory shaft, Lenny lingered a moment to work out which way he'd go about delivering the initial blow. He decided the first and most energetic blow should be delivered plumb centre to the top of the freezer.

Lenny Plant hoisted the sledge over his right shoulder in readiness to commence the swing. His left hand gripped the base of the shaft while his right took hold close to the head of the hammer.

Once he let loose with the swing, his right hand would slide down the shaft to end up next to his left. Lenny focused on the centre of the freezer lid. With his feet shoulder width apart, he closed his eyes and winced against the anticipated clout of solid iron against domestic appliance.

Lenny swung the sledge. Halfway through the arc of the swing; a point where the shaft was roughly perpendicular to the horizontal, Art Schitthelm opened the garage door behind Lenny. Lenny was too focused to hear the door open. The hammerhead gathered momentum as it continued on the latter half of its journey.

Lenny waited for the deafening crash of the sledge making contact with the freezer lid. No such noise was forthcoming – neither would it be. With his eyes still clamped shut, Lenny assumed he'd missed his target. The only sound on culmination of his swing: a dull crack.

It would be his first and only attempt.

Art Schitthelm had stepped into the garage as Lenny swung the sledge. At the start of the swing the freezer lid opened. Animal Androvski stuck his head out for a look around. As he did so the hammer crashed into his skull. Androvski slouched back into the freezer, totally dead.

If things had turned out differently, Animal Androvski would still be alive, and Lenny Plant would now be dead. But things did not turn out differently. By a most coincidental and careless oversight, things turned out the way they did.

The Russians had become overly distracted – and obsessed, with their plan to secure the freezer. In the midst of a quest so hastily cobbled together, both Maxim Yankov, and Operations Director Victor Pavlov, had neglected to observe that on the cusp of Saturday night/Sunday morning, the clocks went forward one hour. In the nanosecond that sits between a tic and a toc, Greenwich Mean Time became British Summer Time.

Through their mutual oversight, the whole operation was now running precisely one hour behind schedule.

Maxim had level transferred Androvski to the freezer at what he thought was 18.00hrs local time. The local time was, in fact, 19.00

hrs – the approximate time Lenny Plant and Three F converged at the destination.

'Keeping busy Mister Plant?' Art Schitthelm's tone was casual.

Lenny opened his eyes as the freezer lid closed. He was unaware that he'd just smashed someone's skull to pieces. On hearing a strangely familiar voice behind him, he turned to see Art Schitthelm standing in the doorway.

People react in various ways when they're surprised: a sober, carefree individual will react in an entirely different way to a stressed-out individual who's half-pissed – but fully pissed-off.

Schitthelm expected Lenny to be suitably startled on being so abruptly disturbed. However he'd sneaked-up on a person who was numbed with alcohol, fatigued with worry, and more or less fucked-off with everything.

As Buddhist monks meditate intensely to reach an ultimate state of consciousness known as Nirvana; Lenny had drunk and fretted himself onto a lofty plateau of indifference. Simply put, he was now immune to any form of shock or surprise.

Schitthelm nodded at the freezer. 'Nice work Mister Plant,' he said, making a sincere reference to the way Lenny had disposed of the Russian.

'I've just seen you on the telly,' said Lenny, matter-of-fact.

Schitthelm was impressed with Lenny's phlegmatic demeanour. The Head of Three F was more used to his presence overpowering and intimidating people when he showed up in such circumstances. But this was Lenny Plant, a man who could kill with anything, from a chopstick to a sledgehammer.

Lenny managed to summon up a little curiosity. 'What happened to Dimblewit?'

'Search me Mister Plant,' said Schitthelm, shrugging his shoulders. 'But if I had to guess, I'd say se Russians got to him – he's upset plenty of people along se way; no doubt he's pissed them off too.'

Lenny wasn't interested in pleasantries; he pointed at the freezer. 'This has to go – it has to be destroyed.'

'You obviously know about its potential to create havoc – I'm impressed Mister Plant. All along I was thinking you were just using it for cold storage. Would you mind if I enquired as to the source of your intelligence?'

Art knew fine well he was chancing his arm with such a question. It was an unwritten law that you neither revealed the source of your information, nor asked another agency to disclose theirs. Lenny was unaware of such etiquette; he answered Schitthelm's question honestly and without hesitation.

'I met an angel in the pub last night; she was wearing no knickers. It was the angel who revealed everything and told me about the freezer.'

Schitthelm threw his head back and belly-laughed with authentic joviality.

'Mister Plant, you are so funny. You say an angel revealed everything to you – is that how come you knew she didn't have here knickers with her?'

Lenny didn't crack a smile. He answered in sober tone. 'She may well have had them with her; but she definitely wasn't wearing them.'

Art, still chuckling, turned to Horace who'd just followed him into the garage along with Ugo Dragonetti. 'Have you heard this Horace, an angel in se pub, with no knickers?' Art wiped a tear of laughter from his eye. 'Se pussy of an angel Mister Plant – it must have been a wonderful sight?'

'Angelic,' said Lenny, imagining what his imagination had imagined.

'What an imagination. Tell me Mister Plant; did se angel tell you anything else about se freezer?'

'Yes she did as a matter of fact – she told me that there are two of these freezers left in existence: this one here, and another somewhere in Norfolk.'

Art's face straightened-out in an instant. Up until now he believed that this freezer was the only such freezer left in the entire world. He was shocked to hear of another one lurking somewhere in Norfolk.

'Another freezer you say?' Art frowned with concern as he thought about the increasing gravity of the situation. 'Hmm – this angel of yours – did she happen to tell you of its exact whereabouts in Norfolk?'

'That's as much as she knew,' said Lenny. He quoted the angel's words from memory: "It's somewhere in Norfolk and it's in brand new condition."

At a hundred-and-fifteen years of age Art Schitthelm could smell bullshit the same way a dehydrated buffalo snorts a distant waterhole. Here in the confines of Ronnie Dent's garage there was no such odour. The war veteran's unfaltering sixth sense had Lenny Plant down as a real-deal kind of person. Yes, it was obvious he was trying to protect his source of intelligence with the angel nonsense; but he didn't doubt Plant's information was reliable enough for Three F to act on.

Art had to think and act quickly – for there was never so much to do, for so many, in so few minutes, by so many members of a comparatively large organisation. He was thinking and talking inside his head like Churchill or Mountbatten; but these guys were only good for talking the walk; when it came to walking the talk, they ran and hid behind themselves.

Art was acutely aware that if the Russians did not already know about the second freezer – then they soon would. Immediately on concluding his business in Locburn, he planned to head for Norfolk. In the two hours it would take Petro Pushkar to drive them there, Art expected to have worked out the exact location of the other freezer.

For now though, Ronnie Dent's freezer needed shifting. Equally as important, Lenny Plant needed taking out of the equation.

Art addressed his son, 'Horace, instruct se snatch team to make se swap – and look sharp while you're at it.' Horace disappeared and returned shortly afterwards followed by two burly men carrying the replica freezer. Lenny cottoned-on to what was happening.

'You're taking the freezer with you?'

'Correct Mister Plant,' said Schitthelm. 'But don't worry – we've got your friend a replacement, he won't notice se difference.'

Lenny raised the sledge and turned to Ronnie's freezer. 'Oh he'll notice the difference alright – coz I'm going to smash the fucker to pieces. It's going nowhere Schitthelm; the problem needs sorting here and now.'

Schitthelm knew Plant would be no pushover. He was prepared for this scenario or something similar. As Lenny readied for another blow Art nodded to Ugo. 'Sorry it has to be this way Mister Plant.'

Dragonetti grabbed the shaft of the sledgehammer with one hand. With the other hand he plunged a syringe into the back of Lenny's neck. The syringe was similar in size to the one used to dispose of Dimblewit. Dragonetti emptied every drop of its contents into Lenny.

Lenny Plant and his sledgehammer dropped to the floor – both equally motionless.

Art focused on the situation at hand. He barked-out a series of orders. 'Okay – listen-up! Ugo: take Plant and his hammer – dump them in se graveyard and get back here on se double. You two, get ready to swap se freezers – leave se body inside for now. Horace, contact our nearest ambulance crew – arrange an immediate rendezvous with se snatch vehicle at se farm track. Tell them to take se body from se freezer and remove and destroy se transponder. Once se body has been transferred, clear se rendezvous zone immediately.'

Two Three F police vehicles were parked in a layby on the Catterick Road. Each vehicle was manned by four armed officers. They would provide an escort for the snatch team vehicle as it made its way to Tyneside. Three F had its own private cargo ship waiting to take the freezer to Rotterdam. From there it would be transported to Three F's headquarters in Geneva where it would be placed in secure storage in a carbon steel vault two miles beneath Art's office.

CHAPTER 24

BARRY SEWELL

Lucy Armstrong ran into the P.I.S.S Academy and threw open the doors to the main hall. She paused in the doorway gulping breath. With an expression set into a panic she glanced around at the surprised faces that had turned to look at her. The hod carrying class was in full swing with another half-hour still to run. It jarred to a silent halt as the class members waited to find out what had got Lucy into such a state.

'Where's Sarah?' she panted. 'Sarah Plant?'

Sarah was at the bottom end of the hall, about to ascend a ladder with a loaded hod on her shoulder. Puzzled, she called up the hall to Lucy.

'I'm here Lucy – what's up?'

'It's your Lenny – he's laid out in the graveyard. I tried to wake him but – but -.'

Sarah handed the hod to her instructor and marched up the hall – her face was crimson with fury. 'If he's off his biscuit I'll fucking kill him – show me where he is Lucy.'

Fifteen minutes earlier a local named Barry Sewell had showed-up at The Haydale Arms. Barry was thirsty, fairly shifty, and slightly out-of-breath. He wore a large Parka coat.

Most people reckoned Barry not to be the brightest light on the Christmas tree. Indeed, most people reckoned that if he were a light on the Christmas tree, he'd likely be a contender for the dimmest light of them all – so most people reckoned.

Barry was, in fact, brighter than most people reckoned him to be, and certainly brighter than he would have most people believe. However, he was not as bright as he liked to think he was.

Barry Sewel was a Ronnie Dent protégé – of sorts; a top of the class underachiever at the wasters' school for urban survival.

Relentlessly calculating and deceitful for every exploitable occasion, Barry was an incorrigible trickster who never liked an opportunity to scrounge, thieve, or con, pass him by. He couldn't help himself to helping himself to that which was not his for helping himself to.

Recent advancements in the study of brain function and behavioural disorders had provided Barry with an opportunity to falsely claim benefits. After much research, and subsequent practising of symptoms, he'd been successful in convincing doctors and psychiatrists that he suffered from Attention Deficiency Hyperactivity Disorder, Asperger's Syndrome, and Chronic Spontaneous Amnesia (which in Barry's case was manifested in a convenient loss of short term memory).

Through the providence of modern medical science and gullible doctors, Barry had managed to get himself diagnosed – and registered, with behavioural disorders and deficiencies that were both familiar, and plausible, to the broader public. These he could hitherto use to offset blame when commissioning his iniquities. Whenever he'd done something naughty, most people would say or think: "he's a bad lad – but he just can't help himself."

Barry was entitled to claim welfare benefits due to his "psychological ailments". He subsidised his tax-payer funded income by conning and thieving from the tax payers that subsidised his income. His benefits also saw their way clear to the rent on a two-bedroomed flat. Barry had created an additional revenue stream by running the property as a cash only Air B&B.

'A pint of lager please Mervin,' said Barry, fetching a five-pound note from his trouser pocket, and at the same time eyeing the plastic charity money box on the top of the bar.

Mervin poured the pint. 'That'll be two-eighty-five please,' said the landlord flatly.

Mervin disliked Barry, and Barry knew it. The problem for Barry was that he could not outwardly reveal his awareness of Mervin's antipathy towards him. To do so would betray a type of sensitivity to emotional and social interaction which Barry knew to be contrary to one of the classic symptoms of Asperger's Syndrome.

Barry had worked hard to mimic the idiosyncrasies of the high-functioning disorder – and so had to behave in accordance.

Mervin had known Barry since he was a youngster – and Barry was aware that, out of all the people that knew him, no one had him sussed like Mervin.

Mervin placed Barry's pint on the bar, took the five-pound note, and slid it into the till. Dickhead Douglas and Ronnie Dent were further down the bar, distracted in conversation with a couple of walkers.

Mervin handed Barry his change. Barry drained half his glass in one go and smacked the froth from his lips. 'Hang on a minute Merv,' he said with deep suspicion. 'This ain't right.'

'What's up Barry?' said Mervin.

'I gave you a tenner – and you've given me change for a fiver.' Barry purposely raised his voice so other customers in the bar could hear. He knew that when you did this the landlord would usually cave in and give the change demanded – just to keep the peace. Barry had noticed that when Mervin opened the till, the respective compartments for twenties, tens, and fivers were handsomely stocked in more or less equal amounts.

Various drinkers, including Dickhead and Ronnie, turned to observe. Instead of toning the situation down, Mervin responded to Barry with equal volume.

'I'm sorry Barry; you're mistaken. I definitely gave you change for the fiver you handed me.'

'Nope,' countered Barry. 'I gave you a tenner – no doubt about it.'

'I bet you didn't,' said Mervin.

'I bet I did,' said Barry, starting to sound aggressive. He now had the attention of everyone in the bar.

'Tell you what,' said Mervin with confidence. 'Let's have a bet on it.'

'I'll bet you the whole contents of your till.'

'You sure about that?' said Mervin. At the mention of a wager Ronnie headed back up the bar with Dickhead in tow.

'Why shouldn't I be?' said Barry.

'Because I have an unfair advantage over you,' replied Mervin, pointing theatrically, however vaguely, at an area of the ceiling roughly above the till.

'What is he talking about,' said Barry, sarcastically addressing the patrons.

'A concealed high resolution camera – that's what I'm talking about Bazzer.'

There was, in fact, no camera – but Barry didn't know that. Mervin was bluffing with an arrogance that would subdue the boldest of confidence. Barry studied the ceiling. Mervin watched him for a few seconds before giving Dickhead a crafty wink.

'You obviously don't believe me Barry. But I'm telling you there's a concealed camera up there and it's got incredible definition – in colour as well. Never misses a trick, if you'll excuse the pun.' Mervin spoke to Dickhead. 'Tell him Dickhead.'

Dickhead was tuned-in to Mervin's subterfuge. 'He's right Barry: a multi-pixel, high intensity micro-lens. It can pick-out whether a blue bottle's foreskin is inside-out or the right way around.'

'What's it to be then Barry?' said Mervin tantalisingly. 'And before you answer, I can tell you we've had a busy day.' Mervin pressed the button that opened the till. Barry stared at the brimming contents. As he did Mervin offered his hand over the bar to shake on the bet.

'No way,' said Barry, keeping his hands this side of the bar. 'You're using cameras – and that's cheating.'

Mervin spoke to his patrons. 'I'm sorry everyone; perhaps I should explain: you see my friend here can't help himself. Sadly he suffers from Attention Deficiency Hyperactivity Disorder, which means he has difficulty maintaining prolonged attention to most forms of order or detail. This simple transaction at the bar tonight has obviously been too much for him.'

Barry Sewell looked at Mervin like he wanted to slit his throat. Mervin continued.

'And another thing you need to know folks: if it wasn't bad enough that Barry has A.D.H.D. he's also registered with the doctor as having Chronic Spontaneous Amnesia – it affects his short-term memory you see.'

Mervin stared Barry square in the eye. 'So I wouldn't worry too much about it Barry. In another five minutes you'll have forgotten all about that imaginary ten-pound note that never existed in the first place.'

Barry clenched his fist in readiness to take a swing at Mervin. 'You're an arsehole Daley,' he snarled through clenched teeth. 'When I'm finished with you you're gonna' wish –.'

The door behind Barry opened. Two police officers walked in. They were Three F police officers.

§

On his way to the pub Barry had taken a detour through the graveyard. He was in the habit of taking this route perchance he might happen upon an aged widow or widower grieving beside their partner's grave. Barry was an expert at comforting the old and vulnerable.

As Barry skirted the southern wall of the P.I.S.S Academy he noticed a body lying between two graves. He strode over and saw that it was Lenny Plant. After a quick glance around, and without thinking twice, Barry stooped over Lenny and gave him a poke in the ribs. Seeing him to be lifeless, he went through his pockets and removed a wallet from inside Lenny's jacket. Barry slid the wallet into a hidden "loot pocket" stitched into the tail of his Parka coat. He checked around for any onlookers and, reckoning no-one had seen him, made haste to the pub.

Problem for Barry was; someone had seen him.

Of the half-dozen Three F police officers that had been despatched to the P.I.S.S. Academy, two now remained. Once Lenny Plant had been "neutralised," Art instructed that two officers stay in the village until further notice. He wanted them to keep watch over the site where Lenny Plant had been dumped. Art knew fine well that once the Russians had stopped receiving transmissions from Androvski's cranial transmitter, another Russian spy would show up in the village inside the hour. If he or she was worth their salt, they'd soon discover Plant and report back that he was dead.

Mandy Seymour also remained in the village. She would continue to carry out surveillance and report back, half-hourly, to Art Schitthelm. There was the risk that once the Russians had discovered Lenny Plant, they would attempt to seize his body to find out what Three F had done to him. Art didn't want the Russians to discover what Three F were using in their syringes, so it was important that Lenny was watched over until he was discovered by the locals.

The two officers, Sergeant Albi Cumming and P.C. Dean Godfrey, had taken up a surveillance post in the Vestry Bar. They each took a stool at the far end of the bar where a small window, situated to their right, gave them a decent view of the eastern end of the graveyard. That was where Dragonetti had dumped Lenny Plant. Though dusk was due to darken-on, there was yet daylight aplenty to observe that part of the graveyard.

Sergeant Cumming had just ordered a couple of beers when P.C. Godfrey, who had been peering out the window, gave him a nudge. He'd spotted Barry Sewell walking towards Lenny Plant.

'Sir,' he said, 'male approaching: slim, six-foot-two, collar length straw coloured hair, with a snake tattoo on his right forearm and a four inch scar on the left side of his neck.'

Cumming looked over Godfrey's shoulder and out through the window.

'I say Godders,' he exclaimed. 'What a spankingly top description old boy. The blighter's got to be over fifty yards away.'

Cumming's father and mother were both retired fighter pilots. 'Do you think he's our Rusky spy fellow chap?'

'No sir,' said Godfrey, 'he's a cunt sir.'

'A cunt you say Godders?' said Cumming, making his way over to the window for a closer look. 'What sort of cunt are we talking about?'

There was an unnerving serenity in Cumming's voice. Leering out the window with a hideous grin, he wrung and rubbed his hands in a manner most disturbing.

'A first class cunt sir – he's also got a lazy eye.'

'Cripes Godders – toppo old bean!' said Cumming, now excited. 'How the deuce can you tell all this?'

'I know him sir – a local guttersnipe going by the name of Barry Sewell – slippery as you like. The local cops manage to nail him alright; but once he gets to court there's a Legal Aid solicitor, a social worker, a doctor, and a psychiatrist fighting his corner – the judge doesn't stand a chance. He gets away with allsorts on account of his A.D.H.D. his Asperger's Syndrome, and some memory disorder that I can't just recall right now.'

P.C. Godfrey was a good Three F cop. He'd committed, to his almost perfect memory, detailed intelligence on every ne'er-do-well in Locburn and its environs. He could describe them, and their methods, in minutia.

'I say Godders old chap,' said Cumming. 'Look what he's doing.'

Godfrey and Cumming huddled closer to the window. They watched as Sewell rifled Lenny's pockets.

'The bounder,' said Cumming. 'Plant's gone and bought it; now the poor old sapper's getting robbed by this guttersnipe fellow of yours Godfrey – it's absolutely not cricket.'

The two cops watched as Sewell secreted Lenny's wallet in the tail of his coat. Cumming turned to Godfrey, his expression over-loaded with excitement.

'Chocks away Godders! Let's get after the scoundrel.'

Godfrey made to leave the bar in a hurry; Cumming placed a restraining hand on his shoulder. 'Not so fast old boy, let's not forget our tipple – hey what?' Cumming raised his glass and waited for Godfrey to reach for his.

'Bottoms-up, chin-chin, down the hatch, and all the rest of it.'

Temporarily forgetting their instructions to watch over Plant, the two officers drank off their beers and headed for the pub.

§

Barry Sewell turned to see who had come in through the door. He looked the two officers up and down with arrogant disdain; then disregarded them by showing them his back and sipping at his pint.

Barry mistook the officers to be the North Yorkshire Police – and you couldn't blame him. Going on appearance alone there was nothing instantly recognisable about a Three F cop that would set them aside from a normal police officer. The attitude and application however, were startlingly different.

'Good evening officers,' said Mervin, with emphatic politeness. 'What can I do for you?'

'And a jolly good evening to you landlord,' said Cumming, with equal deference. 'Since you ask, perhaps you can be of assistance.' He'd recognised Sewell the instant he walked through the door.

'We're looking for a local chappie who quite possibly may have frequented your premises this evening.'

Barry Sewell carried on sipping at his pint, naturally impervious to the presence of the two officers.

'Have you got a description of him?' asked Mervin.

'We've got a ripping description old boy – an absolutely ripping description,' said Cumming, fooling with the situation. 'We've even got the blighter's name and address.'

Mervin was puzzled. 'Begging your pardon officer,' he said, straining with politeness. 'If he's a local just give me his name – I know them all round here.' Mervin Daley was by no means a snitch – he always looked out for his locals. However it was in his interests as a landlord not to be obstructive with the cops whenever they came a calling.

'I can't just give you his name old boy,' said Cumming in jest, 'that would spoil all the fun.'

Hungry for mischief, Cumming raised his voice to address the whole pub. Mervin was beginning to suspect these were no ordinary cops.

'Okay everybody – listen carefully. P.C. Godfrey here is going to give you some really pippin clues about the scumbag we're after; so you can have a go at guessing who you think it is.'

Cumming turned and spoke to Godfrey. 'Now then Godders; I suggest we give them one clue at a time – starting off with the most difficult one.'

Godfrey cleared his throat. 'Well, we know for sure he's a male.'

'There you go ladies and gentlemen – he's definitely a male – so he is.' Cumming took to the centre of the floor and spoke in the manner of a deranged show host. 'I'm not saying we're trying to make it easy for you, but old Godders here has just eliminated three and a half billion potential suspects. That leaves just three billion or so to worry about. Next clue please.'

'He's of slim build,' said Godfrey.

'That's a stonking clue Godders,' said Cumming, looking over at a portly gentleman with a bald head sitting by the fire. 'I think we can rule you out sir. Another clue if you please Mister Godfrey.'

'He's six-foot-two.'

'When you say "six-foot-two" Godders, do you mean he's six-foot two as well – or do you mean he's six-foot-two inches?'

'The latter sir,' replied Godfrey.

'A peach Godders – an absolute peach of a clue,' said Cummins sweeping his eyes about the room. 'Hands-up anyone if you're six-foot-two.'

One of the walkers raised their hand immediately. 'I'm six-foot-two officer,' he proudly announced. He turned to his wife sitting next to him. 'Isn't that right Gladys?'

'Six-foot-two in his sock soles,' affirmed his wife.

'I say, well done old boy,' said Cumming, humouring the walker. 'Did you hear that everyone – he's six-foot-two, hey what?' The walker, a retired civil servant with a dull-normal I.Q. looked chuffed with himself. Cumming continued.

'Fortunately for you sir – you're not our man.' Cummins noticed the walker now looked markedly less chuffed. 'You see, if the pile of shit we're looking for was in this room right now, he would have to be an idiot to own-up to being six-foot-two.'

Cumming turned to Godfrey. 'I think it's time for another one of those cracking clues of yours Godders.'

'Our suspect has collar length, straw coloured hair sir.'

'That's me,' called out the walker, made-up at being back in the reckoning. 'Look,' he said, tugging at his hair. 'Straw coloured hair – collar length as well.'

Cumming strode over to the walker. With his hands clenched behind his back he leaned over to examine his hair from a distance of a matter of inches.

'Hmm,' muttered Cumming, 'something's not right here.' He spoke to the walker's wife. 'If I didn't know any better madam, I'd wager this cad's been at the bottle.'

Cumming studied her face for a reaction. 'Am I right in saying that's not his natural colour?'

The lady put a hand up to her mouth. 'He err – it's umm,'

'Yes or no!' snapped Cumming, becoming slightly nasty. 'We can always get him to drop his trousers?'

'He dyes those too,' she blurted out.

Cumming turned his attention back to the husband. 'You wouldn't, by any chance, happen to be a civil servant?'

'Yes,' he replied boastful, 'retired as a matter of fact.'

'Thought so,' said Cumming, with nonchalant disinterest, 'worst kind.' The sergeant stooped again; this time to have a quietly menacing word in the walker's ear. 'Next time you interrupt my little charade, I'll have you done for wasting police time.'

The portly gentleman by the fire spoke up. 'I used to have straw coloured hair before I – you know, before I –.'

'Before you went bald,' interrupted Cumming. 'We've already eliminated you slap-top; so keep it buttoned – there's a good chap.'

Barry Sewell leaned on the bar; a twinge of suspicion tugging at his guts. The sergeant's exuberant rudeness bothered him. He'd never come across that kind of attitude in a police officer before – he'd also never come across a Three F cop.

Cumming went over to the bar and stood next to Sewell. He spoke to Mervin.

'I say landlord old bean, all this talking's got me a tad dry – thirsty work and all that. I could murder a pint don't you know?'

Although Mervin was a little concerned at the prospect of serving alcohol to an on-duty officer, he thought it best to hold his tongue.

'I rather fancy a pint of this pissywiser stuff. Better get one for P.C. Godders too – he's partial to a drop of the old sparkly apple.'

Mervin dutifully poured the drinks.

Cumming slouched against the bar, adopting the posture of an arrogant gunslinger looking for trouble.He eyed Sewell up and down then took a long draw on his pint. The sergeant savoured the subtle blend of apple, ethanol, and carbon dioxide. Trying his best to appear oblivious to Cumming's attention, Sewell kept his stare locked in the straight ahead position.

Cumming got his face close up to the side of Sewell's. He spoke with a volume barely able to overhaul a whisper, his tone however, heaved with menace, 'six-foot-two, straw coloured, collar length hair.'

Cumming noticed the scar, as described by Godfrey, on the side of Sewell's neck. 'I say old chummy, that's a nasty looking scar you've got there.'

Sewell gave-up pretending to ignore Cumming. He rounded on the policeman.

'Back-off copper – leave me alone.'

Cumming pretended to act startled. He straightened up, almost as if standing to attention. 'Godders my good man, you're spot on with the lazy eye – last time I saw an eye as lazy as that the damned thing was asleep.'

'Not much of a policeman that has to get personal,' said Sewell in a loathsome tone. 'What do you want with me?'

'What do I want?' challenged Cumming. 'Well – if old Godders here doesn't mind too awfully; what I want is to let everyone in on the last two devilishly cheeky clues.'

Sewell didn't reply. He turned to leave the pub. Godfrey stood in his way.

'Hands-up anyone who wants to hear the last two clues?' said Cumming, teasing the locals.

Like a classroom of knowledge hungry kids, everyone, including Cumming and Godfrey, raised their hand. Everyone that is, except Barry Sewell.

'Unanimous,' said Cumming, 'motion passed – and I suspect it'll be a motion-passing moment for the suspect when he hears the last two clues.'

Cumming allowed for a lengthy pause to heighten the drama. 'He's wearing a Parka coat – and he's standing right next to me.'

Mervin grinned at Cumming, nodding his approval at the way he was goading Sewell.

'Right ladies and gentlemen – before I proceed any further, and because you've been so good this evening, I'm giving you a bonus clue – his name's Barry Sewell.'

Barry Sewell fronted-up to Cumming, so close that their noses almost touched.

'Either tell me what you want cop, or get out of my way,' he snarled. 'You're harassing me in front of all these witnesses,' Sewell fetched his phone out and waved it at Cumming like it was a warrant card. 'And I've got a top brief just a phone call away.'

This was always Sewell's first line of defence: standing his ground and threatening with a solicitor. It often did the trick for less audacious acts of crime – especially when challenged by store detectives and inexperienced police officers.

Cumming was done with the fooling. He decided it was time to get down to business.

'Where's the wallet?'

'What wallet?'

'The one you've just stolen from a dead body in the graveyard.'

At the mention of a dead body there was a collective gasp from the locals.

'I've got no wallet – search my pockets all you like,' said Sewell.

With cocky confidence he adopted the crucifix pose in readiness. After failing with his first line of defence, Sewell played his second bluff by ostentatiously offering his willingness to be searched. Such bullish assurance that he had nothing to hide would often subdue threatening suspicion. As a result the invitation to search would sometimes be turned down.

If it did turn out that Barry was searched, his hidden pocket took some finding. To date, it had evaded detection.

'You want me to search you?' said Cumming, pretending to be surprised. 'There's no need for that old chap – surely you don't want to be subjected to such humiliation in public. In situations like this we must strive to maintain a suspect's dignity – so if it's all tip-top with you, be a decent fellow and hand me the wallet.'

Sewell was beginning to think the sergeant might be a pushover.

'I've already told you, you bloody half-arsed toff, there is no wallet.'

'Oh but there is,' assured Cumming, ignoring the insult. 'You see, both me and old Godders here watched you take it from the body in the graveyard.'

Sewell began with his third line of defence – denial. 'I have no recollection of being in any graveyard.'

'Ah – that'll be your memory problem kicking-in old boy,' said Cumming sympathetically. 'But don't you worry; I've got the perfect cure for restoring all your recently lost recollections.'

With disturbing energy Cumming thrust his open hand into Sewell's crotch. With his other hand he took him by the throat and forced him up against the bar. The policeman gripped the suspect's testicles, applying a "stage 1" clamping force. This was a level of grip approved by the Three F Interrogation Standards Unit, and was estimated, by medical experts, as being sufficient to secure the subject's attention whilst partially taking their breath away so as to leave them with sufficient breath to cough-out a confession.

There were five stages of standard testicle grip, with "stage 5" being the most excruciating. Normally the interrogating officer would go in at "stage 1." In extreme circumstances however, there was the option of going straight in at "stage 5".

Three F police were trained in applying the varying clamping pressures using lemons. A "stage 1" grip should squeeze the lemon firmly but without breaking its skin. An increase to "stage 2" should produce stress cracks on the surface of the skin – however it's important that no leakage occurs at this level. A "stage 5" grip should cause ejection of pips and drain the lemon of around ninety percent of its juice.

When a ballet dancer goes "on point" for the first time, it is after weeks, if not months, of intense practise. In less than a second Sewell was up on his toes – a useless reflex reaction to being grabbed by the bollocks with a vicious up-thrusting action. His mouth gaped as he let out a half gasp.

Cumming stared Sewell in the eye. 'Wallet please,' he asked, in a tone as firm as his grip.

'You've got the wrong man,' wheezed Sewell, his expression twisting with the pain.

Cumming considered increasing to a "stage 2" grip, but thought better. He deemed Sewell to be taking the piss in the kind of way that warranted converting pain into agony. He went straight for the "stage 5".

Sewell's eyes bulged so wide it looked like they were ready to drop from their sockets. He tried to say something, but could only manage a faint croak.

Cumming smiled at Sewell. 'How's the memory?'

Sewell was incapable of speech. Cumming threw him a life-line.

'Tell you what old chap,' he chirped, 'I'll ask you a "yes" or "no" question – and you can reply with a nod or a shake of that shit-brained head of yours.'

Sewell nodded keenly.

'Could it be that the wallet is hidden in the tail of your coat?'

Sewell nodded twice as keenly. Cumming let go of his bag and let him fall to the ground. As he rolled around in the foetal position, PC Godfrey stooped to feel his way around the tail of his Parker coat. After some considerable rummaging he located the pocket, which was cleverly concealed in a pleat close to the base of the tail. Godfrey handed the wallet to Cumming who immediately crouched down beside Sewell to show it off.

'Get on with it copper,' groaned Sewell. 'Caution me and charge me. I'm calling my solicitor – this is police brutality.'

'There's no caution or charges for you old boy,' assured Cumming. 'We're Three F you see. This one's getting reported to the Regional Inspector – and he reports directly to Mister Schitthelm who, incidentally, has taken a keen interest.'

Sewell was still curled-up on the floor, nursing his crotch with both hands.

'Caution me,' he repeated, 'charge me – I want to be charged. I want my solicitor, along with a "no comment" interview.'

Cummings stood up. 'We'll be in contact – and when I say contact, I mean physical contact.' The sergeant grinned down at Sewell with psychotic satisfaction. 'I'll warn you now old bean – you're not going to like it.'

Ronnie Dent saw the wallet in Cumming's hand. He'd seen it many times before. It belonged to his best friend, Lenny Plant. On recognising the wallet Ronnie startled himself into sobriety.

'It's Lenny's,' he called out.

'What's that you said Ronnie?' asked Mervin, distracted with the whole scenario.

'The wallet – it belongs to Lenny.'

Ronnie made for the door with the urgency of a greyhound released from its trap. In a couple of seconds Dickhead Douglas and Mervin cottoned-on to what he'd just said. They followed Ronnie out the door with equal haste.

§

Ronnie Dent sprinted towards the graveyard, his short legs moving with such speed they were almost a blur. In his life, Ronnie had never moved so fast – not even when he was escaping from Spiderman. Behind him, some fifty yards, Dickhead and Mervin struggled to catch up.

On entering the graveyard Ronnie paused just beyond its gates. Gasping for air he scanned the graves for Lenny. Down at the lower eastern end of the graveyard Ronnie noticed what he thought to be someone's nose, protruding skyward from the uncut grass that verged two graves. He took a few reluctant steps closer to confirm what he already knew: the nose he could see belonged to Lenny Plant.

Ronnie knew Lenny Plant to have a large, instantly recognisable nose. The reason Ronnie found it to be instantly recognisable was that he'd spent thousands of hours over the years looking at it whenever he and Lenny were engaged in conversation.

No one, including yourself, knows what your nose really looks like, better than your best friend.

Beset with a mixture of fear and foreboding, Ronnie made haste to where Lenny lay. At the same time Sarah came marching round the side of the P.I.S.S Academy, Lucy Armstrong at her shoulder. Dickhead and Mervin ran through the gates.

In the panic no one noticed the Russian spy crouching by a grave on the western side of the graveyard. Dressed in black with a white streak of fresh rook shit on her left shoulder, she posed as a mourner. Anna Ledbedev had already checked Lenny Plant out. She sent a message to her handler in Moscow reporting Plant's status as deceased. Mandy Seymour watched Ledbedev from a thicket of Yew trees at the top of the graveyard. She contacted Art Schitthelm to inform him that the Russians had located Lenny Plant and likely reported him as dead.

Ronnie got to Lenny first; he was dismayed at the sight of his friend lying white-faced and unmoving. The ageing drunk was on the brink of bursting into tears but somehow the pystwiser kept his emotions temporarily in check. Ronnie kneeled down beside Lenny and shook his shoulder.

'Lenny, wake up, it's me – Ronnie,' he said softly.

Sarah Plant and Lucy pulled-up alongside the same moment as Dickhead and Mervin. When Sarah saw the look on Mervin's face she knew something was terribly wrong – something more terribly wrong than finding your husband lying in a graveyard sleeping-off drunkenness. She looked down at Lenny and feared the worst.

Kneeling by Lenny's side Ronnie leaned over so he could hold his ear close to Lenny's mouth. He gently placed his left hand around Lenny's neck to feel for a pulse. Ronnie was no First Aid expert; in fact he hadn't a clue. He was parodying what he'd seen countless times in Sunday afternoon 'B' movies. Sarah and the others stood by. In the grip of morbid anticipation they waited silently for Ronnie to give his diagnosis.

After an eternal pause Ronnie sighed. His sigh was so bereft of affectation, so genuinely un-theatrical, that those who witnessed it – those who'd known him forever, knew that the news would not be good. A large tear leaked from his eye. It trickled down the right side of his nose as far as the nasal hair braid. From there it spiralled till it met with the pink ribbon. The tear fell from the ribbon onto Lenny's forehead.

Ronnie spoke. 'He – he's gone.'

Sarah sank to her knees. She grabbed at her hair in dismay.

'No,' she whimpered. 'Please no.'

Lucy Armstrong crouched beside Sarah, comforting her with an embrace. Dickhead and Mervin were stunned into silence.

'Hang on a minute,' said Ronnie, his hand still around Lenny's neck. 'I think I just felt something.'

It was only the second time that the cocktail injected into Lenny Plant's neck had been used. The temperature reactive enzyme-based protoplasmic adrenalin memory synapse blocker had been signed-off for operational application less than a year earlier.

During its five year development period, Three F's Laboratory Facility in Barcelona had recommended the cocktail be trialled extensively on laboratory mice and rabbits before it was signed-off and entered onto the Three F Approved Combatant Chemicals Register. When he found out the lab's plans for proofing the chemical, a dismayed Art Schitthelm ordered that no such testing on animals should be practised. Art was very much against cruelty to animals and sought to find a more humane way of trialling the substance. After briefly considering the situation he arranged to have a phial of the chemical sent to his address in Geneva.

The potent chemical was designed to have a multi-clinical effect on its recipient. Once it enters the blood-stream of a warm-blooded creature the subject would become instantly "neutralised". The temperature sensitive adrenalin component would act as a universal muscle relaxant, arresting the function of all muscles, including the heart. The synaptic blocking agent would disable the memory, with a permanent recall erase of up to six months – depending on dosage.

To test the chemical, Art treated his son Horace to a weekend of fun and entertainment – one that ought to remain prominent in his memory for years to come. Horace was taken to the funfair, where he rode the merry-go-round, slid down the helter-skelter, and ate candy floss. He had his picture taken with Bozo the Bear, watched Punch and Judy, and spent almost a full hour playing on the bouncy castle with two cheerleaders.

On the Sunday night Art took a mug of hot chocolate up to Horace's bedroom. The drink was laced with the chemical. After two sips the potion had done its work. Horace's eyes closed and his heart stopped beating.

Try as hard as he could, Art could find no signs of life. He checked his son thoroughly for a pulse, fired off a starting pistol next to Horace's ear, and shone a laser-pen directly into his eye to check for any sign of corneal reflex. As a final check Art punched Horace in his guts to see if he could get any reaction. Horace did not respond. Beyond any doubt his son was dead. Art now waited to see if the cocktail did what it said on the tin.

After half-an-hour Horace's body cooled to a specific temperature (precisely five degrees below normal body temperature). This caused the heat sensitive enzyme protoplasmic adrenalin to become activated. Whilst the protein rich enzyme served to oxygenate the blood during the period of "neutralisation," the adrenalin kick-started the heart once the critical body temperature was reached.

Horace gave a gentle cough and opened his eyes. Art, sitting expectantly in a bedside chair, immediately interrogated him about his weekend at the funfair. Horace thought for a while, somewhat confused. He was at a loss to recall the previous 48 hours, and stated that the last thing he could remember was watching a potato spinning in the microwave early Friday evening. The fun-filled weekend had been erased from his memory forever.

§

'I thought I felt a pulse,' said Ronnie. He looked up at the others, an expression of hope blooming on his face. Sarah, still kneeling and distraught, removed herself from Lucy's embrace. She leaned forward to hug Lenny.

Lenny coughed. At the same time his eyes snapped open. Sarah recoiled to observe her husband.

'False alarm everybody,' announced Ronnie, cheery as a drunken Santa. 'He's just pissed.'

Now she knew Lenny was alive, or indeed, was never dead, Sarah swiftly recovered from her state of grief and bewilderment.

Lenny blinked at the fading blue of a late March sky; silhouetted against it: five concerned faces peering down at him. Cold to his bones and disorientated in the extreme, he sat up to take-in his surroundings. Having been dead for best part of an hour – and with his memory comprehensively robbed of the preceding forty-eight, he'd got a lot of catching up to do.

Shivering, and dazed with confusion, Lenny looked about him. He struggled to fathom how and why he came to be lying between two graves.

'What day is it?' he asked.

'What?' demanded Sarah; becoming annoyed with the situation as she saw it.

'Saturday,' said Ronnie, eager to answer a sitting duck of a question. When he noticed Sarah looking at him like she'd caught him urinating on her doorstep, he had another guess.

'Or is it Sunday?' he mumbled, scratching his head and cowering his eyes to the farthest parts of the graveyard.

'What time is it?' said Lenny.

'Somewhere around half-seven or eight-o'clock,' said Dickhead, 'you alright Lenny – had us all worried for a moment there?'

'How come it's still light?' asked Lenny, now rubbing at his eyes like a toddler rising from innocent slumber.

'The clocks Lenny lad – they've gone back one hour – I mean forwards one hour,' said Dickhead, looking at Mervin for confirmation.

'Forwards,' said Mervin, 'definitely forwards.'

'Marvellous,' said Sarah, using a tone all present knew to be a harbinger of withering invective. Ronnie, Dickhead, and Mervin braced themselves for an onslaught of insults and oaths.

'Absolutely fucking marvellous – never mind the time of day, you arseholes don't even know what day it is.'

'Sarah,' appealed Ronnie, 'Lenny's had a busy weekend – he's mended the fence, and fixed the willy on the ceiling, and everything.'

'Fuck off piss-bag – and you two as well!' Both Mervin and Dickhead bowed their heads and studied their shoes. 'How can you stand by and watch your friend get into a state like this? You Mervin – you should know better. It's that fucking pystwiser – everything was okay till you started pouring that down their throats. If I ever catch you serving him another drop I won't be responsible for what I fucking well do!'

'I've fixed the fence and painted the ceiling?' said Lenny, puzzled. 'I can't remember doing that – but nice one anyway.'

'See what I mean – he can't remember a bastard thing.'

Lenny tried his best to recall any of the weekend's happenings. The last thing he could remember was having an argument with Dickhead in the pub on Friday night over who invented the free-range egg.

As Lenny rose to his feet Sarah took him by the arm and frog-marched him home. She scolded him every step of the way.

Mervin, Dickhead and Ronnie retreated back to the pub. At the same time in Church Lane, the Russians were exchanging one replica freezer for another.

CHAPTER 25

NORFOLK BOUND

The Mercedes hurtled down the motorway. Horace studied the expression on his father's face.

'Why just half a grin Father?'

'Half a grin for a half job done Horace. We need to find se second freezer; then you will see a full grin.'

Horace nodded, 'Fair enough,' he said. 'Don't you think we should be making plans to get our hands on it Father?'

'Has it not dawned on you Horace, as to why we might be travelling at almost twice se national speed limit in se direction of Norfolk?'

'Err – let me see now,' said Horace, concentrating madly, 'is it because we used to go there for our summer holidays when I was a kid?'

'No son,' replied Art.

'Oh right – so if it isn't that then, I err, I wonder why.'

'Quit your wondering Horace; it's a waste of time. You heard what Lenny Plant said back there: "Se freezer's somewhere in Norfolk – and it's in brand new condition."'

'So that's it Father, that's why we're going to Norfolk: to find a freezer that happens to be somewhere in Norfolk.' Horace gleefully rubbed his hands. 'How exciting; I've never tried to find a needle in a haystack before!'

'How funny Horace; that you should choose se most un-funniest time in se history of humanity, to say something so unfunny that you actually think is funny.' Art stared at his son unimpressed. 'Wise up – or I'll get Ugo to punch you in se guts.'

Horace shut his mouth while his father sorted himself a cigar. Upfront, Petro Pushkar weaved the Mercedes through the half-busy stream of Sunday evening traffic. Ugo Dragonetti sat next to him. He plucked out a nasal hair, which must have been deeply rooted in the upper reaches of his nose, for it was over two inches long and caused his eyes to water.

Deep in thought Art smoked an inch or so from the end of his cigar. After a silence of some five minutes he spoke.

'Time,' he said wisely, 'is a pisser.'

'In what way Father?'

'Se way you can count on it to see everyone and everything off.'

Horace could sense futility in his father's tone.

'It neither greets you, nor bids you farewell – so fucking rude. On and on it marches, oblivious to what's happened, what's happening, and what will happen. Time is so ultimate – so perfectly insuperable.'

'Eh?'

'You can't beat it. There's no reasoning with it – no escaping it. A deceitful bastard if you please: palpable, ubiquitous – yet it evades se senses. There's neither a beginning nor an end, no in-between. It's insatiable, feasting on one eternity after another. Time came before God, and it'll be there after God. Because when all humankind is gone in se dust, there will be no need for a God. With no mortal being left to lick his arse; and only his own arse left in se whole of se cosmos, God will be fucked for ever and ever. Amen.'

'I've never thought about it like that before,' said Horace.

'Before when?' asked Art keenly.

'Before now,' said Horace.

'And when is now?'

'Just then, when I said "before now,"' said Horace, looking at his father puzzled.

'You're already talking about se past Horace. Se present is nothing but a fleeting state of consciousness, so useless: "Oh look! There was se present, and now it's buggered off into se past – so much for that." As for se future – it's a fantasy, forever beyond reach. Se past is king Horace, se past is reality. Orwell said it: "those who control se past control se future."'

'I see,' said Horace, unsure.

'I'm trying to make a point,' said Art, getting impatient with Horace's grasp of the here and now.

'Se ultimate weapon has to be time travel Horace. To have se ability to travel back in time, to be able to change se past – se very threat of it is enough to subdue se strongest of world powers. Se Russians are desperate to perfect their time travel program, and up until now they were on se cusp of achieving se dominance they crave. However, without se technology unique to se freezer, they find themselves in a dead-end street.'

Art eased back in his seat and allowed himself another half grin; this time on the other side of his face – so as to counterbalance the previous half-grin.

'But how things have changed son; Three F have now have se freezer. We've drawn level with se Russians and overtaken them in one go. Only problem is, if they get to se second freezer before we do, then we will have se equivalent of an arms race on our hands. We need to avoid that at all costs. With both freezers in our possession we can force their hand. By threatening to embark on our own time travel program, we can insist they abandon theirs altogether.'

Horace moved the conversation on.

'Why did you have Lenny Plant killed Father? He might have been of further use to us.'

'We only killed him temporarily Horace. The drug Ugo injected into him was unique; it rendered Plant deceased for little more than an hour. Enough time for a Russian to get to him and report him dead. Believe me, Lenny Plant is alive and well – albeit with a forty-eight hour memory deficit. He won't remember what his knicker-free angel told him in se pub; so he'll be no longer aware of se freezer's significance with regard to world dominance.'

'Very clever Father,' said Horace.

'I like to think so,' said Art. 'And for once you're right Horace. We need to protect Plant – when se future becomes se present, I have no doubt he will be of use to us. With se Russians safe in se knowledge that Plant is dead, and se freezer gone from Locburn, the village is of no further interest to them.'

Art took one last drag on his cigar. He stubbed it out on the back of Ugo's neck and tossed it out of the window. The cigar, not quite fully extinguished, bounced along the tarmac. A following car with a leaking petrol tank drove over it. The car at once burst into flames, then exploded. Its driver, a drug-dealing wife beater from Halifax, was blown out through the car's sunroof. The blast was sufficient to propel him one-hundred foot into the air. During his descent he reflected on his wasted life. The ne'er-do-well took a final puff on his joint before touching down in front of a juggernaut.

'So, any ideas on how we're going to find the other freezer Father?'

'I've worked out roughly who might own it, and where we might expect to find it,' said Art, a hint of confidence in his voice.

'When did you do that Father?' said Horace.

'Just now – I mean, just then, when I threw my cigar out of se window.'

'And how have you worked it out?'

'When I say I've worked it out, I mean I've deduced it by using reasoning from a combination of known facts and suppositions to form my own extrapolation.'

'A bit of a Sherlock Holmes on the quiet Father,' said Horace, humouring his father.

Art leaned forward and spoke to Ugo.

'Ugo, when we arrive in Norfolk, please remind me to ask you to punch Horace in his guts.'

Ugo nodded.

'Are you going to let me know how you've done it Father?'

'If you can find your way clear to shutting your mouth for a few minutes Horace, then I'll enlighten you.'

Horace mimicked drawing a zip across his lips to demonstrate compliance.

'Firstly, let's look a se facts: there's just one freezer left; it's in brand new condition, and it's in Norfolk. Secondly, let's look at near certainties: both freezers were bought back in se seventies. I'm positive se one we have has remained in se same house from new

295

– perhaps for sentimental reasons: a moving-in present, or maybe a wedding present. We do know that se Dents were married back in se late seventies, and that they moved into se late uncle's house around that time.

'Although se Dent's freezer has a scratch on se front of it, it is still in remarkably good condition. When you look at se state of se house and its grounds, se condition of se freezer is somewhat at odds with all se unkemptness.'

Art took a deep breath and continued.

'When I observe such a contradiction Horace, I start to build a mental profile of se kind of person who would hold on to such a relic; and indeed, would take such bother as to keep it in good condition.'

'A person Father; you're talking about an individual – as opposed to a family or a couple?'

'I see a male in his late fifties. Both parents buried in se local graveyard of a quiet Norfolk village – he's a bachelor, reclusive – a loner.'

'Why a loner necessarily Father?'

'Oh he lives on his own alright – there's no wife, no partner. You see your average woman-about-se-house would not tolerate such a relic in her kitchen. Proud housewives are most covetous of one another's white goods. Se kitchen must boast to their contemporaries, se most modern, sleek, and expensive German fridges, freezers, and cookers. A seventies freezer would not cut se mustard Horace – se quintessential housewife would never permit such an embarrassment to be visited upon her.'

'I'm offended Father,' said Horace.

'Offended?'

'Yes, your references to "proud housewives," the "woman about the house," and "the quintessential housewife." Stereotyping woman like that, in this day and age, it's derogatory – you should be ashamed of yourself.'

'Ooh – chase me I'm a daffodil,' said Art, overly camp, but with pointed sarcasm. The take on Duncan Norvelle was wasted on Horace.

'Now you're mocking gays Father. And quite frankly, I'm disgusted.'

'Quite frankly son, you can go fuck yourself,' said Art, frankly. 'Who do you think you are, lecturing me on political correctness? It's so yesterday.'

Horace ignored his father and continued.

'And this business with Three F's new "Toilets in the Workplace Charter," I mean – what's that all about?'

'One workplace, one toilet,' said Art firmly, 'no matter what you're pissing through – or out of. It doesn't matter what's hanging between your legs, or what was hanging between your legs, or what you'd like hanging between your legs – just go and have a fucking piss and get on with your life.'

Art gave a tired shake of his head. 'Straight, gay, bisexual, trans-sexual, gender-neutral, re-assigned, non-binary – be whatever you want, society will accommodate you. There's no need to get hysterical, or precious – no need for mobs of them waving their banners in se city, or lobbying MP's, or running crying to se Union, or complaining to HR.

'Se people I speak of Horace; they're tribal – like Hell's Angels, or Skinheads, Protestants, or Catholics – troublemakers no less. Their compulsion to belong to a group and shout about it, it's a weakness. Damn tribalism! It destroys good society. Can't they see it takes more guts to be an individual? I say to them: "quit your narcissism, show some courage. Exist at se centre of your own universe. People will respect you."'

'But these people Father – they feel they're underrepresented in society.'

'Then what about me Horace? No one represents me – I'm straight and I've got se oldest cock on se planet.

'As for sex: so long as it's consenting and you're above se prescribed age, you can fuck who you want, where you want.'

'So you don't mind if people are having sex in public – like on buses, or in the middle of the market square,' challenged Horace.

'No, you clown; I mean in any orifice.'

'Holy shit,' said Horace, half dismayed.

'Yes, se clergy as well,' said Art.

'Sometimes you disappoint me Father.'

'Always happy to oblige son,' said Art, leaning forward to speak to Petro.

'How long till we reach se border with Norfolk Petro?'

'Just under an hour Mister Schitthelm.'

Art got out his side-valve phone. 'Right Horace, enough idle talk. It's time to make things happen.'

'Who are you dialling Father?'

'Max Jackson,' replied Art.

'What's the point of calling him, a former door-to-door lingerie salesman?'

'Because I need action,' said Art.

'Action?'

'That's right Horace. Max might be from Philadelphia, but he's all about action. That's why he's se Head of Three F's Action Squad. I gave him se job because I was so impressed with how he interviewed. He uttered just one sentence for se whole of se interview. I knew straight away he was se man for se job.'

'What was it he said Father?' asked Horace, intrigued.

'He declared, with se typical verbal racket you'd expect from a braying Philadelphian salesman: "If you're looking for max action – send for Max Jackson!"'

'And you offered him a high profile job on the strength of a one-liner.'

'Have you got a problem with that Horace?' challenged Art.

'Don't you think you were a little spontaneous? I mean, what about his qualifications, his past work experience, his hobbies, his religious and sexual orientation – then there's his dietary requirements?'

'What a turd you are Horace. Can you not see? Whenever I interview someone, I'm looking for attitude, nothing else. Just give me se right attitude – I'll do se rest.'

Horace said nothing.

'So, when I'm interviewing a candidate for Head of Action, I want someone who can supply action on demand.'

Max Jackson answered the phone.

'Art,' he said, with an action-packed voice. 'You gotta be looking for a whole pile of action!'

'That's right Max. And when I'm looking for max action...?'

'You send for Max Jackson!' bellowed Max.

Art laughed. The exchange with Max was a familiar one.

'So how much action are you looking for Mister S?'

'Shitloads,' said Art.

'Fire away!'

'I want you to find some stranger in Norfolk. More precisely, we need to get our hands on se freezer he owns.'

'Not a problem Mister S,' said Max. 'What do we know about him?'

'Nothing,' said Art.

'I see,' said Max, typically unperturbed.

'But I do have my own perceptions – and what better to use to find a stranger than the perceptions conceived in se oldest mind in se world.'

'Too true Mister S. So tell me, what's on your mind?'

'A bachelor – scared of women. He lives on his own, in his dead parents' house, in a small village. He'll be in his late fifties, shabbily dressed, with an unkempt beard. Probably drives a Reliant Robin he parks in a driveway cluttered with junk he's collected over se years.'

Horace stared out the window, shaking his head in disapproval. Art carried on talking to Max.

'Norfolk villages Max; are famed for being picturesque, a comfort of rural Englishness: medieval churches nestled among flint-walled, rose-smothered cottages; their gardens so meticulously manicured you'd be hard pushed to find a blade of grass out of place. And se people who live in them: decent, tidy, clean-living folk, thriving on high-fibre diets. Their bio-digesting septic tanks, they have such an easy time of things – and do you want to know why?'

'I'm all ears Mister S.'

'You see, high-fibre food equals high-fibre shit. Norfolk village gastric waste systems are se envy of se country, a paradigm of responsible bog management; so unlike se city sewers: blocked-up with junk-food stools, bloated tampons, and one-night-stand jonnies.

'Se typical Norfolk village Max – it's a paradise, both for se sewage operative, and se nut-roast munching, hedge-fund brigade.'

Horace cringed and put a finger into his ear.

'However, there's always a blot on se bucolic cossetted utopia – every village has one. That's who we're looking for Max: a hovel-dwelling fleabag, driving around in a three-wheeler.'

'I'm right with you Mister S. We're gonna find this guy so quickly you'll think we found him yesterday,' said Max, with exuberant confidence.

'Okay Max – this is what I want you to do: Get on to our intelligence people, tell them to check se criminal records of all Norfolk residents who live in villages with populations of one thousand or less. We're looking specifically for a scruffy male in his fifties who's got some petty form peculiar to his character type: public nuisance type of stuff – you know – indecent exposure, voyeurism, outraging public decency, etcetera. We need to check out any local enforcement notices issued to smelly, dirty neighbours, to address vermin control issues. If he's scared of women it's highly likely he's a knicker thief. Notify Three F Police and get them to investigate all reports of missing underwear – both from clothes lines, and laundry baskets. My guess is he's using se freezer to store his loot.'

'You mean he could be storing female undergarments in his freezer?' asked Max, amused.

'Only se used ones,' said Art.

'The used ones?'

'Yes Max. Once he's stolen them he'll be keen to seal se un-freshness in.'

'I see,' said Max, trying to hide his bewilderment.

'As soon as we've located him we need to arrest him on some trumped-up charges. We'll hold him twenty-four hours for questioning then drop se charges. Get hold of our Fabrications Team. Instruct them to build a second freezer. It needs to be ready for another swap in less than twelve hours. As soon as it's ready se logistics people will be on stand-by to ship it to Norfolk. When we've made se swap we can release se scruff-bag and he'll be none se wiser.'

'What about the smelly underwear Mister S?'

'That must be carefully transferred to se exchange freezer. Make sure protective gloves are worn and that it's packed in se same order as you found it.'

'You want me to call you the minute we get him?' said Max.

'That would be nice Max – speak soon.'

Art shut the phone off and yawned, 'All this excitement about se forthcoming action Horace. It's got me tired. I'm a bit late for my afternoon nap, so, if you don't mind, I'll take my forty-winks now.'

§

Petro Pushkar eased-off the throttle. He'd just taken the King's Lynn ring-road at over a hundred. Now they'd crossed the border into Norfolk he let the car waft along on cruise control. The wheelman glanced in the rear view mirror and saw his boss was still asleep. He considered asking Horace whether they should park up and wait for instructions, but thought better of it. Petro knew Art's son to have a dodgy track record when it came to making the right decision. As for Ugo, he was only good for beating people up.

Petro decided to head east along the coast road, knowing that most of the county's smallest villages were strung along the north coast. Like any professional wheelman his geographical knowledge of the country was more or less photographic. If they happened to get a location fix away from the coast, he could always cut inland.

The side-valve phone rang; it startled Horace out of a half slumber. Art opened his eyes and sat up. Unlike Horace he was unstartled by the ringing phone. He'd heard gunfire, and bombs, and the dying screams of wounded men: "When you've heard se sound of war, nothing startles you anymore," he would say to people whenever they asked why nothing ever startled him.

Art answered the phone. It was Max Jackson.

'Max – any news yet?'

'We got him Mister S!' said Max, excited as usual.

'You got him,' said Art, equally excited, 'where?'

'Quaint little village by the sea called Weybourne. A man called Cedric Bunsen; just as you described him.'

'And has he been arrested?'

'Already done Mister S.'

'Excellent Max – have we charged him with anything yet?'

'The Three F police have charged with some of those trumped-up offences you mentioned Mister S – funny thing is though he – he err -.' Max hesitated uncharacteristically.

'Is there something wrong Max?' asked Art.

'Well the police aren't sure how to handle this. They're saying they've never come across a situation like it before.'

'How do you mean Max – what's going on?'

'He's owned-up to all the charges – and they don't even exist. The cops are saying they're not sure what to do with him.'

Art thought for a brief second then smiled.

'Tell them to charge Cedric with wasting police time.'

'That's brilliant Mister S – we could do with you on the Action Squad.'

'So kind of you to say Max,' said Art. 'What about se freezer.'

'It's getting loaded into a truck as I speak Mister S. The logistics people will have it down to Felixstowe in just over an hour.'

'And se replacement freezer?'

'They'll have it ready to deliver within the next four hours – it'll be in Cedric's outhouse before daybreak.'

'Max,' said Art, 'You have made an old man very happy. I believe it is your birthday next week?'

'You remembered my birthday Mister S; that's so touching.'

'I'll make sure there's something extra in your pay packet.'

'Why thank you Mister S.'

'Thank you Max.'

Art shut the phone off. He turned to Horace and gave him a full grin.

CHAPTER 26

THE NEO TESTAMENT

Sarah Plant was determined to let the neighbours both see, and hear her, marching Lenny up the front drive. To her mind a dose of public humiliation would shame him into reviewing his attitude, towards his attitude. She purposely pitched her cursing at stentorian volume, so that oath and imprecation carried the length of Willow Gardens.

Lenny shuffled towards the front door, unsteady on his feet. The concoction injected into him was still in his system, and would only dissipate fully after a good night's sleep. Sarah obviously put his tottering deportment down to drunkenness. Lenny was puzzled though. He was in the comfortable habit of succumbing to orderly staggering when full of drink. But this evening his overall disorientation was disproportionate to the volume of alcohol consumed. He'd had plenty of boozy weekends before and was always able to manage his day-to-day functioning. In any case, he'd stayed dry on Saturday night, so, if anything, his total weekend consumption was down on his average.

There was only one thing different about this particular weekend though. And that was that Lenny had been drinking pystwiser.

'I can't remember doing the garden fence?' he said.

'Don't take the piss Lenny,' said Sarah, 'I've had enough.'

'But there was nothing wrong with the old one.'

'I mean it Lenny – shut it,' Lenny knew by his wife's tone that it was best to do as she bid. As they reached the door she stood in front of him and issued him with his instructions for the remainder of the evening.

'Just go inside, get a shower, and fuck off to bed,' she ordered.

Lenny didn't need telling twice. In less than ten minutes his head hit the pillow. Inside another minute he was asleep.

Immediately he lost consciousness, he started to dream.

§

Lenny made the P.I.S.S. Academy with not a minute to spare. Minister Kelly was just ascending the steps to the pulpit as Lenny took a seat in the middle of the front row. Kelly had under his arm a sizeable book that looked much like a tatty old bible. The Minister observed the congregation, his usual kindly expression overwritten with solemnity. He reverently laid the book on the lectern and opened the first page with purposeful ceremony. Kelly spoke to a P.I.S.S. Academy congregation never more intent on listening.

'We have in our possession, a book recently discovered at the bottom of a chest freezer in Norfolk. The writings contained herein date back to the beginning of time – that is, time as we think we understand it. I am about to read to you, with the utmost of gravity, Chapter One of The Neo Testament.' Kelly drew a deep breath and began:

"Many ages ago, when the Earth was young, it was untouched by humankind. Beasts roamed the land, birds flew the skies, and fish swam in the sea. Seasons came and went with predictable grace, and the planet was lush and pure. If one cared to look anywhere, they would behold the flourishing of nature with speechless wonderment.

"But there were none to look with care or speechless wonderment. For Man or Woman did not exist. There was neither a Heaven nor a Hell, and not a soul to send if there were. Goddess and Satan had created the Earth and all its life. Everything was perfect.

"Alas, there came an age when Goddess and Satan grew dissatisfied with their unspoilt creation. For it neither needed nor esteemed them. Both the nettle and the rose thrived without threat, prejudice, or divine management. Creatures existed in accordance with their environment, and among one another, they did behave themselves. No influence could Goddess or Satan impart. Not to bird, bee, beast or fish, for none was necessary.

"With nothing but the company of one another's vanity, the divine nobility found themselves all at sea. In time it came to dawn that their imperious might could bear no influence over the modest indifference of a beating heart. All creatures that on Earth did dwell, were incorruptibly impervious to the threat of death, for they neither contemplated nor feared it.

"With not a sinner or saint to judge, both Goddess and Satan were unfulfilled. A paradise had been created, and for what reason? If one is perfect, then one should not possess the urge to create.

"Goddess and Satan were secretly ashamed, for each imagined the other to be virtuous. Alas, each knew themselves not to be. With un-divine and mutual blindness, Goddess envied Satan's purity, and Satan envied Goddess's.

"In the midst of a barren universe they had conspired to create a most wonderful planet. The Earth, in all its majesty, was their jewel, and they were proud of it.

"But pride was a deadly sin, and so was envy. These sins were invented and committed by Goddess and Satan; borne of their own indulgence. After forty long ages, and fifteen short ones, Goddess and Satan became bored and sloth-like. As pride and envy were deadly sins, so was sloth.

"With nothing to do for an eternity, Goddess and Satan gave in to frustration. In the fullness of two ages, frustration surrendered itself to sinful anger.

"There came to pass, a time when Goddess and Satan turned their attentions to one another. Goddess found herself attracted to the body of Satan, and Satan did admire the form of Goddess; for verily, they did recognise themselves to be different to one another.

"Satan longed to fondle the fulsome bosom of The Lord Goddess. He hungered for the taste of her honey, and yearned to fill her honeypot. And verily, Lord Goddess did become fond at the site of Satan's serpent. She did behold that it was different to the earthly serpent, for it had but one eye, and that eye did survey all before it from a hood of skin that was wrinkly and stretchy.

"At sunrise on the first day of the third eternity, Lord Goddess beheld the serpent of Satan, and she was dismayed. For his serpent had turned a pale red and was stiff and swollen. The Lord Goddess did feel for the serpent, for she understood it to have been beaten, or strangled; or less injured by some other mischief. Lord Goddess didst feel some more, and she did rub it to make it well again. By the will and love of Goddess, and many tears wept from the serpent's eye, the swelling did relent.

"By the sixth day of the third eternity, The Lord Goddess had developed a sincere affection for serpent. The affection did turn to lust, and lust drove her to permit the serpent to ascend her honey pot. Satan was filled with joy, and the Lord Goddess was filled with Satan. The Lord did cometh, and Satan did cometh. Forsooth, the comings did occur at the same time.

"Goddess and Satan were insatiable, and they were greedy, for the serpent was now in daily and hourly employment. There came a time when Goddess did take the serpent into her mouth, and verily, she became so gluttonous that she took it into the depths of her throat. When Satan saw what she had done his knees did tremble.

"On the two-hundred-and-seventy-ninth day of the third eternity, baby Adam didst emerge from the honey pot. He grew to be a man, and was sent out of the way to roam the Earth. From his flesh Goddess did make Eve, so that Adam might have a partner. Adam and Eve did reside in a beautiful garden, and the garden did boast an apple tree that was subject to a preservation order. The Lord Goddess decreed that no fruit should be eaten from the tree; for to do so would violate the conditions set-out in the preservation order.

"There came a day when a two-eyed serpent did venture into the garden. The serpent became the first terrorist, for verily, it persuaded Eve to eat an apple from the tree. The serpent knew that to tempt Eve to take that which was not hers to possess, much less to devour, would plant the eternal seed of conflict in the midst of humankind. Eve did offer the fruit up to Adam, and he too did take a bite from it.

"The Lord Goddess and Satan were filled with joy, for now they had two sinners to judge. Adam and Eve did go forth and multiply, and they were strenuous. In the fullness of time they would go on to breed a family of over seven-billion sinners.

"Thus, the legacy of The Lord Goddess and Satan was nothing more than a vile race, borne of the womb of Eve.

"Come the eve of the fifth eternity, The Lord Goddess gave birth to Virgin Mary. Both Goddess and Satan agreed that their new child should be named Virgin Mary, because she was born a virgin. Virgin Mary was born in Goddess's new house, which was the house of the Lord. The Lord Goddess did name the house 'Heaven,' and this did fill Satan with rage. Satan demanded the house be named 'Hell,' but Goddess would have none of it. There was to follow a great conflict between Goddess and Satan over the naming of the House of The Lord.

While Virgin Mary was still a babe in arms, Satan left the family home. He made a new home for himself and named it 'Hell.'

"The Lord Goddess was keen to let humanity know that she was right, and good, and that Satan was wrong, and bad. So that word might be spread among the people, Goddess sent Virgin Mary to Earth.

"On the sixty-ninth day of the fifth eternity, Virgin Mary fell to Earth. She came-to in a vast, thick forest, where no person lived. Virgin Mary was raised by a family of squirrels till hair grew from under her armpits and from between her legs. On the seven-thousandth day of the fifth eternity, Virgin Mary set off into the wilderness. She walked for twenty days and twenty nights.

"On the morning of the twenty-first day Virgin Mary did reach the village of Nazareth. Virgin Mary wandered into the market place and could not understand why the locals stared at her so.

"Virgin Mary was naked and unashamed, for she had no consciousness of her nudity. The squirrels were not in want or need of cladding; neither too, was the mouse, or the fox.

"The young men of Nazareth did admire the naked body of Virgin Mary, and they did froth with testosterone. Among these men there came forward to Virgin Mary, a man called Joseph of Nazareth, who was son of Ephraim, and third cousin, twice removed, of Bob Martin. Joseph was also young, but he was wise, and his testosterone frothed not for Virgin Mary.

"Joseph took Virgin Mary to his home, for he feared that she might witness the frothing of the testosterone, or worse still, become a host to the froth itself. Joseph was kind to Mary, for he did teach her, and feed her, and clothe her. Joseph lived with Darren, and Virgin Mary did hear Darren addressed by all who knew him, as Daz. Virgin Mary came to know him as Uncle Daz.

"Uncle Daz's testosterone did froth for Joseph, and Joseph's did froth for Daz. Verily, things were frothy.

"One evening, when Uncle Daz was outside squatting over the latrine, the Angel Gabriella appeared to Joseph at the foot of the bed. She did reveal to him that Virgin Mary was to conceive a child, and that the divine froth would come to her through the Holy Spirit. The Angel Gabriella said unto Joseph that he would be the adopted Father, and that he shall proclaim to the village that he did not physically beget Virgin Mary's baby, due to the fact that it was an immaculate conception.

"Joseph was at first dismayed, and he said unto the Angel 'How will the people of the village swallow such hog excrement, for everyone knows that babies are begotten through the froth of the testosterone whenever it is spat into the honeypot from the eye of the serpent? Surely the villagers will know that I am the biological father of the child.'"

"The Angel Gabriella spoke unto Joseph, 'Be not afraid Joseph, worry thou not about your implausibility. For I say unto thee, that the village folk know thou to be a poofter, and that thy serpent ascends only the gastric chamber of another man. I say to you most solemnly, that the baby Jesus will come to save creation, and people will know him to be the Son of the Holy Spirit, definitely not begotten by way of a common fuck.'"

"There came to pass a time when Joseph and Daz went on holiday to the seaside for a week. While they were gone, Virgin Mary stayed at the house of a local priest named Zechariah. Zechariah was married to Elizabeth. Joseph knew the priest to be an honest and reliable man, of excellent repute. His wife was a good cook and kept the home clean and tidy.

"Alas, although Zechariah was a decent man, his serpent was possessed of the same conscience as any other serpent. One of the first night it went a slithering where it shouldn't.

"Joseph and Uncle Daz came home from their week by the sea, both relaxed and invigorated. Mary came home from her week away, both satisfied and impregnated. She had inside her the foetus of our Lord Jesus Christ, wrapped in a swaddling embryonic membrane.

"During the time of her pregnancy Mary had difficulty sleeping, for she suffered badly with wind and heartburn. One evening she rose from her bed and went through to the scullery for a drink of water. While she was up and about she thought she could hear a moaning sound coming from Joseph's bedroom. She went to investigate. Mary opened the door to the bedroom and saw what she reckoned to have seen. She beheld Uncle Daz, kneeling on the bed behind Joseph, and lo, he had ascended the gastric chamber of Joseph.

"As the weeks and months went by, Mary's tummy did grow, and she did blossom. How she looked forward to the birth of her child. Mary was puzzled though, for at first she rejoiced at her discovery that Uncle Daz and Joseph were trying for a baby. She knew that Joseph was bound to conceive any day, as verily, the groaning was in persistence nightly. Mary prayed that a playmate for Jesus was growing inside the tummy of Joseph, and that soon he would give birth to a baby from out of his gastric chamber. Mary didn't mind whether it was a boy or a girl, so long as it was healthy.

"Alas, as time went by, Joseph's tummy did not grow.

"Christmas came, and Jesus was born. He grew to be a young man and started going around telling people that Satan was his dad. Jesus did preach that anyone who believed in him would find life everlasting.

"When Jesus realised he was having difficulty winning people over, he began to fear that he might never become famous, and that no one would revere him. He prayed to Satan for guidance, and forsooth, the Devil did come to him in a dream:

"'Son,' he said. 'Don't wake up just now, for I have something to say to you regarding your chronic narcissism. I've looked into the future, so that I may see how you might make yourself famous.' The Devil revealed his visions to his son. "One day there will cometh a man, and he shall be called Donald Campbell. I say unto thee that Donald will have an obsession with how swiftly he can travel across the water; for he knows that when he is the swiftest of them all, he shall be forever famous. Donald will build for himself a jet-powered death-trap, and it shall propel him across the water faster than a diving falcon. Lo, when Donald realises that the waters are too choppy for his chariot, his vanity shall surely overcome all the good counselling given unto him by Health and Safety people. It shall dawn upon Donald that he will not be the swiftest, unless he does bugger the consequences and give it full throttle. I say unto thee that Donald will have such a huge crash, and that he and his chariot will be smashed to a thousand pieces.'"

The Devil didst get to the point:

"'What I'm trying to say son, is that if you don't get to be famous, then tis best to die trying.'"

"So Jesus went forth and got himself nailed to a cross. In death he found for himself, everlasting stardom."

Minister Kelly turned to the last two pages of the first chapter and read on:

"Come the dawning of the sixth eternity the world found itself in chaos. Both The Lord Goddess and Satan were dismayed. There were Catholics and Protestants, Jews and Muslims, Communists and Capitalists; all of them proclaiming their way to be the most virtuous, and all of them in denial of their foolishness. There was neither a religion nor a government that worked for the good of society, nor the environment. The planet was overpopulated by a vicious race, indifferent to any high moral teachings, and intent only on the destruction of both the ecosystem, and one another.

"The Lord Goddess did strive to remedy the situation, and she did anoint Art Schitthelm as The Holy Ghost. Goddess decreed that Schitthelm shall live for an eternity, so that he may have plenty of time to right the many wrongs. Goddess did also send an angel to Lenny Plant, and the angel did warn him of the chest freezers. Verily, it is written that Lenny Plant is a prophet, for it is he who has led Art Schitthelm to the freezers. Now that Art Schitthelm is in possession of both appliances, he can heal sick societies, subdue tin-pot dictators, and find out who killed the princes in the tower."

§

"The alarm clock did startle Lenny Plant into Earthly consciousness. Till such a time as it was rendered silent it bid him rise from his bed. Lenny scratched at his head, then his orbs, for this did greatly assist in offering-up the wisdom to ponder the meaning of his dream.

He journeyed unto the en-suite latrine, and therein, in the midst of the Stellar Bosch Ceramics, he did rid himself of all the foulness that did reside in his gastric chamber. Lenny cleansed his hair and his skin. He put on his robes and climbed into his chariot. Lenny drove forth to work, for he had advertising sales to manage for the local newspaper."

CHAPTER 27

LOOKING BACK AFTERWARDS

Things eventually settled down in the village of Locburn. The cause of the recent disruption was blamed squarely on the pystwiser. As soon as Mervin Daley returned to the pub from the graveyard he took the cider off-sale.

In less than twenty-four hours he'd replaced it with a medium strength Somerset Dry Cider called "Bramley Bastard."

Edith Dent became concerned about her dramatic weight loss and visited her doctor. He informed her that it was likely she had a tapeworm, but sent her to the hospital for an X-ray as a precaution. The radiologist was shocked to discover a twenty-foot tapeworm that appeared to have a moustache and a small ear-ring. Shortly before his death Vagin Semyon had noticed that both his moustache and left earing had gone missing during his last level transfer.

It took five hours of complicated surgery to remove Edith's tapeworm. It is now on display in a large pickle jar at The London Museum of Health and Medicine.

By the year 2050 there was a network of P.I.S.S Academies in every country in the World. Only a handful of churches remained.

Mick Frost, inventor of rheo-static trickle-volt technology, was posthumously awarded a Nobel Peace Prize. He would be the only person to have it awarded three years in a row. Art Schitthelm gave him the title 'The Godfather of Peace', and ordered that a portrait of him be hung in every P.I.S.S Academy in the World.

By 2024 Three F had successfully converted every golf course in the British Isles to a nature reserve. Former golfers were required to attend a compulsory course run by local colleges. The five-day certificated course enlightened the non-golfing golfers on the damage the game had inflicted on society. On successful completion of the course the ex-golfers were presented with a badge of achievement, and also a sticker for their car.

The Three F police continued to provide an excellent cost-free service to the public. Year on year the crime figures diminished, until the year 2026 when a national zero crime rating was achieved. The Senior Police Force Commissioner, Trudy Mullings, resigned the day after her appearance on The Dimblewit Debate.

Art Schitthelm personally requested that Barry Sewell be randomly mugged three times a year, over a period of ten years. After being thoroughly beaten and robbed, the Three F plain-clothed detectives left Barry with a calling card. The money taken from him was donated to charity.

Maxim Yankov, Head of Time Travel Research, defected from Russia in 2022. He finished his days working for Art Schitthelm on a seven figure salary.

Following the success of the Pocket Sphinculator, Shaun Swill became both a billionaire and a household name. He went on to submit another patent for scrutiny by Three F's Innovation Assessment Committee.

Shaun had come up with the idea of increasing the separation intervals on toilet roll tissues from the average six inches, to a yard in length. This could be easily done during the manufacturing process by adjusting the distance between the linear perforations that assist with the tearing action. Shaun held that the wiping/smudging motion in common use was outdated, inefficient, and clarty. He believed that dragging a lengthy piece of tissue between the buttocks in a one-directional flossing action would render the process more hygienic and efficient.

To avoid unwanted tearing during use, Shaun suggested that the toilet paper thickness would need to be increased from the existing two-ply thickness. Each toilet roll would be sold with a ply rating that would range on a scale, from three, to twelve, according to the size of arse to be wiped.

Ronnie Dent continued with his drinking, smoking, and gambling.

Art Schitthelm got both freezers safely back to Geneva. They are secured in a vault two miles beneath Three F's headquarters. On the last Sunday of every month Art posts a picture of himself sitting between the two freezers. The picture shows him reading the day's Sunday newspaper.

Schitthelm regularly sends out World broadcasts warning of retro-termination for those who behave in a way deemed by Three F to be injurious to good society. From 2025 onwards neither a battle nor a war was fought anywhere on the planet. People respected both one-another, and the environment.

There was never a better time to live in the World.

CHAPTER 28

MONDAY EVENING

'Lenny – is that you back from work?' called Sarah Plant from the kitchen. She was busy pacing to-and-fro gossiping with her friend Claire on the mobile.

Lenny had just come in through the front door.

'Eh,' said Lenny, confirming both that he'd heard his wife's question, and that it was actually him back from work.

'Claire's coming round in an hour for a cuppa, so there won't be enough milk left for your Weetabix in the morning.'

Lenny called back down the hallway. 'How many cups is she having?'

'I don't know – maybe forty or so. Edith might show as well.'

'Bollocks,' muttered Lenny to himself, whilst stooping to re-shoe his recently un-shoed right foot. 'Why don't you just ask me to pop-out and buy some milk, instead of panicking me with a forecast of liquid calcium shortage for tomorrow's breakfast?' said Lenny.

'Get a four-pint one – it'll last us till Wednesday.'

'Fuck's sake,' groaned Lenny. He'd had a busy day at work, and, in spite of an excellent night's sleep, he was tired and overly fractious. He'd spent most of the day trying to remember any small detail of the weekend. Try as hard as he could, he failed to muster the faintest recollection. He eventually gave up and blamed it on the pystwiser.

He put on his jacket and headed out the door for the village shop. Sarah had meant to tell him not to be calling at the pub, but didn't bother. She knew the lambasting Lenny received the previous evening would still be echoing in his ears. He wouldn't dare even think about it.

Lenny walked to the end of Willow Gardens and turned left onto Locburn Lane. Heading down towards the P.I.S.S. Academy he approached the junction with Church Lane. A familiar figure appeared, emerging on foot, from Church Lane.

'Hey-up Lenny lad – how's it going?' said Ronnie Dent.

'Not too bad Ronnie – still feeling a bit shitty from the weekend if I'm honest.'

Ronnie waited for Lenny to join him and they walked together.

'You had us worried for a while there Lenny; thought you'd buggered-off to the Promised Land.'

Ronnie looked at his friend and smiled. The smile was the same as always: enduringly unassuming, unfalteringly reliable, like it was gifted to Ronnie with a lifetime guarantee. This evening Lenny found it intoxicatingly uplifting; more welcome than a mild day in February. It was a poignant moment for Lenny. All day he'd felt depressed, and somehow disconnected from life; like he was observing it from some muted dimension, alone and unseen. A genuine smile from a good friend was all that was needed to rescue Lenny from suffocating morbidity.

'Where're you off to Lenny?' asked Ronnie, fetching out a fag and lighting it. 'Bet it's not the pub.'

'You're joking aren't you? The fucking roasting I got last night.'

'Me too,' commiserated Ronnie, 'Edith seems to be much more vigorous with her scolding these days – it's like she's got a new lease of life – gets physical with it as well.' Lenny noticed one of Ronnie's ears was thicker than the other. The braids and pink ribbons had gone too.

'Sarah's got her friend coming round for tea and gossip,' said Lenny, 'no prizes for guessing who's on the agenda?'

'Don't be surprised if Edith shows-up,' said Ronnie in an unjoking tone.

'I know,' said Lenny, 'three of them. Our ears will be on fire anytime.'

'She mentioned it this afternoon; said she might pop round tonight for a chit-chat.'

'Chit-chat?' said Lenny. 'More like a bitch-fest.'

'You haven't said where you're heading yet Lenny lad?'

'Just off to the shop for some milk. What about you?'

'Shop too – need some fags.'

Lenny and Ronnie passed the snicket that led to the Haydale Arms. They stalled and looked down the alley. From where they stood they could see the front door to the pub.

'I saw Mervin over at Layton's garage this afternoon Len.'

'How was he?'

'He was fine; said he'd gotten rid of that pystwiser stuff.'

'Has he really,' said Lenny, mildly interested.

'Yeah – he told me he's got a barrel of a new cider getting delivered today. Bramley Bastard it's called. Said he'd be trialling it tonight.'

'Tonight you say?'

'Yeah – it's going to be half-price.'

They were still stationary, staring longingly at the pub door.

'Bet you could murder a pint Lenny lad?'

'Not half,' said Lenny. 'But there's no way – Sarah would lynch me.'

Ronnie looked at Lenny and said nothing. The pair of them remained rooted.

Ronnie smiled again, only this time the smile morphed into a grin loaded with mischief.

'Fuck it,' said Lenny.

Acknowledgments

To my wife Barbara; her second opinion is priceless.

To artist Jackie Stubbs – for the deftness of her brushstroke: just and magnanimous.

To publishers YouCaxton: smooth-riding.

Saint John the Baptist Roman Catholic Church, Swatragh, County Derry. God bless the parishioners, the graves, the rooks, and the rook shit.

To Adrian O'Kane; he is the inspiration behind chapter 14.

To all those who asked me: "How's the book coming along?"

Printed in Great Britain
by Amazon